BELLARY BAY

BOOKS BY JOHN WELCOME

JOHN WELCOME

BELLARY BAY

NEW YORK

ATHENEUM

1979

Library of Congress Cataloging in Publication Data

Welcome, John, 1914-
    Bellary Bay.

    I. Title.
PZ4.W4414Bd 1979   [PR6073.E373]   823'.9'14   79-51523
ISBN 0-689-11013-8

This is for Sally
with love

PART ONE

PEACE

1

The Bay lay like a sheet of silver under the slowly fading sun. On either side, tier on tier, colour on colour, the mountains reached up into the clear blue of the sky. Thirty miles away, in the hazy distance three little rocky islands, called locally the Cat, the Kitten and the Dog, guarded the entrance to the great inlet where a whole battle fleet could lie safe at anchor.

The Bay was at peace that day in the early spring of 1914. There was no wind to ruffle the surface of its waters; no squalls came sweeping down through the valleys and gaps in the hills to tear it apart and threaten the unwary sailor. God's Breaths they called these squalls in the Bay, and those who sailed kept a wary eye for the sudden rippling of the water that betrayed their onset.

For the Bay was not always at peace especially in the early months of the year. Then, the Atlantic gales would roar up its length and dash great waves against the granite pier guarding Bellary Harbour and the little town behind it. At other times fog and mist came down to shroud the hills and the woods that bordered its shores.

Frost and snow seldom if ever touched these south-western latitudes. Palms and semi-tropical plants grew in abundance. Rhododendrons and fuchsia in season rioted their colours everywhere. Save in times of storm a sense of peace pervaded the whole landscape of hill and heather, rock and sea.

It was this stillness which above all laid its spell on those who lived there. Wherever they went they carried something of the Bay with them in their hearts. Its isolation made it a self-contained community and created a sense of kinship amongst all its inhabitants, high and low, rich and poor. 'Any news from the Bay?' they would ask when they met in faraway places. 'I'll never see the Bay again,' were the words used by exiles dying away from the place they loved.

It was the peace and beauty of the Bay which had brought the conquerors and adventurers and their descendants to settle and

3

stay there, driving out the mere Irish, and capturing, cutting out or acquiring by purchase the finest sites and best pastures along its shores.

The Old Earl, as they called him, with his shooting lodge far down the Bay beneath the three peaks of Knockbrandon, Knockmaroon and Knockaree, was the greatest of these. There, on the rare occasions of his visits, he had his woodcock shooting in the winter and in summer his salmon river and his trout fishing on a chain of lakes stretching far up into the hills. The Old Earl was a grandee; he had a palace in Derbyshire and a seat in the Cabinet. His origins went back to an English adventurer in Tudor times; his estates here and in North Kilderry had been mainly acquired by judicious marriages or purchase, not by the sword. He was an absentee but a moderately benevolent one; his ancestors had laid out the town of Bellary and had tried without success to develop a mining industry there. He looked with some disdain on the others who had come later to build their mansions and sham castles on the shores opposite him or on the lower ground at the head of the Bay.

The Old Earl was a fishing and shooting man as were his neighbours far down the Bay. The hunting and racing people came from the estates further up, for behind the little town over a saddle in the hills the country suddenly opened out into grassland. This was good farming country, good country for horse-rearers, too, with its rich pastures set on limestone and, above all, for the gentry and sporting farmers, it was good hunting country with its broad sound banks and firm, fresh turf.

Bellary Court was a mellow, red-brick Georgian house built on a bluff above the town. It was glowing in the last of the westering sun when Stephen Raymond let himself in by a side door and walked down a long flagged passage to the gun-room. Once there, he laid down the single-barrelled ·410 his father had given him on his twelfth birthday nearly two years before and pulled the tray of cleaning materials towards him. When he had finished a meticulous cleaning and oiling of the gun he opened the glass-fronted door of the gun-rack and put it alongside his father's matching pair of Holland and Hollands which were now so seldom used. Then he took his game book from a drawer and turned its pages. As he did so the third entry on the first page caught his eye. It was disfigured by a large, heavy scoring out.

Each time Stephen saw this he was reminded of the occasion on which he had had to make it. Shortly after he had been given the gun his father had taken Stephen and Harry French, the agent's son, to shoot the bogs behind Comeragh mountain. Harry was Stephen's best friend but he had missed everything that afternoon while Stephen had shot quite well. When he came to make the entry recording the day he had written: *Harry shot very badly* with a certain feeling of satisfaction.

4

Looking over his shoulder his father had seen the words. 'Oh, no,' he had said in his quiet way. 'That won't do. You must never, never write a criticism of other people's shooting in your game book. Who knows who may read it and would you like it if he wrote that about you some other time? Besides, the game book is a record of your shooting and only yours.' Stephen had scored it through and through and now no one but himself and his father would ever know he had made it.

Smoothing back the page before him, he dipped the pen in the silver-topped ink bottle on the gun-room table and began to write his entry for that day. Just as he finished the door opened and Mikey, the pantry-boy, pushed his head around it. 'Arrah, Master Stephen,' he said. 'How'd ye get on?'

'Only a brace,' Stephen answered.

'Maybe they aren't in it. The weather's too mild.'

'They're there all right,' Stephen said. 'It's just I couldn't hit them today.'

'You're too hasty, that's what it is.'

'Maybe. I don't know. I'll never be as good a shot as you, Mikey.'

'Steady down a bit that's all ye've got to do. It's tryin' too hard you are. Be aisy with yourself and ye'll hit everything that gets up.'

'Perhaps,' Stephen said, looking at his entry. 'I hope so, anyway, Mikey.'

'They're askin' for you in the schoolroom. That's what I was to tell you. There's quality comin' tonight.'

Stephen closed the game book and put it away. As he went up the uncarpeted back stairs to the schoolroom he thought about his shooting. In many ways he was, as he knew, a natural shot. Often, with snipe especially, he would have a good day, swinging the gun automatically and knocking them down as they got up. At other times it seemed as if the actual act of killing became repugnant to him. Then his concentration went and with it his ability. He pulled and poked, did everything wrong and shot nothing. With Mikey, it was different; always he just seemed to swing and the bird crumpled and came down.

The afternoons Mikey spent shooting with Stephen, sharing the gun, were wholly illicit and unknown to his parents. His father, Stephen thought, would hardly worry if they were brought to his notice, but his mother would be furious.

Mikey, like Harry French, was Stephen's friend. He had seen the eager way Mikey had looked at the ·410 when he had been given it; once he had found him in the gun-room with it in his hands, swinging it at imaginary birds. So far from causing wrath and tribulation to descend from upstairs upon the boy, Stephen had offered to share the gun with him one afternoon and, later on, other days had been stolen. It was Rogers, the English butler, who should have supervised Mikey

5

but Rogers was old and slightly dotty and scarcely knew what was going on so Mikey's afternoons of truancy had gone undetected.

Anyway, Stephen thought, as he entered the schoolroom, shooting did not come first in his life. His thoughts went to Pat, his pony, and he smiled to himself. Riding, now, that was different, that was something he could always do. Pat and he seemed to be at one. It came naturally to him to make Pat do as he wished. And tomorrow was a hunting day.

A fire blazed in the schoolroom grate and the heady smell of burning turf filled the room. That was another thing those who lived about the Bay never forgot—the tang of turf smoke that came from their fires and hung all about their homesteads great or small.

An oil lamp had been lighted and stood on the table that had been laid for his tea. Ethel, his sister, was away in Kildare, staying with cousins. He was quite happy to be alone in the cheerful room with the Giles and Alken hunting prints on the walls. The *Boy's Own Paper* had come too, he saw, and had been laid out on the table. The lamplight danced on the bright spines of his other books on the shelves, Herbert Strang, Henty, Marryat and Ballantine. Soon there would be poached eggs and toast and soda bread and raspberry jam. Since his sister was away there would be no interference with his peace by her. And as there was to be a dinner party that night there was little chance of his mother paying one of her infrequent visits to the schoolroom, visits which invariably led to fault-finding and scolding and long lectures about his dreaminess, general inefficiency and inadequacies.

Thinking of his parents brought thoughts of trouble, more particularly in view of what had happened yesterday. He had been passing the door of his father's upstairs study and had heard angry voices inside, or rather one voice, his mother's, for his father seldom if ever raised his quiet tones. The door had not been quite shut. Involuntarily and against all he had ever been taught, he had paused to listen.

'You'll have to do something, Edward,' she had been saying. 'The man is incompetent if not worse. I asked him about those rascally Rossiters at Corravore and he said they were behind in their rent, which is small enough in all conscience. Yet I hear in the village that Larry Rossiter was boasting he had paid up and had a receipt to prove it. If he hasn't they should be ejected.'

'I've said before, my dear,' came his father's tired tones. 'There will be no more ejectments as long as I am here.'

'Then you won't be here much longer, Edward. You owe it to us and the boy to do something.'

'It's a wretched piece of mountainy land. It's of no use to anyone.'

'Then they'd be better out of it. They can go to America like their forbears did. And a good riddance too.'

6

'It's too late for that. And perhaps they have as much right to the land as we have. This government seems to think so.'

'Sentimental rubbish. But in any event it's French I'm really thinking of. It's common knowledge he is playing ducks and drakes with the estates he's supposed to be managing. The Old Earl got rid of him long ago. Sarah Gnowles told me they have just finished with him. You'll soon be the only one left. I shouldn't wonder if he isn't collecting the rents for himself.'

'His family have always been the agents for the Bay and for us.'

His mother had made a peculiar noise through her high-bridged nose. It was half-way between a snort and a neigh and signified that she was really annoyed beyond measure. It was a noise both her family and her servants had grown to recognise and, when recognised, to accept as a danger signal. 'That's purely an excuse for doing nothing, Edward, and you know it,' she said. 'You have to think of the future.'

Stephen heard his father sigh. 'I hope there is a future for us landlords,' he said. 'If this Home Rule Bill goes through—'

'Home Rule or no Home Rule, you cannot go on letting things drift. Pull yourself together, Edward, and do something. You know you have to face the boy's fees at Eton next year.'

'I don't think Stephen will be going to Eton, my dear.'

At the mention of his name Stephen woke out of the almost trance-like state in which he had been listening to the conversation. Guilt overcame him with a sudden shock. He tiptoed a few steps down the landing and then took to his heels and fled to the schoolroom.

So he was not to go to Eton because his father was in some money trouble which he did not understand but which had something to do with Harry's father. He did not mind missing Eton. It had been his mother's idea anyway for him to follow in the footsteps of all those long-striding Delaway men of her family, men who had seized and held India for the Crown and left their health and often their bones on the battlefields of the small wars of Empire.

Stephen had no desire to emulate them. In truth he did not want to go away anywhere. He had no wish to leave the Bay which had already set its spell on him. He loved it in all its changing moods. Getting up from his chair he crossed to the window and pulled aside the curtains. The schoolroom was set in an angle of the house where the servants' wing began and it commanded a view of the whole length of the Bay. Dusk was falling fast but he could see on either side the soft colours of the mountains gradually blending into the misty distance. The wind had suddenly risen and was whipping the surface of the water into a myriad of white horses. An angry mood was coming to the Bay now, for the wind was freshening every minute. Soon it would be rattling the windows in their sashes and tearing at the roofs.

7

The anger in the Bay seemed to Stephen to symbolise somehow what was happening in the house. He had been unable to rid his mind of the conversation he had overheard and all that day he had been conscious of an air of unrest, almost of approaching doom pervading the house. Even Rogers, the butler, seemed to feel it. He had pottered about on his bad feet that bulged with bunions, the leather of his shoes cut open to accommodate them, muttering 'trouble in the house, trouble in the house' as he went about his daily tasks, ineffectually attempting to clean the silver and harassing the maids and Mikey, none of whom nowadays took any notice of him.

It had been partly to escape this atmosphere that Stephen had slipped out to shoot and it was at least to some degree due to the fact that his mind was filled with thoughts of trouble that he had shot so badly.

He wished he had someone with whom he could talk things over, but he could hardly confide in Mikey and Ethel was away. In any event he and Ethel had little in common. She was four years older and resentful, though he did not then know it, of his position as son and heir. Like his mother, too, Ethel was hard, strident and unsympathetic. Ethel would take his mother's side in the argument whatever it was; she would be of little assistance in explaining to him what was happening to them all. His father had said something about there being no future for them. Surely they would not have to leave the Bay?

The storm was building up and as he stood there a sudden gust of rain rattled like smallshot against the glass. In the gathering dusk he could see the downpour crossing Holy Island a few miles down the farther shore. Then for a second it blanked out the white tower of the great mansion Andrew Massiter, a newcomer to the Bay, had just finished building.

The squall swept on and once more he could see the tower above the trees. From the snatches of conversation he had heard among his elders he gathered that Massiter's mansion was enormous. It was bigger even than the ambitious plans Barty Corringer had for enlarging the old house where the Corringers had lived for generations. Those plans coupled with unwise speculations for financing them had broken Barty, and Massiter had bought up his house and lands.

Massiter himself was something of a man of mystery, a talking point in the Bay, or so Stephen had heard. He himself knew him only from seeing him out hunting, where he went across the country like a devil on skates, as an admiring countryman, watching him, had said in Stephen's hearing. There was some sort of rivalry building up, too, Stephen knew, between him and Desmond Murtagh, the gentleman rider, winner of countless steeplechases and second in the Grand National last year, who had reigned supreme as the leading thruster in the County Kilderry hunt until Massiter came along.

It was Massiter who, out hunting, had made the remark about Stephen and Ethel which had come back to the Raymond household by way of servants' gossip as everything said in the Bay always did. Mikey had repeated it to Stephen one day out shooting when Stephen had hesitated to wring the neck of a wounded bird. 'Toughen yerself, Master Stephen, toughen yerself,' he had said. 'Or they'll all be laughin' at ye. D'ye know what that new fellah, Massiter, has been sayin' about you and Miss Ethel?'

Stephen had looked at the bird, soft and warm and terrified in his hand, its blood staining his fingers. 'No, what?' he had said.

'He says Miss Ethel bred to the dam and you bred to the sire and it should have been the other way round.'

Massiter was coming to dinner tonight, Stephen remembered. He thought he had heard words about that, too, between his mother and father. At least his mother's remark: 'That bounder. Why ask him? No one knows where he sprang from,' had, Stephen assumed, referred to Massiter for he had heard similar epithets describing the newcomer from members of the County Kilderry field out hunting, though there they were usually followed by, 'But I'm not denying that the damn fellow can ride,' or some such qualification.

His father had protested that new arrivals, whoever they were, must be entertained at least once and it seemed he had on this occasion got his way for Massiter had been invited.

Faintly Stephen thought he could hear carriage wheels on the gravel in front of the house. He left the schoolroom and made his way to the bannisters of the first landing. There he took up a position, as he often did, looking down into the long hall where he could watch the guests arriving unobserved or so he thought.

It was Desmond Murtagh's carriage wheels which Stephen had heard and he and his wife were the first to arrive. Stephen watched them as they walked the length of the hall, Desmond tall and lean with broad, horseman's hands and long humorous face; his wife, Sarah, her wide mouth made for laughing and her mass of auburn hair catching the glints from the choker of diamonds at her throat—one of the last of her mother's jewels that had not been sold to pay Desmond's gambling debts. It was to be a hunting and racing dinner party Stephen decided, for Grig Gnowles, the Master of the County Kilderry Hounds, silent and saturnine, with his hard-bitten wife beside him, was the next to come.

Then a snorting and a banging outside proclaimed Massiter's arrival. He was one of the few in the Bay who owned a motor-car. It drew up with a scrunch of brakes and a defiant backfire as if proclaiming its owner's disregard for the conventions and the muttered protests of many of his hosts concerning his ruining the gravel with those tyres of his and staining their forecourts with oil.

He strode into the hall stripping off his gloves as he came. With his long blue Melton motoring coat and his pointed imperial jutting out between the wings of its astrakhan collar he did indeed in the lamplight look a bit like a devil, Stephen thought. Massiter was alone, for he was a bachelor. His shirtfront gleamed with two huge diamond studs. 'Overdressed,' the gentlemen would say later over the port at other dinner parties at which he was not present. As he came almost underneath the landing he suddenly looked up. His eyes met Stephen's. They were strange eyes, Stephen thought, tawny and fierce. All at once Stephen felt a shiver of fear run through him. Then Massiter gave a sudden conspiratorial grin and passed on into the round ante-room where the guests were gathered.

2

The round room as it was called had been built on to Bellary Court by Edward's grandfather to command a view of the Bay. A tall window took up one side. Below it the bluff on which the house was built fell steeply to the shore so that, sitting in the sweep of this great window, one seemed to hang suspended in air while all around was the changing panorama of sea and mountain. The heavy curtains were drawn now. Standing in the window's embrasure with his back to them Edward could hear the rain and wind dashing against the glass.

The starched white collar was cutting into Edward's throat and he ran his finger round its edge. It was much too tight. He would have to send to Dublin for some more. He intensely disliked dressing up in these clothes. When they dined alone he wore a smoking jacket. In fact he disliked dinner parties but considered it part of his social duty to give them, and in any event he would be bullied by Honoria if he did not, and he had long since decided that the only way he could secure anything approaching peace in his own house was to give in to his wife.

The assembling of the guests before they went in to dinner was the part of the entertainment which he disliked more than any other. The *mauvais quart d'heure* he had heard it called and he heartily agreed with this description. No drink of any sort was served during it though he had been told by Dicky Belmore back from a visit to the States with the West Indies Squadron that the Americans handed round mixed drinks called cocktails during this time. It was an innovation, Edward thought, which might well be introduced this side of the water. Just the thing that fellow Massiter might well do and he would have Edward's blessing if he did.

He looked at Massiter now and smiled slightly to himself at what he saw. With the unerring instinct of his kind, Massiter had identified his arch-enemy amongst the party and had immediately set himself out to conquer her. The *mauvais quart d'heure* with its restrictions and inhibitions had no effect on him. He was thanking Honoria for putting him right 'in that good hunt we had from Gratton Wood'.

'If you hadn't told me I couldn't get through down by those cabins,

11

I'd have lost it, Mrs Raymond. And that grey of yours; he's quite brilliant. The way he took that big double to get you your start, I've never seen anything so quick and clever. And none of us could catch you, you know.'

Honoria, Edward noticed, was, unbelievably, actually glowing under his praise.

The whole party was assembled now. Save for Massiter who was still carrying on his easy flow of conversation, they were talking stiltedly amongst themselves, the men eyeing the newcomer with wary suspicion. He had somehow drawn Sarah Murtagh into the little group around him and Edward heard her sudden throaty laugh at something he had said.

Edward wished he could look at his watch. It was high time Rogers announced dinner. Rogers—that was another of his worries. He was really becoming too dotty to be kept on any longer. Honoria had been campaigning for his dismissal for months past. But what would happen then to the poor old man? There were no cottages for him on what was left of the estate; he could scarcely be kept on in the house as a sort of permanent pensioner for he would never understand that he had no more duties to perform and would be perpetually interfering to the disruption of the household and the fury of Honoria. Tonight Edward had told him to put out whisky and champagne. He could scarcely go wrong over those—or could he? He had been known before now to put whisky into the sherry decanter and serve it as such. And the port? He had told him to open the Taylor '96 but it was well within the bounds of possibility that he had decanted the hunting port. And one of Edward's few extravagances was that he liked to drink vintage port and to serve it to his guests.

But Rogers, really, was only a minor worry. There was this business of Sterling French, the agent. Honoria had brought into the open what he, himself, had been feeling for some little time now. Things were not what they should be with French's agency. He would have to face up sooner or later to finding out just what was wrong, if only because Honoria would give him no peace until he did.

Edward became conscious that silence had fallen on the round room. The guests had run out of conversation. What *was* Rogers doing? Edward's eye strayed to the long embroidered bell-pull hanging by the fireplace. Then suddenly the tall inlaid doors to the dining room opened and Rogers stood there shuffling on his feet as always. 'Dinner is served, madam,' he said with a slight hiccup. Edward wondered once again about the port.

In fact, as it turned out, he need not have worried. It was the Taylor all right as he knew immediately he put his glass to his lips. And the meal had really gone off remarkably well. Entertaining was, of course, one of the things that Honoria was good at. She saw that her guests

12

were dined a little bit better than anywhere else in the Bay which made her invitations sought after and when issued promptly accepted. She managed the house impeccably, too, and she managed him. For about the thousandth time he wondered why he had married her.

He had gone out to India that terrible time after his first wife's sudden and tragic death, asked by a kindly cousin who had been commanding a cavalry brigade at Meerut. In those days Edward, though always shy and retiring, had been something of a sportsman. He had beautiful hands on a horse, so that all sorts of horses seemed to go for him, and he was above average as a shot. Ever since a kindly doctor had broken the news to him that his beloved Libby was dying, he had lived in a sort of daze and that daze had remained with him during the entire Indian visit.

Once installed with his cousin, he had been introduced to pig-sticking where his horsemanship had stood him in good stead and he had had some success. Similarly he had taken to polo quickly and played with promise. When the hot weather came he had moved to Simla.

It had been Kipling's Simla then—an unreal, artificial, hothouse place of gossip and intrigue, of games of chance between the sexes, married and unmarried, of flirtations and of what they called in those days 'skating on thin ice'. It had all the heady atmosphere of a shipboard holiday prolonged for months. Nothing in Edward's unsophisticated upbringing or his life amongst the simplicities and uncomplexities of the Bay had prepared him for anything like it. Although he did not realise it, his recent widowerhood, his ability as a horseman and a shot, even his shyness, made him into something of a romantic figure amongst the worldly population of that extraordinary Indian resort.

He was never quite sure just how Honoria had come into his life though in his bitterer moments he told himself it had all been arranged by her parents. Her father, General Sir Henry Delaway, scion of an Irish Cromwellian family from County Cavan, was commanding the district; her mother was an older and even more domineering edition of Honoria herself. Honoria even then was not in her first youth nor was she a beauty, but one thing she could do; she rode like a dream. Somehow in the paperchases that took place they always seemed to be thrown together and they were almost invariably amongst the first up. It was but a step to be riding together on the Maidan and then at picnics they began to be paired off. There was no denying, too, that in those days Honoria had both presence and dash and she looked uncommonly well in a habit. Also at that time he had been grateful for the direct and immediate way in which she made his decisions for him. In the haze in which he was then living she had seemed a rock upon which he could lean. But he could never quite

13

recall in what terms they had become engaged. He supposed she had managed that, too.

The night before the wedding he had lain awake, facing reality for the first time for months and realising that he was making a ghastly mistake. Honoria's ways were not his ways, nor her virtues his virtues.

The Raymond family origins went back far beyond the Cromwellian conquest. Somehow they had through the years avoided confiscation, attainder, banishment or flight. They had kept and held their lands, by judicious trimming of their sails to each political wind and calculated changes of religion at convenient times, so their detractors said, but they nevertheless remained safe and secure in the Bay with their holdings intact where others had lost everything and died in poverty or exile. Edward had always faintly despised the Cromwellians with their aspirations to gentility hardly compatible with their origins, their lack of culture or any understanding of the graces of life, their ruthlessness to their tenants and those whom they had dispossessed. He conceded to them their martial virtues which sprang from their origins as Godly colonels or cornets in the New Model Army, but Edward had no martial interests or ambitions. He realised all too late that Honoria was a feminine edition of her hard-fighting brothers one of whom had just been shot in the neck in some border affray and the other, shortly to be his best man, only the other day promoted in the field for gallantry at Omdurman.

The marriage in Christ Church, Simla, had been a grand affair emblazoned with uniforms in all the bright colours of India at the apogee of Empire and dignified by the presence of the greatest of all the Victorian pro-consuls, the Viceroy himself. They had spent their honeymoon in the Vale of Kashmir, shooting, and then sailed for home. Back in the Bay, Edward soon found that in place of his gentle Libby he had installed a tyrant in his house and learnt, too, with bitter self-knowledge, that he lacked the courage to stand up to her.

'Well, Raymond, what do you think?' Desmond Murtagh's voice broke into his thoughts and he came back to his own dinner table with a start.

'Eh, what?' he said hesitantly. He really must prevent himself from going off into day-dreams. It was becoming so frequent as to be embarrassing, a fact of which Honoria was constantly reminding him.

'Is there going to be a war?' Massiter said, clipping the end off a cigar.

Edward sipped his port. 'Johnnie Belmore when he was in here with the Fleet last summer told me there wouldn't be one,' he said. 'He told me we've too many capital ships for them to risk it. If they come out they'd be blasted out of the water.'

'That Kaiser of theirs is a fire-eatin' sort of feller,' Gnowles put in. 'Still, hardly likely to take on the French and the Ruskies—and us, is

14

he?'

'Don't be too sure,' Massiter said. 'Their industrial production is better than ours and the French put together. If it comes buy commodities—they'll be the thing.'

'He won't fight on two fronts,' Gnowles growled, looking belligerently across the table. He did not much care to be contradicted. Come to that he did not much care for Massiter either. Bounderish sort of feller. Always ridin' over his hounds or damn nearly.

'He may not have to. If he moves quick enough he could knock out Russia in a week. Russia is rotten. I was there last year. Spoke to some members of the Duma. The whole system is corrupt. They could collapse like a pack of cards. Then he'd only have the French to deal with.'

'Duma. Damn politicians. Always talkin' damn rot,' Gnowles said scornfully. 'No one has conquered Russia yet. Napoleon couldn't. And what about us? What do you think we'll be doin' eh?' He glared across the table.

'It could be a long war if it comes,' Edward said.

'Nonsense,' Grig declared. 'All over in six months. Modern fire power will open it up and then the cavalry will go through.'

'Yes, but what will they do when they get there?' Massiter enquired.

'Why, exploit the advantage of course,' Grig snorted. 'The rôle of cavalry—'

'Well, Grig,' Desmond Murtagh put in quickly to dissipate the antagonism that was quite clearly building up between the two men, 'If it does come I hope they won't let it interfere with racing. See to that, Grig, will you?'

They all laughed. The potentially dangerous moment passed and they fell to talking of horses, hunting and racing, not unusual subjects over the port where members of that section of the Bay's population were gathered together.

Good fellow, Desmond, Edward mused, going off into another of his reveries. If only he wasn't so damn reckless and feckless. He betted in thousands where he should have wagered tens at the most; he rode any sort of horse with casual brilliance and should have been killed years ago from some of the rides he took and the falls he had had. Women, too, fell for him as easily as horses went for him. He took the ones he wanted and then rode away to return to Sarah who, with the luck these fellows always had, Edward thought, never seemed to lose the love she had for him. She was far too good for him, of course, as everybody said but they also added that nobody could be angry with Desmond for long.

The Murtaghs had come to the Bay four generations before. They had been lawyers or merchants or something in Dublin, had

15

amassed a fortune, bought the old Fitzgarton estate in the Encumbered Estates Court and, by their charm, waywardness and wit, had immediately established themselves. In a way, Edward thought, the three of them sitting drinking port at his dinner table represented a microcosm of Irish society at the time. He thought of himself as old Irish, Gnowles as a Cromwellian if ever there was one, and Murtagh represented a mixture of new wealth and pure Irishness untainted by Saxon blood. But Massiter, what was he? The joker in the pack? The unknown? A newer Ireland still?

Again Edward pulled himself out of his reverie to hear Desmond expatiating on the merits of one of his horses. 'Bred well enough to win the National,' he was saying. 'And made like a National winner too. You mark my words, Grig, this fellow will win good races. I've put him in the Conyngham Cup.'

'The Conyngham Cup,' Massiter said. 'I hope to have a runner in it.'

'Well, keep 'em both on the racecourse then and not ridin' over my hounds,' Grig growled, and on that note Edward suggested that they should join the ladies.

When the guests had gone Edward compelled himself to face the problem of Sterling French. It was only cowardice, he knew, which had prevented him from dealing with it before. That and a reluctance to believe anything bad about an employee who was also a friend. Now he had to face up to it if for no other reason than that Honoria would give him no peace until he did.

He had to find out whether French was in fact playing ducks and drakes with the rents. The agricultural tenants were few enough nowadays since the passing of these new Land Purchase Acts but there were still a few of them left; there was a tithe rental; there were, too, the ground rents from the village of Cloonara twenty miles away and a slice of Dublin property, both the latter having been acquired by some remote ancestor or brought into the family by marriage or devise. They all did or should between them produce a reasonable income. When he came to think of it he realised that he had not seen any rentals or returns for some time.

The records of the property were kept in a room known as 'the rent room' from the days when the tenants had come there to pay their rents. They were, therefore, here in the house, ready to his hand. He hated doing anything that savoured of spying or behaving in an underhand fashion but he saw no alternative. In no time at all Honoria would be demanding of him what he had done and what results he had achieved. Pouring himself a stiff whisky and soda he took the glass in one hand and an oil lamp in the other and left the long drawing room where they had gathered after dinner.

16

The rent room lay at the end of a stone-flagged passage. It had a door opening to the outer world through which in former days the tenants had entered. A mahogany table took up the centre of the room with, behind it, the agent's chair. Behind this again the wall was lined with shelves on which were stacked rows and rows of leather-backed rent ledgers, books containing agents' minutes asking for instructions from the master of the house and annotated and counter-signed by him, together with bound volumes of maps of the estate. Set into a corner on a tripod was a safe of which only Edward and French had keys.

The room was dark and draughty. The oil lamp which Edward had placed on the table cast only a pool of light around it. He had heard that Massiter was installing the new-fangled electric light in his castle and wished he had the money to do it too. Edward sipped his whisky. It was devilish cold. He'd better get on with the job. He sighed and turned to face the shelves.

The current ledgers were immediately behind him, their titles and the years they covered stamped in gold letters on their spines. The one which first caught his eye had the words *Tithe Rents* on it.

Checking the tithe rental should be comparatively easy. They were 'impropriate lay tithes' converted to secular use and ownership at the Reformation. They formed only a small proportion of the total rental. Edward took the ledger down and placed it before him. When he opened it he received the first of the many shocks he was to receive that night.

The rental had not been written up for years. He remembered that French had said that the tithes were becoming very hard to collect as there was agitation about them. This might be so but they were not so bad that something could not have been collected.

With a sinking heart Edward turned to the other ledgers. Two hours later he closed the last of them. He was no expert but the message they bore was all too plain. He had been systematically cheated and, it seemed, of some pretty considerable amounts. In one instance alone a substantial sum of arrears was recorded against a Dublin rental which to Edward's certain knowledge was not in arrear at all. The tenants were distant cousins, always prompt to pay. In fact they had recently written to him about the possibility of purchasing out the rent.

Wearily Edward took a sheet of writing paper from the rack on the table, picked up a pen and dipped it in the ink-pot. Even the ink, he noticed, had not been kept fresh and was beginning to become congealed. When he had finished writing he sealed and addressed an envelope. Going back to the hall he placed it on the table with a message to Rogers that it must be sent down to Mr French first thing in the morning.

Then he went slowly upstairs to bed. Partly, he told himself—as

Honoria would assuredly remind him when she heard about it—this was his own fault. He had never instituted a check on the rents or asked a question. But then he had always regarded French as a friend.

He and Honoria had long ago agreed to occupy separate rooms so he was spared telling her anything that night.

The rain had cleared and the wind had dropped. He pulled aside the curtain in his bedroom to look out at the Bay. It was calm now; the clouds had gone and moonlight was a splash of silver on the water. He could see the top of Massiter's preposterous tower above the trees and far, far down the mass of woods that guarded the Old Earl's demesne. He wondered how much money had gone. Would he be able to stay on here? If he had to leave it would be the worst wrench of all, in fact he doubted if he could survive it. Anyway he would have to call in experts now and that would be for them to find out. It would take some time, he supposed.

He let the curtain fall back into place, undressed and climbed into bed.

3

Grig Gnowles, M.F.H., late of His Majesty's Queen's Bays, sat amongst his hounds on a blood weed bought cheap as a cast off from Desmond Murtagh's stable at the end of last season, and morosely surveyed his field. He wished they would all go home. Then he and his hounds could seek out and destroy his quarry, the fox, without their distracting presence. They chatted when he was casting, getting his hounds' heads up, they headed his foxes, they over-rode his pack, they were a general bloody nuisance. Unfortunately he had to put up with them, even with an ill grace, since they paid the subscriptions which he had to have if he was to continue hunting the County Kilderry hounds.

Grig was a small spare man whose face had as its most prominent feature a nose that had been broken and badly set after some long-forgotten encounter in Indian inter-regimental polo. He had made his name fourteen years before as a leader of a mobile column in South Africa. Back home he had crossed swords with Douglas Haig, and seeing little hope of advancement by ordinary Army steps, he had gravitated to the cavalry school at Netheravon where in the course of time his brilliance as a horseman had brought him the post of chief instructor. There he had enjoyed himself as emperor of his own little kingdom, picking those whom he favoured for advancement and ruthlessly culling any pupil who failed to reach the high standards of equitation and horsemastership demanded by him.

On the death of his father, since the County Kilderry hounds had been hunted by a member of the Gnowles family for the last hundred years, he had sent in his papers and retired to take over the Mastership. Once there he had dedicated himself with the singlemindedness which he gave to everything he undertook, to the task of killing foxes and showing sport. Success, which usually comes to the dedicated, had attended his efforts. He showed such sport as had not been seen for generations. He was rude, arrogant, bad-tempered and overbearing, but he was a member of one of the old families of the Bay. That and the sport he showed made his field tolerate from him the

19

insults, eccentricities and general outrageousness they would never have taken from an outsider.

His bleak and jaundiced eye roving the open space at the little mountain cross-roads where hounds met, fell first on Stephen, who had arrived early and was now doing his best to efface himself. He had felt the blast of Grig's wrath on several occasions and had no wish to do so again. For it was, as he knew, quite unpredictable. Like a heathen God, which indeed in many ways he resembled, Grig flashed fire at irregular intervals, blasting whoever stood in his way.

Not a bad young feller, Grig's thoughts ran on as he looked at Stephen, kept out of the way, didn't try to over-ride hounds, rode nicely too, he could have made something out of him if he'd had him at Netheravon. Trouble was he was too damn nice, would have liked him better really if he had been into his hounds once or twice. No real fire in his belly, just like his father.

Young Raymond was talking to Desmond Murtagh's girl. What the devil was her name—Barbara, that was it. She should make up into something. She'd have a go. Well, after all, she was bred for it. Her father was behind her, just getting up on a big, blood bay, the sort he liked to ride. They said he was going badly, or even worse than usual, was a better way of putting it. Betting, of course. Bloody fool.

And French, over there with his boy. There were rumours about him, too. Good job he'd got rid of him in time. Sterling French. Bad sort of name for a feller like that. Come to think of it he looked pretty shaky. Taking a shot from his flask, too, before they even moved off. Bad sign that. The boy was looking at his father as if he was worried. Miserable-looking screws they were both riding. Couldn't afford to feed them, he supposed.

A snorting and roaring noise broke into Grig's ruminations and the blood weed between his thighs shifted, threw up his head and arched his back. Grig looked over his shoulder. Of course. He should have known. It was that bounder Massiter and his bloody great motor-car upsetting the horses. Upsetting everyone in the calm and well-ordered world of the Bay if they weren't careful. The Corringers should never have sold out and let him in. And now he was putting the finishing touches to that ghastly great house a mile or so along the Bay from where Grig himself lived. And that rubbish he'd been talkin' last night. The Duma indeed! Who the hell worried about the Duma, even knew what they were, for that matter? Lucky he had remembered one of those P.S.C. chaps talking about them one night over the port at Netheravon.

He watched as Massiter's car pulled up by the cross and its owner stepped out. He was wearing a long grey motoring coat and a cap with goggles. Stripping these off, he slipped into a perfectly-cut black hunting coat the chauffeur held for him, then, taking a top-hat from its box, he walked over to where a groom had come on with the horses. Turned himself out properly, Grig had to admit that. And there was nothing wrong with his cattle either. Bought them himself, too, he believed, or with a little help from Bob Ferris the trainer. And the damn fellow could ride wherever he learnt it. He supposed they'd have to think about giving him the hunt button soon.

Grig saw Desmond Murtagh eyeing the newcomer and his mount and permitted himself the slightest of sardonic grins. Desmond did not like to be outshone and Massiter was the sort that always had to be first. Well, if they thought they were going to find out which was the better man across a country by riding over his hounds, they'd soon find they were very much mistaken. He scowled a response to Massiter's 'Good morning, Master,' nodded to Bob Ferris who had just come up on a fat cob, pulled a battered gun-metal watch from his pocket and glared at his first whip. 'Come along, Michael,' he said. 'No sense hangin' about any longer. We'll draw Gahan's gorse first.'

Stephen really loved hunting. It was not the killing part of it; he hated that and never watched it if he could help. That was why, he knew, his father had given it up along with other field sports. Edward had simply decided that he did not like killing things. But Edward was never one to impose his views on anyone, least of all his family, and he had put no obstacles in the way of Stephen and Ethel continuing to hunt. It was the thrill of it, the excitement, the actual riding, the feeling of being at one with your horse and the satisfaction of meeting your fences just right that Stephen loved. Racing, now, if only he could do it, he was sure that would be even better. Desmond Murtagh's ramshackle demesne was in easy bicycling or hacking distance from Bellary Court and whenever he could manage it Stephen was over there watching the horses work and learning what went on in a racing stable, albeit a pretty unorthodox one. He looked now at his idol, Desmond, sitting his big horse with a casual elegance as they hacked to the first covert, and wished with all his heart that he could grow up into someone like him.

Barbara, who was beside him, he liked her, too. She was fun to be with and she rode like her father. She was far bolder than he was, Stephen thought, and she did not seem to mind being cursed by that old monster Grig, which Stephen hated and dreaded. Harry French was usually with them to make up a threesome but Harry had scarcely spoken to him at the meet and now he was somewhere behind with his father. Stephen looked round to see just where Harry was and caught a glimpse of Sterling French sliding a flask surreptitiously back into a case in front of his saddle.

Something was wrong, again Stephen felt it, and for the hundredth time his mind went back to that conversation between his parents which he had overheard. He understood very little of what it meant

21

where it had concerned Harry's father. He only hoped it would not interrupt his friendship with Harry for Harry was the only real friend he had of his own age in the Bay. And Harry was the leader. It was to Harry he went for advice and to Harry that he poured out his troubles such as they were. But he could scarcely go to Harry with this one.

Gahan's was a big gorse clump lying across a narrow valley. Grig drew it slowly, his hounds thrusting through the thick gorse, questing, seeking, not an inch left unexplored. Grig's hounds never drew over a fox. Ever patient with them, never hurrying, never ranting, encouraging them with that musical voice which came so strangely from those bleak and saturnine features, Grig gave them all the time they needed. But Gahan's Gorse, usually a sure find, was blank.

So was the next covert and the next. Grig's expression grew ever more thunderous. There should be foxes here, he knew. This was wild mountainy country, just on the edge of the Bay where the hills ran down and the plains began. The people who lived here were something of a race apart, a clan of their own, a sort of cross between the placid inhabitants of the plains and the feckless, laughing people who lived in the mountains and along the shores of the Bay.

Someone had been at his foxes, Grig was sure. And they had no damn right to for the foxes in all this country were *his* foxes to pursue, match his skills against and kill if he could. If they outwitted him, well, good luck to them, perhaps they'd meet another day. But they weren't here to be shot or trapped or otherwise done away with by some damn countryman. Grig's chin sank deeper into his stock and his brow grew darker.

'Golly,' Barbara whispered to Stephen, 'Just look at him. Someone's going to catch it before the day is out.'

'Not me, if I can help it,' Stephen said fervently.

Beside them Desmond Murtagh gave one of his infectious laughs. 'You'd better keep at your distance, you two,' he said. 'You don't want to bring on a stroke in the Master, do you? All the same,' he added, 'there should be foxes here. I don't remember Gahan's being blank these last six seasons.'

The day was drawing on. Sandwiches were coming out. Sterling French had greater justification now in reaching for his flask. It was much lighter than when he had started out, he noticed, as he slid it back into its case. In fact it must be almost empty. At least its contents were putting a sort of haze between him and the grim reality he ought to be facing. Edward's letter had reached him just after breakfast and it was in his pocket now. Things must be bad to make Edward, of all people, write like that. He knew, of course, that he had dipped in where he shouldn't; he knew, too, that he had picked on Edward because his easy-going nature made discovery much less likely. And he had always intended to pay it back. He would have, too, if those gold shares had come right. That had been the culminating disaster. Could he, though, have taken as much as Edward implied? It had all slipped into his pocket in bits and pieces over the years. And how could he have been so careless over those Dublin rents? He supposed it was because in the last six months he had scarcely known what he was doing.

They were approaching a cluster of cabins set in a fold in the hills. With a shock French recognised them as belonging to the Rossiters, Edward's tenants. He remembered now that Honoria had mentioned this rental to him the other day. And for the life of him, his wits muddled by apprehension and alcohol, he could not recall just how that rental stood or how he had handled it.

As they drew abreast of the cabins he saw one of the Rossiters, he thought it was Larry, the head of the clan, standing in a doorway, watching them. Larry Rossiter's eyes met his and he left the doorway and came across to him. He was a tall, lean man, who walked with the easy stride of the mountainy people. There was no avoiding him for at the cross beyond the cabins Grig had pulled his horse to a standstill and was having a word with Michael.

Larry Rossiter stood beside French and looked up at him. 'I got a demand from ye for that rent,' he said.

French swallowed. 'What rent?' he said.

'Last six gales, the paper ye sent said. I paid ye that rent. I have the receipts kept, too.'

'There must be some mistake—'

'Aye, that there be and it's no mistake of mine. And this isn't the first time. I'm thinkin' of seein' Mr Raymond himself about it. He was always a decent man and his father before him.'

'No. No . . . I'll have it seen to.'

'Ye'd better do that then, French,' Larry Rossiter said with the easy insolence of a man who knows he is in the right. He looked along the line of horsemen to where Grig sat glowering at its head and a gleam of amusement came into his eyes. 'What's he doin' stoppin' here?' he asked. 'Has he any foxes caught, I wonder.'

'Making up his mind where to go next, I imagine,' French said and added with sudden venom, 'Someone's been shooting his foxes. I shouldn't like to be in his shoes if he catches him.'

Larry Rossiter gave a sudden barking laugh. 'Tell him there's a fox in Tubrid Hill,' he said. 'I'll be hearin' from ye, French, or else I'll be makin' a journey to see Mr Raymond.'

'What is it, Father? What did that man want?' Harry had suddenly appeared beside him.

'He says there's a fox in Tubrid Hill.'

'Are you all right, Father? You don't look well. Is anything wrong?'

'Yes, yes, of course I'm all right. Tell Colonel Gnowles about

23

Tubrid Hill.'

But he was not all right. He remembered all about the Rossiter rental now. He had never thought Edward would bother about it for it was a pittance really, coming as it did from this half-starved hillside. If Rossiter fulfilled his threat and went to Edward terrible things might happen. With Honoria pushing him they might even have him on trial for embezzlement and that could mean gaol.

And he was not done with the Rossiters yet. An old crone, wizened and bent and leaning on an ash plant, a shawl drawn tightly round her shoulders, was at Larry's elbow. 'Agents,' she hissed. 'Land agents, they call ye. Ye're only the carrion that picks the bones of the Irish.' She stretched out a long, gnarled finger towards him. 'You put that rent right, French,' she went on in a high-pitched, quavering voice. 'Or I'll call down God's curse on ye. And remember, French, I have four strapping sons—I can spare one for the gallows!' Then she spat on the road at his feet.

Sterling French shuddered and reached for his flask. Tilting it to his mouth, with one despairing swallow he finished what was left of the potent mixture of port and brandy with which he had filled it before setting out.

Harry threaded his way through the field to where Grig sat. He did not much relish his mission and thought Grig might well savage him as soon as he began to speak.

Grig was about to move on when Harry arrived beside him. 'Well, boy,' he barked. 'What is it, boy? Don't stand there like a damned dummy, boy. If you've anything to say, say it.'

'Excuse me, sir, but my father said to tell you a man back there said there was a fox in Tubrid Hill.'

'The devil he did. Who was it? Did you see him, Michael?'

'Larry Rossiter, sir.'

'One of that crew. Thievin' rascals. Shootin' my foxes to save his damned hens like as not. Tubrid Hill, eh? Very well, we'll try it. Get on, Michael.'

Tubrid Hill was a little knoll which jutted out from the main slope of the mountain. There was a lake the shape of a penny below it. A few sparse trees grew along its crest and a tangle of scree and gorse and scrub covered it. From its side just above the lake, where the field was gathered, you could see the sweep of the plains below. The coloured patchwork of fields stretched away into the distance to where a range of blue mountains at the very edge of the County Kilderry country smouldered in a misty haze.

Grig put his hounds in and almost immediately they gave tongue. Stephen saw the fox leave, a big grey mountain fox, slipping away at an easy lope, his mask set for the hills. Then hounds came pouring out and Michael's Gone away! Away! Away!' split the heavens.

Desmond Murtagh and Andrew Massiter, the frustrations of the morning forgotten, the slope of the hill behind them, eyeing each other and ready to ride for their reputations, let their big, blood horses go. They met Grig fair and square as he was jumping a fallen log out of covert, blowing his hounds away.

'Hold hard! Damn you, hold hard!' All Grig's pent-up wrath exploded on top of them. 'God damn you to hell, Desmond, can't you let my hounds hunt their fox?' He galloped on, turning in his saddle and still swearing. 'Haven't found a fox all day and you two bloody tailors try to ride over hounds! Hold hard, damn and blast the two of you!'

'Cutting up crusty. Thought he would,' Desmond said to his companion with an unrepentant grin.

'Daddy's catching it. He won't mind!' Barbara set her pony alight. 'Come on, Stephen.'

It was not the best of the County Kilderry country. The banks were small and dry and stony with an occasional stone wall but the hounds ran true and fast across it without check or hesitation for twenty minutes. Then they poured over a lichen-covered and broken-down demesne wall, crashed into the undergrowth beyond it and fell silent.

'Rochestown, isn't it?' Barbara said to Stephen.

'Yes,' he answered, looking at the tangle of abandoned ornamental trees and the sycamore, ash and elm that had grown wild amongst them. Through the branches he could see the blackened walls and empty windows of the old house. It was a strange, deserted, almost haunted place which had once been a property of some consequence. Long ago, before the famine, in the roistering days of the squireens, the then owner was said to have asked his wife's lover to dinner, made the three of them drunk and then set fire to the mansion, killing them all in the holocaust. No one had claimed the property; it was thought to be cursed and the country folk avoided it. Now what was left of it stood, a deserted shell in the lonely hills, a monument to the follies of an earlier generation.

'This looks like the end of it,' Desmond said, coming up to where Stephen, Barbara and Harry sat talking to Bob Ferris. 'We'll be here for the rest of the day. They'll never get him to leave this place.' He slid a gold cigarette case, a present from some inamorata, out of his pocket and opened it. 'Listen—'

There was a burst of music in covert and then silence again. 'Round and round, that's all they'll do,' he went on. 'Your father's cutting out the work, today, young Harry, isn't he? Going as if the devil was after him. I can't hardly catch him and this thing's got a bit of blood.'

'Are you going to run him at Punchestown, sir?' Stephen asked.

'No. I've a better one for that. Robin À Tiptoe. You can have your shilling on him in the Conyngham Cup. What do you say, Bob? I hear you run one in it.'

'Yes. Mr Massiter's. He'll be sending him along to me any day now, I hope.'

'He has him at home still, has he?'

'That's it, sir. I'm just to get him cherry ripe.'

'Well, if you beat me, you'll win it, but you won't!'

'We shall have to wait and see, sir, won't we,' Bob said. Privately he was wondering just what made Mr Murtagh so confident about his horse's chances in the big race. Bob carried the form of all the horses in the county and most of them outside it in his head. He knew all about Massiter's good horse though he had not yet got him. He was a class horse and to his mind Robin A Tiptoe was a goodish point to pointer but no more.

Stephen had not been giving his full attention to the conversation. He was listening to hounds who were speaking again. It seemed to him that their cry was getting further and further away. 'I wonder, sir,' he said to Desmond, 'should we move on. If they do go—'

'Don't bother your head, boy, they never get out of here.' Then Desmond hesitated and cocked an ear, listening intently, 'B'God, I don't know, you may be right, young feller. B'God, they have gone! Come on!' He kicked his big horse into a canter, leading the way round a corner of the demesne wall.

They jumped a small bank and in the next field Michael came out over a break in the wall. 'Gone for Castle Martin, sir, by the look of it,' he said to Desmond.

'Has he, b'God,' Desmond said, suddenly looking grim. 'That means we'll meet the Still. Look after the children, Bob.'

The next fence was a tall, narrow, stone-faced bank with a rough growth running along the top. Three people jumped it in front and abreast and were lucky to find places to do so. They were Desmond, Andrew Massiter and Sterling French. French's horse got to the top with a struggle and made a desperate blunder coming off it.

'He'll want to put some oats into that brute of his if he's going to go on riding at the top of the hunt,' Desmond thought as he saw the blunder and recovery. 'What's got into him today, I wonder? Never seen him push on like this before.'

Castle Martin was a name given to a rocky formation which towered up in a shape resembling a medieval castle. Its caves and caverns were a haunt of hill foxes. It was guarded by a ravine known for no reason that anyone could remember as the Still. This was only jumpable at all out of one field where it narrowed to a chasm with sheer, steep sides. It was not often met out hunting and less often jumped, for failure to clear it meant instant disaster to horse and man.

The country leading up to Castle Martin was even more stony and trappy than that which they had traversed before. Soon they could see its rocky outlines on the skyline in front of them and there could be no doubt that this was the fox's point.

All the children's ponies were by now beginning to tire. Big Bob Ferris was shepherding them along as best he could. Hounds were down on their left with Grig in close attendance and Desmond not far behind. There was no sign of Massiter and Stephen wondered if he was down somewhere.

The blind nature of the country meant that each fence was only jumpable in one or two places. Stephen had picked what he thought was a good spot in a trappy, narrow fence and was about to face up to it when he heard the thud of hooves behind him. He looked round. It was Massiter. He had been down all right. There was mud on the shoulder of his coat and his top-hat was dented. He was riding hard to catch up and it was obvious that he, too, had picked Stephen's place. 'Get on or get out of the way, boy,' he barked.

Stephen was near enough to the fence not to want to pull out. And in any event it was his place; he had been there first. But he was going slowly on a blown pony and clearly about to hold the other up and cause him to lose time in getting back to the top of the hunt. Stephen heard him swear. Then he shouted: 'Pull out, boy, pull out!' and cut in in front of him.

The big horse landed on the bank with a crash, kicking a stone out of it in the process. A piece of earth, dislodged by the impact, hit Stephen in the mouth. Massiter was over and gone without a backward glance. Pat, Stephen's pony, unbalanced but brave, tried to jump. He made a mess of it and tipped Stephen into the next field. 'You beast!' Stephen exclaimed as he rolled over and picked himself up.

'Are you all right, Master Stephen?' Bob Ferris' face appeared over the top of the fence.

'I'm all right, did you see what happened?' Stephen said, climbing on to Pat. 'Hurry up, Bob, we'll lose the hunt.'

'You're not going to try the Still, Master Stephen,' Bob said firmly. 'Nor any of you, either. Come along with me now, I know a way round.' He popped over the fence, followed by Harry and Barbara.

Bob led them into a little lane at the far side of the field and the four of them clattered down it. The lane ran out into a stretch of open ground carpeted with rough coarse grass and studded with outcrops of bare rock.

They were almost under the grim shadow of Castle Martin now. Directly below them was the Still. On their right, hounds had forced their way across higher up and were running on through a tangled mass of rock and heather driving up into the heart of the natural fortress.

In the field below, leading to the Still, were three riders. Grig, his eyes on the hounds, was in front, galloping steadily down the slope towards the chasm. Nothing ever stopped Grig when he was hunting

27

hounds. Without appearing to take note of the obstacle at all, his blood weed floated over it as if it was not there. Then he was pushing on through the heather towards where his pack, hackles up and ripe for a kill, were hard on their fox.

Behind him, Desmond and Massiter took it almost abreast. Desmond's big horse stood back and jumped it clean but Massiter, driving a tired horse, only just got away with it. His mount dropped a hind leg into it, kicked, scrambled and recovered somehow to slide and stagger on the far side and then roll over. Massiter was safely across but he was down with his second fall that day and Desmond and Grig were alone with the hounds.

Then the watchers saw that another rider had followed close on the heels of the leaders. Sitting loosely in the saddle, his eyes fixed ahead, he was approaching the Still at a point between where Desmond and Massiter had taken it. The reins were slack in his hands and he was making no attempt to pull his horse together and drive him on as a tired horse needed at such a jump. It was Sterling French.

The horse hesitated as he neared the chasm. Then, as if waking from a dream, French sat up and hit him hard, once, behind the saddle. They jumped. Even from the height where Stephen and the others were watching it was evident that they were not going to make it. They hit the far side and horse and rider fell together into the ravine.

For a moment the watchers were too stunned to move. Then Barbara gave a little cry of horror.

'Papa!' Harry cried out in anguish. 'Papa!' He took hold of his pony's head and turned him towards the slope leading to the Still.

Bob grasped his bridle. 'Be aisy now, Master Harry,' he said. 'Stay where you are. And stay with him, Master Stephen and Miss Barbara. Wait till I come back.' Then he was bucketing his cob down the hill.

People, as always, had sprung up from nowhere. Members of the field were gathering around. Black-coated countrymen were running like ants across the fields towards the scene of the accident. Soon the children could see nothing but a crowd of people, some peering into the chasm.

'I must go down,' Harry repeated. 'I must go down.'

'No, Harry, no. Wait. Remember what Bob said,' Barbara told him.

The three of them peered anxiously at the crowd, trying to discover what was going on. Some members of the field had dismounted and were trying to clamber down into the ravine.

Bob reached the outskirts of the crowd, gave his cob to a bystander and began to push his way through it. After a little while they saw him coming back. He took the cob, remounted and cantered slowly towards them. When he came up his face was set. He looked at Harry with sadness written across his friendly features. 'You'd better come away with me, now, Master Harry,' he said.

4

Even Honoria was temporarily subdued by the shock of Sterling French's death. She knew nothing, of course, of the letter Edward had written and he took good care not to tell her. Two days after the funeral she announced her intention of going to the cousins with whom Ethel was staying and bringing Ethel back with her on her return.

Edward to his great relief was then left alone to consider his position and what he should do about it without any interference from his wife. Sooner or later she would have to know but just at this moment he could not face the accusations and recriminations he knew would follow any revelation to her of just how bad things might be.

In any event, he did not himself know the magnitude of the disaster and he had only very hazy ideas about how to set about finding out. The true state of affairs could only be ascertained by an examination of the estate books and bank accounts, which was a matter for experts. Had French lived, the whole thing could, perhaps, have been quietly settled up between them, but that was impossible now. But who was he to call in and whose advice was he to take? He had early on decided against consulting either of the two local solicitors in Bellary and revealing to them the extent of his foolishness and the depth of French's disgrace. His own men of business were two elderly relatives of Honoria's practising in Kilderry. They had, according to their own account, 'come down to the professions'. They appeared to Edward to spend most of their time in the County Club, situated across the Mall from their office, eating fruit cake and sipping port, and discussing endlessly, with anyone who would listen, genealogical details of the local Ascendancy families. Quite apart from their relationship with Honoria, Edward did not feel they were the best people to handle his present pressing problems.

To add to his worries, too, he could not escape the conviction that he was in some way responsible for his agent's death.

Two days after Honoria's departure a letter arrived from his bank manager asking him to call. This threw him into still greater panic than before. If the bank manager had written, things must be even worse than he had thought. In his harassed and confused state of mind he took a sudden decision.

There was only one man in the Bay who had the knowledge, acumen and business background to advise in such a situation as this. That man was Andrew Massiter. Massiter would know what he should do. Massiter was a man of affairs. Look how he had talked at dinner the other night. Buy commodities, he had said, whatever the devil they were. Not exactly the way one expected a guest to talk at a gentleman's dinner but, by George, that sort of knowledge could come in very useful now. Massiter would tell him what to do and advise him whom he should consult. He had made his fortune himself; he knew those who inhabited the great world beyond the Bay.

Edward sat down and wrote Massiter a note. The reply came by return. Massiter would be pleased to see him the following day.

Sitting at his desk the next morning, Edward pondered over how best he should put his problem before the other man. The more he turned it over in his mind the more foolish, it seemed, he would appear, but that, he supposed, could not be helped. With a sigh he crossed the room and pulled the tasselled bell-cord. After an interval it was answered not by Rogers, but by Mikey, wearing a striped apron and looking dishevelled.

'Where is Mr Rogers?' Edward asked.

'He's in bed, sir. Them bunions of his are that bad they're tormentin' him something terrible.'

'I see. Well, tell Mr Hannigan in the yard I want the dog-cart round in half an hour and ask Master Stephen to come here, please.'

When Mikey had left, Edward turned to stare out at the Bay through the tall windows that allowed light to flow through the room. It was a clear day; the storm had long since passed and the surface of the Bay was calm and still. The mountains rolling away into the hazy distance were taking on the colours of spring. As always the beauty of the place took him by the throat. You never forgot it and it never palled or staled. Big white cumulous clouds were piling up on the far side and, even as he watched, beneath them on the hillsides the colours began to blend and change.

It would kill him, Edward thought, if he had to leave all this. But could he stay on? Again his thoughts came back to gnaw at the subject they had rarely left since that night he had spent in the rent room. Was he ruined? Had French's defalcations and his own carelessness brought the whole family to irretrievable disaster?

When Stephen came in Edward turned slowly from the window. He had asked Mikey to send the boy to him partly because he would be company on the drive to Massiter's and, usually a solitary man, he found in times of trouble that he wished for company.

30

More importantly, however, he knew that sooner or later, and better sooner now that Honoria was away, he must tell the boy that he could no longer expect to go to Eton. He supposed, too, that that meant looking for another school, but for the moment that could wait.

'You wanted me, Father?' Stephen's voice broke into his thoughts.

'I'm going over to see Mr Massiter. I thought you might like to come along. Perhaps you'd be interested to see the Castle. It's very impressive, I'm told.' That was Edward's way. Even with his children he never commanded; he asked.

'Of course, Father. I'd love to. Do you think he'll let me see the horses?'

Edward smiled. 'I expect so if you ask nicely. Get your coat, will you, and meet me downstairs. The dog-cart should be round by now.'

Together they climbed into the dog-cart while one of the grooms stood at the horse's head. Edward pulled the waterproof rug across their knees. 'Are you sure you are warm enough, my boy?' he asked.

'Yes, thank you, Father.' This was a great adventure, going with his father to see the ogre's castle, the two of them together. Things were much nicer when his mother and Ethel were away. He didn't like Mr Massiter much and he still remembered that fall out hunting, but his father would be with him so he would hardly, himself, see much of the ogre and his father had said he could probably see the horses. He might even see the 'chaser they were going to run in the Conyngham Cup against Babs' father's horse. Massiter had been training him himself or rather his stud-groom had, for his point to points and early races. He was to go to Bob Ferris for his winding up races and his final preparation, but from what Stephen had gleaned from the conversation between Bob and Desmond out hunting Bob had not yet got him. Merrymaker, his name was, Stephen remembered, and he was useful, all right. Stephen had seen him win those early point to points, one by six lengths and the other by a distance. But they'd never beat Babs' father. No one could beat him. Stephen began to drift off into a dream of his own as his father picked the long whip out of the slot beside him, touched the blood four-year-old between the shafts, and they trotted off down the long avenue.

They crossed the town square of Bellary and began to traverse the extreme tip of the Bay where it ended in a series of rocky coves and inlets. The four-year-old spanked along, his hooves ringing clear on the unmetalled road. Soon they were passing the gates of Grig's demesne. Two stone gryphons snarled at each other from the tops of their piers. A long, straight avenue bordered by churchyard yews, set at regular intervals like a regiment on parade, led to the house itself, a square, grim, cut-stone Georgian edifice. Without portico, cornice or entablature to soften its lines it stared belligerently down the Bay, the embodiment in stone, Edward always thought, of those who had occupied it during the generations since Cromwell had granted their sword and bible ancestor the confiscated lands of the O'Learys and the O'Regans.

A little further along the left-hand side of the road, down almost at the edge of the Bay itself was Maple Villa, the house where the Frenches had lived. It was shuttered now, for the family had packed and gone immediately after the funeral, though the cutter which had been Sterling French's pride and joy and which he had been readying for the summer still lay on the boat slip below the house.

The sight of the shuttered windows and the closed and empty house brought back to Stephen a scene he had been trying to forget. It was a scene which he had entirely failed to understand and which became more incomprehensible the more he puzzled over it.

Before the funeral Stephen had been surprised that none of the French family had made an appearance at Bellary Court. They had been close friends, after all, and he had expected that Harry would be over when he could tell him how sorry he was about the awful accident. He had been even more surprised that, when he had mentioned this to his father and suggested riding over himself to Maple Villa, his father had advised him not to. At the funeral he had made it his business to seek Harry out. Harry's face, taut and pinched and white as he turned towards him, was still vivid in his memory and Harry's words were burned into his brain. 'Go away,' Harry had said between tight lips. 'I hate you. Your father killed my father. I hate you. I'll never speak to any of you again.' There was the memory, too, of Mrs French, dressed all in black, brushing past where he stood with his father and mother, her face averted, and not speaking a word to them. What had it all meant? It must have something to do with that conversation he had overheard between his parents. But who could ever have imagined his gentle father killing anyone?

The sight of Maple Villa, too, had reminded Edward of one of the reasons he had asked Stephen to accompany him. He coughed, cleared his throat and said: 'There is something I must tell you my boy.'

'Goodness,' Stephen thought. 'Is he going to tell me he really did kill Harry's father? If he does, what can I do? But he wasn't near us all day, he wasn't even out hunting. What can it all mean?'

'I'm afraid,' Edward said, 'we won't be able to send you to Eton when you leave Wyston House next half.'

Relief flooded over Stephen. Was that all! What did he care about mouldy old Eton. He supposed he'd have to go somewhere but it was the Bay he loved. He never wanted to leave the Bay and he never would.

'You must remember,' his father was going on, staring straight ahead, 'that there are other good schools besides Eton, though I'm afraid Etonians don't think so. We'll have to find you one. There's been a bit of money trouble, I'm sorry to say. I hope you are not too disappointed.'

'Of course not, Father. I don't mind a bit, really.' Stephen dimly realised that he should say something more. 'I hope things are not too bad, Father.'

'I trust not, my boy.'

'And, Father—' the words tumbled out from Stephen almost before he could help it.

'Yes, my boy.'

'It won't make any difference to our going to Punchestown, will it? I do hope not, Father. You see, Mr Murtagh has a runner in the Conyngham Cup and so has Mr Massiter. Out hunting, Mr Murtagh said his horse Robin A Tiptoe would win. I'm sure it will too if Mr Murtagh rides him.'

'You wouldn't like to miss that, would you?' Edward said gravely.

'Oh, no, Father.'

'Well, we'll have to see. I'm sure we can manage it. Desmond says he'll win it, does he?'

'Yes, Father, and everyone says he is the best gentleman rider in Ireland. I wish I could ride like him.'

'Perhaps some day you will. I don't think I'd copy him in everything though.' This was another puzzling grown-up remark, Stephen thought, but by that time they had arrived at the ornate castellated gateway at the entrance to Dunlay Castle, the seat of Andrew Massiter Esquire.

The avenue curved along by the sea, crossed a bridge and went through a cutting, each side of which was covered by a mass of rhododendrons that had not yet come to bloom. As they emerged from the cutting the immense bulk of the castle rose almost like a cliff in front of them.

It was built on a slight rise in the ground from which lawns sloped down to a private harbour. The avenue ran beside this harbour which, like everything about the place, was built on the grand scale and was almost an inlet in itself. Its entrance was guarded by two groves of conifers that framed a vista of the main waters of the Bay and the mountains. At the edge of the nearest grove the avenue swung round to climb through another cutting and ended in a great sweep of immaculately kept gravel. Confronting them as they pulled to a standstill was the vast arched doorway of the castle, which would not have disgraced a cathedral. The whole thing was crowned by the tall white tower above the entrance.

The house itself was an immense affair of Tudor windows, turrets, battlements, crenellations, galleries and even a sham cloister running along the side that faced the harbour. It was a Gothic extravaganza to

33

end all Gothic extravaganzas and because of its size and the scale on which it had been conceived it was impressive in a slightly shocking way.

Two iron-studded wooden doors filled the great arched entrance. In one of these was a wicket. A groom had appeared from nowhere and had taken hold of the horse's head. Edward and Stephen dismounted and when Edward pulled on the brass bell pull the wicket opened and a manservant admitted them.

Stephen gasped at what he saw. Once through a small entrance hall underneath the tower they were in an immense flagged main hall. On either side were arched galleries supported by pillars of pink marble. These galleries extended to two floors and the rest of the vast space went clean up through the centre of the house to a dome in the roof. Facing them was a massive stone staircase. This divided into two branches with heavily carved marble banisters, which climbed up to meet the galleries. Stephen was entranced. To his romantic eye it seemed the most wonderful place he had ever been in.

Edward stood for a moment looking about him. 'Hm,' he said almost under his breath. 'Bit overdone, I should have thought. Rather on the large size for one man, too.'

'The Master is in the library, sir,' the manservant said. He led the way down the length of the hall to a door beside the stairway. They traversed a short passage and then he opened another door. 'Mr Raymond, sir,' he said.

The library was full of dark furniture. The walls were lined with glass-fronted, gold-wired bookcases filled with sets of books, elaborately bound. Andrew Massiter was in a leather armchair in front of the fire reading *The Times*. He rose as they came in.

'I'm afraid I brought the boy.' Edward said with his diffident smile. 'I wonder—perhaps he could see the horses while we talk?'

'Of course. Ask Leary to look after him, will you, Johnson? Tell someone to take him to the tower, too, if he likes.'

When the door had closed behind them, Massiter motioned Edward to a chair. 'Would you care for anything after your drive?' he said.

'No, thank you, Massiter. It's good of you to give me your time.'

'Time scarcely matters here, does it? It's one of the things I find so attractive about it all'

'I daresay.' Edward in some remote way felt that his beloved Bay was being patronised and he didn't think he cared for it. But he had come to seek help; he had made up his mind that this was the only man who could help him, he must go through with it now. He drew a deep breath. 'I've come to ask your advice, Massiter,' he said. 'If you'll be so kind as to assist me. The truth is I find myself in the devil of a fix. In fact I'm not at all sure I know how or where to start.'

Massiter smiled a little grimly. He pushed a cedar-wood cigar-box towards his guest. Taking one himself, he snipped off its end with a gold cutter. 'It's French, I should imagine, isn't it?' he said.

'How the devil did you know that?'

'I've had time to think a little since I got your letter. When I came here first I made certain enquiries about him. The replies I got were to say the least unenthusiastic. Yours was just about the only agency he had left. The crash was bound to come.'

'Come it has, no doubt about it,' Edward said. With that he poured out the whole story in so far as he himself knew it.

Massiter listened to him in silence save for interjecting a question now and then. These questions were pertinent and to the point. Not wishing to disclose the extent of his own folly and the depths of his ignorance concerning his own affairs, many of Edward's answers were evasive and lacking in complete candour. These rather pathetic attempts to preserve his self-respect did not for an instant deceive Massiter who had from the first read him like an open book. And, while he was talking, Massiter's mind was working to decide what course he could take that would turn Edward's troubles to his own advantage.

When Edward had finished Massiter crossed to a table by the window where a high-sided silver tray was laid with decanters and glasses.

'I'll take a glass of sherry if I may,' Edward said in answer to his question. Then, for the first time since he had entered the room, he became aware of his surroundings. The tall, mock Tudor mullions of the window where Massiter was standing framed a magnificent vista, reaching out over the private harbour along the whole sweep of the Bay right up to the town of Bellary. He gazed out, thinking again that he could never bear to leave it all and hoping against hope that this new chap in this vulgar great castle of his might somehow find a way for him to ride out his troubles.

'You know,' Massiter was saying as a servant poured sherry from a Waterford decanter, 'things may not be so bad as you think. But first you must ascertain exactly how you do stand. After that we can discuss a course of action.'

'I agree, but to be candid I am somewhat at a loss to know how or where to start.'

'You have your own man of business, I suppose?'

'There are solicitors in Kilderry but frankly I don't think they are quite the people to handle a matter of this sort.'

'And you would not care to entrust it to one of the local men, I imagine.'

'Certainly not.'

'I agree. Well, in that case, may I suggest that you consult the man who looks after my affairs, William Hutton of Will Hutton & Co of Dublin. He's a very clever chap. He will get to the bottom of it for you.

And you can trust him implicitly. If you agree I can write to him now.'

'I'd be very grateful if you would.'

'Good, that's settled, then.' Massiter crossed to a desk. 'I'll get him down straight away.' Things, he thought, as his pen crossed the paper, were really turning out very nicely indeed. This was becoming uncommonly interesting.

'Do you think, Massiter,' Edward felt rather as if he were consulting a doctor and asking for an opinion while he awaited a full diagnosis, 'that this man of yours will find a way out?'

'If anyone can, he will. Now, you and the boy must stay for luncheon. I've told them to expect you.'

'You are very kind. Splendid place you have here, Massiter. Quite a change from Barty Corringer's time.'

Massiter smiled briefly. 'I enlarged on his plans a little, that was all,' he said.

When Stephen left the house he was handed over to the care of a groom who brought him down to the stableyard. This had been built in the same castellated style and on much the same scale as the house. An arched gateway with a fringe of fake battlements running along its top led into the upper yard where were the stud-groom's house, the grooms' quarters and the boxes for the hacks and carriage horses. Here Stephen was formally introduced to Mr Morrissey the stud-groom, a wizened little man with bow legs encased in spotless box-cloth gaiters. 'Show him the hunters and the racehorses, Jim,' he said. 'But remember I'm working Merrymaker with Coachman in twenty minutes in the long meadow.' He took a watch from his pocket, consulted it and put it back. 'But I expect,' he said, looking at Stephen, 'the Master will be wanting the young gentleman back at the castle before then.'

There were fifteen big blood horses in Massiter's stables, bought to carry their owner in the first flight with the County Kilderry hounds or to act as replacements for the injuries his hard-riding inevitably inflicted. All of them were solemnly paraded for Stephen's inspection. 'Not a commoner amongst them' he was commending knowledgeably to the groom when he saw two horses with sleek and shining coats being pulled out from boxes lower down the yard.

'That's Merrymaker, the Punchestown horse,' the groom said, pointing to the leader. 'The other is old Coachman.'

Stephen hurried on to get a closer look. Merrymaker was the horse Desmond Murtagh and Bob Ferris had been talking about out hunting. He had come on since he had last seen him point to pointing. He looked all quality and up to weight, too, a real Conyngham Cup horse, Stephen thought judicially and with all the authority of his thirteen years. Coachman he remembered as an old chaser Massiter

36

had bought probably to use as a lead horse. Coachman was past his best but he had won good races in his day and could probably still go a bit.

Two lads swung themselves up on the horses. With their rugs still on them they went out under a farther archway and made their way along a pathway leading through trees and banks of rhododendrons. A moment later Mr Morrissey followed on his hack.

'What are they going to do?' Stephen asked eagerly.

'A rough-up gallop. That's what he says,' was the reply.

Their eyes followed the horses until they disappeared round a bend in the track. 'Better be getting back,' the groom said then.

At the same side door through which he had left the house Stephen was delivered into the charge of a supercilious footman in livery. 'I understand I'm to take you to the tower,' he said, looking at a point somewhere about six inches above Stephen's head.

It was all very gorgeous and grand, Stephen thought, as they threaded their way through what seemed an endless succession of corridors and stairways arched and vaulted and flanked about by Gothic splendours. At length they reached the upper gallery where Stephen could peer down through the vaulting into the gloomy depths of the great hall. At the far end of this gallery they were at the front of the house. Passing under yet another archway, they climbed a narrow twisting staircase, where at the top an iron-bound doorway brought them to the flat roof of the tower. Now, they were at the highest point of the great house and the whole panorama of the Bay lay open before them.

Immediately below him Stephen could see the lawns running down to the private harbour and, beyond the shores of the demesne, the long shape of Holy Island with its causeway. Holy Island had been the scene of sailing picnics when Stephen and Ethel had been younger but somehow recently his parents had lost interest in picnics or maybe Ethel had said they were childish things and had refused to take part in them. It would not be unlike her if she had. But Holy Island with its ruined church, its holy well, its stone circle said to be Druidical at its eastern end and its caverns and caves had always fascinated Stephen.

Beside them on the roof was a powerful, brass-bound telescope mounted on a tripod which Massiter had had set up there to give his guests greater enjoyment of the spectacular view. The footman gave a vague gesture towards it. 'Perhaps you would care to look through that,' he said, and then resumed his bored contemplation of empty spaces.

Stephen bent down, put the telescope to his eye and focused it. Everything suddenly sprang into closeness and clarity. At the head of the Bay he could see the cluster of houses that was the town of Bellary with his own home on its bluff above it. So distinct were they that he fancied he could almost see into his schoolroom window. There on

37

the opposite shore was the Old Earl's Lodge amongst its trees, Desmond's decaying mansion and then, in the distance, the three rocky islands and the open sea. Below him he could peer into every secret of Holy Island, the inlet with its jetty where they moored for their picnics, the boathouse and the paths leading to scattered clearings amongst the tangled trees.

Fascinated, Stephen swung the telescope around. As he did so something moving below him and not far away, beyond the turrets and battlements of the stableyard, caught his eye. Steadying the telescope he looked again. Horses were galloping round the perimeter of a long, oval field. He knew immediately what he was watching. This was the rough-up gallop of which the groom had spoken and such was the magnification of the lens that he might almost be standing beside them. He swung the telescope on its pivot so that he could follow the progress of the gallop.

Together the two horses passed where Mr Morrissey sat his hack. As they did so Stephen saw him raise his hand in what was evidently a signal to the riders. Immediately, in response, the pace quickened. After a few strides they began really to go on. Then Stephen, from his knowledge gained from watching countless gallops at Desmond's, realised something else. This was no rough-up gallop; this was a trial.

Down the far side of the big field both riders shook up their horses. As they turned for home, one began to draw steadily away. When he passed where the stud-groom sat he was fully five lengths in front of the other. Stephen held the big telescope on him as he came back. There was no doubt in his mind which this horse was. It was Merrymaker and he had left old Coachman cold.

The two riders had a brief word with the stud-groom and then passed on into the trees and out of Stephen's view. What made him wait with the telescope still focused on Mr Morrissey he never quite knew. Instinctively he was aware that what he had seen was not right, that something was going on that should not be, and, since Mr Morrissey had not followed the other horses but had remained sitting on his hack as if waiting, that there was more to follow.

His instinct did not betray him. As he watched a figure came out from behind the massive trunk of a Spanish chestnut and walked towards the stud-groom. He was full in the lens of the telescope and Stephen had no difficulty at all in recognising him. They spoke together for a moment or two and then the man on his feet reached up and handed something to the other. That done he turned and walked again into the trees.

Now what in the world, thought Stephen, was his hero, Desmond Murtagh, doing there watching that gallop and handing something to Mr Massiter's stud-groom?

5

Will Hutton stepped off the Dublin train at Bellary station a few days later. He was a tall thin man with a face that might have been made from dried leather. He wore a wing collar with a string tie and carried a Gladstone bag. A long black overcoat encased him like a tube.

Massiter's motor-car was waiting for him outside the station. On arrival at the castle he was shown into the library where Massiter was standing at the window looking out over the Bay and stroking his trimmed imperial. 'Ah, Hutton,' he said. 'You had a good journey, I trust. Come along and sit down. We have something which may be of considerable interest to discuss.'

Massiter and Hutton understood each other very well for they were both on the make, each in his own way.

Massiter had been born the son of a grocer and general merchant far away on the east coast. As he had begun to come to manhood he had been brought face to face with the all-but-feudal power exercised by the Ascendancy families of the day. He had both resented and envied the manner in which they controlled every avenue of power—the Grand Jury, the County Council, the Poor Law Guardians and, of more immediate concern to him and his family, the patronage given to the shop-keepers in the town who competed for their services. The sudden decline in his father's fortunes had been a living instance of this.

For many years Massiter's father and his father before him had been the general providers of groceries and provisions to the nobility and gentry of the area. It had been a prosperous business until one day the wife of the greatest grandee of them all had stopped by the shop to give an order. On the rare occasions when she did this in person Massiter senior was expected to leave whatever he was doing and stand bareheaded by the carriage while he received and took down his instructions.

On the day in question it was raining and he had been in the warehouse at the back of the shop supervising a delivery. The messenger had thought he was elsewhere on the premises and had been slow in finding him. When he did so Massiter had looked for and failed to find his umbrella which was missing from its usual place. All this had meant that the lady was kept waiting for longer than she expected or thought proper for a person of her high station in life. Before he reached the door she had directed the coachman to drive on. The next day Massiter had received a letter asking for her account and stating that she was placing her custom elsewhere. That was bad enough but at tea parties and dinner tables she had proclaimed that Massiter the grocer was getting above himself and had prevailed upon others of her circle to remove their patronage also.

Retainers and dependents followed the example of their betters; the business and profits of A. W. Massiter and Son had declined both sadly and quickly. When his father had died not long afterwards Massiter realised that there was nothing left for him in that town. He sold the shop, paid the debts and with what little was left emigrated to South America to find his fortune.

On the boat going out he had fallen in with another adventurer who had been in England trying to raise capital for an enterprise he was sure would succeed. The railways were expanding fast in South America. In the backward parts especially, anyone who could plot their progress—and he claimed to have access to sources of information which would enable him to do this—would be in a position to buy the land they would cross cheaply and sell to them at an enormous profit.

It had all been too speculative for conservative English minds and he had failed to arouse any interest. Massiter, however, was attracted to the scheme. It was a gamble but then he had come prepared to gamble. If the other man's sources of information were as accurate as he said they were, indeed if only one or two of them were, then the risk was negligible and the prospective gain a goldmine indeed. He offered to put his remaining capital into the enterprise.

With their limited resources their first purchase was a small one. But the information was accurate. They held the railway to ransom and increased their investment tenfold. After that they never looked back. Buying ever larger and larger tracts of land, both became rich.

All this time Massiter never forgot what had happened to his father and why. A burning resentment against a class that had crippled him financially and ruined his life stayed with him always. Another man might have found his revenge, as many Irish Americans did, by turning towards the subversive movements that even then were just beginning to flex their muscles. Massiter never even contemplated this. Instead he determined to return to Ireland, to adopt their way of life and to prove to both himself and them that they could not ride roughshod over him as they had his father.

Money, he told himself, would give him power, for the world was beginning to turn away from inherited privilege to the power and patronage that wealth could buy. In England the scions of the industrial revolution had in many cases already established themselves alongside the great families, or acquired respectability by marrying into them. Edward VII was picking his friends from amongst the international set, financiers and the like, and conferring peerages on them.

He would, Massiter told himself, do all the things they did and do them better. He would have better carriages, faster horses, larger motor-cars and greater houses. And should any of them stand in his way he would ruin them as casually as they had ruined his father. Position and power were his twin aims; the amassing of a fortune was not an end in itself, it was a step on the way to achieving his ultimate goal. Instinctively, too, he realised that a knowledge and mastery of the horse would be an essential if he were to succeed. An ability to ride had in any event been necessary to cope with the long journeys over the roadless Pampas surveying the areas of their prospective purchases. Here he had been lucky, for like many of his countrymen he was a natural horseman and he found sitting into the easy swing and lope of the cow ponies came effortlessly to him. When the heady gambling days of risk, adventure and speculation were over and his money was made, he had taken up residence in Rio and embarked on other enterprises in which he had been no less successful. He had owned and run racehorses also with success and become a member of the Racing Club. Through it all he had never married. A succession of mistresses had satisfied his sexual needs. A wife would have slowed him down. Later, when he was established, he would choose a suitable consort to reign and rule at his side in his castle. When his sexual desires needed slaking there were trips to London and visits to discreet establishments where the requirements of men of his wealth and standing were understood and catered for.

The opportunity to purchase Dunlay had come through Hutton. The firm of which Hutton was the head had lately absorbed another older firm who acted for the Corringers. Barty Corringer had wildly overspent himself in adding extravagant extensions to Dunlay Castle, his family seat. In an attempt to recoup his fortunes he had, ironically, put every penny he had into a speculative South American railway. Hutton had been recommended to Massiter as a sharp and successful solicitor well qualified to look after any Irish interests he might acquire. During an interview on a visit home Hutton had asked Massiter if he knew anything about San Romeo Deferred since he had a client who had made a considerable investment in it, unwisely in Hutton's opinion.

Massiter's mind never missed a trick or the opportunity, however remote, of taking one. By careful and apparently casual probing he had discovered the client's name and after that it was only a small matter to find out the reason behind the investment and the enquiry. As it happened, Massiter knew all about San Romeo Deferred and the San Romeo Railway for that matter, since he was holding a tract of land in front of its proposed development and was waiting for his price. It was one of his more fortunate investments for the land he held consisted of a long narrow valley between two mountain ranges. There was nowhere for the railway to go save through that valley without incurring an expense that would ruin it. Massiter named a price which he knew was far beyond the resources of the railway to meet and from that price he refused to budge. The San Romeo Railway went bankrupt and brought down the Corringers with it. Massiter purchased the shares in San Romeo for a song and allowed it the use of his valley for half the former asking price. He also purchased the unfinished castle very cheaply for no one wanted what was held to be a half-completed monstrosity. He had taken his time consulting architects and contractors about the enlargements and improvements he intended to make for there were his business interests in South America to be wound up as well. During all this time rumour and legend circulated in the Bay about him, as he well knew and rather enjoyed. When the castle was completed he had a country seat of sufficient grandeur to satisfy his ambitions and had returned home to take up residence.

In fact it was not all cupidity and desire for aggrandisement which had inspired his purchase of Dunlay. There was something in him which responded to the grandiloquence of it and it was with genuine enjoyment that he roamed through the great rooms revelling in their size and spaciousness and marvelling at the different vistas of the Bay commanded by the tall windows. And he was beginning to find that the Bay was laying its spell on him, too. The peace and beauty of the place in its periods of calm soothed his restless spirit and the sudden changes of rain and storm matched his own changing moods.

But, having made the purchase, he knew that this was only the first step towards achieving acceptance by the conservative, closed society into which he had come. His ability on a horse helped for he was aware that one of the things these simple people admired above all else was the ability to go well out hunting. His nerve was unshakeable and the banks and stone walls of the County Kilderry country held no terrors for him.

No one but himself knew the true story of his acquisition of Dunlay though Will Hutton had made a pretty accurate guess at it. Since he realised that his chance query might have sparked off the whole thing, Hutton had his own reasons for keeping quiet. In any event Massiter was an important client and it would not be to his advantage to betray him. For Hutton, too, was an ambitious man. He wanted money and he wanted success. The old firm which he had absorbed brought him respectable clients which in those pre-war days it was important to have for both prestige and income, but Hutton was shrewd enough to realise that the fortunes of the gentry were declining. The Land Acts and the Local Government Act of 1898 had cut them off from the base upon which their power rested and men such as Massiter together with the rising merchants and businessmen in Dublin and the provinces were replacing them as a source of both money and influence.

'Is this likely to take long?' he asked now. 'Should I send for someone from the office to take over once I have it started?'

'It depends how bad things are but I don't think so. It's a comparatively small affair but it may be important to me. I would like you to give it your personal attention. I shall see to it of course that your time is not ill-spent. It's about Raymond at Bellary Court.'

'His agent has been cheating him, I gather from what you said in your letter. That's not unusual. Has he given you any details?'

'He's given me everything in so far as he knows it himself. He's a child in these matters.'

'What has he got to meet these defalcations if they are substantial?'

Massiter crossed to the desk and unrolled an ordnance sheet. 'There is the house, Bellary Court,' he said putting his finger on the map. 'I don't know how much land he will be left with after the sales to the tenants have gone through.'

'I've looked into that. I have a contact in the Land Commission. He's in under the 1909 Act with his last and final sales. They'll leave him with about three hundred acres.'

'That's very satisfactory. I'm obliged to you. Now we know where we are as regards the main place.'

'Is it good land?'

'It would be if he looked after it.'

'Any charges?'

'Only to the Bank, he tells me.'

'No other jointures or encumbrances?'

'I gather not but of course you'll find that out.'

'They're probably on the Schedule of Encumbrances in the Land Commission. I haven't had time to have that inspected. Has he anything else in the way of assets?'

Massiter picked up a sheet of paper on which he had made notes during Edward's visit.

'Dublin rents bringing in about £300 a year,' he said. 'Rental of a village near here, Cloonara, say £150 per annum, and a parcel of mountainy land occupied by three families all related and all called Rossiter. Blackguards most of them. I gather it's not in the Land Commission sale for some reason. They're a queer, dangerous lot or so I'm told. No value.'

'There should be money from the Land Commission sales,' Hutton said. 'He may quite possibly have drawn against it in expectancy, however. Do you know who acts for him?'

'A firm called Merrett & Merrett in Kilderry. Are you acquainted with them?'

'I know of them. They're very slow. They're probably just about clearing up the arrears of the Wyndham Act. It will be some years before he sees any of the money coming from the Land Commission, I should estimate. Anything else?'

'A small private income, mostly settled.'

'Has the wife any money?'

'Very little and what there is is in the settlement. She's a termagant, by the way.'

'I see. That gives me a pretty clear picture. I'll look into it all and let you have a report. You want me to start right away?'

'I'll have you driven over this afternoon.'

'You think it might be an investment?'

'There's a war coming. I have no doubt of that. If it does, land and stock will both appreciate. If there is adequate security it could well suit me to see him right, pay off the Bank and the deficit and take a first mortgage.'

'He would have reason to be grateful if you did. Has he much influence in the locality? He is a J.P. and a D.L., I see.'

'The family have been here a long time. He's very well liked.'

'I take your point,' Will Hutton said.

The eyes of the two men met.

6

To Edward's dismay Honoria and Ethel returned from their visit earlier than he had expected. He had hoped that by the time they arrived Hutton would have finished his task and gone, and that he would have been able to present his wife with some sort of *fait accompli*. It was not to be, for when she arrived Hutton was in the rent room working at the ledgers and his presence immediately became known to her.

'Who is this man?' she demanded of Edward, invading his upstairs sanctuary for the second time in the space of a month. 'What is he doing? What is *happening*, Edward?'

Pushing aside the *Annals of the County of Kilderry*, and his notes and records for his own history of the Bay and its peoples in which he had hoped to find seclusion and some sort of solace, Edward rose from his desk and walked to the window. The Bay was at its loveliest, its stillness unruffled, its colours beginning to change and grow as spring crept in. For once, however, it held out little hope of peace for him. Instead it reminded him of all that he would lose if he left it. With a sigh he turned from the window and faced her. Haltingly he related the whole story, or as much of it as he knew. The full facts would only be learnt when Hutton had completed his investigation.

'So,' she said when he had finished. 'It seems that you may have allowed us to be ruined. I hope you're pleased with your handiwork, Edward. And how could you be so foolish as to place yourself in this man Massiter's hands? My cousins could have looked after all this for you. At least, then, our disgrace would have been kept in the family.'

'Hardly our disgrace, my dear,' Edward said mildly. 'The disgrace, I'm afraid, is that of Sterling French.' Privately he congratulated himself that he had at least had the sense not to entrust his affairs to Honoria's cousins. His problems required more urgent and skilled attention than Messrs Merrett & Merrett were likely to give to them.

At his reply Honoria emitted her peculiar half-neigh, half-snort through her high-bridged nose. 'Has this man Hutton been able to give you any idea about how things stand?' she said.

'No, my dear, but I'm sure he will very soon. He seems most capable.'

'Is he capable of holding his tongue when he does?'

Edward was not quite sure whether his wife's chief concern was for her social standing and position or for the future welfare of her family. It seemed to him suddenly that had he ever set himself to think about it he would have realised that it was the former which always had come first with her. 'I understand that solicitors are compelled to be discreet,' he said.

'Discreet! In Bellary! The whole town must know now who he is and what he is doing.'

Edward went to the window again. 'I wonder if that matters very much,' he said. 'So long as he can find out a way for us to stay here.'

'It matters to me very much, let me tell you, Edward, that if we do stay here we should not be said to have been rescued by such a one as Massiter.'

Edward turned again from the window and his beloved vista of hills and sea. 'I think,' he said almost under his breath, 'I should be content to stay here under virtually any terms.'

Honoria hardly heard him and certainly did not heed him. She had made up her mind. 'I shall see this man Hutton, myself,' she said.

She then left the room, went down the broad staircase, through the door at the back of the hall and walked along the flagged passage that led to the rent room with long, swinging, determined strides.

Upstairs in the schoolroom Stephen was being put through his own inquisition by his sister. Ethel Raymond would make her bow to the Viceroy in Dublin the following year but at the moment she was in the transition period when she was neither child nor adult. Her mother, during their stay away, had not taken her into her confidence about the family crisis. Beyond being told that Sterling French had been killed out hunting she had learnt nothing about the calamities his death had revealed. But she was fully aware that something was wrong. The presence of the mysterious stranger in the rent room was alone sufficient evidence of that. In any case, however, the general air of apprehension hanging over the house was almost palpable and had infected the servants.

Rogers, bumbling about on his bunions, seemed even dottier than before. He appeared incapable of answering even the simplest questions and indeed of saying anything save the endlessly repeated, 'Trouble in the house; trouble in the house.' Mikey, on the other hand, was everywhere, doing most of Rogers' work for him, his eyes darting about to see what they could find, his ears obviously strained to pick up what pieces of information might come their way. The maids, too, whenever she saw them, were huddled together in pairs, whispering or giving covert glances.

Ethel, at this stage of her life, considered herself to be above the schoolroom but Stephen was in the schoolroom and Stephen was the only source of information to which she could turn.

Stephen had been trying without success to tie a fly. After several failures he had sought Mikey's help, but Mikey had been too busy in the butler's pantry to come upstairs. Stephen had returned to the schoolroom, and when Ethel found him he was sitting by the window eating toffee and reading a book which in the eyes of his parents he should not have been reading. The book had been loaned him by Harry French who had somehow purloined it from a locked cupboard belonging to his father. It was called *The Blue Lagoon*. At Ethel's entrance he pushed it hurriedly away under a cushion.

'What are you doing? It's not like you to be reading. What are you reading?' Ethel demanded sharply and suspiciously.

'I'm trying to tie a fly,' Stephen answered, his mouth full of toffee, indicating the materials which he had left on the table in front of him to meet just such an emergency.

Ethel was too intent on finding out what was going on in the house to pursue the matter any further. 'What on earth has been happening since I went away?' she said.

Stephen and his sister had never been close and there was more than the gap in ages between them. What Massiter had said about Stephen taking after his father and Ethel breeding true to her mother had much of the truth in it. Stephen had inherited a strain of his father's dreaminess and gentleness while Ethel had the mainstream of her mother's forcefulness running through her. That alone would have accounted for the mutual antipathy that lay between them, but there was something else which increased it. Ethel was jealous of Stephen and the fact that as the only son he would inherit. She felt that had things been fair the rights of the first-born should have been hers and she was satisfied that she could fulfil and discharge the duties that went with them far better than Stephen ever could. She lost no opportunity of belittling him, which Stephen both recognised and resented. Mostly, they went their own ways; when together it was rare for them to remain long in one another's company without trouble developing between them.

'What happened about French?' she said now.

'He was killed trying to jump the Still.'

'But he never went a yard out hunting. And those screws of his wouldn't carry his boots. Were you there? I don't suppose so.'

'We saw it. We were with Bob Ferris.'

'Who's we?' Ethel sniffed. 'Oh, you and Babs Murtagh, I suppose. You two would need old Bob to grandmother you. But they've all gone, the Frenches, haven't they? Bolted, it seems. Why?'

'I think there's some trouble over money.'

'Then that's what that strange man is doing in the rent room. It's our money, too, I suppose. Does Mother know about this?'

'I don't know but I think I saw her going into the study just now where Father was working.'

'Working!' Ethel said suddenly and viciously. 'Working! He's never done a hand's turn in his life. This is all his fault. He's just useless.'

Stephen sat up. 'You're not to say that,' he said. 'Father's so kind—'

'Kind!' Ethel's snort was very like her mother's. 'Kind! What good is that to us? I heard Mother say to Adrian Barrett when we were there that she suspected French was up to something and Father would do nothing about it. Now look at the mess he's landed us in.'

'We don't know how bad it is yet.'

'We'll know soon enough. Even the servants are talking about it. I noticed it as soon as I came back. Of course they always get out of hand when Mother's not here.'

'It would be awful if we had to leave the Bay.'

'Awful? I wouldn't care a bit if it meant we could live somewhere decent like Meath or Kildare.'

Stephen stared at her aghast. 'What on earth do you mean?' he said. 'Leave the Bay? It would be too terrible even to think about. You don't know what you're saying.'

'Indeed I do. I've always hated being stuck away down here. It was wonderful with the Barretts in Kildare. The people are so smart and there are the cavalry officers from the Curragh out hunting. You should see the turn-out. Some of them wear swallow-tails!'

'I don't think I want to be smart. I'll bet old Gnowles shows just as good sport as the Killing Kildares for all their swank and show.'

'Anyway,' Ethel went on as if she had not heard him, 'they've asked me back for Punchestown, thank goodness.'

'But Father said yesterday he'd take us.'

'You can go with him and stay with those mouldy old cousins of his if you like. They're just dull. You've no idea what fun it was with the Barretts. They all think we're frightfully provincial down here. I heard one of the soldiers say only tradesmen hunt on Saturdays.'

'I wouldn't let old Gnowles hear you saying that if I were you. And for all their swallow-tails I'll bet none of them could catch Desmond Murtagh across a country.'

'Babs' father—that flatcatcher!'

'What do you mean?' Stephen, bridling, sat up in his chair and stared at her. He had not the least idea what the word meant but it sounded insulting and, especially after what she had been saying, he was not going to put up with any insults to his hero.

Ethel, in turn, did not know just what the word meant, either. It was an expression she had heard one of the smart guests at the Barretts' using. She thought it sounded rather well and was sufficiently derogatory to suit her purposes of putting down her young brother. Now it suddenly occurred to her that it might be something worse than derogatory and that she had perhaps gone too far. 'You can't be expected to be grown up enough to understand,' she said loftily and withdrew from the room.

When Honoria reached the door of the rent-room she threw it open and stormed in. 'Mr Hutton?' she enquired imperiously, looking belligerently at the figure behind the big desk with its rampart of books and ledgers running across it.

Hutton put down his pen and got to his feet. 'Yes, madam?' he said.

'Mr Hutton,' Honoria continued, acknowledging his acceptance of her address with a brief nod, 'I wish you to know that it is at my husband's choice not mine that you are here.'

Their eyes met across the desk and each of them instantly recognised the other's quality. Hutton saw at a glance that here was an adversary worthy of his steel quite unlike Edward, whom he had mentally dubbed 'that poor creature upstairs'. He told himself, moreover, that here was one with whom he would have enjoyed crossing swords either in the witness box or on the other side of a hard-fought court-room battle. Honoria, for her part, meeting a cold stare that matched her own, knew at once that Hutton was someone whom she could neither bully nor brow-beat, someone, in fact, who had met and stood up to far sterner verbal onslaughts than she could ever launch.

'I understand your interest and your opinions, madam,' Hutton said, a slight smile twitching his lips. 'Nevertheless your husband has employed me and perhaps I should add that until he terminates my retainer I intend to finish my task.'

'And just what is that task?'

'You appear to appreciate frankness, Mrs Raymond.' Hutton was now swinging his pince-nez between his fingers at the end of their black silk band. He was beginning to enjoy the interview. 'I shall be equally frank with you. My instructions are to ascertain the amount of the defalcations made by your late agent, Mr Sterling French, who recently died, as I am sure you are aware, as a result of a hunting accident.'

'Of course I am aware of it. Very well, since you are here I suppose you must stay though I will not conceal from you that I would have chosen differently.'

Hutton's lips twitched again. 'That, if I may say so, madam, was apparent from the moment you entered the room.'

'Are you presuming to be impertinent?'

'Only if a statement of fact is impertinent.'

Honoria paused. She was not accustomed to being stood up to on her own ground. She took a deep breath. 'And just what have you uncovered as yet?' she asked.

'A considerable amount. At least I can tell you that there have indeed been defalcations and I believe I have found the method that was employed.'

'I see. You appear to have done quite well in the time,' Honoria said grudgingly. 'You are not yet in a position to give a final estimate?'

'I am not, but you may rest assured that I shall be and it should not take very long now, I think.'

In fact Hutton had got down to the bare bones of Edward's problem more quickly than he had anticipated. The rent roll was not, after all, a large one. At first the unexplained gaps in many of the rentals and the total absence of any entries at all in the tithe rent ledger had caused him some perturbation for this could have entailed writing round to each tenant asking for his last rent receipt. In turn this would at the very least have meant considerable delay in finalising the accounts.

But that morning Hutton had had a stroke of luck. In one corner of the large room half-hidden by a press crammed with old rentals, record books and agents' submissions for instructions, he had found an old and rather battered iron safe. None of the keys on the ring Edward had given him fitted this safe. That alone was sufficient to arouse his suspicions. Underneath the two windows that faced the courtyard was a desk which had obviously been used by French himself as a sort of personal workbench. Hutton had already been through the drawers and found little to assist him. There were merely sheaves of bills, many of them unpaid, letters to and from tenants, and a few old bank books which disclosed that French for some time had been running his affairs on a considerable overdraft. Now he resolved to examine the desk again.

Mounted on its top were two banks of small drawers with a row of cubby-holes running between them. Beneath these were racks for writing paper and envelopes and a black-japanned pen-tray all recessed into the surface of the desk. Hutton examined the pen-tray. As he knew, such trays often concealed the oldest and most simple of secret drawers or hiding places. Putting his finger on one end of the tray he pushed it down. Immediately its other end sprang up revealing a shallow compartment underneath. In this compartment was a key.

Taking the key, Hutton walked over to the unopened safe. It fitted the lock. With one quick turn the tumblers slid back. Hutton pressed the handle and the door swung open. Inside was a set of ledgers and account books. When he opened them Hutton could scarcely believe his good fortune.

Sterling French had kept these books with care and accuracy. They were replicas of the estate books with the gaps filled in, and they showed exactly where the money he had received and not accounted for had come and gone. Either through carelessness, over-confidence or simply because it suited him to keep them there and made accounting more easy, he had actually stored them in his employer's rent room and underneath his employer's nose. There were even receipt and lodgement books and in effect their discovery did Hutton's work or most of it for him.

French had had authority to draw on the estate account in the bank as well as to lodge to it and this was the one area where his records were incomplete. When he had finished reconciling the true and the false set of books Hutton realised that he must interview the bank manager.

The interview took place that afternoon. The bank manager was sycophantic, helpful and more than a little frightened. It appeared that transfers were made every quarter from the estate account into Edward's private account. Up to a few years ago the estate account had been able to sustain these lodgments and remain in the black. It was now, however, seriously overdrawn by reason of substantial withdrawals made by French. These withdrawals were unexplained but it was obvious on the face of it that they were for his own purposes and not those of the Raymond estate.

The bank manager on being questioned said that he had no authority to query the withdrawals. When Hutton pointed out that the amount of the overdraft far exceeded the security given, his explanation was that he had not liked to press one of the old families of the Bay and that he had been sure it would all come right in time. He did, however, go on to say that his head office had been in touch with him asking for an explanation of the ever-rising indebtedness and instructing him to require either liquidation of the debt or a very considerable reduction.

'How far will they take this?' Hutton asked him.

'In view of what has happened I greatly fear they may go the whole way,' was the answer. 'We hold the title deeds of Bellary Court and the lands.'

'That would mean a forced sale?'

'I hope indeed it will not come to that. I'm sure Mr Raymond will find a way of meeting us. If he cannot then, ultimately, perhaps, yes.'

'And you fear even then that the realisation will not cover the accumulated debt and interest?'

The manager's watery eyes met Hutton's. 'I would be very much afraid that it might not,' he said. 'The way farming is at the moment in this part of the country; and the talk of war—'

'Farming prospers during a war. If your bank forces a sale in the case of a man of Mr Raymond's prominence and popularity, do you really think anyone would bid?'

Hutton knew the manager was a frightened man and he thought it good tactics to turn the screw and increase his fears. Hutton was only too well aware from previous experience that bank managers were slow indeed to press members of the nobility and gentry in the matter of their overdrafts. For, they told themselves, one never knew, the running on of accounts was frequently due to pure carelessness or in some cases a pretentious indifference to dealing with matters as sordid as money; and if the account was ultimately put right the interest earned showed a handsome profit for the branch when the yearly accounting came. But, even more important, was the risk entailed in 'acting the usurer' as the manager had heard one of the Ascendancy caste describe a colleague who had pressed him. These people still held considerable power and patronage in their hands. Push one too hard and he would tell his friends and employees with a consequent loss of accounts and business to the branch, which did not commend itself to the Board of Directors. Many of them, too, had friends and relatives in high places, some of them even on the Board itself. Every conceivable area of influence was somehow covered by their net-work of intermarriage and nepotism.

'Have you any other security?' Hutton asked him.

'Some scrip. It is not of any great value.'

'The market is down at the moment. If your directors are pressing I imagine you will be instructed to sell these even at a loss?'

The manager coughed. 'I'm afraid I have a letter this morning indicating the advisability, in fact the necessity, of taking that course.'

'I thought as much.' Hutton got to his feet. 'I'm obliged for your assistance.'

'I hope you will explain to Mr Raymond,' the manager said as he bowed him out, 'that none of this is of my making. The matter is out of my hands. If by any chance things should take a turn for the better I trust he will not think any the worse of us.'

'I shall certainly deliver that message,' Hutton said gravely.

That night Hutton sat up late in the rent room completing his accounts and making up his report. The following morning he presented it. The interview took place in the library at Bellary Court and, as he expected, Honoria insisted on being present.

Hutton sat at a sofa table between the tall windows, his back to the view. His working papers, covered in his neat, meticulous hand-writing, were stacked on the table in front of him. Although his first professional responsibility was to Edward on whose behalf, technically, he had carried out the investigation, he knew what his real master, Massiter, wanted. Therefore he made no effort to soften the impact of what he was about to say or to mitigate the seriousness of the situation. As it happened, he was rather looking forward to another encounter with Honoria. Edward's wife, he knew very well, would take the leading part in the interview. There was bound to be a clash of wills in which, he comfortably reminded himself, he would be in the position of a poker-player who not only holds all the winning cards in his hand but who knows it.

He cleared his throat. 'According to your instructions, Mr Raymond,' he began, 'I have now carried out a thorough examination of the estate books. I was fortunate in discovering a duplicate set of books kept privately by Mr French for his own use and this considerably simplified my task.'

'Do you mean,' Honoria demanded, 'that the wretched man actually kept an account of what he had stolen?'

'That is approximately correct, madam. It is by no means an unusual situation. Embezzlers often do it.'

Honoria sniffed. 'You seem to speak from experience,' she said.

'It has fallen to my lot in commercial transactions to find that not everyone is as honest as complete trust demands and here we had a situation of complete trust.'

'Unfortunately, yes.' Honoria sniffed again and glanced contemptuously at her husband who was sitting slumped in a chair, gazing through the windows down the Bay.

'However,' Hutton continued, 'that is not all. Mr French, it appears, also had authority to draw on the estate bank accounts. He did so, frequently and substantially. The account is now heavily overdrawn.'

'Are you quite satisfied that your results are correct?'

'From the information given me and the records supplied or discovered, yes, madam. In round figures.'

'Very well, in round figures, what is the amount?'

'Thirty thousand pounds, madam.'

'Thirty thousand pounds!' Edward gasped. 'I had no idea—' He seemed to grow smaller, to shrink as the shock hit him and to subside further into the chair.

Honoria for her part sat up straighter. She looked Hutton unflinchingly in the eyes. 'That is a substantial sum indeed,' she said. 'Is there any way of meeting it? My marriage settlement?'

'That cannot be touched, I'm afraid. There are limitations over to the children. Your husband's liquid assets are not such as to cover this debt. Even if they were a sale would leave no resources to run this estate and provide for living expenses.'

'And what will the Bank do now, pray? Can they force a sale?'

'They can and it seems probable that they will. There is a mort-gage.'

'Mortgage?' Honoria turned fiercely on her husband. 'Mortgage? I knew nothing of this.'

'French arranged it about two years ago. He said it was only a for-mality.'

'Formality!' Honoria snorted.

'I've always heard,' Edward said, speaking very slowly, 'that, on a forced sale by a Bank, if the owner appears and bids, then no one will bid against him.'

'That is so,' Hutton said. 'And I've seen the tactic used myself. But—'

'Stuff and nonsense!' Honoria interjected angrily. 'As if we weren't ridiculous enough already. It would be reducing ourselves to the level of tenants—of peasants even. Well, Mr Hutton, you appear to have remarkable experience in these matters. Have you any suggestions?'

Hutton had to tread carefully. He knew just what Massiter wanted. Massiter wanted the Bellary estate as a hedge for his money but he also wished the locality to know that it was out of the goodness of his heart that he had masterminded the rescue. Thus at one stroke he could secure himself both prestige and profit. But for this to be done successfully the goodwill of the Raymonds, especially Honoria, had to be secured.

Hutton coughed. 'Have you any relatives or close friends, perhaps, who might be induced to help?' he asked.

'None in a position to meet this,' Honoria replied.

'I see. There is a possible way out which might or might not appeal to you. As you know Mr Raymond took Mr Massiter completely into his confidence in the matter, which is how, indeed, I came to be employed. Mr Massiter has instructed me to say that if the debt was not of gargantuan proportions—too large in fact—and I may now with safety add that for this purpose it is not—then he would be pre-pared to fund it—'

'Never!' exclaimed Honoria promptly.

Life and hope seemed suddenly to have returned to Edward. He was sitting up in his chair, staring at Hutton. 'Let Mr Hutton finish, my dear,' he said. 'What are Mr Massiter's terms?'

'Mr Massiter proposes,' Hutton said, turning to this unexpected ally, 'that he should clear your debt with the Bank. In return you would give him a first mortgage on this house and lands. The interest rate would be considerably lower than that charged by the Bank.'

'It would be exchanging whips for scorpions,' Honoria said de-fiantly, looking indeed, Hutton thought, rather as her covenanting ancestor must have looked as he laid his sword about him in Cromwell's campaigns.

Edward sat up still straighter in his chair. 'I do not intend to leave this house until I am carried out of it in my coffin, like my ancestors before me,' he said. 'It seems to me that Mr Massiter is behaving very handsomely.'

'Handsomely! That man!'

'Perhaps we had better discuss it, my dear. Mr Hutton can wait in the morning room.'

'There seems to be nothing to discuss. But—oh—very well.' Honoria crossed the room and tugged savagely at the bell pull. When Rogers tottered in she said: 'Show Mr Hutton to the morning room and bring him some refreshment.'

When the door had closed behind the solicitor she turned on her husband. 'Haven't you caused enough trouble already, Edward, with your foolishness?' she said. 'This man Massiter is only interested in what he can get. If we go through with this, our last state will be worse than our first. It is time to make a clean break. We must sell. Let him buy at the auction, if he will. Much good may it do to him!'

But for once she found Edward uncowed and immovable. His house meant everything to him. No price was too high to pay for the privilege of living on in it surrounded by the sea and mountains he loved so much. He was adamant, however much she ranted at him. Eventually she gave up. Had she been another woman she would have dissolved in tears. Instead she stared contemptuously at him as he sat in his chair with the look of a man who is driven hard but on this one occasion determined to stand his ground. 'So be it, then,' she said. 'And on your head be it, Edward. When the worst happens, do not say that I did not warn you.'

Edward crossed to the bell pull. When Hutton reappeared he said to him: 'You may tell Mr Massiter we accept his terms. The details, I assume, will be worked out between you and our own men of business.'

'Merrett & Merrett of Kilderry who are relations of mine will represent us,' Honoria said. It was the one small solace she had snatched from defeat. At least she would have some say in the final negotiations.

Hutton dined that night at Dunlay Castle. The huge dining room, panelled in dark oak, was lighted only by candelabras that stood in a row down the heavy mahogany table. Dinner was served by silent footmen directed by the English butler. Neither man spoke of anything other than trivialities until the table cloth had been removed, the port was on the table and the servants had left the room.

'So,' Massiter said, lighting a cigar. 'You've pulled it off. That was well done.'

'I hope you're satisfied with the deal. The concession on interest will

55

be considerable.'

'If there is a war, income tax rates will go up. I doubt if I shall lose much, if anything. It's a reasonable business risk.'

'At one time, you know, I felt sure we had lost. I spent some anxious moments in that morning room, let me tell you. You were quite right about the wife. She's a tartar if ever there was one. I didn't think he had it in him to stand up to her.'

Massiter chuckled. 'Everyone has a sticking point somewhere,' he said. 'That is his. These people, you know, they love their houses more than their wives. And this place—' he waved a hand about him to indicate all the country that lay beyond the dark curtains. 'They love it best of all. I'm not sure that it isn't beginning to get to me too. The rhododendrons will flower shortly. They set the whole place ablaze. You should stay to see them.'

Hutton looked at him curiously. He was a city-dweller. Streets and buildings and bustle were everything to him. He disliked mountains and remoteness, rivers, rocks and streams. Empty spaces and elementals such as storms and wind-lashed shores frightened him though he would not have cared to admit it.

'So you're becoming one of them,' he said.

'Not yet. You know what they say of strangers here? "Is he one of us? Is he from the Bay?" Not yet. But I shall.'

'And this deal will help?'

'I can't see it failing. Land and cattle, they always appreciate in a war. And Raymond, poor simple fool that he is, will never stop being grateful.'

'But what about the wife?'

'She'll put a good face on it. She could never openly admit that this one time he stood up to her and defeated her.'

'So you win both ways.'

Massiter's strange eyes gleamed. 'I usually do,' he said.

'And will your horse win the Conyngham Cup?'

'Bob Ferris has him now. He says he will.'

7

In that golden spring of 1914 when the old, secure, Edwardian world was dying in a blaze of fashion, splendour and flamboyance, Punchestown was the highlight of the Irish sporting and social season.

Summoned by its spell, hunting and racing people from all over Ireland mingled with the wealth and riches of smart Dublin society. Every country house within driving distance held a house party; special trains delivered the Dublin contingents at Naas station where carriages waited to carry them the few miles to the course. Once there, the occupants, if socially acceptable, could make free of the many club and regimental tents. There was a stand reserved for the members of the Kildare Hunt and their guests, and a special stand for the Lord Lieutenant. Men wore morning dress and top-hats; women their Ascot finery. The Lord Lieutenant himself in a landau flanked by outriders drove down the course each day to lend a final touch of dignity and distinction to the occasion.

Outside the enclosure, across the gleaming green of the course, was all the fun of the fair. Here hurdy-gurdies, swing-boats, and merry-go-rounds competed with the bookmakers for the spending money of the crowd. Three-card men and thimble-riggers plied their trades unhampered by the attentions of the Royal Irish Constabulary.

Set in the lush grassland of the plains of Kildare with a far background of blue mountains, the gorse running like a living flame across the nearer ridges and hills, Punchestown was a fit setting for the festival of steeple-chasing, the apogee and culmination of the jumping season, which took place in the late April of every year.

Part pageant, part social occasion it was indeed, but, nevertheless, for those concerned with the real and basic reason for its existence, racing, it was a deadly serious affair. And for the jockeys and gentlemen riders who rode over a course unique in the three kingdoms it was a test of nerve and skill and a battleground for bravery.

Except for two flimsy brush fences at the finish and a stone wall built of loose stones which had to be replaced after each race when the horses had crashed through them, the races were run entirely over banks. These were big, solid, earth-built obstacles on which the horses had to change legs at racing pace. Dominating all these was the Big Double, a fearsome obstacle, which was as typical of the course and as famous in Ireland as Bechers Brook in the English Grand National.

The Big Double was a bank four feet high on its landing side and six and a half feet wide on top. It was guarded on either side by ditches three feet deep and six and a half feet wide. A path led from the stands to the Double, and crowds gathered at it as they did at Bechers, to watch each race that crossed it. To see a bunched field come racing into this obstacle, rise to it, and sweep over it in a tide of bright colour was one of the highlights of the meeting.

The chief event at Punchestown was the Conyngham Cup, run over a distance of four and a half miles and ridden by gentlemen riders. It was in this race that Andrew Massiter and Desmond Murtagh had entered their horses, Merrymaker and Robin À Tiptoe.

Because of the upheaval in their affairs, neither Edward nor Honoria considered it advisable to make the journey to Punchestown that year. Ethel had, however, already been asked to stay by her cousins, the Barretts, and because Honoria, to use her own words, did not want Stephen 'hanging about the place' whilst business discussions were going on, she persuaded the Barretts, much to Ethel's disgust, to fit him in, too.

The Barretts lived in a big square house about five miles from the course. It was crammed with family, relations, and guests, all staying for the meeting. A tremulous, almost hectic gaiety pervaded the house party that year. Apart from the glamour and excitement of the racing which inevitably heightened the atmosphere, especially when certain members of the party were owners or riders, underneath the swagger and the security strange currents were stirring and, almost unconsciously in certain cases, some of them realised it. Foreboding filled the thoughts of those who allowed themselves to think on events and to ponder where those currents might eventually bring them. No one among them contemplated for a moment that they would eventually sweep their whole caste or class completely out of existence.

It was not so much the thought of a European war which disturbed them. Only a few of the more serious-minded amongst the soldiers prepared for that. But recently something had taken place nearby, only a few miles away, in fact, which none of them could overlook.

The 'Curragh Mutiny' had ended in confusion and recrimination a bare month ago. Mishandled and bungled on every level, it had been an unsatisfactory affair for all concerned. There had been hard feelings and in some cases hard words in the messes of even the most united of cavalry regiments. The reverberations were still echoing in the Garrison and many of the guests were fearful about their future

and the effect it would have on their careers.

The Curragh Mutiny, of course, had sprung from the business of Home Rule and the question of the coercion of Ulster. Religion and ties of blood and history made the members of the house party, almost to a man, sympathetic with the mutineers. The names of politicians were mentioned only with execration. One of them, Stephen noticed, from chance-heard conversations, appeared to attract especial obloquy. It was a name which once heard was difficult to forget—Winston Churchill.

'That damned hot-head. Never know what the feller will do next,' he heard one cavalry colonel with a drooping moustache remark to another over a whisky and soda. 'Can't think why the Boers didn't keep him when they had him,' was the reply. 'Didn't want him, I suppose. Can't say I blame them.'

Stephen was not happy nor at ease in the house party. There was no one of his own age amongst them and Ethel had immediately disowned him. The old schoolroom had been re-opened for him and his meals were brought up to him there by a bad-tempered and overworked maid. When the carriages came round to take the party to the races he had to take care lest he be overlooked entirely and left behind.

Once at the course it was different. There he knew his way round from previous visits and could go off by himself to watch Bob or Desmond saddling their horses, discuss prospects with the stable lads or survey with a knowing eye the runners in the parade ring.

On Conyngham Cup day he was keyed up with excitement. Near the weigh-room he met Babs Murtagh. 'Babs! What fun!' he said. 'Let's watch it together. Is your father going to win?'

'I hope so.'

They went towards the parade ring and secured a place on the rails where no one could interrupt their view of the horses. Merrymaker was a bright, hard-looking bay, full of quality; Robin À Tiptoe a chestnut with a shade of flashiness about him. 'Like his owner,' Stephen heard someone behind him in the crowd remark as the horse passed them. He turned to see if he could identify the speaker but he was only one voice amongst many. He wondered if Babs had heard. Then his thoughts came back to the race again.

The morning papers had mostly given The Pilgrim, owned and ridden by a Captain in the 16th Lancers, stationed at the Curragh and said to be a coming man amongst the younger G.R.s, as the likely favourite. Listening with one ear to the shouts of the bookmakers, however, it seemed to Stephen that Robin À Tiptoe was shortening in the betting all the time and might well start if not favourite then at a very short price.

Standing in the ring beside Andrew Massiter, Bob Ferris also listened to the betting. As he followed it a puzzled frown appeared on his face. 'They're backing Mr Murtagh's with pounds, shillings and pence,' he said. 'I don't understand it. He shouldn't beat us. Nor Captain Jarvis either, for that matter.'

'Is it his money, I wonder?' Massiter said.

'If it is, it shouldn't be,' Bob answered.

At that moment the riders came into the ring. Tim D'arcy, one of a famous racing triumvirate of brothers from Meath, was to ride Merrymaker. He crossed to where Bob and Massiter were standing, nodded to Bob and touched his whip to the peak of his cap in the traditional salute to his owner. 'Nice day for it,' he said. 'The ground is good, too. It never really gets heavy here.'

'This fellow stays forever,' Bob said. 'You can come away as hard as you like from the stone wall. If you're there or thereabouts then you should just about win it.'

'They're backing Desmond's as if he was past the post already.'

'So I see. I don't understand it.'

'You never know with Desmond. He could have something up his sleeve. Though he's made no secret he fancies his.'

'I know, and that's not like him, either.'

The saddling bell went. Bob whisked his jockey into the saddle. He slapped Merrymaker on the rump. 'Good luck,' he said. 'Come back as quick as you can.' It was his inevitable little joke when he had one he fancied. Then he made his way beside Massiter to the owners' and trainers' stand.

Stephen and Babs, after a lengthy and serious discussion, had decided to watch the race from the Big Double. As soon as the riders came into the ring they made their way across the course through the thronged crowds 'outside' to the path that led to the fence. Hardly had they arrived at it and taken up their positions when the first of the runners came down, for the start was there too and the horses lined up 'tails to the double'.

Soon all the twelve runners, the cream of Irish hunter-chasers, were walking round waiting for the arrival of the starter.

Stephen wondered what it would be like, sitting there, waiting for the off. He had heard it said that this was the worst time of all, these stretched moments of nervous tension, until you got used to it, and that some never did.

'Gosh,' he said to Babs. 'It is marvellous, isn't it? I wonder if I'll ever—' And then a thought struck him. 'Do you remember last year when Harry and I were saying that sometime we'd ride against each other here? What's happened to the Frenches, Babs, do you know? Have you seen Harry?'

'He's not here, I'm sure. I looked for him.'

'So did I.'

'They must have gone to ground somewhere. Wasn't it awful about his father? They say, Stephen, that it's something to do with your family, that he took money—'

'There's terrible trouble at home, I know that. That's why my parents couldn't come. And there's the queerest sort of old man from Dublin sitting in the rent room doing the books.'

'It's awful, isn't it. Poor Harry—'

As she spoke those words all of a sudden Stephen felt a twinge of something which he could not put a name to. Long afterwards he recognised it as the first stirrings of jealousy and that even then he resented anyone else occupying Babs' interests and affections. 'Look out,' he said, changing the subject quickly. 'Here's Major Reynolds. They'll be off in a minute.'

The starter, resplendent in top-hat, morning-coat, dark breeches and shining butcher boots, his furled red flag under his arm, had just cantered up on his hack. He commenced to call the roll. 'Mr Murtagh, Captain Doyle, Captain Jarvis, Mr Donegan . . .'

That finished, he slid the piece of paper back into his pocket. 'All right, line up now, gentlemen, please.'

The colours shifted and sorted themselves into a line. The Big Double loomed up behind them. The starter raised his red flag. 'Come up, Captain Doyle. Very nice. *Now*, Gentlemen . . .'

The red flag swept down and the twelve runners surged forward.

The starter sat still for a moment as he watched them go. 'Off with you then and good luck to you, you lucky devils,' he said. Then he kicked the hack into a canter and set off back to the stands.

Stephen raised the binoculars he had borrowed from his father and peered through them. At this point of the race, since he was on the same level as the runners, he could not see very much. As they made the turn back towards the stands he caught a flurry of falling colours. 'One of them has gone,' he said.

'It's not Father, is it? Quick, Stephen, tell me.'

'No, of course not,' Stephen said stoutly though in truth he had no very good idea who the faller was. When he could identify the runners properly on the hill past the stands he was relieved to see Robin À Tiptoe still there, galloping on strongly in third place.

Then they were coming down the hill, jumping out of the Herd's Garden, and beginning to turn towards them. The field had thinned to nine and a loose horse was with them, but the three fancied runners were still there.

Now they were almost abreast, facing the Big Double. On they came at it, their hooves drumming on the sound turf. They rose to surge over it like a wave, their riders' faces strained and intent. A smash of hooves, a creak of leather, a rasping of breaths and they were

61

gone. One of them was down, coming short off the bank, hitting the edge of the far side ditch and cart-wheeling into the next field.

In an instant, it seemed, they were at the stone wall, smashing through it in a cascade of flying stones. This was where the real race began.

'He's well there. He'll win it,' Stephen said, jumping down from the bank where he had been standing. Together they commenced to run towards the packed stands.

Up in those stands Bob Ferris was watching the race with tense concentration. Neither as a rider nor as a trainer had he ever won the Conyngham Cup. He badly wanted to win it now and he considered that with Merrymaker he had the best chance of bringing it off that had yet been offered to him.

As the field left the stone wall behind them Bob saw that the three fancied horses, Merrymaker, Robin A Tiptoe and The Pilgrim, had drawn ahead of the rest. There was a faller at the wall but it was no concern of his. His glasses remained on the leading three. Now was the time for Tim D'arcy to go on, to make use of Merrymaker's endless stamina. Merrymaker did not have a great deal of pull out at the finish but, Bob told himself, if he was ridden right that should not much matter at the end of four and a half miles.

As he saw Tim begin to draw away from the others Bob gave a little sigh of relief. You never knew with these damn gents. Some of them thought they knew it all, far more than you did; they did something damn silly and then came in and told you your instructions had been all wrong. But Tim was riding to orders, Tim knew his job, Tim would do what he had been told.

They crossed the pond fence and turned towards the straight. Robin À Tiptoe had closed the gap a little. Captain Jarvis on The Pilgrim was hard at work and making little impression on the leaders. Bob discarded him in his mind. He was beat.

At the two brush fences Robin À Tiptoe was closer still. As they touched down in the straight Bob's eyes narrowed. Tim D'arcy on Merrymaker was making the best of his way home but, three lengths behind him, Desmond Murtagh had not yet moved.

The crowd were already shouting Merrymaker home. But Bob's eyes were focused on the second horse. What in hell was Desmond doing? Two seconds later he knew.

When it seemed that he must have left it too late Desmond sat down and asked Robin À Tiptoe to go. The response was instant and electric. In three strides he had closed the gap. In another he was in front. He won by a neck.

'Cheeky bugger,' Bob muttered under his breath. 'But what a jockey! A neck after four and a half miles!'

But coming down from the stand Bob was frowning. He would not have believed there was a hunter-chaser in Ireland who could do that to his horse over that distance. After all, The Pilgrim, a useful horse well ridden, had been beaten out of sight. The more he thought about it the more he was certain something was wrong. What it was he could not for the moment imagine but with every step he took he became more certain that there was more behind the result than met the eye and more determined, too, to find out what it was.

As he walked towards the unsaddling stalls he hardly heard the commiserations that were being given to him by friends and relations. Vivienne Gnowles, however, planted herself firmly in front of him. 'Marvellous result for the Bay, wasn't it, Bob,' she said. 'First and second.'

'Yes, ma'am,' Bob answered. 'I'd have as soon had the order the other way, though.'

Massiter had somehow become separated from him in the crowd. But he was there in the place reserved for the second when Bob reached it.

'No disgrace in that defeat,' Massiter said. 'He ran a great race, Bob. That must be a good horse of Murtagh's. Is he for sale, I wonder?'

'He's a good 'un all right,' Bob said. 'But I—' Then he resolved to keep his thoughts to himself.

Merrymaker was the first to come back. Tim D'arcy stripped the saddle off him and said as he did so: 'Just too bloody good for us, I'm afraid. Don't know where he came from. This fellow is as game as a pebble. He'll win good races for you, Mr Massiter.' Then he disappeared towards the weigh-room. As he left, Desmond Murtagh rode Robin À Tiptoe into the winner's stall. He slipped to the ground to the accompaniment of a little ripple of clapping. Then, he, too, had gone towards the weigh-room.

Bob remained on looking at Robin À Tiptoe, puzzlement in his eyes. He saw with some surprise that it was Desmond's head lad who was at the horse's head.

There was some fiddling with a buckle as they put the horse's rug on to lead him away. 'Hurry up, can't ye,' the lad said. A cloud had come over the sun and Bob saw the head lad looking anxiously at it. Then his glance met Bob's. 'The Bay done well today, Mr Ferris,' he said.

'Aye, Jerry Jack. That's a good one you have there.'

'That he is. Come on, can't ye?' he barked at the lad with the rug.

The horse was getting restive, too, and then, somehow, the lad with the rug succeeded in pricking him. Robin À Tiptoe lashed out and his head came up, tearing the leading rein from the hands of the head lad. Bob found himself two inches away from Robin À Tiptoe's broad

63

forehead, staring at it. It was only there for a second or two but it was enough. Bob knew in that instant what was wrong and why he had been beaten.

The head lad cursed savagely, retrieved the rein and tugged Robin À Tiptoe's head around. Then he had him out of the stall and was walking him away through the crowds towards the boxes. Bob's eyes followed him as he went. He turned to look for his owner but Massiter had left the unsaddling stalls.

Bob hurried away. He had to find Massiter. He had not much time to do it in and he did not know where to look. He went along the line of bookmakers scanning the groups standing round waiting to be paid, hoping, though he knew it was unlikely, that Massiter might have had a cash bet and be amongst them. But Massiter was not there.

Bob himself had no right of entry to any of the tents or marquees and he did not know to which, if any, Massiter himself would be admitted. Choosing some of those he believed to be the less exclusive he enquired from the attendants if anyone answering Massiter's description had recently gone in. Here again he drew blank. Time for an objection was, he knew, rapidly running out. Almost in despair he returned to the weigh-room. And there by a lucky chance he met Massiter leaving it.

'Ah, Bob, there you are,' Massiter said. 'I've been looking for Mr Murtagh but he doesn't seem to be anywhere about. I want to ask him if he'll sell that horse.'

'You won't find him,' Bob said grimly. 'And you won't buy him, sir. That horse isn't Robin À Tiptoe.'

'What?'

Bob drew Massiter aside towards a space in the crowd where they could talk without being overheard. 'Listen to me, sir,' he said. 'You must object and quickly too before they give the winner all right.'

'Object? What is this, Bob?'

'I'll tell you what it is, Mr Massiter, sir. That's no more Robin A Tiptoe than I am. He stuck his head into my face half a minute ago and I could see where they had dyed out half his blaze.'

'Dyed? But, good God, man—'

'I'm as sure as I'm standing here,' Bob interrupted him hurriedly, 'that that horse is Canvasser, that top-class chaser they had last year that Mr Murtagh was second in the National on. They put it out that he'd got a leg and they'd have to put him by. They put him by all right—for this. He's no more got a leg than I have. If it'd been a handicap he'd have been giving us a stone. No wonder they backed him.'

Massiter hesitated. 'Proof, Bob, we've got to have proof.'

'Put in an objection now and I'll get you proof. Besides, I had Canvasser myself as a three year old on the flat and he was bloody useless. I know that horse. I thought there was something funny about the whole thing from the very beginning and I should have seen it sooner. The stewards have only to look at the horse for themselves—'

'If we can get them to do it. They're all friends of his, remember. They won't want to move.'

'If we don't do something soon, sir, everyone will lose their bets.'

'Damn the bets. I don't keep my horses for the public to bet on,' Massiter said sharply.

'Maybe not, sir, but there are others. And he'll collect, too, and it's a dead swindle.'

Massiter stroked his beard and then made up his mind in the sudden way he had. 'No, Bob,' he said. 'It won't do. I know how you feel but it still won't do. I'll lay anything that horse is off the course by now. Even if the stewards did move quickly they wouldn't be in time. And they wouldn't move quickly. They'd be on his side. Look at their names on the card. They'd say I was doing this because I couldn't take a beating. They'd make me into a laughing stock—'

At that moment they heard the 'Winner all right' being shouted to the bookies.

'It's too late now anyway,' Bob said, an unusually surly look appearing on his good-natured face.

'It's not too late,' Massiter said quietly. 'Under the rules we still have a fortnight to object in a case of this sort. Get me proof, Bob, good solid proof that will make them act, and then perhaps I'll think again.'

A week later Bob was shown into Massiter's library at Dunlay Castle.

'Come along in, Bob,' Massiter said. 'It's about this business at Punchestown, isn't it?'

'Yes, sir, that's just what it is. It was Canvasser all right, sir. I have proof of sorts. I don't know if it will satisfy ye, but it's good enough for me.'

'Sit down, Bob. Before you start there's one thing I must clear up with you. We were both a bit strung up and upset at the time, I think. I said something to you about betting. If you had a bet yourself I won't see you at a loss. Did you?'

'Yes, sir, I did. I had fifty pounds at five to one on Merrymaker.'

'Very well.' Massiter went to his desk, wrote out a cheque and handed it to him.

'Thank you, sir. That's very handsome of you. But you'd have saved yourself that if you'd have objected.'

'I'm not so sure about that. Now, let me hear your story.'

'Well, sir, it's this way. It's very hard to keep a secret in racing, as you must know. You have to take someone into your confidence if you get up to something and this time it was the head lad, Jerry Jack Regan. He's called Jerry Jack to distinguish him from his father Jerry Regan who's a keeper with the Old Earl and then there's his own son

Jerry Jack Tom who's with Mr Raymond—'

'Yes, Bob. I've been here long enough to learn about the nomenclature in the Bay. Do get on.'

'Well then, sir, you'll know, too, that it's very hard to keep a secret in the Bay. Nearly everyone is related to each other somehow. My wife's sister is married to a cousin of the O'Regans', Tommy Naylor, that is; he has a few acres up by Postheen. And Jerry Jack, he takes a drop now and then does Jerry Jack and he was taking a drop after Punchestown.'

'I'm not surprised.'

'Tommy Naylor was coming back from Clogheen fair last Wednesday. He'd sold his cattle well and he went into Julia Lacey's which is where Jerry Jack goes when he's takin' a drop if ye follow me, sir. The two of them got to talking and naturally like they had to talk about the race and Mr Murtagh's big win. Jerry Jack's pockets were stuffed with sovereigns and when he gets a drop in him he gets talkative and confiding like if you follow me—'

'I do. Go on, Bob.'

'It was Canvasser, all right, sir. Jerry Jack couldn't help himself when the drink was in him, and he was so full of it and the cleverness of it and how they'd hoodwinked the big fellows, and you, too, sir.'

Massiter suddenly looked grim. 'I see,' he said.

'After what you said about proof at the races, sir, I was a bit puzzled myself and wondering if I could have made a mistake. After all I'd only had that quick look at him. And there was another thing that made me worry whether I was right. Canvasser had a white snip on his off fetlock. It wasn't there when I watched him walking away. If they'd painted it out down there I wondered how it would stand up to the pushin' and scratchin' it'd get in a race. Well, d'ye know what they did?'

'No, Bob, you tell me.' Massiter was all attention now, leaning forward, his chin resting on his hand.

'Mr Murtagh found out from one of his lady friends—' here Bob coughed delicately, 'that there was a hairdresser man in Dublin had a new dye that wouldn't wear off whatever happened. He got him down from Dublin and it was the hairdresser who stained out the snip and the blaze!'

'But, good heavens, man, did the hairdresser know what he was doing?'

'They paid him well and they told him it was for a practical joke on another gentleman.'

'Do you know where the hairdresser came from?'

'Somewhere in a street called Westmoreland Street, sir. I have it written down.' Bob produced a sheet of paper which he handed to Massiter. 'I don't know Dublin much meself. Would it be easy to find,

66

sir?'

Massiter glanced at the paper. 'There shouldn't be much difficulty about that,' he said.

'And another thing, sir.'

'Yes. What is it?'

'Perhaps it's not my business but I've said so much I might as well say more.' Bob's good-natured face was set in determined lines. 'I think you should sack your stud-groom, sir.'

'And why, pray?' Massiter looked grim. He did not care for interference in his affairs more especially when it came from an employee.

'Just before ye sent Merrymaker to me he told ye he was going to give him a rough-up gallop with old Coachman.'

'That is correct.'

'He didn't. He tried Merrymaker with him. He set Merrymaker to give Coachman a stone and Merrymaker lost him. Mr Murtagh watched that gallop, and he made it worth your man's while to do it. He was very frightened of us, and he was desperate. He was up to the neck with the books you see, sir, and they were after him. He had to win that race. That's why he took the chance he did with Canvasser. Are you going to find the hairdresser, sir?'

'I'm not but I know someone who will,' Massiter said, thinking of Hutton.

'And you'll object, sir. We're still in time.'

Massiter stared out of the window for a moment or two and then brought his gaze back to meet Bob's. 'No, Bob,' he said. 'I won't object.'

'But, why, sir? Is it because you think the hairdresser man won't say he done it?'

'No, it's not that. The hairdresser will talk all right when my man tells him he's taken part in a fraud. I've no doubts about that.'

'Why not then, sir?'

'I've given it a lot of thought since the race, Bob. I don't for a moment doubt from what you have told me that I could object and they'd have to give me the race. But they'd have to warn him off, too. And they'd never forgive me. He's one of themselves. I'm not. I'm still an outsider.'

'He's not one of the old gentry, sir.'

'He's near enough. They've been here for four generations. They've accepted him. And at the back of it all, too, you know, Bob, they'd admire him for it. They'd think it an almighty clever thing to do. And they'd be delighted he'd skinned the books. Half of them are up to their necks with the books themselves. Somehow they'd make it not worth my while ever to run a horse again. And you, too, Bob. It wouldn't do you any good either.'

'What do ye mean, sir?'

'You'd have to give evidence. You're the man who discovered it all and started it all. They'd see to it none of them or their friends ever sent you a horse to train again. And what would they say in the Bay if you or I ruined Mr Murtagh? Have you thought about that, Bob? You could go out of business and I might as well sell up and go away.'

Bob sat without speaking for a moment or two while the weight of these words sank in. He had been so intent on exposing the fraud which had lost him a race he had spent much of his life trying to win that he had overlooked the wider implications of it all. Now, pondering Massiter's words, he had to admit that they carried the truth in them.

'So you'll do nothing,' he said slowly.

'Oh, no. I didn't say that. Not by any means. I don't like being beaten, Bob, but if it's fair and square I've schooled myself to take it. But I've been cheated, Bob, and no one, no one, ever does that to me without paying for it. It may take a long time but they pay and pay dearly in the end.'

'What will you do?'

'I'll get that signed statement first and then somehow,' he banged a closed fist into the open palm of his other hand, 'somehow, I'll find a way to use it.'

Bob, looking directly into the blaze that had suddenly come into the tawny eyes of the man opposite him, all at once felt a tremor of fear run through him, not for himself but for those whom his enquiries had exposed.

PART TWO

WAR

8

War came to the Bay that golden summer of 1914 but at first did little
to disturb its way of life. The sun shone and the place lay bathed in its
beauty and stillness far from the thunder of the guns and the holocaust that was about to consume Europe. The Howth gun-running
away on the other side of Ireland had little impact on the Bay and its
people, who looked west not east. Redmond's ill-advised pledge of the
Irish Volunteers to fight for England had even less effect. There were
few, if any, volunteers in the Bay but some of the hungrier, the hardier
and the more adventurous spirits, among them Larry Rossiter, enlist-
ed.

Then, one evening, as if to remind them all of the reality of war, six
sleek grey shapes slid out of the mist, took up their station at the head
of the Bay and dropped anchor. They were the forerunners of a de-
stroyer flotilla which was to use the Bay as a base for anti-submarine
patrols for the rest of the war.

Grig went back to his regiment, leaving his beloved hounds in the
charge of his wife for the duration, Massiter appeared briefly in naval
uniform and was said to be employed in intelligence; and Stephen
went to school.

The negotiations which had followed Hutton's departure and the
drawing up of the necessary deeds and mortgages had been prolonged
by the reluctance of Messrs Merrett & Merrett to proceed at anything
other than their accustomed pace of writing and answering one letter
per week. As a result, the question of Stephen's further schooling had
almost been overlooked. At the last moment Honoria suddenly awoke
to the fact that the new school year was approaching and that nothing
had been done about finding a public school for him. There was then
very little time left to secure an entry anywhere, but in the end one of
Honoria's many martial cousins had come to the rescue. He had
served in South Africa with the chairman of governors of a school in
the North of England called Sellingham; so, by a judicious pulling of
strings, a late entry for Stephen had been made and accepted. Because of the special nature of his entry he was placed in the School

71

House presided over by the headmaster.

Neither parent had bothered to enquire as to the suitability of Sellingham as a school for their son's further education during his formative years. Honoria's only object was to get him out of the way and Edward, after his brief flash of defiance which had secured him his house and lands, seemed to have sunk even deeper into apathy.

Although Sellingham prided itself on being a tough school and the game of rugby football, played in all weathers, was elevated into a sort of tribal ritual with the oval ball as its totem, Stephen did not find that the actual external circumstances of life there imposed any real hardships upon him. Hunting had accustomed him to being outdoors in all weathers and to stand up to physical injury when it came his way. All this enabled him to bear with stoicism the frost and snow of the harsh Northern climate and also the considerable bullying of new boys and fags. He had no desire to be a blood, no ambitions to wear the gaudy ties and blazers sported by the beefy bruisers of the first fifteen. Although he was not actively unhappy, all he really wished for was to be back in the Bay between the mountains and the sea with his horses and his dogs.

Throughout his first few terms he was in a state of constant homesickness. It took at least a fortnight for the worst effects of this to wear off and for acclimatisation, such as it was, to begin. All the time it seemed to him as if he was not quite sure just where he was. While his physical presence moved aimlessly through the bleak buildings, his thoughts were occupied with the house and the people and the animals he had left behind him in the Bay.

It was only in the holidays that he really came alive, especially now that Bob Ferris was allowing him to ride work. Almost every day he would bicycle over to Bob's stables in time to go out with the string, and Bob was glad enough to have him for the war was now working its changes even at the Bay. Owners had cut down for the duration or in some cases even gone out of racing altogether. The hounds were only hunting three days a fortnight. Grig had gained a D.S.O. in the 'race for the sea' and had then been given the command of a Yeomanry brigade.

Desmond Murtagh was also in France with the 5th Royal Irish Dragoons. He had survived so far but since that victory in the Conyngham Cup things had not gone so well for Desmond as might have been expected. Both his popularity and his standing had suffered because he had not sprung to the colours with the alacrity expected of one of his class and caste. Desmond, whose interests were dominated by horses, racing and women to an extent that left him little time to think of anything else, had confidently expected the war to be over by Christmas. Thus, in his opinion, it could well be left to the professional soldiers, who, after all, were paid for that sort of thing. When he awoke to his mistake and to the fact that there was scarcely anyone of his own sort left in racing, and that some of his friends had already been killed, Christmas had come and gone and pointed remarks about slackers and dodgers were beginning to be made in the coffee rooms of the better clubs, parade rings and owners' and trainers' bars.

It had proved, too, as Bob had foretold, impossible to keep the story of the Robin À Tiptoe coup quiet. Had it not been for Desmond's apparent reluctance to go for a soldier this might not have mattered. People would then, as they had so often in the past, have laughed it off as another of Desmond's escapades, especially as it had been the outsider, Massiter, who had been caught. But now things had altered and a sterner spirit was abroad. This time, it was held, Desmond had gone too far. Furthermore the elders in racing began to nod their heads sagely amongst themselves and to say that that fellow Massiter had really behaved very well in not objectin' and causin' a scandal, that Desmond had been damn lucky to get away with it and he might not be so lucky the next time.

Massiter himself had been sent abroad on some mysterious intelligence mission said to be connected with his knowledge of South America. Certainly he had been in Chile about the time of the Battle of Coronel and in Patagonia when Von Spee's victorious squadron lay in St Quentin Bay. The Bay, who loved to claim prominence for its inhabitants even if they were outsiders, stoutly maintained that it was information supplied by him which enabled Sturdee to bring his adversary to battle and to destroy him. The story had, in fact, some substance of truth. Massiter had been sent out to ascertain from his contacts the strength or otherwise of the neutrality of the South American Republics. German agents had been at work there for some time and any shift in allegiance could endanger British trade routes. During his tour of duty he had used his sources to ascertain Von Spee's movements and to transmit the information home.

So, in one way or another, Massiter was gaining both esteem and prestige in the Bay while Desmond Murtagh was rapidly losing both. Desmond had not helped matters much, either, in the way he had eventually answered the call of duty. Without informing his family or anyone else, he had sold his two best horses and gone off with the proceeds for a final spree in Dublin, leaving his wife to grapple as best she could with the problems of maintaining his decrepit demesne.

Some of this Stephen learnt from remarks dropped by his elders in the holidays, some from the long letters his father wrote every week during term time telling him what was happening at the Bay and how the war was affecting its people's fortunes.

Gradually as the terms slipped into years, acclimatisation to school and its routine came more quickly to him and lasted longer. In this his surroundings helped for Edward and Honoria had, entirely by accident, placed him in a school set in some of the most beautiful country in England. Sellingham itself was a hamlet in a fold of the Yorkshire dales ringed about by fells and hills which the boys were encouraged to explore when they were not playing Rugby football. As time wore on Stephen came to love those lonely fells and the little rivers that tumbled through them. Especially in the summer when the sun struck colour and contrast from hill and heather, the beauty and spaciousness of it all reminded him in some way of his home and went at least some distance to console him for his absence from it.

Summer for Stephen was unquestionably the best time at Sellingham. Cricket was compulsory only in name, fishing and fell-walking were encouraged and on most free days Stephen found himself free to throw a fly in the mountain streams.

That was until Conway became house captain, which happened in Stephen's second summer term. Conway was all sorts of a blood. He was a football colour of two years' standing and the captain designate of the school fifteen next season. He also had his cricket colours as a hard-hitting number four bat, and was heavy-weight boxing champion of the school. He was a worshipper of the public school ethic which Stephen, if he thought about it at all, looked upon with a sort of hazy distaste.

Conway was the son of a West Riding parson with strong Calvinistic leanings which had led to his banishment to a remote parish in the fells. His mother had died when Conway was a child and the boy had been brought up to a doctrine of hell-fire and damnation, a doctrine enforced by frequent use of the strap. The Reverend Horace Conway, though he struggled against them manfully, was a man of strong sexual desires. After the death of his wife he refused to take unto himself another, holding that sexual satisfaction even when hallowed by wedlock was a gratification of the flesh and therefore an occasion of sin at all costs to be avoided. His son suffered for this since Mr Conway's tenets were thrashed into him, thus affording the father, though he could never have admitted it to himself or his God, some release from the inner tensions and the passions that constantly tortured and preyed upon him.

Conway had inherited much of his father's sexual drive and he adopted the same methods of combating sin. He lusted after small boys but he exorcised the temptation to touch their nubile flesh by beating them unmercifully at the least excuse and for the slightest offence.

A temporary house tutor with horsey pretensions, observing all this and being about to leave for the Front, had taken the unusual step of going to the headmaster and telling him of his doubts and fears concerning the house captain. 'Conway is too fond of the stick,' he had said. 'And he's getting worse. It may lead to trouble later on.'

74

And earlier that term it very nearly had. A boy had complained to his parents after one of Conway's beatings. As a result they had descended on the headmaster demanding retribution. It had taken all the headmaster's tact and diplomacy to persuade them not to make a public issue out of the matter, which had ended comparatively peacefully by their removing the boy. Conway had, however, received a stern warning and the headmaster had instituted a beatings book in which all school prefects were required to record their punishments.

So far Stephen had avoided any of Conway's attentions and beatings but, though he did not know it, Conway had had his eye on him for some time.

Stephen had, in fact, come to Sellingham from his private school with something of a reputation as a fast bowler. Since he loathed all games he had done his best to conceal his ability and live down the reputation, fooling about on the cricket field and refusing to concentrate when called upon to bowl. All this was anathema to Conway who sensed the ability underneath Stephen's antics; and Stephen made it worse by airily telling Conway after one practice that holding slip catches was a bit like shooting snipe on a good day. Conway senior had taught his son to regard field sports as inventions of the devil and all those who pursued them as eternally damned, so it was not surprising that Conway regarded Stephen as one who delighted in flaunting all that he held to be both right and respectable.

Conway was determined to make not only his house captaincy but his future leading of the fifteen next term triumphant both for his own glory and for that of his father who he knew had scraped and saved to send him to Sellingham. The public school code of games and teamwork and playing hard and praying hard all meant much to him. He believed passionately that any boy who did not give himself wholeheartedly to playing games, thus increasing the glory of house and school, was not only a slacker but actively sinful. The fact that Stephen was Irish made things even worse for that implied in Conway's mind that he must somehow be connected with the Catholic church, the scarlet woman, the whore of Babylon, against whom he had so often heard his father rant and rail.

All this made it certain that Stephen and Conway were set on a collision course.

One bright sunlit day, far too fine for fishing, when no self-respecting trout would leap to his lure, Stephen had put up his rod and was walking a narrow twisting lane that led to the fells when he heard the unmistakable clatter of a horse's hooves coming along towards him. From the sound of them the horse was galloping loose and shouts coming down from above seemed to confirm it.

In a moment the horse came into view round a bend, riderless, reins and stirrups flying. Stephen moved to the centre of the lane and held

75

out his arms. The horse checked in his stride, snorted, swerved and then pulled up, propping himself on his forelegs, his shoes shooting sparks from the stones. Then he commenced to graze on the grass growing from the bank beside him. Approaching him quietly and talking to him Stephen soothed him and soon he had the reins in his hands. He was gentling him when a man on a thickset cob came round the corner followed by another thoroughbred with a frightened boy perched on it.

The man pulled up beside Stephen. 'Thank 'ee, young sir,' he said. 'You be one of the young gents from th' college, eh?'

Stephen admitted that he was.

' 'Tis not all but can catch a loose horse. Used to horses, be you, then?'

'I've ridden a bit,' Stephen said.

'Wilt ride t'horse back for me then? Charley, here, slippery arsed booger that he is, he'll take t'rod.'

Another boy, looking even more frightened than the one perched on the horse, had come up by now and was standing by, panting from his run to catch up and nervously rubbing a thigh bruised from his fall. Stephen handed him the rod, turned the horse down the slope of the lane and, putting his hands on his withers, vaulted into the saddle.

The red-faced man's name was, it transpired, Walker. He farmed some miles away and kept a few horses which he raced for his own amusement. The boys were his sons whom he bullied unmercifully and over-horsed.

When they had arrived at the farm and put the horses up, Stephen was brought into the house and sat down to a huge Yorkshire high tea. There was no rationing here. Hams and cold cuts, cakes and scones, jams, honey, butter and apple cake all abounded.

'Aye, th'd think it'd all fatten 'em up, wouldn't tha, but it don't,' Walker said to him, looking at his sons.

His wife was a small fragile-looking woman and it was obvious that both the boys had taken after her. 'He thinks everyone as strong as himself,' she said to Stephen wistfully, gazing at her husband.

'Nay, not that, but strong enough,' Walker said, and then, turning to Stephen, 'Wilt come and ride for me again, lad?'

Stephen, his mouth full of apple cake, said that he would love to – if he could.

The upshot of his visit was that his fishing rod was discarded and whenever he could he slipped away to ride Mr Walker's horses. After a week or so of this Walker propounded a plan.

Owing to the war there was no racing under Rules anywhere within travelling distance and as a result the farmers in the dales were running meetings amongst themselves. These were unauthorised 'flapping' meetings and strictly speaking anyone taking part in them should

76

have suffered the most condign penalties which the Jockey Club could impose. But there was a war on, West Yorkshire was remote. The racing authorities, operating with skeleton staffs, were busy elsewhere and a blind eye was turned.

All this meant that Walker and his friends had found an opportunity for sport amongst themselves, for running their horses and for having a gamble. Walker thought that the horse which Stephen had caught might be something more than useful and he wanted to run him at one of these flapper meetings. The trouble was that he had no jockey since neither of the boys was strong enough to do justice to the horse or indeed to hold him at all. Walker watched Stephen ride and one afternoon as he slipped off he said to him: 'Wilt ride him at Heythorpe next Friday for me, lad?'

It seemed to Stephen that he should be able to manage it; he had played cricket earlier in the week and he was pretty sure he would not be wanted again. It meant cutting roll-call but afternoon roll-call in the house was only a formality and he knew he could get someone to answer for him. It also meant that he would be back after lock-up but this again should not present many difficulties since one of the library windows was on the latch and he had used this method of entry before.

So, on the following Friday afternoon, he drove over with Mr Walker in his trap to Heythorpe races.

He was beaten a length and a half by something which had been backed down from twenty to one to near evens. When he came in Walker was looking thunderous and he began to be concerned about his reception. He need not have worried. His owner's wrath was reserved for others. 'Tha rode him reet well, lad,' Mr Walker said. 'Those boogers. Stopped him for three months and then let him go today. I might a' guessed it. If we had some fookin' stewards instead of this lot of boogers good for nobbut save boozing in th' beer tent . . . Have a glass of beer, lad, and then we must be gettin' you back to college.'

The journey to Sellingham took some time especially since Mr Walker had partaken heavily of the strong local brew in the beer tent and followed it by 'a little brandy to quieten me stomach like'. Their progress was erratic and punctuated by frequent stops to allow Walker to relieve himself. By the time Stephen reached School House it was well after lock-up and later than he expected. He should be in prep and he might have difficulty getting into it unobserved.

He made his way quickly through the house garden to the library window. It slid up at his touch, and with a heave and a jump he was inside. To make his way to the dayroom he had to pass the entrance to the prefects' studies. Ordinarily, their doors would be shut and they would be working themselves or pretending to. But on this occasion the door to Conway's study stood open. Hearing Stephen's step, he appeared menacingly in the passage.

77

'Where have you been?' Conway demanded.

'In the library. I was looking for a book.' It was the best he could think of and even as he said it he knew it was not going to work.

'You're lying. I had you down for house cricket practice. There's a trial for the house eleven tomorrow. You're down for that too. You cut roll-call and you've been out after lock-up. Where have you been? What have you to say?'

Stephen had nothing to say. He was caught red-handed and he knew it. Moreover he was frightened. He did not like the look in Conway's eyes. For the first time he took stock of those eyes. They were a pale, icy, washed-out blue.

'I'm asking you again. Where have you been?'

'I—I was on the fells, Conway.'

'On the fells to this hour? What made you miss roll-call? Were you in a pub, drinking?'

'No—no, Conway.' In his fright Stephen blurted out the truth. 'I was riding a race—'

'Racing! You cut cricket and roll-call to ride in a race!' Conway stepped nearer to Stephen and sniffed his breath. 'You have been drinking.'

'Only a glass of beer, Conway. I was thirsty.'

'I should send you through to the headmaster but I'll deal with you myself. See me in the bathroom before lights out.'

The bathroom was the place where the ritual beatings took place. Conway had introduced a refinement of cruelty into these by decreeing that the victims presented themselves in their pyjamas just before bed, thus ensuring that his strokes inflicted the maximum hurt and injury.

Swallowing hard and finding his knees shaking under him, Stephen crept into evening prep. He was in for it now and he knew it. Conway's beatings were legendary, and this had all the appearance of being an extra special one.

For his part, sitting in his study, Conway brooded on Stephen, his character and his offences. In his eyes what Stephen had done amounted to the worst crime in the calendar. If he tried, Stephen had in him, Conway believed, the ability to help them win the house cricket cup. He had put him down for house nets that day. Instead he had affronted his authority and gone off racing. Racing! The sport of fast men and loose women. Conway resolved to give Stephen such a hiding as he would never forget and which would cure him once and for all of his slacking and cutting games. As he thought it over he wondered just what Stephen had been up to. All sorts of strange fancies connected with those who frequented racetracks and their way of life crept into his mind. Sexual desires had been tormenting him lately. Getting up from his chair he went to a corner of his study, picked up a swagger stick and swished it experimentally in the air.

Stephen presented himself in the bathroom just before lights out. Conway, burly in the shadowy light of the one electric bulb, was standing on the duckboards, the swagger stick in his hand.

He made a frightening figure. Stephen shivered. His thin pyjamas would afford him no protection at all. The back of his thighs were shaking.

'Bend over the bath,' Conway said. He was smiling slightly.

Stephen went slowly to the bath and leant over its wide mahogany ledge.

'Further,' Conway said. 'Tighter. That's better.'

Stephen set his teeth as the cane came down. It hurt even more than he had imagined. A searing pain ran across his buttocks and then seemed to go right through him. He had hardly time to think before the second one landed. It was exactly across the first, making the pain even greater. Two. Then three. It must be six he was going to get. Well, he'd stick it out; he must but, God, it was awful. Conway was an artist. He had heard about this. As well as the strength with which he administered his beatings he could land each stroke on top of the other. Four. And now, suddenly, a new dimension of pain was added. It was as if something was tearing his flesh each time the cane landed. Five. Six. That was it then. He'd done it. He'd stuck it out, he'd won in a way. He hadn't moved or moaned. He began to straighten up.

And then something seemed to possess Conway. That Stephen had taken one of the savagest beatings he had ever administered without a whimper appeared to him to make his offence all the greater. There was an evil spirit in Stephen and he would exorcise it by thrashing it out of him forever. 'Stay where you are,' Conway said. 'And don't move until I tell you.'

The swagger stick rose and fell; it was the sword of the Lord and of Gideon. In the person of Stephen, Conway was smiting the Amalekites, the Philistines and all the ungodly who worshipped strange idols and indulged in unclean practices such as horse racing, and all that went with it—gambling, drinking and whoring after loose women.

Again and again the cane came down, searing into Stephen's flesh. And again. And again. Stephen lost count, lost consciousness of anything save an agony that burnt through his whole body, until at last he slid along the side of the bath and fell, sobbing, to the floor.

Conway stopped then. He had won. He had exorcised the evil spirit. He put the swagger stick under his arm. 'That may teach you to behave when you're at school whatever you get up to at home,' he said. 'See that you turn out for the house trial tomorrow.'

Stephen never knew how he got back to his cubicle. Climbing in agony into bed, he lay face downwards and, much later, some sleep did come to him though it was only in patches shot through with pain and distorted by dreams in which Conway's face seemed always to be hovering threateningly over him.

When morning came he had made up his mind on two things. He would play in the house trial come what might and not give Conway the satisfaction or the opportunity of punishing him again, and he would give Conway back something of what he had given him. He was a fast bowler of sorts. He would bowl to hurt Conway as Conway had hurt him; he would maim him if he could.

Somehow he got through morning school and changed into his flannels. The house tutor was captaining the house Possibles which was Stephen's side, and Conway, as Captain of the house, led the Probables. The headmaster in his capacity as housemaster of School House always came down to watch this match and was sitting in a deck chair by the pavilion steps. Conway won the toss and batted first. He opened the Probables' batting so that he could keep an eye on the batting and fielding form of both sides.

The house tutor threw the ball to Stephen to open the Possibles' bowling. He failed to catch it and it hurt horribly as he bent to pick it up. Observing this and the stiffness of Stephen's movements, the house tutor called, 'Are you all right, Raymond?'

'Yes, thank you, sir,' Stephen said. He wasn't going to give away this chance of getting back at Conway. Slowly he paced out his run.

His bottom was hurting fearfully now. It would, he knew, burn into him every stride he took. It didn't matter. Nothing mattered save the strip of green turf and the man at the other end.

He turned and began his run. His stride lengthened as he came up to the wicket. The ball was a full pitch, very fast and it hurtled dangerously near Conway's head, missing it by inches. The second hit a bare patch on the pitch and lifted. It took Conway bang on the navel and doubled him up. That's one for last night, Stephen thought, as he watched Conway drop his bat and, hands on his midriff, gasp in pain. But it did not last long. Conway picked up his bat again and faced him. Stephen walked back. The third ball was another full pitch, waist high. No one could ever accuse Conway of cowardice. He stood up to it and hit it into the pavilion. Damn him, Stephen thought, if I could only land one on him again. But he was coming to the end of his resources. The pain was frightful. It was slashing through his buttocks. But he would not give in. Concentrate, he told himself, concentrate. Make the bastard feel what it is like to be hurt as he hurt me. He ran up. But even as he did so he knew that it was no good. His arm came over, the ball flew wide. The bright colours of the day merged into a swirling mass. The ground rose up around him and he fainted.

The house tutor reached him first. 'Take him to the pavilion,' he said.

In the changing room the house tutor was joined by the head-master. Both of them stared at the red stain beginning to seep through Stephen's flannels. 'Get him up to the sanatorium immediately,' the headmaster said. 'And go for the doctor. Tell him I'll meet him there.'

The school doctor, an elderly, kindly dug-out with snow-white hair and a stoop, had reached the sanatorium by the time they brought Stephen in. As soon as he got him to bed he banished the headmaster from the room. 'Come back in an hour and I'll see what I have to tell you,' he said.

It was exactly an hour later, for the headmaster was a punctual man, that the doctor met him at the door of the sanatorium and brought him into his little surgery. 'Well,' he said. 'Young Raymond. I've washed and cleaned his wounds; there's no infection so far as I can see.'

'What does he say happened to him?'

'He says he committed an anatomical impossibility.'

'What?'

'He told me he was climbing on Blayfell. He slipped and tore himself on some sharp rocks.'

'Very ingenious. Could it be true?'

'Of course not. Schoolboy ethics. Thou shalt not sneak. He's been submitted to a savage and irresponsible thrashing, and indeed rather more.'

'What do you mean?'

'Those prefects' beatings which, incidentally, I've never held with, are administered with a Corps swagger cane, I understand?'

'That is so.'

'In this instance I think what must have happened is that the ferrule had worked itself loose and one of the edges of the joint was expanded. In addition to the beating it's as if he had been slashed with a knife.'

'Can I see him?'

'I'd rather you didn't. He's still in some shock. I've given him a sleeping draught. Come back in the evening.'

The headmaster had formed his own idea of what had happened and on returning to the house he went immediately to Conway's study. In a corner amongst a huddle of other athletic oddments he saw three Corps swagger canes. Picking them up he examined them. The second one proved the doctor's guess to be correct. The joint of the ferrule had separated making it loose on the shank. The separa-tion had left exposed a cutting edge of metal as sharp as a knife. As if to place matters beyond doubt there was a tiny piece of cloth adher-ing to this part of the ferrule. Putting the stick under his arm the head-master went back to his own study where he opened a drawer in his desk, placed the cane inside and locked it. He then consulted the beatings book and found, as he thought, that no entry had been made concerning Stephen's punishment.

The headmaster was a worried man. He was now convinced beyond any doubt that the thrashing had been administered by Conway. The earlier incident where the boy had complained to his parents was only too vivid in his mind. If this boy were to do the same, heaven only knew what trouble would erupt. There might be a civil action against the school and it could even be that the press would get hold of it, with untold consequences. His own position would certainly be in peril. To make matters worse he now remembered that this boy, Raymond, had been sponsored by Colonel Fraser, one of the Governors. His parents were probably people of some importance but whether they were or not Fraser would not take kindly to the treatment and injuries which the boy had received.

The headmaster knew that he must act quickly. If he were to take immediate and determined action to rid the school of Conway's presence then he might forestall much of the unpleasant consequences of this beating.

In fact Stephen had no intention of complaining about his injuries to his parents or to anyone else. In some obscure way he felt that this was an issue between Conway and himself and that by bowling at Conway and nearly knocking him out he had gone some distance towards settling it. What Conway would do to him when he returned from the sanatorium was a matter which did cause him some uneasiness. He knew in his bones that Conway was not a man to let bygones be bygones, to stretch out a hand. And all the cards would be stacked on Conway's side. But none of this altered his determination to remain silent. So, when the headmaster returned that afternoon, Stephen was quite adamant that he would not alter his story.

As the headmaster was leaving, the doctor intercepted him and drew him into his surgery. 'Has the boy told you anything of what really happened to him?' he asked.

'No. He still says he fell when he was climbing.'

'Silly young fool. This stupid code of honour.'

'I suppose you must admire him for it in a way.' The headmaster was, in fact, profoundly grateful for it.

'It's too serious for any of that now,' the doctor said. 'Whoever inflicted those injuries may do it again. In my view he should not be at large, certainly in a school and with powers to administer corporal punishment.'

'I'm inclined to agree with you there.'

'Very well, then. Have you made any enquiries since I saw you?'

'I have indeed,' the headmaster said. But he had no intention of confiding in the doctor what he was about to do. His mind was made up and what the doctor had said confirmed him in the belief that his decision was the right one. Conway must go and he thought he had found a way of ridding the school of him with the least risk of dangerous publicity.

Back in his study he put a call through to the officer commanding the depot of the Westmoreland Fusiliers who was himself an old Sellinghamian.

'Not a hope, I'm afraid, of an immediate commission just at the moment,' was the reply. 'He could enlist, of course—'

But the headmaster wanted to save face both for the school and Conway if he could, and enlistment in the ranks after leaving in the middle of term would imply that something was seriously wrong. Sensing the headmaster's disappointment, the colonel went on: 'Is this important to you, Headmaster? Does it affect the school?'

'Yes,' the headmaster replied with a sigh. 'I'm very much afraid that it does.'

'Why not try the Flying Corps? They're killing them off like flies. They'll grab at anyone provided he's fit. There's a johnny in the War Office, a captain on the Staff, an O.S., too. He's in charge of interviewing candidates. I'll give you his name. He'll fix it for you.'

Later that evening the headmaster made another telephone call. He was lucky; he found the Old Sellinghamian captain still at his desk. In reply to the headmaster's enquiry he sounded enthusiastic. 'Play games?' he asked. 'What—Rugger and cricket colours? Sounds just the sort of chap we're looking for. Send him along. No trouble at all. Glad to help.'

For the first and only time the headmaster had reason to be thankful to the war. When he had put down the receiver he sent for Conway.

Although he was both mentally and physically tough, Conway was, after all, still only a boy. He was no match for the formidable personality of the headmaster, exerted in surroundings which gave it every conceivable advantage. Confronted with this and the evidence of the swagger-stick, in a few minutes Conway had admitted everything.

Conway had not known of the loose ferrule when he had administered the beating. He made an effort to explain this to the headmaster who, however, was in no mood to accept any plea in mitigation.

'I'm sacked then, am I?' Conway said miserably when the headmaster had finished. 'And my pater—he was so proud. The disgrace—'

'There need be no disgrace,' the headmaster said sternly. 'I have asked your father to come and see me as soon as possible. I shall tell him the facts. I shall also tell him that the Flying Corps will take you. I shall recommend that he agrees to remove you for that purpose. Nothing further need be said or done.'

When he arrived next day, Conway's father heard the headmaster out with a strange expression on his gaunt features. The headmaster wondered what it presaged but the Reverend Horace Conway was in fact remembering an incident in his son's childhood when one of the villagers had given him a white rabbit as a pet. The rabbit had been found later with its neck wrung and one of its legs all but torn off. The father had said nothing but had visited on the boy one of his more terrible thrashings and thenceforward pets were banished from the house.

'It is ordained,' was all he said when the headmaster finished. 'Everything is ordained as the sparrow falls.'

'You consent then,' the headmaster said. 'It means that the boy must leave as soon as the interview is arranged. Within a week, I'm told.'

The old man rose from the chair. Madness, the headmaster suddenly thought, lurked somewhere in his strange eyes, eyes that were not unlike those of his son. 'It is not for me to consent or refuse,' he said. 'We are only instruments of His will.'

The headmaster coughed. 'Er, yes,' he said. 'I am, then, taking that as consent. I think the boy is waiting for you.'

The Reverend Horace Conway went back with his son to the house Captain's study. By now Conway had convinced himself that he was the victim of an injustice and that Stephen was the author of all his troubles. It was Stephen with his wicked ways, his refusal to conform, who had brought all this down upon him. Stephen had received the punishment which he richly deserved and now it was he, Conway, who was suffering for it. It was never in Conway's nature to admit that he could be wrong and it did not take much to convince himself that in this instance he was in the right and that somehow Stephen should pay for it. He endeavoured to explain all this to his father, laying emphasis on Stephen's iniquities.

'The boy is possessed of an evil spirit,' his father said when he had finished. 'It should be driven out. But it is clear you were not the chosen instrument. Now, let us pray.'

During the days of waiting, Conway's resentment against Stephen grew. He could not reveal to the house the real reason why he was leaving but he made dark illusions to his fellow prefects who guessed that his departure was not entirely voluntary that 'that little swine Raymond' was responsible for it. The house as a whole made a hero out of him. The headmaster had allowed it to get round that he had insisted on taking the opportunity of accepting an immediate commission in the Flying Corps in order to fight for King and Empire and had sacrificed the chance of a school career which held out prospects of unrivalled athletic distinction.

So, when the cab turned into the house yard to take him away to the station, it was to find the whole house drawn up in two ranks

84

stretching from the gate to the boys' doorway. Eager hands seized Conway's trunk for him and placed it on the box. Then he came from the entrance like a conqueror dressed in his best Sunday blue suit and wearing an Old Sellinghamian tie.

As he emerged, cheering broke out. It continued, rising to a crescendo as the cab trundled its way towards the gateway.

Stephen, who had just been discharged from the sanatorium, was walking down the road to the house when he heard the cheering commence. Puzzled, he hurried on to find out what was happening. He turned in at the entrance of the yard at the very moment the cab was leaving it. The cab-horse was old and slow and starved, the incline was steep and the cab was barely moving.

With a last wave to the cheering crowd, Conway threw himself back on to the cushions. As he did so, he saw Stephen and their eyes met. The laugh vanished from his face. Stephen was close enough to remark again on the icy coldness of Conway's eyes. They were eyes that would always be strangers to compassion or mercy and as Stephen watched they filled with naked hatred.

9

'So you want to fight for the Empire, England and the Pax Britannica?' Edward looked quizzically at his son across the big desk in his upstairs study.

Stephen had never given a thought to what he and his like were fighting for. In addition to the escape from Sellingham it offered him, he had accepted without questioning that he would go into one of the Services if the war lasted until he had reached the necessary age. It was more a matter of caste than anything else. All his contemporaries joined up unless they were medically unfit. Never for an instant had he considered the alternative of refusing to do so though he was vaguely aware that there was a miserable group called conchies who did evade military service. Now, suddenly, an entirely different aspect of the matter was being presented to him. 'I never thought of it that way, father,' he said. 'I just though I had to go like everyone else. I'm not sure that I do particularly want to fight for England. I don't seem to get along with them very well—or some of them anyway,' he added.

'You are not alone in that. Our family, you know, my boy, have never been unquestioning loyalists. Some of your ancestors fought with the Wild Geese. It's different with your mother's family. They're Cromwellians—warriors all of them. Most Cromwellians have the mentality of mercenaries. That's what makes them such good soldiers, eager to do England's fighting for them. Gough, Wolseley, Roberts, Kitchener—it's almost like a roll call, isn't it? But we belong to a different culture. Some of our roots go right back to the beginnings of this land.' Involuntarily his eyes strayed to the sea and the mountains lying in the sun beyond the tall windows.

'Do you mean you don't want me to go, father?'

'No. If I were your age I'd do as you are doing. But I want you to know why you are doing it. This isn't only England's war. It's a war for civilisation, perhaps to end all wars if that is possible. But what will become of all of us here when it is over, or perhaps before, I am sometimes afraid to think.'

'What do you mean, father? Surely nothing can happen to us here?

86

The Germans won't come.'

'It isn't the Germans I'm thinking of. That terrible business in Dublin last year and the brutal retribution the Army exacted. It's made martyrs of the rebels and crystallised the feeling for revolution that's never far away in this country. We're sitting on a powder keg and sooner or later, sooner, I'm afraid, than anyone thinks, it is going to explode. Sometime someone will have to pay for those centuries of oppression and persecution, for the evictions and the emigrations. We were always good landlords but I doubt if that will protect us when the holocaust comes.'

Both of them were looking out of the windows now, at the sweep of sea and hills and heather. Two destroyers of the anti-submarine flotilla were sliding slowly towards their moorings. Below them their own boats, the ketch and the little twelve-footer, lay at anchor just off the Bellary Court jetty.

It was Stephen who raised the unspoken thought in both their minds. 'But, father, we can't leave here—'

Edward looked again at the destroyers as they came past Holy Island towards the head of the Bay. 'I hope not, my boy. But I'm afraid in the last resort we rely on England to keep us here, and will she go on doing it? I doubt it. But let's not speculate. This is all in the future. It is the present that concerns us. You don't want to go back to school. You haven't been happy there of late, I think.'

Stephen looked at his father in surprise. So the old man had guessed. He saw much more than those around him gave him credit for. 'I hate school, father,' he said simply.

Edward sighed. 'I didn't much care for it myself when I was there,' he said, 'but you're too young to join up. They won't take you until you're eighteen.'

'I'm over seventeen. I'll be eighteen in a few months. They're taking people of seventeen in the R.F.C.'

'The Flying Corps?'

'Yes, I want to fly, father.'

'Desmond is in it now, I seem to have heard. He transferred from the cavalry. He was always something of a hero of yours. Is that the reason?'

'No, not really. I think I could fly. It's a bit like riding races they say. You know I've always wanted to do that. And it's, I don't know, it's a cleaner way of fighting.'

'I can understand all that. I think if I had to go to war that is the way I should want to do it. I don't see how I can stop you.'

'Thank you, father.'

'But I don't in the least know how you go about it. Perhaps Mr Massiter does. He's at Dunlay on a few days' leave. He is coming to lunch tomorrow. He seems to know everyone and everything these days. We must ask him. And you must tell your mother.'

'Yes, father.'

Honoria was in the conservatory with secateurs in her hand. She was surveying her carnations with the air of a sergeant-major drawing up a battalion for inspection. 'Of course you must go,' she said briskly when Stephen announced his intention. 'I'll write to your uncle immediately. He'll arrange for a commission for you in his regiment. There will be no difficulty at all.'

'I'm sorry mother, but I want to fly. I've spoken to father about it. I want to go into the R.F.C.'

'The Flying Corps! But they're only mechanics!'

'They're the cavalry of the air, mother.'

'Cavalry of the air, indeed!' Honoria gave one of her peculiar snorts. 'This is all quite ridiculous. I'll speak to your father myself.'

'But, mother, Mr Murtagh is in the Flying Corps now.'

'Desmond!' Snip, snip, snip, went the secateurs as if they were taking off Desmond's head and the rest of the Flying Corps' with it. The carnations fell into the gardening basket in a heap of bright colours. 'I can't say I think *that* much of a recommendation. Which reminds me. Sarah was to come over to discuss the canteen for the sailors.' She glanced at the little gold watch that was pinned to her blouse.

At that moment Mikey came in to announce that Mrs Murtagh and her daughter had arrived and were waiting in the round room.

Stephen had not seen Babs for over a year as she had been away during his recent holidays. Now she had suddenly sprung up into a young woman and a very attractive one. Her russet hair and wide laughing mouth were much as her mother's must have been before the years had faded their freshness and care coupled with marriage to Desmond had etched lines of strain and age on to her face.

Babs was laughing at some shared joke when Stephen and his mother entered the room. Stephen was struck anew by the gaiety and vitality that seemed to surround her.

'Well, Sarah, we must get to work,' Honoria said. 'The first thing to decide is where we are going to buy the food for these people. Hennessy's in the Square, I think. They always seem to me to give the best service. And young Hennessy, I'm bound to say, is uncommonly helpful and civil.'

Stephen looked at Babs and their eyes met. In hers he saw an unspoken plea for escape. She no more wanted to spend the afternoon planning meals for sailors and running errands for her elders than he did. 'Look, mother,' he said. 'I don't believe Babs can help you much with your old canteen—' Seeing the look in his mother's eye he hastily stopped and started again. 'I mean she'll be no help about shopping in the village, I'm sure. She'll only be in your way. I'm going sailing.

Why not let her come?'

Babs' eyes lit up. 'Oh, do,' she said. 'I'd simply love to. What fun, Stephen!'

'I don't know.' Sarah was doubtful. 'What about the weather, Stephen? I dread these squalls. Remember what happened to that poor fellow last year. How safe are you in a boat, Stephen?'

'Of course he's safe,' Honoria said sharply. Whatever private thoughts Honoria had about their abilities she would never admit to anyone else that her children were other than supremely competent in whatever they wished to do.

'The glass is high,' Stephen said. 'There won't be any squalls.'

'Of course we'll be all right, mother dear,' Babs put in. 'Please do be a sport—'

Having been moved to defend her offspring by Sarah's implied criticism, Honoria could scarcely do other than give her blessing to the proposed expedition. 'They'll be quite safe,' she said. 'And Stephen is right in a way. I don't suppose Barbara would be much help in what we have to discuss, Sarah.'

As usual she carried the day. 'Very well then, though I do hate boats,' Sarah said.

But by that time Stephen and Babs were running together across the lawn, and down the terraces that ended in the flight of stone steps leading to the jetty.

The twelve-footer had a single lug sail. Stephen had it up in a few minutes. The light breeze took them out from the shelter of the bluff on which the house stood. Then the wind filled the sail, Stephen paid out the sheet and they went scudding along into the sunlit afternoon.

Babs dropped her hand into the water and looked at Stephen as he sat with his hand on the tiller. 'And how is school, Stephen?' she asked.

'Horrible,' Stephen answered. 'I hate it. I'm leaving.'

'But what are you going to do? You're not old enough to join up, are you?'

'I'm going into the Flying Corps. They'll take you at seventeen. That is if mother doesn't mess it all up.'

'Why? Doesn't she want you to go?'

'She's decided I'm to go into some silly grand cavalry regiment with her beastly old brother. He commands it. He's all covered in whiskers and talks as if he had two hot potatoes in his mouth. No one can make out a word he says. "Pop, pop, pop. Paw, paw, paw," that's what he sounds like. Father says he supposes his horses understand him but nobody else can.'

Babs laughed. 'But how can she stop you, Stephen?'

'You don't know mother.' Stephen was plunged into sudden gloom. 'She can do almost anything she wants to. Do you remember

89

that terrible row over the Frenches and Harry's father being killed out hunting?'

'No one in the Bay will ever forget it. What really did happen, Stephen?'

'All I know is that old French was pinching our money. He took an awful lot, I think. Mother wouldn't give father any peace until he'd threatened Mr French with something awful, like going to prison.'

'Goodness! And do you know what happened to Harry?'

'No. He and his mother just disappeared.'

'Someone said he was in the army.'

'He might be. He's a year older than me.'

'But, Stephen, if you lost all that money, what happened? How was your father able to carry on?'

'I think in some way Mr Massiter rescued us. Just before he finally went I heard old Rogers say to Mikey that if it hadn't been for Mr Massiter we'd all be in the poor house, himself included.'

'Mother dear says Mr Massiter will own the whole Bay before he's finished.'

'I think mother still hates him. But he's so rich and grand and everything now that she almost accepts him. He's coming to lunch tomorrow.'

'Why don't you get him to help you? I'm sure he could get round your mother for you.'

They were almost abreast of Holy Island now, the prow of the little boat lifting and banging against the light waves. Babs looked up at the great tower of the castle. 'Let's pay a call on him, Stephen,' she said. 'It'll be bearding the ogre in his den. We'll persuade him to help you at lunch tomorrow. What an adventure, Stephen!'

'But we can't do that, can we?' Stephen protested. 'What's he going to say?'

'He won't say anything. It's the best chance you have. Be brave, Stephen!'

It was what they used to call to each other out hunting when approaching a difficult fence. Stephen looked at the wind, looked at her laughing face and knew he was lost. He put about and they came around the head of the island. In its lee the breeze was very light. They drifted slowly along through the calm, clear water, past the causeway connecting the island with the mainland, and so approached the entrance to the private harbour.

The harbour had been constructed on the same scale as the castle. It was fully five hundred yards long with walls of cut stone lining its sides. The open doors of two big boat-houses stared at them from its head. On one side a slope of lawn reached up to the castle; the other was covered with banks of rhododendrons. Massiter's cutter, its brass and paintwork gleaming in the sun, lay at her moorings along with a

90

steam launch and a whole host of smaller boats. Stephen dropped the sail and secured it. Then he took out the oars and rowed towards where a boat slip and a flight of steps were let into the wall nearest the castle.

A figure was standing at the head of the steps, watching them. It was Andrew Massiter, resplendent in a yachting cap, a blue double-breasted blazer and a pair of spotless white duck trousers. Stephen was immediately conscious of his old jersey and worn grey flannels.

Massiter made no move to greet them in any way, either hostile or welcoming, but stood watching them in silence as Stephen brought the boat alongside the slip and secured the painter to an iron ring. With his trim imperial jutting out over his collar he looked, Stephen thought, the embodiment of piratical self-possession. Neither his attitude nor his surroundings did anything to increase Stephen's confidence in the successful outcome of the visit.

'And to what do I owe this pleasure, may I enquire?' Massiter asked as they approached him.

Stephen hesitated. He could hardly plunge in and say straight away that he wanted him to intercede with his mother so that he could join the R.F.C.

It was Babs who answered. 'We were sailing by,' she said smiling. 'And we thought—well, Stephen has something to ask you—a favour.'

'And you aren't worried that this might be taken as an intrusion?'

'Oh, Lord!' Stephen thought. 'Now we've torn it. He's going to warn us off. I knew we shouldn't have come. Now he'll back mother up just because he's cross with us.'

Babs looked Massiter squarely in the eye, and gave one of her dazzling smiles. 'Divil a bit,' she said in the vernacular.

Massiter laughed. He really does look like a fox, Stephen thought, and barks like one too. All at once he appeared to be recognising Babs as a woman and not as a child. His tawny eyes ran over her. Watching him, for some reason he did not understand, a small shiver ran across Stephen's shoulders. But whatever had been in Massiter's eyes was gone in an instant. 'I'm about to have tea,' he said abruptly. 'I hope you'll join me. Come along.'

A stretch of lawn divided the head of the harbour from a sunken garden where trim box hedges guarded beds of begonias and roses. Under the spreading arms of a copper beech a table was laid for tea. Basket chairs with deep cushions stood around it. Massiter motioned them towards these with a wave of his hand.

After tea had been carried on to the lawn with impressive ceremony by the English butler, and a retinue of footmen and parlour-maids, Massiter turned to Stephen. It was, Stephen noticed, the first time his glance had left Babs since they had sat down. 'Now, young man,' he said. 'Just what is this favour you want to ask of me?'

Though he did not care to admit it, Stephen was still slightly frightened of Massiter. Tongue-tied in his presence and over-awed by the grandiloquence of his surroundings, he did not know where to begin. Babs, however, had no such inhibitions. She was enjoying herself and was entranced by everything about her. Eyes dancing, she looked around her, taking in the evidence of wealth and luxury in all that she saw, so different from the fallen glories of her own home. Then again her eyes met those of her host. 'He wants to go into the Flying Corps,' she said.

'A most laudable ambition, I should have thought,' Massiter said gravely. 'And why can't he?'

'My mother is all against it,' Stephen blurted out, and even as he did so realised how childish the words must sound.

Massiter raised his eyebrows. 'Your mother, dear me,' he said. 'But these are apron strings, surely?' His voice held, Stephen thought, a note of quiet contempt. 'And why, pray, is she so much against it?'

Stephen knew that he was being more than gently mocked, shown up as a child before Babs. It made him more tongue-tied than ever. 'She wants me to go into some beastly cavalry regiment,' he said sulkily. 'Her brother is the colonel.'

'And why do you imagine I can help?'

Stephen had no idea how properly to frame an answer. He was thoroughly hating this whole interview. 'We . . . I . . .' he began, and then started again. 'Babs and I . . . you see . . . we thought . . .'

'What he really means, Mr Massiter,' Babs said laughing, 'is that you're going to lunch at Bellary tomorrow and he hopes that you will use your influence with his mother to persuade her to change her mind.'

Massiter looked at Babs. His lips twitched slightly as he turned to Stephen. 'You have a most able advocate,' he said gravely. 'It seems I must do what I can.'

Massiter had exchanged his noisy and largely unreliable Panhard-Levasor, which had so irritated Grig Gnowles at his meets before the war, for a steel-grey Phantom Rolls. His connections in high places had secured for him a plentiful petrol ration and now the Rolls purred along the narrow twisting roads that would take him to Bellary Court.

By arrangement with Edward he arrived early, for they had matters to discuss. Always anxious to supervise the security of his investments he had had the Bellary Court farm and rental accounts submitted to him and there were one or two points arising from them which he wished to talk over with his host.

Edward was waiting for him in the upstairs study when Mikey showed Massiter in.

'You've lost Rogers, I see,' Massiter said as they shook hands.

'Yes. He really got too decrepit. It was a problem to know what to do with him. Fortunately we found he had a sister in Tunbridge Wells and she took him in. It's a case of cutting down all round now with this ghastly war. But the boy is shaping up quite well.'

'He is of military age, though, surely?'

'I suppose so. He doesn't show any signs of wanting to go. I can't say I blame him. It's not their war, is it? The Cabinet can't be so foolish as to insist on conscription here, or can they? It might be the spark to set everything alight.'

'Like the cartridges in the Indian Mutiny? I'm not sufficiently in their confidence to say what they'll do though the more out-and-out Conservatives want it, I know. They may have to in the end. The manpower situation is looking extremely serious.'

'The losses on the Somme last year were terrible. Even in the village we felt it. Three killed in a little place like this. It brought it home.'

'There's talk of another big push. The French can't hold without it, they say.'

'The French? We always blame the French, don't we? However, I don't suppose you came to talk about the war, Massiter. Have you anything particular on your mind? Hutton tells me the accounts all went to you a little time ago.'

Edward had been dreading the interview. Farming was prospering in the changed circumstances thrown up by the war. The demand for meat had vastly increased the prices that could be obtained for livestock; especially cattle. Grain crops, too, had been profitable. The weather had held for the last two harvests and the yield had been good. Nevertheless, Edward knew that Massiter would not have suggested this meeting for no reason at all. Something must have come out of the accounts that was bothering him.

'The figures for the farm are very satisfactory,' Massiter said. 'I am not, however, so happy about the rents.'

Edward heaved a mental sigh. The rents. The eternal problem. Massiter had insisted on dividing the agency. Where Sterling French had had complete control of the entire estate, both farm and rent collection, Massiter had put in a manager to look after the day-to-day running of the farm while an agent in Kilderry was given the collection of the rents. Hutton was in charge of the legal side, looking after renewals of leases and such sales as there were, and maintained an overall supervision.

The farm part worked very well but Edward was not so satisfied with the manner in which the rent collection was conducted. The Kilderry agent was, in his opinion, out of touch with the situation. He was far away, he was impersonal and he was tough. It was Edward's firm conviction that the Kilderry rents, such as they were, required

93

the personal touch.

Massiter took the folded rental out of the leather attaché case he had brought with him, and spread it on the table between them. 'In certain cases,' he said, 'the arrears are mounting up. Yet I understand from Hutton that you are not anxious to sue?'

'Some of them . . . you know how it is,' Edward said. 'They've run into bad times. They nearly always pay in the end.'

Massiter's pencil ran down the list of names and, with a sinking heart, Edward knew just where it was going to stop.

'These Rossiters now, at Corravore,' Massiter said. 'It's quite three years since they paid anything?'

Edward's heart sank still further. He had guessed correctly. The Rossiters at Corravore. That was where it had all started. It was the Rossiters and their rent which had brought about the undoing of Sterling French and the entry of Massiter into his life. The Rossiters had never been anything but a cause of trouble. 'It's not a large rent compared with the rest,' he said weakly. 'And it's bad, mountainy land.'

'That's hardly the point, I'm afraid. Hutton tells me that if we let this state of affairs go on much longer we'll find the rent statute barred. They might even acquire what I understand is known as a squatter's title.'

Edward profoundly wished they might acquire a squatter's title or anything else which would take them out of his concern. 'Things are not good up there, you know,' he said. 'And they're a dangerous, difficult lot.'

'Laurence Rossiter is down here as the tenant. Is he the head of the clan?'

'Larry? He is but you won't reach him. He's joined up.'

'What? If they're all you say they are I should have thought his sympathies would lie the other way—with the Volunteers or Sinn Fein. Joining up would be the last thing he'd do.'

'He says he did it to get a decent meal for himself and provision for his family. But there's a much more sinister story going round. It's said he's going to get military experience for the coming war against the British.'

'That experience could be bought at too high a price. He may not return.'

Edward raised his head to look out of the window. Symbolically, it seemed, a dark cloud had come over the sun, blotting out for a moment the view of the hills and sea. A few drops of rain spattered against the glass. The room darkened. 'I have a feeling,' he said sombrely, 'that he'll come back. They always do, the Rossiters.'

The Captain of one of the destroyers, a Commander with three gold rings on his sleeve, along with his wife who was staying in Bellary

94

while the ships were stationed there, were also guests at lunch.

The conversation was all about the war, the prospects, the coming push, whether America would come in, and the anti-submarine activities of the destroyers themselves.

It was Massiter who introduced the subject of using aeroplanes to assist the fleet in combating submarine attacks. From there he led the conversation to flying in general and thence to the R.F.C. Stephen, sitting silent, realised that, whatever else could be said about him, in this instance at least he had not forgotten his promise.

'Splendid chaps,' the Commander said, unwittingly helping the plot along. 'Used to see something of them at Pompey. Came over from Calshot. Got a cousin with them, as a matter of fact.'

'My son says he wants to join them,' Honoria said.

'Does he, b'Gad. Couldn't do better, young feller,' the Commander boomed at Stephen.

'It's a silly notion,' Honoria said flatly. 'A neighbour of ours, Desmond Murtagh, has just become attached to them from the Cavalry. He's some sort of schoolboy hero of Stephen's. That's all it is.'

'So Murtagh has joined the Flying Corps, has he?' Massiter said, and Stephen saw a sudden flash come and go in his eyes at the mention of Desmond's name. 'You don't by any chance know where he is?'

'Somewhere in France, no doubt,' the Commander boomed again.

'I haven't the least idea where Desmond is,' Honoria said. 'Nor, so far as I know, has Sarah. In any event Stephen would be far better off in the Cavalry.'

'But I do assure you, my dear Mrs Raymond,' Massiter said, 'lots of cavalrymen are transferring to the R.F.C. There is an affinity, you know. The cavalry of the air, they're calling them now. Indeed, I believe they're beginning to pick and choose.' Massiter looked at Stephen. He would never do anything so vulgar as to wink but a faint smile touched the corners of his lips.

'Indeed,' Honoria murmured. 'You surprise me. Well, of course . . .'

Another ally came to Stephen from a totally unexpected quarter. 'Do let him go if he wants to, mother,' Ethel said. 'I know Johnny Winters is jolly keen to join.' Ethel was herself campaigning to get away from the Bay by entering one of the women's services and if Stephen went she felt they could scarcely refuse her.

'Johnny Winters? General Winters' son?' For the first time Honoria began to weaken.

Perceiving this, from the head of the table, Edward spoke up. 'Can you help us, Massiter?' he said. 'Put in a word for the boy, or something? I'm afraid I know less than nothing of how to set about it.'

Massiter looked again at Stephen. This time his strange eyes lingered on him for a moment as if sizing him up. Meeting his glance, it seemed to Stephen almost as if the older man was considering him in some way as a possible adversary, a future threat to some plan he had in mind.

'Of course I can,' Massiter said, and then, turning to Honoria, 'And, may I take it, dear lady, that you give your consent?'

Honoria, for once totally out-manoeuvred, capitulated, though not very graciously. 'It seems I must,' she said.

'That's settled, then,' Massiter's eyes came back to Stephen. 'I'm off the day after tomorrow. I'll be in London the following day and the day after I don't know where I'll be. He'd better come with me.'

The forty-eight hours that were left for Stephen at the Bay passed as if they were seconds. He bicycled over to say goodbye to Bob Ferris and found him in one of his gruffer moods. 'Goin' to fight for them Saxons, are ye?' Bob said. 'Ye're daft! Why don't ye stay here and make a name for yerself ridin' races while all the other lads are gone?'

Seeing the lean heads of the thoroughbreds looking out of Bob's boxes, Stephen was assailed by the temptation to stay. No one could compel him to go, after all. But the thought went almost as soon as it had come. 'But, Bob, I've got to go,' he said.

'No one in this country has to go, boy. Ye're fightin' another man's war for him and little thanks ye'll get for it, I'm tellin' ye.'

'I'm going to fly, Bob. They say it's a bit like riding.'

'Fly? In them crazy things? Now I know ye're out of your mind. And what'll I do for an amateur jock? I was hopin' ye'd ride for me this winter.'

'Keep them for me, Bob. I'll ride them all winners for you when I come back.'

'Aye, boy,' Bob said to himself as he watched Stephen bicycle away down the avenue. 'Perhaps ye will, but it'll be a different Ireland ye'll come back to, I'm thinkin'—if ye come back.'

Leaving Bob and the horses with a pang of regret Stephen went on to the Murtaghs'. Babs was alone in the morning room and in a whirl of excitement. She, too, had persuaded her mother to allow her to go and do war work. 'I'm going to join the WAACs,' she told Stephen. 'I'll try to get into the R.F.C. section. Who knows we might meet— you and I and father all together again, Stephen!'

'Oh, Babs, if we only could!'

Her eyes were dancing. 'Fly away, Stephen, in your flying machine, fly back to me, tra la la,' she carolled, pirouetting on her toes. She came to a stop very close to him, laughing up at him. Hardly knowing what he was doing he bent down and kissed her. Instantly her arms were around his neck and her mouth opened under his. Her tongue was like a live thing; she was clinging to him, pressing herself against him. Then the door opened, a maid came in with tea and they sprang apart.

After that the hours flew by even faster until they ran right out and the Rolls was at the door.

Stephen said his goodbyes. He kissed his sister formally on the cheek. His father's handclasp was warmer than customary and held longer. 'Good luck, son, and God go with you,' he said gruffly.

Honoria was as stiff and erect as if a bayonet had been thrust down her back. Her eyes were as stern and unblinking as ever. 'I trust,' she said sternly, 'that whatever happens you will do your duty.'

Then he was running across the gravel to the car. There was time for one quick look at the sweep and curve of the Bay before he clambered in.

Mikey was putting his bag into the empty front seat beside the chauffeur. When he had finished securing it he turned to Stephen. 'Good luck, Master Stephen,' he said. 'And come back safe to us now.'

The Rolls purred into motion. The little group by the door waved. As the car turned the corner of the avenue and the house disappeared from view Stephen felt lost and frightened and very alone. The blue mountains brooded in the sun. He looked around him absorbing all he could, storing the scene in his memory. He wondered if he would ever see it again.

10

The School of Aerial Fighting at Ayr had not been long established when Stephen arrived there a few months later.

It was at Ayr that a pupil pilot completed the last stages of his training before being posted to a fighting squadron at the Front. During the course, the pupils were initiated into the techniques of fighting in the air by instructors who had done at least one tour of duty over the lines. They flew the type of aeroplane in which they would be called upon to fly and fight in action when they joined a squadron—if they survived the course. The first-line fighters currently in service with the R.F.C. were the Sopwith Camel, the S.E.5a and the two-seater Bristol Fighter. Although the age for entry to the R.F.C. had been raised to eighteen, Massiter had experienced no trouble in arranging Stephen's enrolment, and over the past months Stephen had found to his delight that, in this instance at least, he had not erred in his assessment of his own abilities, for flying seemed to come instinctively to him. Later, he was to hear the romantically-minded rhapsodising over the actual physical sensations of flying—the feeling of aloneness, of communication with the elements, and of the fantasies presented by scenes of cloud and sky never before opened up to the eyes of man. None of these meant anything to him. Quite simply, he loved flying different types of aircraft, divining their secrets, then mastering each one until it became almost an extension of himself.

Beginning on a Farman, or Rumpty as it was called, he had gone on to fly anything he could lay his hands on. By the time he arrived at Ayr he had flown Avros, Spads, One and Half Strutters and Pups, but he had never flown a Camel. He had heard all too much about them, however, since amongst the fledglings of the R.F.C. the Camel had an awesome reputation. It was held to have killed more men in training than had perished in action against the enemy. Although Stephen had passed all the tests so far put to him with a fair amount of ease, and had come to the School, he knew, with commendations from his instructors along the way, he was by no means confident of his ability to master a Camel.

The basic difficulty about flying a Camel was caused by the fact that it had a very short fuselage and a very powerful rotary engine. As a consequence, the machine itself was inherently unstable and, further, the torque or twist of the rotary engine was such that, at the least excuse or mismanagement, it corkscrewed violently to the right. Thus, before one mastered it, any turn to the right had to be treated with extreme caution for the Camel would spin sharply and without warning. It was this characteristic which claimed most of its victims. It was an unforgiving aeroplane to the unskilled or unskilful. One mistake low down was enough; the pilot would not live to make another.

Stephen knew all this for he had listened carefully to the talk of old Camel hands in an effort to divine the machine's secrets. He had learnt, too, that the converse applied. Once you had mastered a Camel, they said, you would never want to fly anything else. The difficulty was to stay alive long enough to acquire that mastery.

The pupils on the course were quartered in a large house standing in its own grounds not far from the race-course which had been converted into an aerodrome. When Stephen arrived he found a room allotted to him. It was bare of furniture save for two beds, a washstand and a couple of rickety chairs.

An orderly was bending over one of the beds. Personal belongings were laid out on it and he was packing them into a battered leather suitcase. As Stephen entered he straightened up and came to attention.

'All right, carry on,' Stephen said. 'Someone leaving?'

The orderly had a long lugubrious face and when he spoke he made a hissing noise through his teeth. ' 'E's not leaving, 'e's left, sir.'

'Gone to a squadron, has he?'

'Gone west, sir. Killed 'imself in a Camel this morning 'e did, pore Mr Johnston. Never a nicer man you could wish to look after. Spun in 'e did. That's the third this week. It's fair cruel the way them Camels is killing the orficers off.'

Stephen watched the belongings, a service tunic, a pair of silver-backed brushes, the photograph of a laughing girl, disappear into the case. It was not the first time he had been present on such an occasion, for accidents and flying training were all but synonymous. You accepted their inevitability very quickly or you cracked and got out or were put out. It did nothing nevertheless to increase his confidence in his own chances of survival and he felt a small tremor of apprehension.

As the orderly was about to leave the room the door opened and another officer came in. He was wearing an R.F.C. tunic and wings, riding breeches and field boots. The breeches were the pale pink colour favoured by the smarter cavalry regiments, the tunic was exquisitely cut, the field boots had been carved to his legs by one of the more exclusive makers. He had fair hair slicked back straight from his forehead, a patrician air and a condescending manner. He looked the embodiment of upper-crust English arrogance and Stephen disliked him on sight. 'De Vaux,' the newcomer announced, gazing down his nose at Stephen. 'Pronounced with an oh and spelt with an x. Deuced difficult to explain sometimes. And who may you be?'

'Raymond,' Stephen said. 'Spelt that way and pronounced that way. Deuced simple, really.'

'Told a soldier servant fellah down there to bring my kit up,' the other went on, entirely disregarding Stephen's reply. 'He seems to be takin' his time.' He stared around him at the bare walls of the room and the sparse furniture. 'Not quite the accommodation to which I'm accustomed,' he said. 'Still, better than the trenches, what?'

'You've been out?' Stephen said.

'Yes. Short time, don't you know. Twenty-seventh Lancers. No cavalry work in this war. Very boring except when they shoved us into the trenches. Mud, don't you know. Horrible stuff, mud. Not the thing at all. Besides—Lancers—well now, what, I ask you, will a lance do to a tank? Asked m'Colonel this one night after a couple of glasses of port.'

'What did he say?' Stephen was beginning to like his room mate rather better.

'Didn't care for it at all. As a matter of fact, old bean, m'Colonel and I never saw exactly eye to eye. A man of no consequence at all, m'Colonel. Can't think where he came from. Told me I rode badly too. Letting down the tone of the regiment, he said. Wanted to make me machine gun officer or some such rot. Put in for a transfer after that, and he seemed quite anxious to let me go. Surprisin', really.'

At that moment an orderly came in with de Vaux's trunks and valise. He put them on the bed and left. 'Scarcely expect him to unpack for you, I suppose,' de Vaux said, looking at his luggage with some distaste. 'Beastly chore.' Then he turned to stare at the empty bed. 'What happened to my predecessor?' he said.

'Killed himself in a Camel this morning,' Stephen said promptly with a touch of malice. 'Spun in. Third this week.'

'Fancy!' De Vaux passed a hand across his fair hair. 'Horrible things, Camels. Throw oil all over the place, I'm told.' He sat down on one of the chairs and crossed his elegant booted legs. As he did so the double-breasted tunic billowed in front of him. 'Horrible things these tunics, too,' he said, smoothing it down. 'All but impossible to get a decent cut. No wonder they call them maternity jackets.' He looked at Stephen, a gleam of acuteness coming into his rather vague eyes. 'Any chance of getting on to S.E.'s?' he asked.

'I don't really know,' Stephen answered. 'I only arrived just before you did. But I did hear that a whole Squadron has just gone out on S.E.s. I should think it's pretty certain to be Camels for us.'

De Vaux took off his Sam Browne and threw it on to the bed. 'That being so,' he said, 'let us go below and search out strong drink.'

The ante-room of the mess was in the former dining room of the house. It was a pleasant, panelled room with electric light coming from two chandeliers which through some oversight had not been removed before the military moved in. There were easy chairs and one or two sofas scattered about. *The Tatler, Sketch, Illustrated Sporting & Dramatic News* together with other papers were on a table near one of the curtained windows. In one corner was a bar. Officers stood about talking or sat reading papers. Most of the newcomers were in a little group by the bar.

'What will you have?' de Vaux said.

Stephen was only beginning to be initiated into the business of drinking. Whisky was, by and large, the staple drink of the R.F.C. but at that time it tasted to him like old iron filings and made him feel sick. He asked for a gin and vermouth which someone at another station had advised him to begin on and which seemed to go down all right.

As de Vaux brought the drinks a voice from the group said: 'I hear we're going straight on to Camels tomorrow.'

'Sweet Christ,' another voice, an American one, answered him. 'Say, we'd better have another drink—quick.'

'When the hell are they going to give us dual Camels?' the first speaker said.

'What are you getting cold feet about?' the truculent tones of a third speaker put in. 'Cold feet, that's what kills men on Camels. Any fool can fly a Camel.'

Heads turned to look at the owner of the voice. He was a short, ruddy-faced man with protruberant eyes and a spiky, toothbrush moustache. He held a large glass of whisky in his hand. Stephen guessed it was not his first.

'Ever flown one yourself?' someone asked him.

'Not actually. No. But I've flown every other service type. Some of the things I've flown I tell you if you can fly them you can fly anything. Ever been upside down in a Pup at five hundred feet? Don't get wind up. That's all there is to it.' He hiccupped slightly. 'Have another drink?'

During this harangue Stephen saw an officer come to the bar and order a pink gin in a quiet voice. When he had been served he stood, drink in hand, surveying the little group. He was wearing a full-skirted cavalry tunic with the distinctive skull and crossbones badge of the 17th Lancers on its lapels. R.F.C. wings were sewn above his breast pocket, with, beneath them, the Mons star and the purple and white ribbon of the M.C. On his sleeve were the three stars of a captain. For a few moments he stared briefly and bleakly at the speaker. Then, taking a copy of *Sporting Life* from the table, he moved away to one of the empty armchairs.

'And who?' enquired de Vaux, surveying the red-faced man with a look of patrician distaste, 'might this enthusiastic and loquacious individual be?'

'Bill Baxter,' the American said. 'He was at London Colney with me. This is how he is after a few drinks.'

'Indeed. Well if he flies as well as he talks we have amongst us a future terror of the Hun. But I can't say I care for the cut of his jib. Let us,' he said to Stephen whom he appeared to have adopted, temporarily at any rate, 'keep our distance.'

The following morning immediately after breakfast they were driven to the aerodrome in a Crossley tender. The rumour of last night that they were going straight on to Camels appeared to have been confirmed and there was a general air of tension. No one spoke very much. Even Baxter was silent.

The aerodrome was a long oval inside the racecourse. They were taken straight to one of the hangars. A Sopwith Camel with chocks in front of the wheels stood at the edge of the tarmac. From somewhere nearby came the stuttering roar of an engine being run up.

Stephen looked with a nostalgic eye at the rows of empty and decaying stands. Then he turned towards the Camel, his glance taking in its trim businesslike lines and the slight hump on the fuselage which had given it its name. The way he was feeling, he thought, must be just like before riding in an important race, only far worse. He found that his mouth was dry and he swallowed several times.

As he wondered to himself who would be the first to go up and try his luck, a motor-cycle combination came to a stop near where they were standing. Out of the sidecar stepped the man Stephen had seen surveying the new intake in the ante-room the night before. This morning he was wearing an old, oil-stained tunic with leather at the cuffs and elbows. He walked towards them with that peculiar cavalry swagger which denotes an intimate acquaintance with the horse. On his head was a battered cap with the wire taken out of its rim. It bore a 17th Lancers cap-badge which Stephen was sure was against whatever few dress regulations existed in the R.F.C. 'All right, gentlemen,' he said. 'Stand around please and listen to me.' He had, Stephen noticed, a distinct cockney twang to his voice and his H's were often astray. 'My name is 'Aynes,' he went on. 'And this 'ere's a Camel.' He gestured towards the little machine behind him. 'I'm 'ere to teach you to fly it. They say we're going to get dual Camels soon. We haven't got 'em yet and it's my belief that we never will. Put another seat into a Camel and you'll change the 'andling characteristics so much you'll kill yourselves a bloody sight quicker when you go solo in one. So just

102

listen to me and pay attention to what I say. Some of you may think flying a Camel is too damned easy and some may think it's too fucking difficult. It's neither the one nor the other—'

There was a roar of engine noise as, further up the field, a Camel commenced to taxi out. Raising his voice a little, Haynes went on: 'All you've got to do is treat her gently. Touch the harp gently, my pretty Louise. Stroke the stick as if you were fondling a maiden's tit. The trouble is 'alf you male virgins have never touched a tit in your lives. Then imagine you're touching it. Don't try to turn—'

Behind him the engine noise rose to a crescendo as the Camel began to race forward to its take-off. It held a straight course for a moment. Then it started to yaw to the right. Soon it was going crabwise across the field. It was almost into a hangar when the pilot pulled on the stick. The Camel leapt into the air with its nose pointing skywards. For a single instant it hung stationary in the sky. Then the nose came down and it went into a sudden, vicious spin. Still spinning it disappeared behind the stands. There was a rending crash and a column of smoke crept slowly upwards. Someone shouted: 'Ambulance.'

Stephen felt he might well be sick. He stole a look at the others. Beside him de Vaux was staring out ahead with his teeth gnawing his lower lip. Baxter's ruddy cheeks had gone white. What, Stephen wondered, did he think of flying Camels now?

Captain Haynes ran his eyes over them. Then he turned and strode to the Camel, shouting to the mechanics as he did so. He swung himself into it. A mechanic ran out and swung the prop. The engine fired, Haynes shouted 'chocks away' and taxied out. The throttle opened and the grass around the little machine flattened. He had scarcely begun to move when he was taking off, and he was turning almost before he had left the ground. It was a right-handed turn, too, Stephen noticed. The Camel seemed to pivot on one wing-tip and that wing-tip was a bare few inches from the earth. Then it came screaming straight for them.

They threw themselves flat just as he swept over them, his wheels all but brushing their backs. Haynes went up in a zoom, and half-rolled off the top. They were just climbing to their feet when he was amongst them again, spreadeagling them once more. 'God darn it, we'll be dead before we ever start to fly,' the American's voice said in Stephen's ear.

For ten minutes Haynes threw the Camel about the sky over the aerodrome. He looped, he rolled, he spun; he put her through every stunt in the book and a few more besides and never seemed to be higher than five hundred feet. Then he landed. The Camel came to a standstill a few yards from where they were standing. 'Say, that's flying!' the American said. 'He's done everything with that Camel except make it talk!'

Haynes walked towards them. 'That, gentlemen, is the way to fly a Sopwith Camel,' he said. 'And that's how easy it is. Now then, first man—' He walked along the line. Suddenly his stubby finger shot out. 'You—' he said.

It was Baxter.

Stephen heaved a sigh of relief. At least it wasn't him. He could see someone else having a first go. It was a reprieve. Then he heard a crash. Everyone's head turned. There was a supine figure lying on the tarmac. Baxter had fainted.

Haynes stirred him with his foot. 'Take him away, someone,' he said, and began to come further down the line.

A sixth sense told Stephen what was about to happen. It did not deceive him. Haynes stopped opposite him and looked at him. The finger shot out again. 'You—' he said.

Stephen swallowed twice and stepped forward. At least he hadn't fainted. Together they walked towards the Camel. When they reached it Haynes paused and put his hand on the fuselage. 'Frightened?' he said, surprisingly gently.

'Terrified,' Stephen said.

'No need to be. You've ridden, haven't you?'

'Yes.'

'Thought so by the way you walked. Besides I've had a look at your papers. I was a rough rider in the Seventeenth before I joined this crowd. Ever ridden a horse that is too good for you?'

'Often,' Stephen said, thinking of some of his experiences at Bob's. 'Too often.'

'It'll feel like that at first. Don't panic. That's what that silly bugger did just now. The torque takes them to the right on take-off. Use your left rudder to keep her straight. You've flown a Pup, haven't you?'

Stephen nodded.

'Then you know a bit of what it's like but these are even more sensitive. You've got to stroke 'em. All the weight's in front. That's why they're so unstable. And don't try to do a thing until you've got to four thousand feet. Then you can try turning right-handed. That's what kills most of 'em and you've got to learn it.'

'Yes, but what do I do?' Stephen said desperately.

'Hold off and ride her round. Everyone does it differently. You've got to find your own way. As long as you have height you'll be all right. She's bound to spin at first. When she does, get your stick back into your crotch and pray. As soon as she comes out, go back and do it again. It'll come quick enough but for the love of Christ don't try to turn low down until you've got the 'ang of 'er. All right. Get in and I'll show you the gadgets.'

Stephen climbed in. The cockpit was full of the smell of oil. It would probably make him sick. Concentrate, he told himself, concentrate. But even so it was in a sort of haze that he heard Haynes saying, 'Watch the mixture when you're taking off. Right oh, then. Touch the 'arp gently. Good luck. Off you go.'

Stephen taxied out. At least he could do that all right. When he reached the centre of the field he looked to see if there was anything coming in to land behind him. All was clear. The only thing on the circuit was a Bristol Fighter and it had not begun its landing approach. He took a deep breath. Here goes, he thought. Concentrate now. He turned into wind. The mixture and throttle controls lay under his left hand. He pushed the throttle forward.

The instant response took his breath away. There was a roar from the engine, the back of the seat hit his shoulder blades and the little machine hurtled down the field. Watch that swing! Use your left rudder! He had her now and she was straight. The tail was up. God, this thing was fast! It was more than fast, it was bloody well alive. He touched the stick and she sprang into the sky. Christ! Haynes had been right. She was bloody well too good for him. The sensation was uncannily like riding something you couldn't hold and that took off two strides too soon.

He was at a thousand feet in half a second, it seemed. The nose was still pointing skywards. His angle of climb was too sharp. This was what had happened to the other fellow. Next thing he'd stall like him and that would be finis. He eased the stick forward. The nose went down, there was nothing in front of him and she screamed towards the earth.

Slowly, stroking the stick, he got her back flying straight and level. Easy now, easy, he told himself. At least he had her on an even keel. He started to climb again, beginning to understand and anticipate her instant responses. At four thousand feet he began to feel more confident. It was time to try turning. First to the left. She came round as quick, responsive and as vice-free as a well-trained polo pony. That was simple enough. Now for the other one, the difficult one, the killer. He moved the stick over and pressed on the rudder.

The Camel whipped to the right with the speed and suddenness of a dog chasing his tail. Then he was spinning, cartwheeling wildly round with the earth a blur of colours far below. He centred the controls and pulled the stick back to where his stomach should have been if it had not been left behind five hundred feet above. She came out so quickly and went into a dive of such steepness he thought the wings might come off. A glance at his altimeter told him he was down to two thousand feet. No wonder they told you not to try to do anything under four thousand!

He began to climb again. This time he went right up to five thousand feet. He had to master right-hand turns if he was to fly and live.

105

He knew that. His second attempt was better. He only lost five hundred feet.

He stayed on, feeling her, easing her, gentling her as he would have done a horse. Gradually a sense of oneness with the machine began to come to him. He lost all sense of time until a quick check on the fuel gauge told him he should be getting back. It was then that he realised he had not the least idea where he was.

Ayr was by the sea. He had taken off in a northerly direction. Therefore, if he got the sea on his right and flew south, he should come out over the aerodrome sooner or later. He looked down and for a moment saw nothing but cloud beneath him. Fear came again then, for he knew that even experienced Camel pilots did not care for flying their unstable machines in thick cloud. To his relief he spotted a break in the cloud-bank about a mile away to his left and dived for it.

Once through the cloud he picked up the shore-line. A winter mist was creeping in from the sea and he knew he had to get down before it covered the aerodrome. Where the hell was the aerodrome? He stared downwards at the unfamiliar landscape and all at once there it was, plumb underneath him.

Although he was now more confident of holding her in a right-hand turn Stephen had no intention of risking one on his approach. Shutting off the engine he came in on a long glide.

For all its vices the Camel was not too difficult to land. But in his anxiety to keep below stalling speed Stephen came in too fast. The fence flew beneath him and he began to float across the aerodrome. He pushed the stick forward and she dropped like a stone. At the last moment he hauled it back. Wheels and tail-skid hit simultaneously, she bounced once, came down again, lurched and ran on, miraculously in one piece. Stephen blipped the engine and taxied back.

'Born in the vestry that one,' Haynes said. 'Anyway, you can walk away from it. 'Ow was it?'

'I might just be able to fly one side of her in a week,' Stephen said.

Haynes looked at the mist sweeping in across the aerodrome. 'You were lucky,' he said laconically. 'Made it with about five minutes to spare. The last man caught out by one of these mists went into the 'angars.' He turned to the waiting group and waved his hands. 'Wash-out,' he said. 'No more flying. Try again after lunch.'

For the next seven days Stephen flew and flew and flew. After they had achieved some sort of mastery over their machines, pupils were required to go up and take part in mock air fights with their instructors. Baxter was tried out in an Avro, crashed it and was sent away. Two others of the group killed themselves in Camels, both in right-hand spins. De Vaux smashed one up on landing, but he and Hank Jarman, the American, were, with Stephen, the sole survivors of their intake to fly on and fight their mock fights.

Because Hank, being American, refused to accept the formalities and conventions of the English public school way of life, he insisted on finding out and using the others' first names. De Vaux's was, he assured them, St Clare. 'Not Sinclair, St Clare. After the third Earl, don't you know. Always called Clare, as a matter of fact. Family custom, don't you know.' All this, combined with the fact that they alone remained out of their intake set them in some way apart and formed them into a close-knit companionship of their own.

Remembering de Vaux's confidences concerning his lack of success on a horse, Stephen had wondered how he would manage the fierce and unforgiving Camel, when his turn came to take it up. In fact, however, he need not have worried. De Vaux took to it quickly and flew every bit as smoothly and well as the other two save for his difficulty with landings. On Stephen's mentioning his doubts to him, he looked at his fingernails in the way he had and drawled, 'Nothing wrong with my hands, old bean. It was my seat that was the trouble. I couldn't sit on the dam' things. You can't fall off an aeroplane, now can you? I mean to say, you're strapped in. Chief reason I chose this branch of the Service. Not, mark you, that I intend to emulate the things our Captain 'Aynes does in them.'

Stephen had by now all but abandoned his first impressions of his room mate and had come to regard him with a sort of bantering affection. He recognised that there was a steeliness of purpose and an acuteness of character underneath the cloak of patrician haughtiness with which Clare surrounded himself. Clare had been a failure with his regiment and he knew it. Ascribing that failure to his lack of horsemanship and his consequent clash with his colonel, he had chosen the R.F.C. to prove to himself and everyone else, but especially the regiment he had left, that there were other things besides a horse which he could master and at which he was just as good as the next man. All this came out, by inference mostly, during the conversations they had in their room or waiting for flights, since there is nothing like proximity and shared danger for promoting confidences. There were, however, certain things about his friend which Stephen found difficult to stomach. The chief of these was Clare's class-consciousness which, even under the stress of war, infused and governed his every action. He had only admitted Stephen to such intimacy as he did because, Stephen was convinced, he had discovered by speedy and skilful cross-examination that his background was acceptable. As an American, the standards he applied to Hank were not so strict though it was at least a help that he came from Massachusetts and had been to Harvard. Others who did not measure up were simply ignored. His 'soldier servants' as he insisted on calling them, regarding the use of the word 'batman' as 'too common for words, dear boy', were treated as if

107

they were beings from another lesser world, as indeed to him they were. But the person who was the chief object of his disdain was Captain Haynes. 'Our driving instructor, Captain 'Aynes,' was his accustomed method of referring to him but he did not hesitate, nonetheless, Stephen noticed, to profit from the instruction given.

For Haynes was an outstanding trainer of pilots. Unlike some of the other instructors Stephen had encountered on his way to Ayr who referred to the pupils as Huns, despised them and left them much to their own devices to learn to fly or kill themselves in the process, Haynes really took trouble in preparing his pupils for the task of flying and fighting over the lines.

It was a quiet time at the front just then and there was not a constant call for replacements. Haynes was determined that his men should not be sent out lacking all knowledge of tactics and with only a few hours' flying in their log-books before they faced the Germans. In the hangar which housed his flight he had installed a series of blackboards. On them were drawn diagrams to show the correct way to attack a two-seater and the incorrect way to leave a dog-fight. 'Now, you young blighters,' he would say, banging on the ground the butt of the billiards cue he used as a pointer. 'There's only one golden rule of air-fighting. As expounded by the great Mick Mannock, it's this and this only: *Always above, sometimes on the level, never underneath.* Write that on your 'earts, my likely lads, and you may live. Never dive away from a dog-fight or you'll die—'

'Quite,' drawled Clare, who loved teasing him. 'But Captain Roggin of the S.E. flight says Camels are no good now. They can't get high enough to be above the Hun, so where does that put us with your golden rule? In fact like Admiral Fisher and the battleships Captain Roggin says Camels are too old to fight and too slow to run away!'

'Balls!' There was always considerable rivalry between Camel and S.E. pilots and any reflexion on his beloved Camels was bound to get a rise from Haynes as de Vaux well knew. 'Up to ten thousand feet the Camel can lick anything the Hun has got or any S.E. either. 'E said that, did 'e? I'll have that bugger Roggin's guts for garters. Too slow to fight, by God! Where is 'e?' Haynes threw down the billiards cue and strode out of the hangar.

Outside they could hear him shouting for Roggin and bawling at mechanics. Then there came the noise of engines starting up. They all crowded to the entrance to see what was happening.

A Camel and an S.E. were in the act of taking off, the S.E. into wind, the Camel cross-wind towards the hangars. They were hardly off the ground when the Camel dived like a wasp on the S.E. For the next ten minutes they chased each other around the sky over the aerodrome. As an exhibition of flying it left the staring pupils breathless. Then the engine of the S.E. coughed, the prop stopped and it

108

disappeared in a long glide behind the suburban houses. The Camel landed and taxied to the tarmac. Haynes got out and walked over to them. 'See what I mean?' he asked de Vaux. 'Cost you a bottle of fizz, that will, when we get back to the mess and another one from your pal, Roggin.'

'Where is he?' Hank asked him.

' 'E's all right. 'E's down on the sands.'

Roggin, an eye-glass stuck in his eye, an open bottle of champagne in front of him, was, in fact, waiting for them when they got back to the mess. 'Ha,' he said. 'Think you've licked me, do you? Engine failure. Means nothing. You may get away with all this splitarsing low down on your ruddy Camels but the battle is now raging at seventeen thousand feet and these poor birds you're training will never get there. Have some fizz?'

Clare called for another bottle and then Haynes opened yet another. Stephen had never drunk champagne before. It tickled his nostrils but on the whole he found it delightful stuff. He drank quickly and each time he finished his glass someone refilled it. Very soon he found himself floating in a haze of dancing bubbles.

Lunchtime came and went without their leaving the anteroom. The weather closed in as it was apt to do at Ayr. There would be no more flying that afternoon.

The haze around Stephen extended and deepened. He heard someone in a voice he vaguely recognised as his own calling for another bottle. He knew he was getting drunk. It had never happened to him before but he might as well go through with it to see what it was like. He found he had no inclination to become boisterous, or argue, or throw things about as he had heard others did when in liquor. All he wanted to do was to sit back quietly and smile on the world and watch what was going on in a tolerant sort of way.

Haynes and Roggin had continued their argument about the respective merits of Camels and S.E.s. Then, as the wine mellowed them, they began to reminisce. They talked of F.E.s and Gun Buses, and Pfaltz and Tripes and Circuses and crashes and dogfights and flamers. Now that the champagne had loosened their tongues it was clear that what both had dreaded above all was the thought of going down in flames, of burning in the air, of the long descent to death without chance of rescue or escape. 'Even Mick Mannock,' Stephen heard Roggin say. 'It's got to him too and it's become a sort of obsession with him. He keeps saying that when he goes he prays it won't be that way. Yet when he gets a Hun he always wants it to be a flamer.'

' 'E really hates 'em,' Haynes said. 'Why the 'ell won't they give us parachutes?'

'Because the buggers at G.H.Q. have never flown since the B.E. was our first line aircraft and they shot at each other with rifles,' was the reply.

This conversation led Stephen's floating thoughts to his own position. He loved flying; he didn't want to die; but he didn't want to kill anyone, either. The thought of being shot down in flames terrified him but, equally, the idea of inflicting that terrible death on another, be he Hun or not, was utterly repugnant to him. It was all very difficult. He drank some more champagne and gloomy thoughts floated away on the haze to be replaced by more cheerful ones. Perhaps the war would be over before he had to fire his guns in anger. Clare, laughing, was refilling their glasses. He lifted his to his lips. It really was delightful stuff. If only it didn't get into his nostrils and make him want to sneeze—

All at once Stephen noticed that the lights in the ante-room had been turned on. They had drunk the whole of the afternoon away. The others were putting down their glasses and getting to their feet. 'Let's move on,' they said. 'Where will we go?' 'What about Mary's place? There are some damn fine girls at Mary's.'

They moved towards the door and Stephen got to his feet to follow them. As he did so the floor gave a sudden lurch and he grabbed at a chair to steady himself. The pictures on the walls appeared to be about to leave their frames. He closed his eyes to a squint in order to bring them into focus. It didn't seem to work. Rather like a bather testing the water he put out a foot to see if he could walk. The floor tilted underneath it.

Of one thing Stephen, even in his fuddled state, was now quite certain. He could not go with the others and must, somehow, get to his room. He was never quite sure how he did it but some minutes later he was standing beside his bed and the walls were spinning about him. With a sigh of relief he collapsed fully clothed on to the bed. It, too, revolved rapidly on its own axis underneath him. Then sleep swept over him.

Hours later he awoke. It was pitch-dark, he had a villainous taste in his mouth and his head was splitting. Still not very sure of his feet he groped his way to the washstand, and, tilting the ewer, drank deeply. As his eyes became accustomed to the darkness he saw that de Vaux had not yet returned. The luminous dial of his watch told him it was half-past one. Searching in his kit he found aspirin and swallowed some. Then he stripped off his tunic and trousers, put on pyjamas and got back into bed. But he could not sleep.

He supposed that Clare and his companions had found women for the night or part of it and were with them. He was the youngest of the group and by far the least experienced in the ways of the world. Coming as he did from the remoteness of south-west Ireland, compared with most of those whom he had met in his army career in matters of sex he was almost unbelievably naïve and unsophisticated. Yet

110

he knew that just like all or most of his contemporaries he wanted to sleep with a woman, to experience sex before he died if die he must. He knew, too, the nightly torment sexual longing could bring. But he was not satisfied to initiate himself with casual sex as most of the others seemed to be. He would, he told himself, start with someone whom he wanted and who wanted him. But he had not found her yet and time was running out. For these romantic aspirations were of little help to him on lonely nights when a spinning Camel might kill him in the morning, or the wings might come off in a dive or the sea-frets swinging in across the shore-line bring death on landing.

The aspirins had done little to help his head. He tossed and turned and still sleep would not come. He forced his thoughts away from what his companions might be doing and the imagined delights he might be missing, to think on the events of the day so far as he could remember them.

Clare had certainly succeeded in making Haynes rise to his fly with that remark about his beloved Camels. As for Haynes—God, how he could fly! And he could infuse in you his own enthusiasm for flying, even perhaps for fighting. But, as Stephen could dimly see, as an instructor Haynes had the defects of his qualities. Like many another brilliant teacher he played favourites and devoted his talents to making the best better. After Stephen's intake another lot of pupils had arrived. Few of them were any good. Haynes had cursed them, culled them unmercifully and shifted the remainder to a more junior instructor. All this did not make for his popularity. And, in addition, there was then a considerable amount of public school snobbery in the R.F.C. Many of the pupils deprecated Haynes' accent and the fact that he had risen from the ranks. Taking their tone from Clare it became their custom to refer to him behind his back as 'Captain 'Aynes' and to imitate his accent.

That Haynes was conscious of all this Stephen was pretty sure, and it could explain the fact of his concentrating his energies on his best pupils. Like Clare but for different reasons he could not afford failure. Outside flying he kept himself pretty much to himself. The drinking session in the mess today had been a rare occurrence perhaps inspired by his defeat of Roggin in the mock fight. Mostly he only came in to have a quick look over the new men or to glance at the sporting papers. Rumour said that he was besotted with one of the sergeants' wives and that he was sleeping with her day and night since the sergeant was away on a course. But then rumour said a lot about Haynes, including the fact that he was due to get his majority and go back to France in command of a squadron but that two crack squadrons had refused to have him on the grounds that he was a ranker.

Whether there was any truth in the rumours or not it was the case that

111

Haynes made few overtures of friendship outside working hours. Stephen was therefore surprised when one evening a few days later he came up to him in the ante-room and asked him to have a drink. His surprise grew when, after the drinks had been served, Haynes said to him: 'Come over 'ere a minute, will you, I want to have a word.'

He led the way to an empty table in a corner and, picking up his drink, Stephen followed him. Once there, however, Haynes seemed curiously slow to come to whatever it was he wanted to discuss. 'Like the old Camel, now then, do you?' he said. 'Think you've got the 'ang of 'er?'

'I hope so. You were right. It's like riding something too good for you. But she seems to be going for me now.'

'Don't get too confident. That's a killer at your stage.' Haynes stared into his drink. Silence fell between them, which Stephen did not know how to break. He wondered what was coming. Then Haynes raised his head and looked Stephen full in the eyes. 'I'm going to France in command of a squadron,' he said. 'How about it? Would you like to come with me? Have me as your C.O.?'

In his eyes Stephen saw something vulnerable; he knew about those jibes, and he was ready to be hurt. But Stephen had no doubt about his response. 'Gosh, sir,' he said. 'I'd love to.'

'Bugger the sir, I'm not a major yet. Would the others come, d'ye think—Jarman and de Vaux?'

'They'll be bloody fools if they don't.'

'I wouldn't be so sure. That there de Vaux 'e looks at me as if I was something the cat 'ad brought in. Where was 'e at school, Eton, I suppose?'

'Harrow, actually, I think.'

' 'Arrow—'Arrow on the 'Ill and Oxford, too, I'll be bound.'

'I believe so. The House.'

' 'Arrow and Oxford. Do these buggers learn anything at those places but 'ow to look down their noses at the rest of us?'

'I shouldn't think Clare learnt anything anywhere. He was born that way. He's a nephew of the Earl of Mulcaster. At least that's what he says.'

'The dickens 'e is. 'E'll think 'e's too good for the likes of us, you'll see. Anyway that's settled with you, then. Get yourself another drink. 'Ere's to all the 'Uns we'll bag.'

Stephen went to bed that night walking on air. He had often wondered where he would be sent when the course was over, what sort of a squadron he would be posted to and what kind of C.O. he would have. From talk in the mess he knew how a squadron commander could make or break an outfit and that some of the older commanding officers who had finished with combat flying in 1915 were regimental to their fingertips and had no conception of the new and fast-developing

112

business of aerial fighting. Now he was to go out with someone he knew and trusted and who was moreover the finest pilot he had yet encountered.

Clare was out to dinner with friends he had found who lived some miles away in the country, the daughter being 'a rippin' sort of girl', and he had not yet returned when Stephen went up to their room. There was, however, a letter from his father in the rack and he took it with him to read before he turned out the light. As usual it was full of news about the Bay.

Things were quiet at the moment but his father was worried about the state of the country. A noted rebel, de Valera, had been elected Member of Parliament for East Clare, and another hothead, W.T. Cosgrave, for Kilkenny. Edward was concerned, too, that the English Government would pursue the insane policy of enforcing conscription. Perhaps because this had set up a train of thought in his mind Edward went on to say that Larry Rossiter was in the trenches and doing well. He had been awarded the Military Medal and recommended for a commission. Massiter had fulfilled his ambitions, or one of them anyway, by securing the nomination to a safe liberal seat. He had won a by-election and was now an M.P. He was said moreover to owe all this to the friendship and patronage of Lloyd George—'Birds of a feather, your mother says, and she may be right.' Ethel was doing war work in England and Babs Murtagh was, Edward had been told, a W.A.A.C. driver in France.

So Babs had got to France before him. Perhaps they would meet somewhere. But his father's letter brought the colour and sweep, the calmness and solitude of the Bay back to him. A wave of homesickness swept over him. He hated the idea of killing anyone, of fighting, even in the air with its so-called code of chivalry. Richthofen didn't display much chivalry to a crippled foe from all he had heard and he doubted if Mick Mannock with his almost pathological hatred of the Huns did either. For the thousandth time he pondered on what it would be like when he came to pit himself against the Hun to see which of them would survive. It might not be him, he knew that. He might never see the Bay again. With a sigh he pushed the letter under his pillow and went immediately to sleep.

Clare was still sleeping when Stephen got up and dressed next morning. He was early for he had a date with Roggin of the S.E. squadron. Roggin had promised to lend him one of his machines so that he could find out what flying an S.E. was like. 'You won't care much for it after a Camel,' Haynes had commented when he heard of this. 'It's like driving a bloody bus.'

The S.E. did indeed prove to be heavy on the controls and unresponsive compared to a Camel. On the other hand it was safe, stable and easy to fly and it was far more comfortable. You sat in comparative luxury in a spacious cockpit quite unlike the Camel's where the padded butts of the twin Vickers and the base of the Aldis sight all stuck into your face and the instruments seemed to have been pushed in haphazard wherever room could be found for them. The S.E. held her performance, too, at a much greater height, and dived like a gannet. He had been warned they were tricky to land but he was now sufficiently experienced to put it down without difficulty.

As he made his way back to the mess he wondered if his chances of survival would be better in an S.E. It was the case that almost everyone, save a few skilled fanatics like Haynes, now said that the S.E. was a better, safer aeroplane and it was also true that almost all the big scores were being put up by S.E. pilots. But his die was cast; his fate lay with Camels and in the hands of Captain Haynes.

In the ante-room he found Clare reading *The Tatler* and refreshing himself with his mid-morning coffee and kümmel. 'Has Haynes spoken to you?' he asked.

'Captain 'Aynes? Yes, dear boy, he has.'

'And you'll come, of course?'

'Oh, I don't know about that, don't know about that at all, don'tcha know.'

'But, Clare, why on earth not? He's the best there is.'

'Perhaps, dear boy, perhaps. But he's a ranker, don't you know. Two squadrons have already turned him down. That's why he's getting a new one to take out.'

'That's only a rumour,' Stephen said hotly. 'It's probably not true.'

'It's true all right. Met a man at dinner last night. Commands some infanteer battalion round here. Friend of our Commandant, it seems. He knew all about it. My people, y'know, they wouldn't care at all for my serving under a ranker.'

'No, nor your last Colonel either, I suppose,' Stephen said furiously. 'Well, I'm going anyway and I'll bet Hank is too. If you want to know what I think, I think you're being bloody cheap, Clare.' And he walked away.

Clare extracted a silk handkerchief from his sleeve and dabbed his lips. 'Don't be so hasty, dear boy,' he said. 'Made an excuse, don't you know. Said I'd think about it. Told him I didn't care much about Camels. Thought I'd be safer in Bristols.' But he was talking to Stephen's retreating back. 'Irish!' he said to himself and shrugged his shoulders.

Stephen was still burning with indignation on Haynes' behalf when he found Hank.

'Sure I'm going,' Hank said in answer to his question. 'Who wouldn't?'

'Clare for one. Says he won't serve under a ranker.'

'That's a swell line. Who does he want to lead him—the Prince of

Wales? I haven't heard Haynes singing the Eton Boating Song in his bath come to think of it, if that makes a difference. Maybe it does to you English.'

'I'm not English, damn you. I'm Irish.' Stephen was still boiling.

'Oh, pardon me, MacMurphy. Why aren't you back there behind the barricades then?'

'Because, hell, it looks like I'm the kind of Irish that's English in Ireland and Irish in England.'

'I'll puzzle that riddle out some other time. Say, MacMurphy, has it occurred to you we're due to fly in five minutes?'

At the hangar they were joined by Clare; as they watched a Bristol Fighter being wheeled on to the tarmac, they fell to discussing amongst themselves the pros and cons of flying two-seaters.

'Y'know,' Clare drawled. 'I'm not sure old Roggin isn't right. The Camel has had its day. Now there before us is what I'd call a safe sort of aeroplane to fly—'

At that moment the motor-cycle combination drew up beside them. Haynes, looking thunderous, stepped out of the sidecar and walked over to them. He ignored Hank and Stephen and glared at Clare. 'Don't care about flying Camels, eh?' he said stabbing his finger at him. 'That there is a Bristol Fighter. Suit you better, so I hear. Let's see 'ow you like it then. Get in.'

He left them and walked to the Bristol, clambering immediately into the pilot's seat. A mechanic swung the prop. Without a glance over his shoulder to see whether his passenger had secured himself in the rear cockpit he waved the chocks away. Then he banged on the throttle and the Bristol went bumping out across the field.

The Rolls engine gave a mighty roar as Haynes opened up. The next moment he was taking off, one wing down, cross-wind. The watchers on the ground saw Clare clutch wildly at the Scarff ring of the gun-mounting as the big two-seater surged into the sky.

At five hundred feet Haynes was looping. Stephen and Hank afterwards swore that they saw Clare's frightened features staring at them upside down and on the same level as their own faces. Later he told them that he had not had time to fasten his safety belt, he thought his feet were outside the cockpit and his head inside but he wasn't quite sure. Holding on with his teeth, fingernails and eyebrows, he said, was the only thing that kept him in place.

One loop was not sufficient. Haynes did two more. Coming out of the last one Stephen could have sworn his wheels just brushed the far rails of the racecourse. After that they saw the Bristol climbing away from the aerodrome. In the middle distance, at about two thousand feet, Haynes deliberately, scientifically and with great skill turned the Bristol inside out. At the top of a zoom, he appeared to see something on the road outside the town and went down on it in a screaming dive.

115

He flew along the road at nought feet for some time before they caught sight of him again, climbing steeply upwards and half rolling at the top of his loop.

'I reckon Clare wishes he was back right there on the playing fields of Eton,' Hank said.

'Harrow,' Stephen said. 'As he constantly reminds us. But I expect Eton would do for him just now.'

The Bristol, flying straight and level for once, was returning. It was almost opposite where they stood, making its approach, when Hank grabbed Stephen's arm. 'Look!' he shouted. 'Look! For Chrissake, what do we do?'

Stephen followed where he pointed. The near wheel of the Bristol's undercarriage was missing. 'Great God,' he said. Both of them stared around, desperately. Haynes had to be warned—but how?

Captain Roggin, however, who had been lounging by the S.E. hangar, had also seen it. He was already running out to the aerodrome holding a wheel aloft in his hands. Others followed him. Someone set a hooter off and every mechanical vehicle in the place commenced to sound its horn.

Haynes was coming in and was over the fence when the commotion below attracted his attention. The engine of the Bristol roared as he took her up to go round again, warned, at least, of what he had to face.

'What would you do?' Hank said to Stephen.

'I'd sit well back and let go of her head. That's what he told me to do when I asked him how to make a forced landing.'

'And pray. Don't forget that.' Roggin, eyeglass firmly clasped in one eye, had walked across to join them. 'He's got a bit of wind. That'll help him.'

They all turned to stare at the french letter or effell—which was what they called the windsock. It was pointing across the aerodrome. Haynes would have to land crosswind to get it under the wing where the wheel was missing but he would have the length of the field if he wanted it.

He was turning now. The little group of watchers had been joined by others. The ambulance started up.

'I hope he's cut his switches,' someone said.

'He will have,' Roggin said. 'And he's got to get it right. He can't go round again.'

The Bristol had a very steep gliding angle. Each of them knew that and knew too that it made Haynes' task all the more difficult. Stephen spared a thought for Clare in the back seat, knowing that there was no margin for error, no second chance and with nothing on which to concentrate to avoid anticipation as the pilot had. All he could do was to sit and wait and, as Roggin had said, pray.

The Bristol was dropping quickly. It was over the far fence and

116

coming in—fast. The crunch was approaching.

Haynes had his right wing down and into the wind. As his speed dropped the wind got under it and held it. So far he was making no mistakes at all. But the moment of truth would come when she touched. If the wing hit first they were probably both done. The watchers held their breaths.

The left wheel was inches above the turf. It stayed poised there for a moment. Then it barely brushed the ground, settled, and she rolled. He had done it.

For a few yards the big Bristol ran on upright, the wind holding the wing above the missing wheel. Then, as the impetus fell off and the machine slowed, the wing dropped. Its tip touched the ground. The whole machine slewed violently to the right. With a crash of disintegrating spars and fabric it collapsed into an ungainly heap of wood and canvas. The left wing still pointed defiantly upwards.

Stephen found himself running across the aerodrome with Roggin and Hank on either side of him. The ambulance went racing past.

A figure jumped down from what was left of the pilot's cockpit. But the occupant of the rear seat had not moved. As they ran Stephen saw to his horror a tongue of flame lick out of the engine. The figure on the ground saw it too. He was beside the wrecked fuselage now, pulling at the slumped object in the back cockpit, kicking and tearing at the canvas and broken struts.

'If that flame gets to the gas tank they're done,' Hank panted to Stephen as they ran.

But Haynes had Clare clear now and was dragging him by the shoulders, away from the wreck. They were ten yards up-wind of it when with a great 'wumph' the petrol tank blew and the whole of the wreckage disintegrated in flame.

When they reached them Haynes was bending over de Vaux who lay inert on the grass.

'Forget to cut your switches, old boy?' Roggin enquired.

'I cut 'em all right. These cows of Bristols burn if you look at 'em.'

Hank was kneeling beside Clare.

'How is he?' Stephen said. 'Is he—'

' 'E'll be all right,' Haynes said. ' 'E'd have walked away from it if 'e hadn't 'ad 'is 'ead on the gun-mounting. 'E was a bit sick like before,' he added with a grin. Clare opened his eyes and got groggily to his feet. He stared at the blazing wreck of the Bristol for a full minute. Then he turned to Haynes. 'Thanks,' he drawled stretching out a limp hand. 'If you still want me I'll be glad to join. I believe on the whole I'd feel safer in Camels.'

11

When No 245 Squadron R.F.C. landed at Bessières aerodrome in Northern France it was winter. The weather was bad and the days were short. There was little time or opportunity for taking offensive action against the enemy, who was in any event also enduring the same weather and was not disposed to leave the comfort and security of his quarters. In addition therefore to the usual short working-up period granted to a new squadron, Haynes was given a respite in which he could attempt to lick his command into shape. And he needed it, for by and large the members of 245 squadron were a pretty scratch lot.

Soon after the Bristol crash Clare, Stephen and Hank had followed Haynes to London Colney and reported to him there. They found him in a foul temper. He thought he was going to be fobbed off with used and patched-up Camels which had Clerget engines with the early and inferior interrupter gear enabling the guns to fire through the propeller arcs. He had just got rid of his first recording officer whom he described as 'a damned stuck-up Guardsman with a face like dog-shit', and had not yet found a replacement; and, although he did not say so, he was not too happy about some of the flying personnel he had been allotted.

'Go away' were his first words of greeting to the three. 'Go away, goddamn you. I'll be damn lucky to be ready in a week and it looks more like a fortnight. Leave me an address, go to London, get drunk, get a woman and get one for this little male virgin 'ere.' He glared fiercely at Stephen. 'Blood him, will you before 'e comes out.'

'Yes, *sir*,' Clare said, bringing his field boots together with a snap and saluting with a wide sweep of his arm. He had lately taken to wearing an eye-glass and was looking more exquisite than ever. 'Any more advice – *sir*.'

Since the crash a sort of amiable bickering intimacy had grown up between Clare and Haynes. Clare still teased him but now instead of disdain there was amused affection in his drawled verbal darts. Haynes for his part had lost his ability to be ruffled by Clare and treated him as he would a rather unruly nephew. He had also taken to

118

addressing him as 'de Vawks'.

'Yes,' he growled now in answer. 'Get yourselves general service tunics for flyin' in. Over there you'll be turning your heads all the time tryin' to spot 'Uns. Those high-collared maternity jackets'll cut your necks off in a week if you live that long. Keep 'em for guest-nights, girls and Generals. And – de Vawks?'

'Sir!'

'Where the 'ell did you get that pane of glass in your eye?'

'Found it in a knocking shop, —sir.'

'Go and lose it in another one then. Now get the 'ell out of 'ere the three of you, I've got work to do.'

Once in London Clare airily beckoned up his 'man of business' and obtained a short letting of a sumptuously furnished flat in Clarges Street whose occupants had removed themselves from London to avoid the bombing by Gothas which was becoming more frequent and intensive.

Because of those raids, London at night was a city of darkness save for the glimmer of light that came from the shrouded street lamps. But behind the darkness the inhabitants rioted with the feverish gaiety of war.

The R.F.C. was at the height of its popularity just then. The press were writing its members up as heroes and intrepid birdmen; its aces—a term borrowed from the French—Bishop and McCudden and the like, were becoming household names, gladiators who brought with them the scent of victory and romance lost and buried for so long in the tedium, death and failure of trench warfare. The public loved them and all the girls were after them. The wings on a pilot's tunic were a passport to every sort of worldly delight.

They had money to spend too for aviators were better paid than the men on the ground. Stephen himself was not short of money for Edward had placed three hundred pounds to his credit before he left Ireland and he had hardly spent any of it. Even so he was by far the least well-off of the three. Clare had private means, presumably inherited, and Hank received large drafts of dollars every month from his father, a corporation lawyer in Boston.

Thus the three of them were well equipped for going on the town, and during those hectic days they made the most of it. Crates of champagne were delivered daily at Clarges Street from Fortnum's, and bacchanalian parties raged by day and night. Through it all, sustained by champagne from hangovers and exhaustion, Stephen walked largely untouched. He opened the cases and the bottles, poured the drinks and handed them round or helped Hank to mix villainous concoctions in a large china bath they found in the house. Hank called them cocktails and the only time Stephen tried them in any quantity they made him violently sick.

The girls that came and went seemed scarcely to notice him. It was Clare's lazy drawl and Hank's pungent idiom and confident way with him that brought them flocking around. Stephen did not mind his relegation to the background. He was, he told himself, still searching for someone who would light a spark between them. But time was running out. Meanwhile he slept by himself when there was time for sleeping, which was not very often.

One evening, when Stephen was opening yet another case of champagne and Hank was setting out drinks on a side-table, Haynes appeared.

'We're off tomorrow,' he said, accepting a tumbler of whisky from Hank. 'Eleven nought nought hours from London Colney and don't you forget it, me lucky lads.' He looked around him, taking in the subdued lighting, the ornaments and bibelots, the glass panels in the walls protecting the more valuable pieces of porcelain. 'Seems a bit like a tart's parlour to me,' he said. 'And as for you, de Vawks, I thought I told you to get rid of that eye-glass.'

'I did,' drawled Clare. 'But the girls told me I looked undressed without it and gave me another one. Stay around and join us tonight, won't you?'

'No, thanks. Bit too la-di-da for me. I'm off to another place I know.' He winked, put down his glass and left.

'So,' Clare said quietly, lifting his glass to the light and watching the bubbles dancing in the wine. 'Tomorrow we go to grapple with the Hun.'

A silence fell between them. The same unspoken thought was uppermost in each of their minds. Given the law of averages and the short lifespan of a fighter pilot at the front, it was all but certain that at least one of them and quite possibly all three would not return. The mathematics of fate alone would determine which would be the first to fall. Their eyes met and in silence they raised their glasses. Suddenly Stephen remembered the lines of the song of the Lafayette Escadrille which he had once heard someone maudlinly chanting after a guest night. Dismissed by the R.F.C. as too sentimental and never sung in front-line squadrons where, as was the English way, the accent was on the ribald and the irreverent, nevertheless to his romantic nature the lines seemed apt to the moment:

'Then stand to your glasses steady,
The world is a world of lies,
Here's a toast to the dead already,
Hurrah for the next man who dies.'

Then the doorbell went. The first of the girls came in. The brief moment of silence and solemnity flowed away in laughter and

120

champagne.

That night they went to Murray's, a night club which was a particular haunt of R.F.C. officers. Everyone went there—aces, fledglings, test pilots, scout pilots, bombers and observers. The only people whom one was unlikely to encounter at Murray's were stuffy senior officers who would have been in danger of having champagne poured down their necks or crème de menthe used for their hair-cream.

It was a rowdy party. Stephen, as usual, was floating in a mist of champagne. Later, when he came to look back on that time, he could remember very little of what went on in the flat in Clarges Street during the week, but the events of the last night were to remain etched vividly in his mind.

He was laughing at one of Hank's sallies when something, he never knew what it was, made him look up. Across the room a couple were getting up from their table, preparatory to leaving. The man was wearing pilot's wings with, underneath them, the purple and red ribbon of the D.S.O. The girl was smiling at him as she picked up her handbag.

It couldn't be—but it was. Even through the dim lights and the haze of smoke Stephen was certain of it. It was Babs Murtagh.

Together they began to make their way across the room towards the door. Stephen pushed back his chair and got to his feet. The girl beside him caught his sleeve. 'Where are you going, dear?' she asked him.

'I won't be long,' he said, disengaging her fingers. 'I think I see someone I know.'

But the delay cost him his chance of catching up with them. When he had threaded his way through the tables and reached the door, all he could see was the red tail-light of a taxi disappearing down the street. 'That couple who left just now,' he said to the doorman. 'Do you know who they were?'

'Don't know the lady, sir, but she's been in a couple of times with 'im. He's Captain Martin, the Australian ace, sir. Thirty 'Uns 'e 'as now. Going back tomorrow, 'e is. The 'Uns 'ad better look out.'

Stephen returned to the table, his mind in a whirl. His father had said that Babs was in France, but, of course, that might not mean anything. It was possible that she had not been there at all, or she could be on leave or have been posted back. But what was she doing alone with that Australian?

'Stop looking so bloody miserable,' the voice of the girl beside him broke into his thoughts.

'Sorry,' Stephen said. 'I just thought I saw someone from home.'

He glanced again at the girl—or was she a girl? She seemed a bit older than the usual run who frequented Brook Street. And even under the dim lights and to his unsophisticated eye the paint on her face was obvious.

'I'm a war widow, dear,' she said, as if reading his thoughts. 'Simon was killed on the Somme.'

'I'm sorry,' Stephen said inadequately.

'Don't be.' Again she laid her hand on his arm. 'We're all going to die, only you're going to die sooner. Never been out, yet, have you?'

'No,' Stephen muttered. He was sobering up. He hated this sort of conversation. He thought she was getting drunk.

'Know what your expectation of life is in the Flying Corps? Same as an infantry subaltern. That's what Simon was—a poor bloody infantry subaltern. Three weeks. That's it. Three weeks. So you've got to live while you can, dear. Take all you can when it's there for the taking. That's all that's left. Pour me some whisky.'

As he did so, Stephen refilled his own glass. Shortly afterwards the party began to break up into its component parts. Back in Clarges Street couples began to drift off to various rooms until Stephen found himself alone with his companion from Murray's. They were sitting on the deep sofa in the window recess, a bottle of champagne between them.

'Don't look so glum, silly boy,' she said to him. 'It's your last night. Enjoy it.' Her fingers were stroking his cheek. It was rather pleasant. The big sofa was as soft and deep as a bed. He lay back and she slid down beside him. Her fingers were now groping at the buttons on his tunic.

Her mouth opened under his. It tasted, he thought, of tobacco and whisky, but her probing tongue fired excitement through him. His hand went up to her shoulder strap. It came down, and the flimsy dress slipped away.

It was the first time Stephen had ever seen a woman's breast. He stared at it in fascination. As he touched it the rosy nipple swelled and tautened under his hand. She laughed and sat up. With a shrugging motion of her shoulders she slipped out of the other side of her dress. Both her breasts, heavy and round, fell forward into his hands. Her fingers were tearing at his tunic. 'Never done this before, little boy, have you?' she said, her voice husky and panting.

The light was full on her face as she pulled him down to her again, her hand reaching for his groin. Her mouth was a scarlet scar drawn back in a rictus of lust.

Stephen never quite knew what it was that came over him then. All he knew was that he couldn't go through with it. He pulled himself away and got unsteadily to his feet. 'I've drunk too much, I'm going to be sick,' he said.

She fell back on the sofa and for a moment they stared at each other. Then she sat up. Her eyes were blazing.

On a small table beside the sofa was a porcelain figure in a crinoline carrying a parasol, and apparently surveying the ridiculous scene with serene detachment. Stephen's companion hurled it at him. It sailed past and crashed through one of the glass wall panels, shattering both it and the precious bibelots inside. 'Take yourself and your useless cock out of here,' the woman shouted at him. Then, suddenly, she threw herself back on the cushions, turned her face to the sofa and began to cry, with great wrenching sobs. 'Oh, God,' she moaned between sobs. 'What is happening to me? What am I? What am I doing to myself?'

Stephen fled.

The following morning they took off for France.

12

Stephen, Clare and Hank shared a Nissen hut with Davis, their flight commander. Davis was a long, lugubrious man who had been a schoolmaster in private life. He had done a previous tour on F.E.s and he made no secret of the fact that he did not think he should have been sent out again. He detested and despised the higher direction of the war, especially where it concerned the R.F.C., and he said so openly. His first tour had been at the end of 'Bloody April' in 1917 when the Germans, by reason of superiority in machines and fire-power, had decimated the R.F.C. and all but grounded it. This had left scars which Davis never forgot, and he blamed Trenchard's policy of sending out obsolete machines and untrained men on offensive patrols or long reconnaissances far over the German lines for the butchery which had taken place. 'Callous, bloody murder,' he called it. 'And what did it accomplish? I'll tell you the answer in one word—nothing. And they'll do the same again. Wait until this new push comes and you'll see. All so that they can tell their political masters, "the spirit of the Flying Corps is unbroken," and get another set of letters to put after their names.'

Trenchard was the main target for his reasoned calumny, after that came all generals and brigadiers, politicians, war profiteers and 'the effete upper class who were running and losing the war'. Clare, of course, came into the latter category: 'Into the tumbrils with you, de Vaux, when they roll down Piccadilly after the war.'

He had brought with him a small library which included the works of Karl Marx and Engels from which he was fond of quoting aloud. No one could maintain that he had an encouraging or bracing effect on the morale of the squadron.

Shaw, the commander of A Flight, was a dour Scot who had also been out before, on Camels. He had been wounded and sent home but not before he had a few Huns to his credit. He spoke very little, but his general attitude seemed to indicate that he did not think much of the human material he had to lead. The third flight commander had had his engine fail when crossing the French

124

coast on the way out. Making a forced landing on the beach, he had hit a piece of soft sand and turned over, breaking his arm. They were at present waiting his replacement. Haynes had, however, secured as his recording officer an old friend from his former days in France. 'Uncle' Warmsley had done one tour as an observer, during which he had been badly shot up and grounded as a result. A solicitor in private life, he delighted in paper work, and that department of the squadron at least functioned smoothly.

But, one way or another, Haynes had plenty to occupy his mind during those first few weeks before the squadron went into action. Determined to weld it into an efficient fighting unit, he made every man study the maps of the immediate front and identify landmarks. He himself led in turn each of the flights to the lines and cross-examined the pilots on their return as to their knowledge of the terrain. Two blackboards were erected in the mess on which were to be recorded squadron and individual scores. He also insisted on each pilot personally synchronising his guns and practising his shooting on the ground target laid out beyond the big Bessonneau canvas hangars that housed the aircraft.

But he knew that he badly needed something to give the squadron a sense of unity, to make them feel they were as good as anyone and better than most, as the crack squadrons did. And a few days later he thought he had found it or the beginnings of it.

Bivouacked nearby was a Yeomanry Brigade. It was a very grand Yeomanry Brigade indeed. They kept themselves to themselves and spoke to no one but themselves. They were popularly supposed to dine in full mess kit every night, each regiment's silver having been brought over from England, with the regimental bands playing soft airs to assist their digestion of the regimental port. No one in the R.F.C., however, could vouch for this since they were never asked to dine on guest or any other nights, probably, it was supposed, because they did not possess mess kit and would badly let down the tone of the occasion.

It was the S.E. squadron who occupied hangars on the other side of the aerodrome and who came to call on 245 who told them all this. The only contact they had had with the Yeomanry, they said, was a series of complaints from one of their adjutants concerning machines flying low over his horse lines and upsetting the horses. They added that on one of the rare occasions when the officers of that particular regiment patronised a local estaminet one of them had been heard to remark that officers of the R.F.C. were 'uncouth fellows who smelt of oil'.

The R.F.C., in fact, were encountering a snobbery greater than their own, one based on class not caste, and they did not like it.

'I know those buggers and their Brigadier too,' Haynes remarked on hearing this. 'They'd be better off getting some trench mud on their boots.'

'They're having a race-meeting next week.' the S.E. Major said. 'I suppose they'll let us in as spectators.'

'A race-meeting. Are they now, that's interestin'.' Haynes looked thoughtful as he said goodbye to his visitors. Later he repaired to the squadron office where he was seen to be having a consultation with Uncle Warmsley and then to be holding a long conversation on the telephone. The squadron office clerk when questioned said he thought the call was to someone in the remounts.

The following morning Stephen took his Camel up for firing practice. He had only made one run at the target when the guns jammed. On landing he sought out the armament officer, for this was the second time it had happened in three days. Lieutenant Heal was a refugee from the trenches, who had a fondness for whisky and a contempt for all young temporary officers. In Stephen's opinion he was one of the misfits foisted on Haynes who did not properly know his job and covered up by being obsequious to senior officers and offhand with his juniors.

As Stephen was remonstrating with him about the stoppages all at once he saluted, staring at someone over Stephen's right shoulder. Stephen turned to see Haynes approaching. 'All well, Heal?' Haynes said.

'Yes, sir. Just making sure with Raymond that his guns are absolutely full out, sir.'

'Good. That's the spirit.' Haynes beckoned to Stephen. 'A word with you,' he said.

When they were a few paces away he stopped and looked at Stephen. 'You've ridden work with a trainer, I think you told me.' he said.

'Yes,' Stephen answered, wondering what on earth was coming next. It didn't sound as if it had much to do with the prosecution of the war.

'And races—two or three point-to-points, wasn't it?'

'That's right. And one National Hunt flat race—and a flapper.'

'You ought to be warned off. Still, that should do. It'll have to do. Come along then and we'll have a look.'

When Haynes was being mysterious, no amount of questioning would make him reveal his intentions and he was, besides, his senior officer. Stephen followed him to the squadron office. Outside was a motor-cycle combination Haynes had scrounged from somewhere while he waited delivery of the official squadron commander's car. 'Can you drive this damn thing?' he said.

'I think so,' Stephen said dubiously.

'Very well. Get on with it then.' Haynes was climbing into the sidecar. 'We're going to see a pal of mine in the remounts.'

After a distinctly uneasy ride and some bad language from Haynes in the sidecar, they arrived at the remount depot. Horse lines were laid out, men bustled about with buckets, the ammoniac tang of horse piss came refreshingly to Stephen's nostrils after the sickly smell of castor oil which permeated the cockpit of a Camel.

'I 'ope you ride better than you drive,' Haynes said as he heaved himself out of the sidecar. 'Mornin', Archie,' he went on as a Captain with a leathery face and very bandy legs came up to them. 'This 'ere's young Raymond, one of my officers. 'E'll ride this 'oss for us. At least I 'ope 'e will. 'E'll need to be a better 'and at it than drivin' this machine. Never been so scared since I 'ad three 'Uns on me tail.'

Archie grinned. 'He takes a bit of a hold, this horse,' he said. 'But you'll be all right, I expect. You've ridden a bit, I understand.'

'What *is* going on?' Stephen asked, but neither of them bothered to answer as Archie led the way towards a long low building at the far side of the compound. It was a converted barn. Inside was a row of stalls. At the end stall Archie stopped. Here a trooper was holding a horse by the head. The horse was saddled and had a rug on him.

'All right, Johnson, let's have him out,' Archie said.

The trooper stripped off the rug and what he saw made Stephen hazard a guess at what was afoot. The horse was a big raking bay with steeplechaser written all over him. He had obviously been done far better and had had more work put into him than the usual run of remounts for he was well muscled up and his coat shone.

'What is he and where did you get him?' Stephen asked.

'Never you mind,' Haynes said. 'If you can ride one side of him that should be enough.'

Behind the barn was a big ten-acre paddock, down one side of which three schooling fences had been built. Here, another horse and rider were waiting for them. Haynes nodded towards the rider. 'Ben Webster,' he said to Stephen. 'Morning, Ben.'

'Morning, sir.'

Stephen recognised the name. Ben Webster had been a useful professional under National Hunt Rules before the war.

'Put him up,' Haynes commanded.

Archie's hand went under Stephen's leg and he was slung into the saddle. Instinctively, his hands went to his girths and leathers.

'Ready, sir?' Webster said.

'Yes, if you'll tell me what I'm supposed to do,' Stephen answered.

'Take him round with me in a steady canter,' was the reply. 'Then we'll begin to go on a bit. Second time round we'll pop over those fences nice and easy like.'

'Christ!' Stephen thought. 'And I haven't been on a horse for months.'

The big horse did take a hold. But, slight as he was, one of the gifts Stephen had been born with was the ability to hold a hard puller, an ability which has little to do with physical strength. All the same he was breathing hard and his muscles were beginning to ache as they came round for the second time and turned towards the fences. They were going fast now, the drum of their hooves banging up from the firm turf. Stephen knew what was happening; he was being tried out to see if he could steer this big horse and sit on him when he jumped at racing pace.

He was upsides with Webster then and they were going into the first fence. The big horse measured it and jumped out of his stride. He threw a hell of a leap, but Stephen had schooled even bigger jumpers than this with Bob Ferris. He did not move in the saddle as they landed and galloped towards the next. The big horse flung the other two fences behind him, and then they pulled up and were walking back.

'This is the hell of a horse,' Stephen said. 'What is he?'

'Did you ever hear, sir, of a horse called Black George?'

'Good God, yes. Third in the National just before the war. The weight beat him.'

'And the distance. I don't think he quite got the trip. Of course no one knows for certain but they do say, sir, that's what he is.'

'Great heavens. But where did he come from?'

'I've heard he got lost somehow early in the war when they were requisitioning remounts. The Captain, here, he found him. We've been getting him straight for a bit of fun, like. Now your Major, it seems, he's got a job for him.'

They had rejoined the others by now. Ben Webster slid to the ground and slapped his horse on the neck. Then he looked at Stephen and nodded. 'He'll do,' he said.

'Just what is going on?' Stephen said.

Archie laughed. 'Come into the mess and we'll tell you,' he said.

Once there, with glasses before them and cigarettes being lit, Haynes said to Stephen: 'Well, what do you think of 'im?'

'That horse? I wouldn't mind riding him in the National.'

'Wouldn't you now. You're going to ride 'im in something a damn sight simpler than that. Those Yeomanry buggers are holding a race-meeting next week. They've got an All Comers Chase because the Corps Commander wanted it and 'e's given a cup. They've made it the chief race on the card so as to please the bleeding' brass hat. There isn't another cavalry brigade in the area and they think it's a million to a monkey they'll win it themselves.'

'It's to be level weights like a point-to-point,' Archie put in with a grin. 'They want their Brigadier to win it. He's got something he thinks can go a bit.'

'Who is he?' Stephen asked.

' 'E's a proper bastard,' Haynes said. 'I served with 'im at Netheravon. Name of Gnowles.'

'Not Grig Gnowles?' Stephen said faintly.

'That's 'im. You know 'im?'

'He comes from where I live. He hunts our hounds.'

' 'E's a bastard wherever 'e comes from. Treated us like dirt, 'e did. N.C.O.s and men, we all hated 'im. How 'e wasn't shot in the back during the retreat I'll never know.'

'But, look,' Stephen protested. 'He was a bloody good G.R. before he started hunting hounds and gave up. He's won lots of races. He'll be fit and I'm not.'

'That 'oss outside could give three stone and a beating to the sort of cattle 'e's got to pick from. You could fall off and carry 'im 'ome and win it.'

'He's right, you know,' Archie put in reassuringly. 'And Gnowles isn't as young as he was. This is a sort of show-off for the General. He was adjutant to one of those Yeomanry regiments some time before the war.'

'It'll be the 'ell of a kick in the teeth for them,' Haynes went on. 'And do us no end of good. They're going to run the books themselves, too. Think it's a sort of regimental benefit, see? But us and the S.E. blighters, we're going to back your 'oss off the boards and bust them, see?'

'They'll have to pawn the mess silver,' Archie said happily.

'We'll dress you up a bit,' Haynes went on, looking at Stephen, 'to make you out an even bigger mug than you are.'

It was, Stephen had to admit, a well-nigh watertight scheme. The race was for All Comers, at level weights. No one could object to the horse, who had been renamed Plum and Apple after the ration jam, because no one could say for certain who or what he really was. Haynes could not ride himself because someone in the Yeomanry Brigade was bound to recognise him and realise that something was hatching, so Stephen was the obvious choice as the jockey. But, just the same, Stephen knew only too well how racing good things had a habit of coming unstuck, and Haynes' next words did little to reassure him. 'And if you fall off, me lad, or make a muck of it,' he said, 'I'll 'ave you posted to an R.E.8 squadron before breakfast.'

Haynes planned the whole affair as carefully as if it had been a military operation. Since they kept themselves so aloof from other, lesser mortals it was unlikely that the Yeomanry would learn of the plot. Nevertheless, if the entire squadron was let into the secret, there was an outside chance that an unwary officer or other rank might let slip some remark in a brothel or estaminet which would reach their ears and put them on their guard. Thus, he decided that only those

129

immediately concerned should be told of what was afoot and they were pledged to secrecy.

Stephen did, however, insist on being allowed to take Clare and Hank into his confidence. He pointed out that, since Haynes was determined to keep in the background and not to be seem to play any active part in the matter, then he would need someone to help with the saddle and that Clare with his cavalry training was the only person qualified to do so. He went on to say that if he told Clare they could not keep it from Hank and Haynes reluctantly agreed, threatening them with boiling oil and brimstone if they breathed so much as a word outside.

The night before the race Haynes disclosed the plot to the C.O. of the S.E. squadron, who received the idea with delight. Together they decided that the betting should be done by the flight commanders and that out of the proceeds a fund would be set apart for the other ranks.

The following morning a conference, presided over by Haynes, was set up in 245 Squadron mess. The C.O. of the S.E. squadron was present, as were Hank, Stephen, Clare and Captain Archie Mulholland of the remounts. The flight commanders were then summoned to attend.

When Haynes took his seat at the head of the table, he looked around him counting heads. 'Where's Davis?' he asked as he finished.

'In the hut reading Karl Marx,' Clare said promptly.

'Karl Marx? Who the 'ell is he? Sounds like an 'Un. Go and fetch him, de Vawks.'

'Shall I tell him why he's wanted?'

'Yes, if you like.'

In a few minutes Clare returned, smiling faintly.

'I regret to tell you our flight commander refuses to have anything to do with us,' he said.

'Why the 'ell not?'

'If I quote him correctly he says that horse-racing is a capitalist ruse to exploit the working class.'

'What in 'ell does that mean?'

'I'm not at all sure but he went on to say that he considered betting immoral. It is, he said, an opium used by the upper classes to persuade the workers to be content with their lot.'

'He can't be a bloomin' red, can 'e?'

'Clap him in irons,' the S.E. major suggested.

'We'll see to that later. This is more important. Now then, de Vawks, you'll 'ave to share in the bettin' then. No, you're travellin' head lad and groom and helpin' with the saddle. What about you, Jarman?'

'Sure thing,' Hank said.

' 'Ere's 'ow we'll go about it, then. Now, listen carefully—'

130

Despite all he had said about keeping out of the way, Haynes could not resist attending the meeting, supervising the preparations and watching the fun. From sources unknown, he had acquired an enormous, full-skirted Guardsman's great-coat and had exchanged his usual Middleton cap with its 17th Lancers' cap badge for a fore-and-aft Flying Corps forage cap. With the collar of the coat turned up around his ears and the forage cap set squarely on his head, banged down and almost inside out, he looked about as unlike his usual damn-your-eyes swaggering self as could be imagined.

Stephen could scarcely restrain his laughter as his commanding officer stumped along beside him towards the fields where the meeting was to be held. Haynes' head was hunched into the collar of the greatcoat, his eyes peering this way and that from behind its wings, taking in everything they saw. As they reached the edge of the field where they were to await the arrival of Clare with the horse, he stopped in his tracks and stared intently at something on the road. 'Now what the 'ell is 'e doing 'ere?' he said.

A motor had pulled up not far away from them. It looked like a staff car and an officer was getting down from it. Stephen recognised him immediately. It was Desmond Murtagh, elegant as ever. A dashing-looking woman with a large hat and a motoring veil remained in the back of the car. He turned to say something to her and Stephen saw her look at him and laugh.

'You know him?' he said to Haynes.

'Know 'im? Of course I know 'im. Everyone in racin' knows 'im. 'E's as 'ot as 'ell. Pulled a right one at Punchestown before the war from all I hear. Why?'

'He comes from where I do.'

'Does 'e? And Gnowles too. Right nest of robins you 'ave there then. Wait 'ere and I'll have a word with 'im and see what he's up to.'

In a few minutes Haynes was back. 'I 'ad to cut 'im in,' he said gloomily. 'He 'as something 'ot in our race. Or 'e says 'e 'as, you never know with 'im. Says that thing of Gnowles' can go a bit, too. Maybe it's better than we thought. He says 'e'll look after 'im for us if anything looks like goin' wrong.'

'You're not going to find any more National runners and riders for me to beat, are you?'

'Don't be bloody impertinent or I'll have you orderly dog for the next three weeks. Now, cut along and walk the course.'

The fences, Stephen found, were well made and on the soft side as was to be expected where the class of horse would be very moderate compared to steeplechasing at home. There were two open ditches and one rather nasty looking drop. About half a mile from the finish the ground dipped and for some little distance the horses would be

131

invisible to the spectators. In this dip Stephen encountered Desmond Murtagh. He was standing at the bottom of the slope leading out of it, looking thoughtful. 'Well met, young feller me lad,' he said as Stephen came up. 'Heard any news from the Bay lately?'

'My father writes regularly. Things seem pretty quiet. Mr Massiter's an M. P.'

'And getting richer and richer while fools like us get poorer and poorer—or get killed.'

'How is Babs?'

'On the rare occasions that I hear from her she seems all right. As a matter of fact I saw her the other day. She's driving a general—a staff-wallah in Paris.'

'I didn't know Babs could drive.'

'Massiter's chauffeur taught her before she left home. She seems to have hooked up with some Australian in one of their Camel Squadrons. She's having the time of her life.'

'Oh!'

'Anyway this coffee-housing here won't do. Let's get to business. Haynes tells me you'll win this race.'

'He seems to think so,' Stephen said cautiously.

'This is where the action will be last time round. I'll take care of Grig if he's looking dangerous. And when I say "Go", go like hell.'

'These Yeomanry sods think they have it all to themselves,' Stephen said.

'That's a bad sort of way to go into a race. I want to see old Grig's face if this comes off.'

'If it does,' Stephen thought glumly to himself. Rather too much was resting on his shoulders, but at least he had Desmond as an ally and not a rival, and if anyone could help to ensure success Desmond could. With that thought his spirits rose slightly and he took himself off to change.

The changing room was in an old barn with a shell hole in its roof. Stephen found himself amongst a clutch of Yeomanry subalterns engaged in putting on the smartest of racing breeches, boots, silks and jerseys, all no doubt brought over in their kit for this precise purpose. They had no middle-class shibboleths about the use of christian names and the air was thick with Alastairs, and Gileses and Perrys and Percys as they hailed each other across the room.

Haynes had borrowed for Stephen a pair of the baggiest artillery breeches he could find. His colours were an old and faded red polo jersey with a white silk sash stitched untidily across it. All this was in marked contrast to the spotless white of his competitors' breeches and the high shine on the products of the best bootmakers which they wore on their elegant legs. To complete the required picture of utter inexperience and general muffishness, he had no racing scarf round

132

his neck and his jersey was worn outside his breeches.

Except for a few disdainful glances in his direction, the Alastairs and Perrys ignored him completely. To his pleasure and surprise all this helped to put him on his mettle. After making what he hoped were several convincingly ineffectual efforts to tie the tape on his racing cap, he turned to the nearest exquisite. 'I—I say,' he said. 'I don't seem able to manage this. Can you do it for me?'

'Can't you?' the elegant one drawled, running his eyes over him. 'Not entirely surprised, I must say. Flying Corps, aren't you? Oh, very well, then. Here, let me.'

'I say, thanks awfully,' Stephen said.

'Not ridden much, have you?' the elegant one went on.

'Oh, no. Hardly at all. I suppose you fellows are frightfully hot. It's all, a bit, well, alarming if you see what I mean, isn't it?'

'One gets used to it,' came the reply in the same languid drawl. 'We do quite a bit here, you know, amongst ourselves. Helps to keep us fit.'

Stephen picked up his whip. Holding it upside down he made for the door.

'That's one we won't have to worry about,' he heard the Perry or Percy he had been talking to say.

'What a frightful Charlie,' another voice replied, and a general laugh followed.

Never one to suffer particularly from conceit, Stephen still did not particularly care for being referred to as a frightful Charlie. It was their arrogance that infuriated him. Had he really been a mug they could, after all, have shown him some kindness instead of this offhand contempt. 'I'll put you over the rails, my beauty, if I get the chance,' he thought savagely to himself.

When Stephen reached the ring, Plum and Apple was being led round by Clare, who was himself disguised in another rank's tunic and breeches. Haynes had procured from somewhere an immense waterproof sheet which stretched from withers to croup and reached almost to the ground. In addition he had covered his head with a hood. Virtually the only parts of Plum and Apple which could be seen were his hooves. Stephen and Clare had been instructed to wait until the others had mounted and were about to leave the parade ring before stripping the horse lest some sharp Yeomanry eye should observe his conformation and condition and make his own deductions.

Haynes had, in the event, been unable to resist concerning himself with the action and Stephen found him standing beside him as he prepared to get up. 'Worked like a charm,' he said. 'Twenty to one and all takers. Remember what I said now, young feller. Win this unless you want a squadron lynching party tonight and a posting to two-seaters tomorrow.' He bent to put Stephen up and as he did so his forage cap fell off and his head shot out of the enveloping wings of the collar.

133

'Careful, sir, someone might recognise you,' Stephen said with a grin.

'Too late. The money's on. Remember now. Them R.E.8's are fair buggers to fly, and they burn like blazes.'

With these encomiums ringing in his ears, Stephen went down to the start. Once there, he tried to keep as far away from the other riders as he could, and especially out of the range of Grig Gnowles' eye. His clothes might be ill-fitting and all wrong, but he knew very well that he could not disguise from any knowledgeable glance that he knew how to catch hold of his horse's head and to hoist his bottom out of the saddle.

To his dismay he found Grig glaring at him. 'What's that horse?' Grig barked, moving over towards him.

'Plum and Apple, sir.'

'Doesn't look much like a charger to me. What are you doing here anyway?'

'Riding a race, I hope, sir,' Stephen answered. The pretensions of these people were beginning to make him really angry.

'Who was that officer who put you up? I thought I recognised him.'

It didn't matter telling him now. The money was down. Maybe it would give him something to think about. 'Major Haynes, our C.O., sir. I think the starter is calling us in.'

There was no time for further conversation. The flag fell and they were off.

For the first two rounds all went swimmingly. The big horse took a hold but Stephen kept him in the middle without much difficulty. It was at the last open ditch, three from home, that the trouble began.

Grig had gone on, with Desmond tracking him. Stephen still had the comfortable feeling that he was galloping over his field and could go and take the other two whenever he liked. No one else looked in the least dangerous. Many of the Yeomanry had fallen, the one beside him was labouring. They came into the wings of the fence.

Then Stephen saw that the other rider was even more tired than the horse. He was rolling about in the saddle. Any semblance of control he had once had had long since been lost. Horse and rider were coming across on to him.

'Keep your bloody horse straight, damn you,' Stephen shouted in the approved fashion, as he had himself so often been addressed on Bob's gallops. It was to no avail. He saw the astonishment on the Percy's face at being sworn at by this Charlie and then they collided in mid-air.

The Percy's horse came down with a crash, shooting its rider clear. Plum and Apple landed all asprawl. He staggered and lurched and Stephen was sure they were gone. It was the horse's strength and experience and only those that kept him on his feet. He shook his big

134

head and remained upright but they were all but brought to a stand-still.

Stephen picked him up. A couple of strides to recover himself was all he could allow him. He had to get back into the race and there was no time to lose. He could see the backs of the other two well ahead. He kicked on.

The big horse pulled himself into his stride. Whether he was Black George, the National horse, or not Stephen knew that he would never sit on a gamer one or one more prepared to give everything he had. He flung the second last behind him, and they came thundering down into the dip.

Desmond was upsides with Grig. 'Where the hell were you?' he said to Stephen out of the corner of his mouth as Plum and Apple forged alongside him. 'Go on, boy, go *on*. I'll see to this.'

Stephen needed no second bidding. He kicked again and got the response he wanted. They sailed over the last. Behind him he thought he could hear some bad language flying about. The post seemed miles away. Then it loomed up and flashed past. He had won.

Haynes was waiting for them in the winners' enclosure. He was wearing a broad grin and his best tunic with wings and decorations. His cap with the 17th Lancers badge was back on his head.

Grig rode into the second horse's berth, looking thunderous. 'What's going on here? What horse is that? Who owns it?' he barked as soon as his feet touched the ground.

'Plum and Apple. Belongs to Captain Mulholland of the Remounts, sir,' Haynes answered.

'The devil he does. It's you, Haynes, is it? Up to your games again, I see.'

'Games, sir? Games? I think I must 'ave misheard you, sir.'

Suddenly realising that he was in the process of making a fool of himself, Grig swallowed twice. Then, putting his saddle over his arm, he made his way to the weighing tent.

'What the hell happened to you?' Desmond said to Stephen as they walked together after Grig.

'Some bloody Percy nearly knocked me down. I never thought I'd catch you. That's the hell of a horse. What did you do to the Brigadier?'

'I squeezed him a little. It'll be a nice touch, and by God I need it.'

As he was leaving the tent after weighing in, Haynes came up to Stephen. 'The presentation is after the last race,' he said. 'Cut off and put on your most split-arse tunic, best breeches and spurs. I want to show these buggers a bit of style.'

'I haven't got any spurs.'

'I know. I told my servant to put a pair of mine on your bed. And tell that de Vawks I want him there with you, and properly dressed, too, in field boots and spurs. And listen—'

'Yes.'

'Tell 'im to put that pane of glass in his eye and to look at 'em like he used to look at me.'

Clare and Stephen split a bottle of champagne as they were changing and Clare needed no urging at all to do as he was told. 'What quite dreadful fellows,' he drawled as they walked together back to the course. 'Don't think my Colonel would have cared for them at all. They don't ride well enough for one thing. Fancy letting some little Flying Corps subaltern in baggy breeches wipe their eye. Fancy!'

'Here's Hank,' Stephen said.

Hank was carrying a satchel stuffed with notes and coin of all descriptions. 'Skinned those guys alive-oh,' he said happily.

'Grocer's port on guest nights from now on,' Clare drawled.

Half an hour later, in their smartest high-collared, double-breasted maternity jackets, their field boots shining and spurs on their heels, Stephen and Clare stood with Haynes and Archie Mulholland waiting the arrival of the General to present the cup. On one side of them were the serried ranks of the two Flying Corps squadrons, on the other the Yeomanry, looking decidedly glum.

Clare surveyed the Yeomen through his eyeglass. He had, Stephen noticed, put the collar badges of his old regiment for the first time on to his R.F.C. tunic. 'Rather a mixed crowd, Yeomanry, I've always thought,' he said in a drawl that could be heard ten yards away. 'Much like Gunners, don'tcha know.'

There was a titter from some of the Flying Corps officers at this sally and then the General was bustling up with his A.D.C. behind him.

'Badly fittin' boots that fellah's wearin',' Clare said loudly in Stephen's ear as he stared critically at the General's turn-out. It occurred to Stephen that half a bottle of champagne might be making Clare overplay the part Haynes had indicated for him and that if he went on the way he was going they'd all end up under arrest for insolence.

Whether the General overheard the remark or not, he did not seem in a very congratulatory mood when Stephen and Archie walked up to receive the cup. He had protruberant blue eyes, drooping white moustaches and a high complexion. He looked fierce and fiery and stupid. Stephen wondered what Davis would have to say about him and determined to find out on his return to the aerodrome. He had never encountered a general at close quarters and in full plumage before.

As the old boy drew his white eyebrows together in a frown and glared belligerently at him, he began to feel vaguely frightened. But at the same time his hackles rose. No doubt the General had been given a highly-coloured version of the affair from Grig, who had also almost certainly filled him full of port and brandy in the private tent to which

136

R.F.C. officers were neither asked nor admitted. If Grig had been squeezed he was supposed to be able to look after himself; it was all part of the game which no one ever pretended was conducted under the same rules as ring o' roses. Why then couldn't this crowd admit they'd been properly had without the conditions of the race being infringed and that they'd been beaten by a better horse?

It seemed they could not. There was silence from the Yeomanry ranks in response to the clapping from the R.F.C., and the General glared even more ferociously as they approached him. 'You're Mulholland?' he barked as they both came to attention and saluted. 'Don't I know you?'

'I served under you in India, sir.'

'What? Piffers? Frontier Force?'

'Sam Browne's Cavalry, sir.'

'Racin' regiment. Might have guessed it. Here's your cup, Mulholland. You may think yourself lucky you're not facing an enquiry. Very sporting Brigade to let you get away with it. That horse a remount?'

'Yes, sir.'

'I'll have the Divisional Inspector look him over, and you, too, for that matter. As for you, young man—' He turned his fierce glare on Stephen.

'You may have been taken by the Flying Corps. They're not too particular about their officers, I understand. You dressed up like a fool yet you ride like a professional jockey. Are you one?'

Streuth! Well, it's a sort of compliment, anyway, Stephen thought, though Bob Ferris wouldn't agree with him. 'No, sir.'

'Then I suggest you'd better become one. You would seem more suited to that than wearing the King's uniform.'

They both saluted and turned about.

'I think the old bastard's drunk,' Archie said as they retraced their steps. 'You could set up a bar on his breath.'

A storm of cheering and clapping from the Flying Corps greeted them on their return. Some of the other ranks had already been celebrating in the beer tent. 'Good old Plum and Apple,' one of them shouted. 'Three cheers for Plum and Apple and when the 'ell is he going to be strawberry!'

The Yeomanry drifted away in silence. 'Licking their wounds,' Archie said. 'Now, back to your mess and the champagne and filling this ruddy mug.'

As they made their way towards the aerodrome Stephen came face to face with the rider who had all but knocked him down. It was the same officer who had tied his cap for him. Stephen stopped. 'Those races of yours you were telling me about,' he said. 'You'll find it a help in them if you keep your bloody horse straight. By the way, is your name Percy?'

'No,' the other said stonily.

'I just wondered,' Stephen said. 'I gather mine is Charlie.'

When they reached the mess, there was no sign of Haynes. Clare had gone off on the motor-cycle combination with instructions to fill the sidecar with champagne but search as they would they could not find their C.O. to help them celebrate. Half an hour later a lone Camel droned out of the evening sky, landed and taxied to the hangars. It was Haynes. He had been out by himself and bagged a Hun. It was the squadron's first victory. The number 1 was proudly chalked on the blackboard and Haynes decreed a binge.

They started with gin and vermouths at the bar and a fierce concoction of Hank's which he christened Yeomen's Blood. Stephen avoided the cocktail and the gin, contenting himself with vermouth and waiting for the champagne.

By the time they moved into the mess the binge was well under way. Stephen was happy and exhilarated. 'You've done us a good turn today,' one of the S.E. pilots said to him. 'Tomorrow and the next day you look after the Huns low down and we'll take care of you upstairs.'

'Are they good, the Huns?' Stephen asked, tentatively.

'No. Not this lot opposite. There're not many of them about and those that are don't seem to want to fight. There's a rumour they've withdrawn all their best men to form circuses to cover this new push everyone's talking about. Anyway—who cares about Huns? Drink up!'

'My sentiments exactly,' Clare said from Stephen's other side. 'Not quite vintage, this stuff, but the best I could get. What do you think of the table decorations? Wouldn't do for the Yeomen, perhaps, but they serve very well, wouldn't you say?' A line of champagne bottles with candles in their necks had been placed at intervals along the table-cloth.

As the pâté was followed by roast beef and bottle after bottle of champagne, the party grew more boisterous. Soon there were calls for speeches. Haynes said 245 Squadron was going to be the best bloody Camel squadron on the Western Front. If they'd started off giving their friends a licking, what weren't they going to do to the Hun? Cheers and clapping greeted this, and someone shouted 'Where's the jockey? Speech from the jockey!'

Stephen sat staring at his plate. He had never made a speech in his life and he did not know where to begin. Clare dug him in the ribs. 'Go on, get up,' he said, 'say something. It doesn't matter a damn what it is.'

Pushing back his chair, Stephen got to his feet. His head was singing and he could scarcely see across the table through the haze of candle and cigarette smoke. Dimly he remembered that he should address senior officers first. 'Major Haynes and Major Cutforth,' he

138

said. 'And assembled gentlemen or should I say temporary gentlemen which was what the General thought of us today—'

Shouts and uproar greeted this. Someone threw a bread roll at him. 'Did he say that?' Archie's voice demanded.

'No, but he would have in a minute. He called me everything else, including being a professional jockey.'

Haynes gave a roar of laughter.

'And a bloody bad one, too,' he shouted from the head of the table. 'You wouldn't have won if Murtagh hadn't squeezed the Brigadier!'

Two hours later, slightly unsteady on his feet, Stephen made his way back to the hut. Behind him he could hear echoing out the chorus which was almost always sung sometime or another at these binges. It was the original song of the R.F.C. written or strung together when the Corps was in its infancy and brought with them by the first squadrons to land in France.

> "Take the cylinders out of my kidneys,
> The connecting-rod out of my brain (my brain),
> From the small of my back take the crankshaft,
> And assemble the engine again!"

Stephen laughed to himself. Champagne was splendid stuff; he had won his race; he felt good. Best of all were Haynes' parting words to him as he left the mess: "You're coming to look at the lines with me tomorrow, young feller me lad. With any luck we'll bag another Hun."

Davis had left the binge early and was still up when Stephen entered the hut. He was writing letters by the light of an oil lamp. 'So,' he said, not unkindly. 'The hero of the day enters.'

'We took from the rich and gave to the poor. I thought you'd have approved,' Stephen said.

'The sentiment perhaps if not the method. I gather the General didn't think much of it either.'

Stephen sat on the edge of his bed and began to take off his shoes. The champagne was dying in him and he began to feel, if not quite sober, then remarkably clear-headed. He told Davis what the General had said.

'Lieutenant-General Sir Cedric Littleton-Smailes, K.C.B., D.S.O., neither of which decorations were earned in action or as a result of it,' Davis said. 'A Boer war survival and a fool. A believer in the well-bred horse, the well-bred man and the *arme blanche*, which is the smart way of describing the cavalry sword.'

'How do you know all this?'

'My brother served in a very minor position on his staff when he had a Division. Even though it was a minor position he hadn't been to the right schools so the General unstuck him—had him kicked out. My

139

brother had been wounded twice and got an M.C. on the Somme. He went back to the line and was killed at Cambrai.'

'I didn't know. I'm sorry—'

Davis did not seem to hear him. 'They're like the Bourbons,' he said. 'They've forgotten nothing and learnt nothing. And like the Bourbons they'll come to dust. We may not even win this war. If we don't it will be they who have lost it—the ruling class. If we do, sooner or later Nemesis will overtake them. Do you know why?

'The sin of pride, that's what will bring them down. It will eat them out from within even if socialism doesn't destroy them from without. They may cling on for years because they open their ranks to a selected few and the new ones are worse than the old. Once they're in they cling more greedily to their privileges than if they were theirs by birth. If my brother had been to Eton or Charterhouse or Rugby he'd be alive today. And what gets them in? Money. And who has the money now? The war profiteers. They're tomorrow's ruling class.'

'You may be right, I suppose,' Stephen said.

'I know I'm right. Look at Haynes. The best scout pilot in France and they wouldn't give him a squadron because he speaks with the wrong accent and when they had to they fobbed him off with this lot.'

'They certainly think they're God's anointed,' Stephen said.

'You're Irish,' Davis went on. 'You've been persecuted for generations. What are you doing here anyway?'

'Hank asked me that the other day and I'm beginning to wonder myself. Some of my ancestors did the persecuting and some of them were persecuted. Now, sometimes, I feel like killing some of my own side rather than the Huns.'

'A more treasonable expression I never heard.' The door opened and Clare came in. 'The doctrine according to Marx is not one that I favour and I don't recommend it to you either, young Stephen.' He looked steadily at Davis as he began to unbutton his shirt, as if challenging him to say something, but Davis merely bent his head over his letters and went on writing.

In a few moments, both Stephen and Clare were asleep. Davis put down his pen and looked at them. They'd be dead soon, he thought, they'd all be dead. He'd seen it before, that terrible April. Britain was squandering its manhood and its youth, and all for nothing. At least it could be said of the Germans that they knew how to husband their resources, especially in the air. Ironically it had been left to an aristocrat—Lord Lansdowne—to protest about it all in that peace letter of his. But nothing had happened, the generals, the war-masters, the profiteers had all been too strong for him. Soon they would be flying their first offensive patrols and Davis knew what that meant—forays far into Hunland and with every possible geographical disadvantage of sun and wind and weather against them, with the Huns waiting for them high up in the sun, ready to pounce on the unwary and to kill, and then another ten miles to fight one's way back through Archie and flaming onions and possible ambush from other Huns. And all to maintain 'the spirit of the offensive'. Davis had long ago lost that spirit and now he hated with a deadly hatred the generals who inspired it from their safe châteaux far behind the lines. The thought of leading one of those patrols made Davis' gorge rise with fear. He knew he had, in the argot of the day, got cold feet. He didn't care. He shouldn't have been sent out again. He had protested but his C.O. at Home Establishment, another fire-eater, had disliked him and wanted to get rid of him. Perhaps he had talked too much, aired his political opinions too loudly. He remembered the gloating look on his C.O.'s face when he told him he had been posted to France again.

Davis turned the wick down and blew out the lamp. He undressed and got into bed, but it was a long time before sleep came to him.

After lunch next day Stephen and Haynes took off together and climbed to five thousand feet. It was a bright February afternoon that carried with it the first hint of spring. The sun was a blazing ball moving towards the west. Down far below men were killing each other. Up here, Stephen felt divorced from everything, alone, isolated, the only realities the aeroplane, himself and the sunlight that touched the clouds with fire. The Camel was almost part of him now; he could fly it without conscious thought, responding to it just as it answered each touch of his hand. The euphoria of yesterday's success, the congratulations, the champagne, and the binge were still with him. He was not concentrating as he should have been. Thoughts of war were far away. There was peace up here and sunlight and the beauty and brilliance of the sky. They had been out for the best part of an hour when Stephen awoke from his daydreams. Haynes was waggling his wings. It was the signal that he had sighted something, probably an enemy. He was looking round at Stephen and pointing down and to the right.

It took Stephen a moment or two to pick out what had caught Haynes's attention. Then, far below, he saw a black speck against the white of a cloud. It was just on their side of the lines moving away from them.

The nose of Haynes' machine went down and he dived. Pushing the stick forward Stephen followed. There were never any half-measures about Haynes going into action. Once the decision had been made the approach was immediate and flat-out. The needle on Stephen's airspeed indicator was nearly off the dial as he strove to keep up with Haynes' dive.

The wind was shrieking through the wires. The machine began to shake and he wondered if the wings would come off when he tried to pull her out. This was his first experience of the real thing and he was not sure that he liked it.

The black speck grew larger and resolved itself into a Hun two-seater, an L.V.G., doing a job over the Allied lines and trying to slip back to safety. In a moment Stephen could see the black crosses on the fuselage. It was his first glimpse of the enemy. He caught his breath.

Haynes was attacking and the rear gunner was firing at him. Then, suddenly, he swung away and underneath. Behind him Stephen was perfectly placed for the kill. The rear gunner was slap in his sights. He could see him struggling desperately to bring the gun back to bear on him after trying to follow Haynes' dive. Stephen's fingers moved to the triggers on his spade grip. The Hun observer was not going to get the gun round in time. He was cold meat; he was a dead man.

And then Stephen knew he could not do it. He was so close he could see the fear on the observer's features. He could not kill this frightened member of his own species in what amounted to cold blood. His fingers fell from the triggers. The two-seater dived into a cloud and escaped.

Haynes turned back towards the aerodrome and Stephen followed him. They landed and taxied towards the hangars.

Haynes got out of his machine and strode over to where Stephen was standing, pulling off his helmet and goggles as he came. 'What the hell happened to you?' he barked. 'Did your guns jam?'

Stephen swallowed. He was in trouble and he knew it. All the way back to the aerodrome he had been anticipating this. He swallowed again. 'N—No,' he said. 'I'm sorry, sir. I just couldn't—'

'Couldn't what?'

'I—I just couldn't shoot at him—kill him.'

'Listen, you young fool, this is war. It's not rounders or a girls' outing—it's war—see? If you don't kill him, that blond Teuton behind his guns will kill you. Perhaps it's a bloody pity 'e didn't. He's not a man. 'E's the enemy—see? And what's more I put him up for you and let him take a crack at me while I was doing it. Christ Almighty! Now you listen to me, Raymond, you may be still wet behind the ears but you do that again or anything like it and I'll post you home— without your wings. Remember that.' He stumped off towards the squadron office.

Stephen found that Heal was standing beside him. The armament officer must have seen and heard everything that had passed. He looked at Stephen superciliously. 'No trouble with your guns this trip, I hope,' he said.

Without answering Stephen went miserably to the hut and took of his Sidcot flying suit. No one else was about. They were all either in the hangars checking their buses or their guns or in the mess playing cards or ping pong. Stephen sat on the edge of his bed and put his

142

head in his hands. All of yesterday's euphoria had gone as if it had never been. He had failed his first real test and Haynes was not likely to forget it. And, of more immediate importance, what the hell was he to put into his report?

It was Uncle who solved his difficulties for him. Haynes had left the squadron office when Stephen got there. Uncle was alone, surrounded by piles of forms and reports, and busily writing.

Stephen sat down and stared at the blank sheet of paper in front of him. Twice he picked up his pen and put it down again.

'In trouble, are you? Can I help?' he heard Uncle say.

'Well, yes, look, did he tell you what happened?'

'Some of it.'

'How am I to write a report saying I funked firing?'

'I wouldn't do that, certainly. In any event, you didn't. It wasn't funk, I'm sure. The first taste of action takes everyone differently. It was bad luck in a way that you came across a sitting duck. If it had been a dog-fight it would have been easier for you. Here, let me have a go at drafting it.' He pulled a form towards him. 'Where were you, do you know?'

'I'm not sure. Somewhere east of Armentières, I think.'

'That'll do. Now, then, how about this?' Picking up the paper, Uncle read what he had written: '*Line patrol. Clouds at 1000 feet. Indecisive encounter with enemy two-seater, L.V.G. which disappeared into clouds.*'

'But what about the Major? What'll he say when he sees it?'

'He never looks at them. I write up his reports for him and he signs them without reading them.'

'Gosh, thanks, Uncle. Is he furious?'

'He's pretty angry. You see, you were a sort of favourite son. You'd done everything right so far. Now he feels let down about it. As you'll learn later on in life when favourites fall they fall harder than most. But don't worry about it. He'll get over it. Especially when you start knocking down Huns.'

'If I ever do. You sure he won't want to vet this before it goes to Wing?'

'Absolutely certain. He won't see it, I tell you. He hates paperwork and he's no good at it. That's why he got me here so that I could do it for him. All he wants to do is to fly and bag Huns. Not like a lot of commanding officers of squadrons which I could mention, incidentally. Now for heaven's sake stop brooding and go and get drunk.'

'Uncle, you're a brick. I'll try not to let you down.'

An orderly came in and passed a sheet torn from a message pad to the Recording Officer. Uncle read it, looked up at Stephen and smiled. 'You're going to have your chance sooner than you thought,' he said. 'The squadron's now on a war footing. We go into action tomorrow.'

13

Then began for Stephen a period of nerves, frustration, anxiety—and fear. The first day had been typical. Each flight flew two patrols. Haynes, leading B Flight in the absence of a replacement Flight Commander, bagged a Hun; Shaw with A Flight claimed one out of control. C Flight saw nothing.

It soon became apparent that Davis was a poor patrol leader. Either his eyesight was not what it should have been or else he had no gift for spotting the enemy. Frequently, others in his flight with less experience than himself had to call his attention to the presence of German aeroplanes by flying alongside him, waggling their wings and pointing. When he did engage he invariably opened fire too soon and from too great a distance so that the Huns were given every opportunity to escape. Had it not been for the fact that at this moment in the air war the Germans were suffering from an inferiority in men and machines C Flight would have been badly mauled. But the enemy pilots, especially those in Pfaltz which had the reputation of being unable to stand the strain of dog-fighting with Camels, for the most part avoided combat when they could, even ten miles inside their own lines, where Trenchard's policy of the offensive at all costs decreed that his squadrons should carry out their patrols.

Such engagements that did take place Stephen seemed invariably to miss. Twice he had had to give the dud engine signal and turn back. One of these occasions had been a squadron patrol led by Haynes. During that job, due to their leader's skilful use of cloud and height, a flock of Pfaltz had been brought to battle and five of them had been shot down. Both Clare and Hank had opened their score. Clare's victory had been confirmed while Hank had shared one with Shaw.

Another time his guns had jammed during an inconclusive and largely ineffective dog-fight into which Davis had somehow blundered, and once his engine had died on take-off. He had had to put down quickly into a field in front of him. At least, he told himself, he had not turned back and crashed. He had landed safely without damaging the bus and had walked away from it.

But despite the German lack of offensive spirit or perhaps because of it, the other flights, aggressively and skilfully led by Haynes and Shaw, were doing well. Haynes' personal score was mounting. He now had seven more victories to add to his previous tally of ten and Shaw had five. In one week the squadron shot down fifteen and Wing telephoned its congratulations.

C Flight, however, was not keeping up. Clare, who was anxious to get into the thick of it, cursed Davis continually and would scarcely speak to him in the hut. 'He's just a ruddy Red,' he exploded one evening to Stephen and Hank when they were changing. 'He doesn't want to fight. Look what happened with those Albatros over Ploeq Street yesterday. He didn't want to see them. He's got cold feet, that's his trouble.'

'He must have been a good man once,' Hank said consolingly. 'He was out on F.E.s when they were being shot the hell out of last April. And he came through.'

Davis came in then and put an end to the conversation. Stephen had not joined in. He knew there was a lot of truth in Clare's fulminations but he felt that he was not the person to endorse them. C Flight was not keeping pace with the others and of C Flight he was, he told himself, the most useless and ineffective member.

The following day his engine failed again. It was a broken feed pipe. He put down on an aerodrome near Poperinghe where there was a Canadian Camel squadron whose air mechanics fixed it for him. After a drink in their mess he flew back and landed at Bessières. Haynes was in the squadron office talking to Uncle when he handed in his report. He took it from Uncle and glanced at it. 'Another engine failure,' he growled. 'You seem to be making a habit of it. What was it this time?'

Soon Stephen began to imagine that the whole squadron was looking at him and despising him. He knew that the story of his abortive encounter with the two-seater had got about. Heal would have seen to that, he told himself. Haynes now almost openly ignored him. Nothing would go right. That brief moment of glory after the race had long since faded. He was angry with everyone but most of all with himself.

As a result he kept himself to himself. He did not even join Hank and Clare when on dud days or off days they went into the village or further afield in search of dinners and drinks and feminine company. In his self-imposed loneliness he even began to try to read Davis' books.

Although he did not realise it, his own conduct made his position worse. By isolating himself he produced the very situation he dreaded and made himself the target for looks and remarks.

Clare was not much consolation to him in his troubles, for Clare was preoccupied with his own ambitions and the thwarting of them by Davis. It was the easy-going and kindly Hank who tried to take him out of himself. 'Say, kid, what's eating you?' he said one afternoon when the rain was slanting down. Flying had been cancelled and Stephen was lying on his bed staring at the ceiling.

'I don't seem to be able to make a go of anything,' Stephen said.

'So, you haven't started. What's that to a row of old tin cans? Mannock was a slow starter. Did you know that? And look what he's done.'

'There's a rumour that he's coming out again to take a flight in a squadron,' Clare said. 'Why the hell can't we have him or someone like him instead of that wind-up merchant Davis? How Haynes hasn't rumbled him beats me. He ought to be court-martialled. There's a tender going into St Omer. Let's get out of here and go and split a few bottles.'

'Coming, kid?' Hank asked.

'No thanks, Hank. I don't feel like it. I'll hang around here for a bit.'

When they had gone Stephen picked up *Das Kapital*, opened it and tried to read it. After a minute or two he threw it aside. He put his hands behind his head and stared at the ceiling, listening to the rain drumming on the roof. He too wondered why Haynes went on tolerat-.ing Davis.

What none of them realised was that Davis' reports were models of self-exculpation. Davis' hatred of the authorities combined with his own and his brother's treatment at their hands had made him determined, in so far as it was possible, to ensure that he survived the war so that he could preach his doctrines after it. His command of the written word was such that he was able to write into his reports the implication that it was his flight which was letting him down not, as was the truth, the exact opposite. Reading the reports, Uncle's legal training had made him sense their falseness but they were so cleverly and carefully worded that he could not find in them anything which would justify his bringing the matter before his squadron commander. To his dismay, too, he saw that Haynes, so far from forgetting the incident of Stephen and the two-seater as he had hoped, was turning more and more against his one-time favourite. In fact he was beginning, quite illogically, to attribute C Flight's failure to Stephen, which made him all the more ready to overlook Davis' lack of leadership.

Alone in the hut, Stephen was bored and miserable. He tried *Das Kapital* again and could make nothing of it. Putting it aside he went to the door and opened it. The clouds were low and the rain was still slanting down. He could not even take his bus up to test his guns on the fixed target. The whole afternoon stretched before him with

146

nothing to do. Glumly he wandered over to the mess to read the illus-trated papers. The anteroom was empty. Everyone was evidently either catching up on their paper work or had gone into St Omer in the tender with Clare and Hank. Collecting copies of *La Vie Pari-sienne, The Tatler* and *The Sketch,* he pulled an armchair in front of the stove and sank into it.

The naked beauties of *La Vie* fascinated and tantalised him. He stared at them hungrily. That was another thing which was bothering him. The incessant talk in the mess and out of it about sex and tarts and who had done what and would do with whom on leave and rest days excited him and left him feeling inadequate. He wished now he had not been so scrupulous or so stupid with that woman in Brook Street. The luscious breasts she had flaunted at him came back with startling vividness. He had been a fool to run away. He wouldn't do it again—or would he? Throwing aside *La Vie,* he picked up *The Sketch.*

There were the usual pictures of shows and actresses which he turned over without paying much attention. Then came a page of photographs entitled *Roll of Honour.* Below were portraits of the gallant and distinguished who had been killed in action. As he glanced at them a face which he recognised leapt off the page at him. He had only seen it once but he was unlikely to forget it. It was a head and shoulders portrait. There were wings on the left breast and a row of medal ribbons under-neath them. It was the Australian airman who had been in Murray's with Babs Murtagh.

Captain O.F. Martin, D.S.O., M.C. 717 Squadron A.F.C. he read. *Killed in action February 2nd 1918. Credited with thirty-four enemy aircraft shot down.*

Babs' friend. What had they been to each other? What would this mean to her and where was she now? He longed to see her again. She was someone with whom he could always feel happy and at ease. Her presence, too, brought with it brightness and a sense of eagerness and fun. He remembered that last day together at the Bay and their visit to Massiter's castle. From this his thoughts drifted to the Bay. Would he ever see it again, he wondered, feel its peace envelop him, dream in its beauty and quietness? It was then that the sound of his own name being spoken behind him broke into his thoughts.

'What about young Raymond then?' he heard Haynes' un-mistakable voice say. ''As 'e got cold feet?'

There was a pause, the scratch of a match on a box and the sound of a pipe being puffed. Then Davis' voice came. 'It's very difficult to say. He's given the dud engine signal twice recently. Mag trouble. You know what these bloody magnetos are like. They're always cutting in and out. It's hard to be definite. One at least was genuine, I think.

147

And that fuel pipe breakage was, too, I checked with the Canadians.'

'Heal tells me he came back once saying his guns were jammed. They weren't. Heal says 'e 'adn't pulled up the cocking handle.'

'He can fly all right.'

'It's no bloody use 'is flying' like the Archangel Gabriel if 'e 'asn't got the guts to go in and shoot. That's what matters right now.'

'He's Irish. You never know with them. Perhaps his heart isn't in it.'

'I thought every bloody Irishman was spoiling for a fight. What about Mannock and McCudden? They're Irish, aren't they?'

'They were born into the service. Bred to it. He's a different sort of Irishman. He did say once he didn't know which side he was fighting on.'

''E said that did 'e? Bloody rebel, is 'e? I'd never 'ave thought it. What's 'e doin' 'ere then?'

'I didn't mean that.' Davis obviously thought he had said too much. 'I was only trying to explain. Perhaps he has wind-up. That's the obvious answer.'

'We'll soon see. Wing have been on. There's a squadron patrol at dawn tomorrow. We're to go far over and flush out anything we can see. Wing think the 'Un is moving 'is squadrons into circuses to cover this new push. We're to try and see whether they're 'ere or down south. I'll keep an eye on 'im. You do too.'

They left the mess and Stephen sat on, staring at the squat black body of the stove.

So it was true then. They did think he had cold feet. It was the monstrous unfairness of it all that lighted a cold, slow anger in him. In the first place it hadn't been funk that had stopped him shooting down that L.V.G. It had been compassion. Davis should have understood that if anyone did. Davis, in fact, had made no real effort to defend him. He was, Stephen saw, protecting himself at Stephen's expense, taking the opportunity offered him of switching his own deficiencies on to Stephen. He had even used against him that remark he'd made after the binge when he'd been half-tight. He'd almost forgotten he'd said it until he heard it again. As for that smirking swine Heal—his guns *had* jammed. It was a break-down in the Constantinesco interrupter gear which enabled the guns to fire through the arc of the propeller without hitting it, and he couldn't have cleared it in a million years. Heal must have said that to curry favour with the C.O., knowing Stephen was in his bad books. And he could do nothing about it. He could not go for Heal because that would mean disclosing what he had heard. Damn them all. So there was a squadron offensive patrol at dawn tomorrow, was there? They said he could fly. Decent of them when he could fly rings round anyone in the squadron. Tomorrow he'd show them he could shoot. He got up, left the mess, and walked over to the hangars. He was going to make sure his guns didn't jam this time.

14

In the half-light of the very early morning, Stephen sat in the mess eating a boiled egg and drinking tea. Bleary-eyed with drink or sleep, his fellow pilots sat around him. Beyond a request to pass the salt or the milk no one spoke very much. One or two made forced jokes or conversation which was greeted in silence. The early-morning job was always inclined to be a twitchy business and this, as they all knew, was to be a deep offensive patrol. They were to go in looking for trouble so as to identify for Wing, if they could, in what strength the enemy were along this portion of the front. Haynes would seek out the Huns and bring them to action if any man could and in all probability they would have to fight their way back.

After breakfast Stephen returned to the hut. He pulled on his flying suit and wound a scarf round his neck. Taking his helmet and goggles he made his way towards the line of waiting Camels.

Somewhere buried deep in Stephen was a strain of his mother's hardness and ruthlessness. It had come out in him with his final dealings with Conway when he had bowled at him to hurt, and it was in control of him now. Concentrate, he said to himself as he had been accustomed to say when he was shooting snipe and shooting well—concentrate. He had only one aim: to show these doubting bastards that he was not a coward and that anything they could do he could do better. He walked past where Heal was standing by the machines without noticing him or nodding to him, and climbed into his Camel. Reaching down he pulled up the handle on the Constantinesco reservoir. When it had sunk back into position to indicate that the gear was functioning normally he snapped down the cocking levers of the guns. Heal was not going to be able to say this time that he had not activated them. He confirmed that the magneto switches were off and methodically went through the starting drill. Then he was ready.

'Contact!' The ack emma swung the prop. The rotary engine coughed and fired. He blipped it and taxied out. Setting the fine adjustment, he checked the wind and turned into it. Then the throttle wide open; the wheels left the grass; he was over the fence and soaring

150

up in a climbing turn.

The squadron formed up at three thousand feet, Haynes at its head, his leader's streamers taut in his slipstream. Archie—the German Ack Ack—greeted them as they crossed the lines. Black bursts appeared all around them. Archie rarely hit anything but the 'Woof!' and 'Wang!' as the shells burst and the dangerous click and crash of a near one added to the general strain on an airman's nerves and courage.

Haynes kept climbing steadily. Soon they were deep into Hunland. Each one of them was constantly scanning the sky about them, turning their heads this way and that to search for the presence of hostile aeroplanes and from time to time covering the ball of the sun with thumb or hand to try to spot Huns lurking in its shelter and ready to pounce.

On Davis' left Stephen sat watching the sky. His engine was running sweetly. No mag trouble this trip. His guns were loaded. He was ready. On either side of him Clare's and Hank's Camels lifted and swayed in the thin air of the heights. He kept one eye always on Haynes as they penetrated further and further into enemy territory.

But there seemed to be no Huns about. Maybe they had all gone south for the new push. Even as he thought that, Stephen saw Haynes waggle his wings. At first, look as he might, he failed to spot the enemy. Then, there they were, to his left and below the squadron, a cluster of black crosses against a huge white cumulus, for all the world like flies on a tablecloth. They did not seem to have seen the Camels yet. Haynes climbed to get more height.

Stephen's mouth was dry. In an instant he would be in action. He was going to find out whether he could kill or would be killed. This was it then. He'd show them.

Haynes went down in a screaming dive. The whole squadron tumbled out of the sky after him.

The German leader turned to meet them. Whoever he was he did not shirk combat as so many of them did at this stage. He was ready and willing to engage. His followers grew from specks into aeroplanes frighteningly quickly. They came up at them as if lifted on strings. Christ, they were triplanes! Tripes! Richthofen's lot! No. Couldn't be, they said he had changed to Albatros because the triplane's wings were prone to come off in a dive. Or was that another rumour? Maybe he was there. If so they were in for trouble. Shut up. Stop your thoughts running away with you. Concentrate. Concentrate. Then they were into them and the world was full of milling aeroplanes.

A red triplane with black and white chequerboards along its fuselage flashed across in front of Stephen. He kicked the rudder bar. It was a full deflection shot. His fingers squeezed the triggers. The twin Vickers chattered and he saw his bullets hosing down the length of the enemy from prop to cockpit. A burst of flame shot out of the engine. The triplane reared up. The pilot flung a hand in front of his face as the flames licked back at him. Then it plunged away and down gushing black smoke and flame. He'd got one!

Rat-tat-tat. Rat-tat-tat. A rent appeared in his lower wing; something tugged at the shoulder of his sidcot. One of them was on his tail. He shoved the stick over into a tight turn. The Boche was on his tail all right and after his blood. Well, a Camel could out-turn anything, even a triplane. Or could it? He'd soon see. At least he hadn't dived away. The turn had been the instinctive result of those lectures at Ayr and the mock dog-fights with Haynes. Concentrate. The bastard was taking pot shots at him. Turn, turn, turn, as tight as you can make them. By God, he had out-turned him. Bastard couldn't fly. Frightened his wings would come off more than likely. Anyway there he was bang in front of him. Let him have it. The twin Vickers chattered again. Pieces flew off the triplane's centre section. The top wings folded like a broken butterfly and it crumpled earthwards, pieces falling from it as it went. Two! A brace! This was like shooting snipe! Exhilaration gripped him and then again came that deadly rat-tat-tat behind him. Another of the bastards was after him. Turn, for God's sake—turn. As he did so a Camel with streamers on its struts shot down from above. There was a chatter of guns. The Tripe on his tail spiralled down in front of him flames bursting from it. Haynes had picked him off and scored another victory. And then, as quickly as it had all begun, the sky emptied. Stephen looked about him. Above him and to the east he saw three Camels and climbed to meet them. As he did so he was joined by another. It was Clare, who waved to him.

Then a Camel with leader's streamers picked them up. They formed on him and resumed the patrol. After another thirty minutes Haynes turned for home. Except for the Archie, which they twisted and turned to avoid, the return flight was uneventful. Once down they crowded round Haynes, talking about the flight.

'They're weak on this front,' Stephen heard Haynes saying to Shaw. 'They must be. Apart from that scrap we met no opposition. There were six Pfaltz over Roubaix but they scarpered too quick for us. There was nothing else. They must be reinforcing down south.' He broke off to watch a Camel coming in. The approach was far too fast. The pilot despairingly tried to lose flying speed. He came in over the fence, stalled low down and stood on his nose. 'Masters again,' Haynes said. 'Mutton-fisted bugger. He's cost us more planes than the 'Uns. Don't know 'ow 'e ever got out on Camels.'

'That was a good scrap,' Shaw said. 'Those Tripes put up a stout show. How many did we get?'

'I got one certain, a flamer. Young Raymond bagged a brace.' He turned to Stephen. 'A right and left,' he said. 'And I'll confirm 'em for

152

you. That's the stuff, me lad. I was beginning to think you 'adn't got it in you.'

That night his name was chalked in on the scoreboard in the mess. But the sight of the German pilot throwing his hand over his face to shield it from the flames was still with him when the jubilation had died and the reaction had set in. After dinner for the first time in his life he got very drunk on whisky.

15

Stephen sat in the cockpit of his Camel at eight thousand feet and watched his leader's streamers, above him and to the right. To his left was Clare; behind and to their right Hank and the ham-handed Masters.

His own Camel had a damaged undercarriage and he was flying someone else's. It always took him a little time to get accustomed to a different bus for, Camels being what they were, each one had varying characteristics. But this one seemed to handle well enough. He had, however, noticed with disgust that the padding on the right-hand gun was worn and thin, and mentally cursed Heal's idleness in not having it replaced.

He was an experienced pilot now. Six weeks had gone by and he had survived. He had done more than survive for he had nine Huns to his credit. Haynes said that he was the best shot in the squadron and in a way it was true. It *was* all a bit like shooting snipe and on his good days he did not seem to be able to miss. Moreover the fact that his life depended on it compelled concentration and with concentration, as it had done in those long-ago days in the snipe bog, came success.

The squadron as a whole had been lucky. The anticipated German push had fallen on the Fifth Army on March 21 and many fighter squadrons had been moved south to meet it. This meant their being employed in low work—trench strafing and bombing which everyone loathed and dreaded. Two forty-five had, however, been kept up north. Uncle, who had with Haynes attended one of the conferences when plans were being outlined, told Stephen that the C-in-C was still concerned about a possible drive for the Channel ports. The squadron's task was, therefore, to ascertain by reconnaissance whether there were any troop concentrations in the area and also to maintain 'command of the air' on this front so as to prevent the enemy in his turn obtaining information as to the movement of British troops.

Because there were only a few fighter squadrons left to fulfil these tasks and since the days were lengthening, they flew long hours, three

154

or sometimes four patrols a day, and, although the crack German formations and pilots, Richthofen amongst them, were all down south, the strain of war, of constant alertness, of sudden and intense combat was always with them.

On this front the Germans had mostly to be sought and brought to battle. They seldom attacked themselves and when they did their tactic was to use overwhelming numbers, to mass their machines and to strike down out of the sun. The squadron had had losses but not many. One man from C Flight whom Stephen scarcely knew had gone down in flames in a dog-fight; B Flight had lost their new commander who had simply disappeared and been posted as missing. His replacement, a round jolly man, had arrived and made himself popular with everybody and seemed to be doing well. Shaw had had two casualties in A Flight. Against these the squadron could put a formidable tally of victories.

It was, of course, Haynes who inspired them and carried them to their successes. He was a leader and he was in love with flying. Every opportunity he had he was in the air leading the squadron or going out on his own in search of Huns. He was cunning and he was quick and he was a deadly shot. The speed of his reactions in a dog-fight, the way he could pick a target, destroy it in one swift, killing burst and then switch to another, never ceased to astonish Stephen. He knew now that he himself was above average both as a pilot and as a shot but he also realised that he could never hope to rival Haynes. Huns might be scarce on that sector of the front but somehow Haynes sought them out and found them. His score went up from twenty to twenty-five. A bar to his M.C. came and more congratulations from Wing.

Sometimes Stephen thought his C.O. was driven on by demons. He was determined, Stephen was sure, to show what he could do with the squadron for which he had waited so long, and in addition his mounting score of victories was bringing with them the ambition to make himself the highest scoring Camel pilot in France. Stephen had heard how these supermen became hypnotised by their scores and he thought that he saw this beginning to happen with Haynes. Whenever he entered the mess his eyes went first to the personal scoreboard as if seeking some reassurance there that his name stood well on top. Shaw, who scarcely ever spoke and spent his spare time doing flight commander's paperwork or tinkering with his bus, was second with fifteen, and Stephen, to his great surprise, came third on the list.

Davis, too, had survived. The squadron's present task might have been made for him. If he was careful he could avoid action almost at will. Clare's fury with him grew greater every day for Clare, too, had ambitions. He was as near to being openly rude to his flight commander as was possible without being insubordinate. In the mess he

155

looked down his aquiline nose at him or surveyed him bleakly and dismissively through his eye-glass. Much of Clare's patrician manner had been stripped away by the strain of war which was indeed beginning to tell on all of them, each in his own way. A few days before Davis had been complaining about the shortcomings of the Camel and its lack of performance compared with the S.E. 'When are we going to get Snipes?' he had said. 'They've been off the drawing-board for months. It's the bosses. They won't let them be built. It's cheaper to build Camels rather than develop something new. All they care about is their profits. It doesn't matter to them if they go on sending out obsolete machines for the fighting man to be killed in. They don't worry. They only feed on us and get fatter—'

Clare had turned on him savagely. 'It's not the bosses,' he said. 'It's your friends the strikers. They're the people who want the profits. Higher wages and to hell with the man at the front. And as for fighting and getting killed it seems to me you're scarcely the one to—'

Stephen opened his mouth to speak. Clare had gone too far this time. But it was Hank who avoided the trouble which hasty words might have brought. He was washing in a corner of the hut. There was a crash as the whole washstand tilted over and fell to the floor. Water poured round their feet.

'Look out,' Stephen shouted. 'Those are my best shoes!'

Everyone grabbed their belongings to avoid the flood. 'Gee, boys, guess I'm sure sorry,' Hank said as he bent to pick up the remains. Catching Stephen's eye as he did so he gave him a broad wink.

Clare, however, was not placated. 'I'm going to look over my bus for tomorrow,' he said shortly and left the hut.

There were strains, too, in the friendship between Clare and Stephen. Clare was not a natural shot and despite spending hours firing at the stationary target laid out beyond the hangars he did not seem to improve. He had four Huns to his credit but two of these had been shared with Hank. Stephen knew that Clare envied him his success and was jealous of the fact that Haynes took him up 'Hun-hunting' alone and that it was from these expeditions most of Stephen's victories had come. At times, Clare's airs and graces would return and he would drawl remarks about 'Palace favourites' and 'Our Major 'Aynes and his left half-section Deadshot Stephen'.

It was the quiet-spoken, easy-going Hank who kept the three of them together. He was always ready with some new drink or new joke to make them laugh. 'We're alive. We're running our luck, don't push it,' he would say to Clare when he was becoming ever more indignant about Davis' lack of offensive spirit.

But Haynes was at last becoming aware of Davis' deficiencies. The previous afternoon had been wet and cloudy and all flying had been cancelled. Haynes had spent it with Uncle poring over C Flight's records. From them it had been easy to see that such scores as had been made by its individual members had come not from C Flight's patrols but in squadron or individual shows. 'Not enough 'Uns,' he had said to Uncle and had sent for Davis. From the interview Davis had emerged looking pensive and had returned to the hut to immerse himself in his books and letter-writing.

They were fairly far over, much further than usual with Davis leading, Stephen thought. He hoped Davis was keeping a good look-out. At this depth with everything in their favour the Huns might well attack. As these thoughts went through his mind he saw a whole flock of Pfaltz crossing in front of them dead ahead. Automatically Stephen turned to search the sun, covering its ball with his thumb. They were there all right, the rest of them, black specks, high up, lurking in the shelter of the sun, waiting.

But Davis had not stayed to look for them. He was diving on the Pfaltz. Uselessly Stephen shouted a warning. Davis was leading them into a trap and there was nothing he could do. Clare had seen them too. Stephen saw him firing his guns in a hopeless effort to attract Davis' attention. But Davis was going straight on down. Half-turned in his seat Stephen watched the others high-up in the sun. Perhaps they'd stay there; perhaps they hadn't seen them. But they had. There were ten or more of them and they were coming down like murder with all the advantage of height and sun behind them.

The Pfaltz were trying to get away. They'd done their work. One of them was slap in his sights. Stephen's guns chattered and the Hun dived away. A Pfaltz could out-dive a Camel but this one wasn't going to. It was a perfect non-deflection shot. 'Got you, my beauty, anyway,' Stephen muttered as he fired again. The Pfaltz fell away and went into a spin, smoke pouring from it.

A machine with a nose like a shark and painted all the colours of the rainbow came down on him from above. Albatros! Where had they sprung from? They were supposed to be all down south helping Ludendorff and killing Camels doing low work. He fired and missed. Rat-tat-tat. There it was again, that deadly sound from behind. He keeled over into the steepest turn he could hold. Albatros were all about them and the criss-cross of tracer was everywhere. Beside him he had a glimpse of a Camel going down in flames. That was what was going to happen to them all. This was it. They'd be wiped out. They hadn't a hope. Damn Davis and damn him again and all his works. He was turning now as he had never turned before. But they seemed to be shooting at him from all angles. Was he the only one left? No, there was another Camel in the scrap and occupying some of them. He supposed he could go on turning until he got tired or they did or he ran out of petrol. But if there were enough of them they'd be bound to

157

break his circle. In fact that's just what they were doing. Something hit one of the guns and went screaming off; another smashed his Aldis sight.

Then six aircraft that had not been there before appeared from nowhere. More Huns. So they *were* done for. But those weren't Huns. There were roundels on their fuselages. They were S.E.s! An Albatros plummeted past him going down fast, spinning and trailing smoke. A second later there was the hell of a clang in front of him: the engine coughed once and stopped. That last burst he had taken must have hit something vital.

He put the nose down and looked around him. The dog-fight had disappeared. He was alone in the empty sky. Thank God for that and thank God, too, for the S.E.s. But he had to get back, and where were the lines?

The wind for once was in the east so they had drifted towards friendly territory during the fight. Shortly he began to pick up landmarks. In a minute or two Zillebeke Lake and the smoking ruin of Ypres came into view. He was easy meat for any Huns that came along, but, since he was nearing his own lines, with any luck they wouldn't. He looked around again. The sky was still empty.

He was beginning to lose height fast. There was no sound save for the sighing of the wind in the wires. Clearly now he could see the lines and the torn, pock-marked soil stretching back from either side of them. Holding the Camel at the extreme edge of her gliding angle he came down as slowly as he dared. He was a sitting duck for Archie but for some reason Archie was silent. Looking for bigger game perhaps.

The lines were coming up and a German machine gun was shooting at him. They were letting fly with everything they had. The whole bus shuddered as something smashed into the fuselage behind his seat. Another one like that and he'd break up in the air.

Then he was over and across. He was safe now if he could put her down. He had no height at all. There seemed to be the hell of a lot of mud round here. It would have to be a pancake landing. Concentrate. Easy now. Gently he held the stick back. The nose came up, the Camel dropped, hit and turned over.

Stephen was thrown forward. His head struck the offside Vickers in the exact spot where the padding was weak. 'I'll murder that bastard Heal', was his last thought before he passed out.

The blackout only lasted a minute or two and when he came to he found he was hanging, held by the safety belt, head down in a shell hole. Loosening the belt he crawled out. Then he remembered the watch. They always said if you crash get the watch and bring it back for it was the first thing the troops stole from the wreck. Bending down, he freed it from the instrument panel and put it in his pocket. After that he clawed and slithered his way through the mud to the edge of the shell hole. A few yards away a communication trench ran back from the front line. A head popped above the sandbag parapet and a voice shouted, 'Run like 'ell, sir.'

A shell came over and burst a few yards from the crashed Camel. Stephen jumped out of the hole and tumbled into the trench. A sergeant in a tin helmet helped him to his feet. 'Are you 'it, sir?' he asked.

'No, I'm all right. Got a bit of a bang on the head, that's all.'

'I'll take you to the officer, sir. He'll want to see you.' He led the way up the communication trench and turned into the front line. After rounding a couple of traverses he stopped and drew aside the gas curtain at the entrance to a dug-out. Pulling off his helmet Stephen went down the steps.

'One of our gallant aviators,' a faintly mocking voice said.

Peering through the murky light of the dug-out Stephen saw a man with Captain's pips on his shoulders pouring whisky into an enamel mug.

'Have some whisky,' the infantry man said. 'I expect you could do with it.' He pushed across the mug and Stephen gulped it gratefully. Reaction was setting in; his knees were shaking and his head felt muzzy.

The captain refilled their mugs. 'How many Germans have you shot down?' he asked.

They all ask this, Stephen thought. 'Nine,' he said. 'Ten if the one I got today is confirmed.'

'Ten dead Germans. Ten little niggers,' the infantry captain said. 'All dead, and we'll all be dead soon enough. Yes, sergeant, what is it?' An N.C.O. had appeared at the entrance to the dug-out.

'Battalion Headquarters. The Colonel's on the line, sir.'

Stephen finished his second large portion of whisky and put down the mug. 'Thanks for the drink,' he said. 'I'd better be getting back.'

In the trench a Tommy on the firestep was staring up at the sky where an R.E.8 was droning homeward from an artillery observation job. 'There 'e goes,' he said. 'Back to 'is nice warm bawth.'

Stephen laughed. It was always interesting to hear the other chap's idea of your job. He wouldn't be in the trenches, he told himself, for all the gold in the Bank of England. Then he began to make his way down one of the communication trenches. After trudging for what seemed miles he came out on to a road and flagged down an A.S.C. tender. This took him to a Service Corps mess where he phoned the squadron for transport. The Service Corps officers plied him with drink, asked him what it was like to fly a Camel and how many Huns he had shot down. His head was definitely feeling most peculiar now and he was not sure whether it was the whisky or the knock it had taken. A large and painful bump was forming on his forehead where it had hit the gun-butt.

The squadron tender arrived at last. It was late when he got back. Clare was sitting on his bed holding a glass of whisky in his hand. 'So you're back,' he said dully. 'We heard you were O.K. Some Service Corps people rang up. Have you got the watch?'

'Yes.' Taking it from his pocket, Stephen threw it on the bed. 'What happened to the others?'

'Masters has gone west. In flames. Hank's missing. There's been no news. He must have gone too.'

'Hank! Oh, God.'

'It's that bastard Davis. He led us into it. Damn and blast him to hell. He killed Hank as surely as if he'd shot him down himself. He killed him, I tell you.' Clare's voice became shrill.

Stephen sat down heavily on his bed. His head was throbbing; and he thought he was beginning to see double. Certainly his vision was hazy round the edges. So Hank had gone, kindly pleasant Hank who had a good word for everyone in his slow New England drawl. He looked at the bed and washstand in the corner with its shaving articles still laid out on it. Soon they would have the melancholy job of going through his effects. 'And Davis?' he said dully. 'What about him?'

'What do you think? He got back all right. Nice safe blighty one in the shoulder. He's gone off to C.C.S. with a happy smile on his face to preach revolution to his striker pals at home.'

'Anyway he's gone. I wonder who we'll get.'

'Whoever we do he couldn't be worse. Poor old Hank.'

There was something nagging at the back of Stephen's mind. Mentally he mulled it over and then he understood what it was. 'Did you see that one I got? Can you confirm it?' he said.

'No, I can't confirm it. You're always going on about your score. What the hell does your score matter? Hank's gone and that's what matters. You and Major 'Aynes, you're both so bloody busy about your score that you think of nothing else. 'Aynes should have unstuck Davis weeks ago if he'd been doing his job instead of counting how many Huns he'd shot down.'

'That's bloody unfair. In the end it's the number of Huns a squadron gets that matters. We've shot down as many as any other Camel squadron and more than most. Haynes is the best patrol leader in the business. You wouldn't want to change him for your old Colonel, would you, even if he doesn't speak the King's English?'

'The King's English? So that's how it is—' Clare's voice had taken on a dangerous edge to it. 'Davis has brought you round to his way of thinking, has he? And that's not the first time you've slung my old Colonel in my teeth. Let me tell you I don't much care about it—'

The door was flung open behind them. 'Say, you guys angry about something?' a well-known voice said.

'Hank!' They both sprang to their feet. 'Hank! We were sure you'd

160

gone west. Where were you? What happened to you?' They dragged him into the hut, slapping him on the back and cheering him in their relief and delight in seeing him safe.

'I've been doing a little serious drinking with my friends and fellow countrymen,' Hank said, and told them of his adventures. His bus had been shot as full of holes as a collander and his engine had conked. He had escaped into a cloud, come out of it completely lost and just managed to get down into a field up north, fortunately on the right side of the lines. Some villagers had taken him to a nearby aerodrome. It turned out to be the home of a Camel squadron, several of whose pilots were American volunteers like himself. They had greeted him uproariously, swapped yarns, filled him with drink and forgotten to telephone his whereabouts. Finally the squadron commander had intervened and had sent him home in his car.

'Did you bring back the watch?' Stephen said.

'Sweet Christopher, I forgot. What will the C.O. say? What happened to your head?'

'That bastard Heal didn't replace a worn pad and I hit the gun-butt when I force-landed.'

'All this talking makes me thirsty. Any whisky left in this place? Strong drink is raging so they say, so let it rage say I.'

They invaded the mess and called for whisky. There appeared now to be a sort of curtain between Stephen and everything else and he was having difficulty with his speech. After a few more drinks he was not making any sense at all. When he began to fall over the furniture, they took him off and put him to bed.

Next morning Stephen had no recollection of the events of the night before. In fact he had only a very hazy memory of anything that had happened after he had left the dug-out. There was a foul taste in his mouth. When he tried to get up he found that he had difficulty in focusing his eyes, that his head seemed about to fall off and that he appeared to be moving through a haze mostly comprised of cotton-wool.

Hank took him firmly by the shoulder and pushed him back on the bed. 'Stay there,' he said. 'I'm going to see the M.O. has a look at you.'

'I'm all right,' Stephen said. 'I don't want any damn M.O. If he puts me off duty I'll get posted away. I'm O.K., I tell you.'

'If you're all right my old man's a monkey. My guess is you've got concussion. That's how you acted last night for sure.'

'What did I do?'

'You were going to get Heal court-martialled or keel-hauled or hung, drawn and quartered, you say it, you take your choice. You said it times over and in spades.'

Stephen made another attempt to get up. The hut revolved around

161

him. It was no good; he could not get up and dress and he realised it. But he was determined not to let the M.O. see him. If he were to be posted away as sick the chances were he'd never get back to the squadron. The squadron was where his friends were. Friends kept you going.

'O.K. then,' Hank said. 'But you'll be off flying. We've no flight commander so I'll have to see the C.O.'

'No doctor, damn you, Hank.'

'I'll tell the C.O. that's what you say. He's not a great one for doctors himself, I guess.'

Stephen lay back and closed his eyes. An orderly came in with tea and biscuits from the mess. There was the noise of engines taking off as one of the flights went on a job. Stephen dozed and sipped the tea. Gradually his head cleared. About lunchtime the door opened and Haynes came in.

'Well then,' he said. ' 'Ow are you now?'

'Better. I'm sure I could fly.'

'And I'm bloody sure you can't from what Jarman tells me, and I'm the one that decides that round 'ere. You're off flying for today anyway. Bang on the 'ead, was it? Jarman says the padding 'ad gone soft.'

'Yes. I got down in a shell hole and turned arse over tip.'

'I've sent some ack emmas up to see what they can find if the 'Uns have left anything. I'll 'ave a word with Heal about that padding. Jarman says you don't want the M.O.? I can send for the Wing M.O. you know.'

'I don't want to leave the squadron. They'll think I've got cold feet.'

'Not with ten 'Uns, they won't.'

'Ten? Who confirmed it?'

'Davis before 'e went. I'll 'ave another look at you tomorrow. No liquor, mind. Did nobody in racing never tell you whisky and bangs on the 'ead don't mix?'

Stephen dozed and slept for the remainder of the day. Next morning his head felt clearer and he insisted on getting up. He was still shaky on his feet but the cotton-wool which had surrounded him the day before had disappeared. After breakfast Haynes sent for him.

'And 'ow are you now?' he asked, picking up a pile of returns and throwing them across the table to Uncle who was sitting opposite.

'Quite fit again, sir.'

'That so? You still look groggy enough to me. Now listen 'ere, me lad. Some American general has sent for Jarman. He's his uncle or 'is father's cousin or 'is brother-in-law or something. Wants 'im to be 'is A.D.C. Jarman says 'e won't go but orders 'as come through for 'im to report to Paris today. The Brass 'At is sending his car for 'im. Do you

162

follow me?'

'Not exactly, sir. Is Hank going to be posted away?'

'Not if he or I can 'elp it. But 'ere's a chance for me to stop you flying and dodge the doctor for a day or two. I'm sending you down with 'im. Officially you've gone to St Omer to pick up a replacement bus. You can take forty-eight hours doing it by way of Paree, see?'

'Yes, sir. Thanks.'

'Know anywhere to stay?'

'No, sir.'

' 'Ere's an address. It's clean and it's cheap and it's a good place to take a woman and don't say that won't bother you because it ought ter.'

Stephen felt himself blushing. An ace—or nearly one with ten victories—and never had a woman! He saw Haynes looking at him, grinning.

'Know what the Frogs say are the four words of love?'

'I'm afraid not, sir.'

'*Touche, bouche, louche, douche*—understand?'

'I think so, sir.'

'If you go on with much more of that sirring you'll start shitting yourself. You don't want to leave the squadron?'

'No, s— No, I don't.'

'Glad to 'ear it. You've been in since the beginning, you and the other two. And, Raymond?'

'Yes—Yes, Major.' What on earth was coming next, Stephen wondered.

Haynes was looking at him with a broad grin on his face. 'Congratulations on your M.C.,' he said.

If he had been in a daze before, Stephen was doubly so now as he walked towards the hut. It seemed the whole squadron knew before he did. Those who weren't on jobs crowded round congratulating him. He was touched that they all seemed genuinely pleased. The awards had come through from Wing the night before. Haynes had a D.S.O. and Shaw a bar to his M.C. There would be an immortal binge tonight. With his head, he was just as well out of it. Perhaps Haynes had thought of that, too.

Back in his hut, he began to take off the oil-stained tunic he wore for day-to-day flying. He was very proud of those oil stains for they stamped him as a veteran. The older and dirtier a tunic became it also became an emblem of experience and seniority. But it would hardly do for Paris. Taking up his best R.F.C. jacket, he found that Hank had already had someone stitch the purple and white ribbon below the wings. It was typical of Hank to take that trouble, he thought, as he looked proudly down at the decoration. He certainly had never believed he could win one. Briefly for a second he allowed his thoughts to dwell on the look of astonishment that would cross his sister's face when she heard the news.

Then there was only just time to push his overnight things into a bag before the U.S. staff car arrived.

An American sergeant in one of their tall cowboy hats stepped out, saluted and opened the door of the back seat for them. The two young officers got in and, amidst friendly jeers and catcalls from their fellow pilots, were borne off on the long road to Paris.

'I don't give a good Goddam what the old man says,' Hank said vehemently to Stephen as they went. 'I'm not going to leave the squadron. He can't make me. I came over to fight not to push a desk. You guys have meant it all to me. I like the British. You've made me one of yourselves, no kidding.'

Stephen thought of pointing out that he was not British or only half-British or only British when he was at home, but it didn't seem to matter at this juncture. He was a member of 245 squadron as was Hank. They were fighting a war together. That was what mattered. 'I'm not going to leave the squadron either,' he said.

'He's a great guy, Haynes,' Hank was going on. 'He's made the squadron. We weren't too hot when we started, you know. What about the flight now Davis has gone? Will they give it to you?'

'Me?' Stephen sat up, startled. 'I hadn't thought of that. No, I'm sure they won't. I'm far too young. Anyway, I don't want it. I couldn't shove you and Clare about.'

'Say, listen, I'm sharing a suite at the Crillon with the old man. Why don't you move in there? It'll all be on Uncle Sam.'

'No thanks, Hank. Those Brass Hats would terrify me. I'll try the address Haynes gave me.'

'O.K. then but there's a party tonight. Come to that anyway. Could even be horizontal talent about. I'll mix the drinks.'

'You do that and you're dead sure of a return ticket to the squadron.'

Stephen was in two minds whether to go to the party or not. There would be Brass Hats abounding, he felt sure, and his one encounter with a general at the presentation of the Yeomanry Cup had not left him with any very kindly feeling towards high senior officers. Apart from that, much of what Davis had said coupled with his own experiences had convinced him that the higher direction of the war was mostly in the hands of fools or knaves. He had seen too many pointless offensive patrols, and the squandering of men and machines that should have been husbanded, to think otherwise. Moreover whether Davis was right and that it was due to the bosses or Clare that the fault lay with the workers, the plain fact was that they were not getting the Snipes they had been promised. And whatever Haynes might say the

164

Camel was becoming obsolete. There were rumours that the Germans were waiting for the new Fokker which was said to be something special and if they got it before the Camel squadrons were re-equipped with Snipes it would be April 1917 all over again.

On the other hand the cold air in the back of the general's Cadillac had been a tonic. He was feeling fit again. For two nights he could sleep undisturbed by the thoughts of tomorrow's jobs. He had two days before him free from the strain of constant watchfulness in a hostile sky, of the bang and bark of Archie and the deadly rat-tat-tat of Spandau guns. He luxuriated in a warm bath and decided to go.

The party was in full swing when he arrived. Hank introduced him to the general, a tall scholarly-looking man with greying hair, in the drab, high-collared American uniform. There were many smart and soignée women who were after bigger game than a young and naïve Flying Corps lieutenant, and an M.C. carried little weight here amidst the galaxy of orders and decorations splashed across important chests underneath red-tabbed collars. Feeling shy and lost he stood by himself fiddling with a cigarette. A waiter came by balancing a tray of champagne glasses. He helped himself to one and took a deep swallow. He finished it and took another. He wondered what would happen if he tried to start a conversation with any of these intimidating women. Were they all French? Should he use Haynes' remark as an opening gambit? He grinned to himself and reached for another glass. As he did so he heard a voice beside him say: 'And how are things at the Bay?'

Turning, he saw her. 'Babs!' he exclaimed. 'Babs!'

'Stephen—and a medal too!'

'It came up with the rations. Babs—how wonderful.' He put out a hand to touch her as if to reassure himself she was real.

Isolated in that roomful of people, they stared into each other's eyes. Something electric passed between them. They both knew then with an unspoken certainty what was happening.

Stephen put down his glass. 'Let's get out of here, quick,' he said.

They found a restaurant. It was in a tiny cobbled courtyard off a street leading from the Place de la Concorde. Because he knew of no other wine Stephen ordered champagne. They drank and laughed. She, too, he learnt, was on a forty-eight-hour pass and he never bothered to ask who had brought her or how she came to be at the party.

Afterwards, by some miracle in that darkened, sombre city, they found a taxi willing to take them to Stephen's hotel. The bed in the room was warm and wide and inviting. They fell into it together, hungrily embracing.

Later she lay in the crook of his arm and they slept. When he awoke it was early morning. Putting out a hand to reassure himself that she was still there and that it had not all been a glorious fantasy he found the bed empty. He sat up and brushed the sleep from his eyes.

She was standing by the window, naked, looking out over the roofs of Paris. The morning sun bathed her whole body in a golden glow. She turned to face him and smiled. He stared at her in a surge of wonder and desire.

'Come here,' he said.

He pulled her towards him down into the bed. 'God, I'm lucky,' he whispered. 'How lucky I've been to find you.'

'We've found each other,' she said.

For the remainder of the leave they scarcely left the room, caught up in each other, exploring, revelling in themselves and their bodies. Though they tried to hide it, there was, too, something desperate about their love-making, for behind it lay the knowledge that this might be the last as well as the first time. Even in Paris they could hear the muted roar of the guns.

That she was the more experienced of the two Stephen knew and accepted. From the first it had been she who had guided him, helped him and taught him. He asked no questions. The present was enough. Those would come later if at all.

And then it was time to pack up and part, to return to the squadron and to concentration and strain and to the nagging dread, however much you tried to push it away or disguise it, that death would claim you somewhere, some day, over the lines.

Stephen put on his Sam Browne and straightened his tunic. Together they went downstairs, out through the little foyer and into the street. It was a day of brilliant sunshine; the air had the translucence of Paris in the spring. From the café across the street came the aroma of roasting coffee and croissants. A camion laden with Poilus rumbled by.

'I love you, Stephen,' she said. 'Come back to me.'

He watched her walk away from him, the trim figure that had been so passionate in his arms a few hours back, very straight in its severe uniform. She turned the corner and was gone.

As arranged, Hank was waiting for him at the Crillon. He was in high spirits. 'You can't win this war without me,' he said. 'I'm coming back with you.'

'The Brass Hat has relented, has he?'

'I told him he wouldn't want you guys to think his sister's son was yellow. But I really got to him when I asked him what way he'd have gone when he was a shavetail in the Philippines if they'd offered him a desk job. So here we go and look at the goodies I've got.'

In the hall were two cases of champagne and an assortment of hampers filled with the loot of the best Paris food-shops. And the general had been so pleased with Hank's enthusiasm for the war that he had again put his car at their disposal.

At St Omer Stephen found the replacement Camel ready for him. He lunched in the mess, signed the clearance papers and took off.

The brilliance of the day had not faded. The sky was a deep cloudless blue stretching from the earth to infinity. As he walked out to the machine Stephen heard a lark singing. Spring was on the way. He was still filled with the wonder and glory of what had happened to him and the day fitted well with his spirits.

He pointed the nose of the Camel up into the blue. Once he had height he dived and looped. Again and again he went up and over just for the joy of it. Then he half-rolled off the top and dived towards the ground. Picking up landmarks he contour-chased home. In a field he saw a platoon being drilled. Skimming over the hedge he flew straight at them. They scattered like toy soldiers. He chased a car along a road. It ran for safety into a coppice and his wheels brushed the tops of the trees as he pulled up to clear them.

Then he was over the aerodrome. The field was empty save for a lone figure crossing from the hangars to the mess. He dived on it. His wheels were all but touching the grass. The roar of the engine made the walking man look up. Then he threw himself flat. Stephen zoomed, half-rolled and came back again. The figure was making with what dignity it could for the sanctuary of the mess building. Two yards from the doorway Stephen flattened it again. He came round on one wing to see a booted leg disappearing into the doorway and the door being firmly shut. He landed laughing.

Heal came up to him as he left his machine. 'The C.O. has spoken to me about that pad on the gun,' he said.

There was something particularly oily about Heal that always made Stephen bridle. 'Did he?' he said. 'Bloody bad show, I call it. It nearly did me in.'

'That's not the point. You had no right to complain behind my back and I won't forget it. In any event it was Corporal Bates' machine and I've had him on the mat about it.'

The old army law, Stephen thought. When you get kicked, kick someone lower down. Basically it was Heal's responsibility whether or not it was Bates' machine. And he hadn't complained; he'd done a bit of drunken talking, that was all. But he was too happy to bother further about Heal. After all, though he couldn't know it, Heal had just given him the most wonderful forty-eight hours of his life.

In the hut he found Clare packing. 'What's up?' he asked him.

'The Huns have made another push. We're moving. We've got a new flight commander, too. They say he's a fire-eater. I think you've met him.' Clare gave one of his slightly malicious smiles.

'Met him? I've only just landed.'

'That's it. Saw you through the window. With that pretty bit of flying of yours you flattened him or thereabouts.'

'Christ! Anyway I'd better tell Uncle I'm back.'

Haynes was with Uncle in the squadron office. The recording officer was sorting records and files and packing them up for the move. Haynes had his feet on the trestle table and was making caustic remarks about the amount of paper it took to fight a war. 'So you're back,' he greeted Stephen. 'What about Jarman?'

'He's on his way in the general's car. Told him the British couldn't win the war without him and the Brass Hat believed it. Oh, and he's got two cases of champagne with him and a few hampers. Present from America.'

'Could be we'll need 'em. Bloody Portugoose 'as cut and run. The 'Un has captured Armentières and we 'ave to go back.'

'That's his second breakthrough,' Uncle said quietly. 'We try for three years and he does it twice in three weeks.'

'That's why we've got to stop 'em,' Haynes was studying Stephen as he spoke. 'What's 'appened to you? You look different some 'ow?' Then he gave a great roar of laughter, sat up and slapped his thigh. 'You've been 'ad, my lad! Looks a bit shot up round the eyes, doesn't 'e, Uncle? 'Asn't been off the nest for forty-eight 'ours or I miss my bet, eh, Uncle, eh?'

Uncle smiled. 'Enjoy your leave?' he said quietly.

But Haynes was going on. 'No stoppin' 'im now,' he said, pointing his pipe at Stephen. 'Virgins and demi-virgins, that is if there are any left, take cover. But listen to me, young feller me lad. Know what 'appened to Uncle Claude and Aunt Mabel?'

'No, I don't believe I do.' Stephen was grinning sheepishly.

Haynes threw himself back in his chair and declaimed rhetorically: *'Uncle Claude and Auntie Mabel fainted at the breakfast table. Let this be a dreadful warning, never do it in the morning.* 'Ullo, 'ere's your new flight commander.'

Stephen turned. Conway was standing in the doorway.

16

Conway had changed little since Stephen had last seen him. His beefy face had lost all trace of the puppy fat of youth and the cheeks were now hard and firm; the burly frame had fined down but he was still a big man. Above all the eyes that stared bleakly at Stephen were the well-remembered, cold, washed-out blue. He gave no sign of recognition. 'You seem to like low flying,' was all that he said. 'I'll see that you get your fill of it.' Then he turned to Haynes. 'They've just about finished fitting the bomb racks,' he said. 'We'll be ready to take off in an hour.'

Their new aerodrome was ten miles back and further south. The pilots' accommodation was in tents hurriedly erected, for the field had not been in use for some time. The mess was in a large marquee and the squadron office was a dilapidated hut. It was in marked contrast to their former comfortable quarters at Bessières but they were given little time or opportunity for contemplating their surroundings.

New maps were issued at once and they were told to mark on them the present positions of the front lines in so far as intelligence had been able to ascertain them, since the word was that the German push was still rolling inexorably on. Tomorrow they would start ground-strafing in support of the hard-pressed infantry and in an effort to hold up the advance. C Flight had the dawn job.

Everyone knew what was coming and everyone dreaded it. When flying offensive patrols above the lines, skill, straight-shooting, quick-thinking and cleverness combined with luck all gave a fair chance of staying alive. Low down, ground-strafing, none of these counted save luck. With the Hun throwing everything he had at you, small-arms fire, massed machine guns and flaming onions, the greatest skill in the world availed you nothing.

When the batman called him at five a.m. Stephen climbed slowly into his tunic and flying clothes. Then he walked across to the marquee for tea and an egg. There was mist curling round the tops of the hangars but it would not stop them flying. The roar of the guns up front seemed to be rising to a crescendo. There must be the hell of a battle

169

going on up there. At least he was out of that. His one brief glimpse of the trenches had been enough to convince him that the infantryman's war was not for him.

During breakfast Haynes and Uncle came in. They were told to remark their maps. Wing had telephoned to say that a critical gap had opened near Bailleul. Every available machine was to be thrown in to bomb and ground-strafe the area. All the other flights' jobs were being brought forward. They were being called now and would follow C Flight as soon as their machines were bombed up.

Some flight commanders, when detailed for ground-strafing, stayed at a thousand feet, selecting targets, and dropped their bombs from that height. They argued that it was at least as effective as going in really low since it gave them more time to choose valuable objectives and to do something about aiming their bombs. C Flight soon learnt that Conway was not one of these. He went right down on the floor, attacking everything he saw.

The din was tremendous. Stephen thought every German on the front must be firing at him personally. He had never experienced anything like it. Holes appeared in both his lower wings; a bracing wire twanged loose. He saw transport moving up and supposed that this was what Conway was attacking. In an instant he was over it himself. He let his bombs go and fired his guns. Conway zoomed, turned and came back over the advancing Germans. Stephen could see them scattering, saw a machine gun team desperately trying to bring their guns to bear on him. He pressed the triggers again and saw men fall.

There was no lack of targets for there seemed to be Germans everywhere. And always they were advancing, pushing on, regaining ground won so slowly and desperately by Allied troops in the past three years.

They were hurling flaming onions at them now, big blazing balls of fire curling lazily upwards to engulf them in flame. The whole thing was impossible. No one could live through this. Near Stephen a Camel exploded in the air from a direct hit. They were right on the ground now and Conway, his streamers flying, was still attacking.

After almost an hour of it, bombs gone, ammunition expended, Conway led them back. Stephen's wings and fuselage were full of holes; an interplane strut had been all but cut through. 'Get another bus' was all that Conway said curtly.

The following day Stephen did nearly seven hours' flying and the squadron total was just over eighty hours in the air. C Flight was the first out and the last in and Conway pressed his last attack home as relentlessly as his first. Haynes had found time in between ground-strafing to shoot down two enemy two-seaters. All flights had losses. B's flight Commander and another man had gone. A had two pilots missing. Stephen could not believe he was still alive.

The next day they did it again and the next and the next. Hurled in without rest or relief the squadron was decimated. New faces came and went. Both Hank and Clare were shot down but made their way back. Everyone had machines shot to pieces. Stephen smashed an undercarriage on landing; Hank stood one on its nose; Conway brought back machines so full of holes that it was a wonder they flew at all, but he survived untouched. Always he was in the thick of it. He never looked for soft targets behind the lines but went down where the fire was hottest and placed his bombs where they would do the most damage. Haynes thought the world of him. Stephen found his loathing for him beginning to be coupled with a reluctant admiration.

As for himself Stephen was so tired he could hardly speak. Every evening he drank several whiskies in the mess before throwing himself on his bed and trying to sleep. But sleep was slow to come. Always in his ears was the murderous cacophony of ground fire; ever present, haunting him, was the belief that the continued miracle of survival could not go on.

And then came the lull. The German advance had been checked, at least temporarily. Taking stock in the mess, Stephen found that very few of the old hands were left. Haynes and Shaw were still there but save for Hank and Clare there were not many familiar faces. Everyone shared the relief of being back doing patrols again. And to make things even easier there seemed to be few Huns about. They, too, presumably, had had enough for a bit or were re-grouping in preparation for their next push.

For Uncle warned them that it might only be a very temporary lull. There were strong hints from Intelligence of a build-up preparatory to another attack. As an omen of this, intense balloon activity began on the German side of the lines. Some of them were brought right up almost to the front line where they could observe the British positions and much of the back area behind them. Orders came that these balloons must be attacked, and by C Flight of 245 Squadron.

Conway, in the lead, climbed quickly to four thousand feet. They caught sight of the balloons immediately, a line of silver sausages gleaming in the morning sun. Archie battered them as they crossed the lines, betraying their position. But, with any luck, the gunners guarding the balloons would think they were on ordinary line patrol. Conway held on, gradually working his way north. He was being both sensible and clever, Stephen thought. Remembering how he had gone down through everything they could throw at him when ground-strafing, Stephen had anticipated that he would go bald-headed for the objective. Instead he was clearly trying to persuade the Germans that they were no threat to the balloons. When he had worked the flight into position he would attack from their side of the lines. From there he would for once have the sun in his favour with the German gunners looking straight into it. In addition he would have a good chance of catching them unawares. It would be just as well if he did, Stephen thought, for they had no escort. The general, who was a great believer in expending his forces in penny packets, having read somewhere that it was a Wellingtonian ploy to send boys on men's errands, had told Wing that machines could not be spared.

These balloons must be important to the enemy, Stephen reasoned, so it was more than likely that they had a circus lurking somewhere high up to deal with any attack. He scanned the sky anxiously for the black dots that would be enemy machines waiting in the sun, ready to pounce. He could not see them but in his bones he felt that they were there somewhere lying in ambush.

He cleared his guns. The belts of his Vickers were armed with flat-nosed Buckingham incendiary bullets. Rumour, totally unsubstantiated, had it that if you were brought down in one piece and the Germans found these in your guns, they held it to be a breach of the Hague Convention which justified them in shooting you—and they did so.

Looking across to where Hank was flying beside him Stephen waved and received a grin and a wave in return. Then Hank pointed downwards to where the balloons, nearer now, sat swaying gently on their cables a thousand feet below. Conway must be coming very close to his attacking position. It was time to concentrate and watch every move the leader made.

Conway turned and the flight turned with him. He waggled his wings and raised his right arm. It was the signal to attack. As always Stephen's mouth went dry and he felt his stomach muscles tighten. This was it; they were going in.

The nose of Conway's machine went down and he dived on the balloons. On his right and just behind him, Stephen followed. They were going down very fast indeed. The pitot needle raced round the dial. The wind screamed in the wires. Like Haynes, Conway never did things by halves. And he was right. Full throttle, flat out and hope for surprise was their only chance of getting away with this job.

For a moment Stephen thought that they had succeeded. In fact Conway's tactics of working round and coming in out of the sun had momentarily thrown the defence off balance. They were just that little bit late in coming into action, which gave the flight an even chance of getting through. But, when it came, the barrage was bad enough in all conscience. As well as machine guns and flaming onions, Archie was there to lend a hand with heavy stuff. The bang and slam was deafening.

And then, somehow, Stephen was through it. The curved side of a balloon envelope jumped into his sights underneath him. He pressed his triggers and saw his incendiaries going into it. A blast of hot air that rocked his machine shot upwards. A sheet of flame and dark smoke engulfed the balloon.

Slamming into a vertical bank, Stephen pulled away. He was very low now, beneath the balloons, almost on the floor. Looking back he saw two of them in flames and the others being hauled rapidly down. As he watched, fire enveloped one of these and a Camel with streamers on its struts zoomed out of the smoke. The observers and crew of the balloons had taken to their parachutes and were floating towards the earth.

Then Stephen saw Conway turn sharply and go back in. He did not realise what his flight commander was doing until he heard the rattle of his guns. Conway was pumping incendiary bullets into the defenceless observers and their parachutes. He saw one parachute dissolve in flames and the observer go plummeting earthwards; the body of the other twisted and kicked as Conway's bullets went home.

Feeling sick, Stephen turned away. At the same moment an ominous rat-tat-tat came from behind him and something cracked unpleasantly close to his head. So they had been there after all, waiting for them. And now he was right down on the ground with no room to manoeuvre.

He went over into a bank and kicked his tail to throw off the aim of the Hun behind him. Looking back he could see two gaily painted Pfaltz closing in. They were further away than he had feared. They had opened fire too soon which at least gave him some sort of a chance. He zoomed to get height and turned again. Christ, there were more of them coming down! Tripes this time. He hadn't a hope. Where were the others? Gone for home more than likely and good luck to them. He took a snap deflection shot at a Tripe and thought he hit him. Machine gun fire was all around him. This couldn't go on forever. Ought he to make a break for it and try to get home contour-chasing on the floor? Not a hope. With their numbers they'd head him off and get him for sure. But they mightn't cross the lines all the same. They were never anxious to do that and they must be just about over the lines now.

Then, in front of his very eyes, a Tripe and a Pfaltz collided. They were crossing each other to get into a position in front of him to turn him back into the guns of their comrades. The Pfaltz smashed into the Triplane's fuselage behind the pilot's seat. Locked together they plunged earthwards. The firing behind him slacked off.

Afterwards Stephen could only assume that the Huns were so appalled by what had happened that they broke off the attack. Then, he did not stop to think. Putting the nose down and slamming the throttle against the stop he dived for the ground and headed for home with every needle nearly off its dial. He was still shaking when he landed. That had been his nearest thing yet.

Conway was waiting for him. 'You let me go in by myself after those balloon merchants,' he said grimly. 'Why didn't you follow me? If you had we'd have got the lot.'

Stephen had had two months of war flying behind him and an M.C. on his chest to prove it. He was not a terrified boy any longer. He was still boiling with a mixture of fright and fury and he had no intention of allowing himself to be overborne by Conway. 'I didn't know it was part of our policy to shoot unarmed men,' he said.

'You're not paid to think about policy,' Conway said, thrusting his chin out at Stephen. 'Your job is to do what I do and what I say—understand?'

'As it happens, I was rather busy avoiding the attentions of some unfriendly Fokkers.'

'Huns? I didn't see any Huns.'

'No. You were otherwise engaged.'

'I'm putting all this in my report—including your not coming in.'

'If it interests you, so am I.'

Conway glared at him and walked off towards the squadron office. Stephen started to follow him when he noticed a Camel some yards away, its propeller motionless. The pilot sat on at the controls. Recognising it as Clare's by the letter on the fuselage Stephen ran towards it.

Clare sat on staring out between the guns. 'Engine conked,' he said slowly. Then he pushed up his goggles and looked at Stephen. 'Hank's gone,' he said.

'Hank? God, Clare, what happened?'

'There's no mistake this time. I saw it. He went straight in.'

'Did he get caught in the barrage?'

Clare pushed himself out of the seat and jumped down.

'He went in again to back up that murdering swine when he started to shoot down the parachutes. They turned their whole hate on him. He just went on down and broke into pieces. He had no chance at all.'

17

Hank's death had the effect of drawing Stephen and Clare closer together. It banished forever the feelings of constraint which had begun
to grow up between them.

That night they went through his effects and packed them up.
Amongst them was a sealed packet addressed to them both. Inside
was a letter to a girl they did not know and one to his parents in Massachusetts. There was also a note for them. In it he thanked them for
everything. It had been his good luck, he said, to have the British train
him and go to France with them. The British had made him one of
themselves. They had seen to it that he had never felt different or out
of it. They were a swell lot—'And I'm including you in this,
MacMurphy'—and if it had not all been worthwhile before, then
being with them had made it so. There were two bottles of a very
special brew in his kit. He'd been keeping them for the victory march
but if he didn't make it then they were all theirs.

They both got very drunk in the mess that night. Those few still
remaining in the squadron who had been in since the beginning saw to
it that they were left alone.

But the R.F.C. never mourned its dead. That was not its way. The
empty chair was filled; the vacant bed occupied. The gramophone
ground out no melancholy notes but instead played the Cobbler's Song
from *Chu Chin Chow* or 'Sister Susie's Sewing Socks for Soldiers'. The
dance with death went on.

By the end of the month the German attacks on the Lys had been
held. The squadron moved north again and resumed patrolling. It
had not been heavily engaged in the final battles round Kemmel Hill
and casualties had been light. It began to cohere into an entity again;
the new men gained experience and the old hands settled down.

The weather which had been mixed began to pick up. The days,
too, were lengthening towards full summer. With the better weather
and longer hours of daylight came more jobs, more patrols and
greater physical and mental strain on the pilots.

Soon Stephen found that although everyone was spending long hours in the air he was being required to do more flying than the others. If anyone in C Flight was sick or out of action for one reason or another it was always he who was detailed to stand in. He never seemed to be given the usual time off, being on call each and every day. It took him a little time to realise that this was a deliberate policy on Conway's part. Never once did Conway betray by any sign or indication that he and Stephen had met before but, just as Stephen had not forgotten him, it seemed also that he remembered only too well the part that Stephen had played in the abrupt termination of his school career. He had been given the chance of making Stephen pay for it and was taking it.

There was nothing Stephen could say or do to alter this state of affairs. Any protest or complaint would be put down as the dreaded disease of cold feet. Conway was gaining in reputation every day as a skilful and aggressive patrol leader. An adverse word from him in Haynes' ear would carry weight. Signs of cold feet, nerves or 'hot-airing' were always being searched for by commanders of every grade and rank. They were held to be a betrayal of the spirit of the offensive dictated by Trenchard and pursued by his disciples, many of whom in the higher echelons had not flown for years and not at all in the conditions and under the stress currently suffered by pilots in fighter squadrons.

Stephen took what consolation he could from the fact that his flight commander, however skilful as a pilot and leader, was not a good shot, and his personal score remained low. Conway could bring his flight to battle under the most favourable conditions but he seemed unable to score himself. There were pilots like this, Stephen knew, who, however gallant they were in pressing home their attacks, could never, apparently, hit an enemy in a vital spot. Paradoxically enough Conway's skills in leadership and his ability to get his flight into the best positions for attack had the effect of enabling Stephen to increase his own score. This did not make for better feelings between them. And even when in the heat of battle Stephen shot a Triplane off Conway's tail, an action he was later bitterly to regret, he received no word of thanks for it nor any mention in Conway's report.

Now that they had been brought into contact again Stephen for his part found himself unable to rid his mind of what Conway had done to him and the resulting tortures he had gone through at school. He held him responsible, too, for Hank's death and he could not and would not forget this. But far more than anything he was revolted by Conway's attitude to killing. Conway delighted in and dwelt on accounts of Germans being brought down in flames. Most pilots tried to divorce themselves from thinking of their adversaries as people. To them they were inanimate objects, part of their machines, to be destroyed if possible because this was war and if you did not kill them they would kill you, but the act of destruction was never dwelt upon.

176

That was not Conway's way. He would go over and over the details of each kill made by his flight especially if it had been a flamer. 'Flames,' he would say licking his lips, 'Flames. That's the way to get them.' And it must have galled him exceedingly, Stephen thought, that he did not himself contribute in any number to their deaths.

One evening, returning from patrol, Stephen shot down a Halberstat two-seater near the Forest of Nieppe. There were no Huns about so he followed it down to confirm his kill. Both pilot and observer were alive and struggling to free themselves from the wreckage of their machine. Having seen enough, Stephen zoomed away. As he came off the top of his climb another Camel flashed past him. It was diving on the wreckage, its guns blazing. The streamers identified it as Conway's machine. Even as Stephen watched he saw the bodies of pilot and observer slump and fall and a sheet of flame swallow up the Halberstat. When he landed he walked past Conway without speaking, went to the mess and ordered a double whisky.

It had been Clare's day off and he had not been on the patrol. The following day the mist and rain of Flanders returned. Cloud shrouded the aerodrome and all flying was washed out. After lunch Clare and Stephen went to the hangars to test the rigging of their machines and to check their guns. That done, they chatted to the ack-emmas for a few minutes and then lounged in the doorway looking at the rain and talking the perennial subject of the R.F.C.—flying shop. Stephen told Clare about the events of the previous evening.

Clare was silent for the moment staring at the effell hanging limp on its pole. 'You know,' he said quietly. 'That day at the balloons when Hank was killed I called Conway a murdering swine. I thought so then and I think so now. But this is war and a bloody one and it's gone on too long and Conway may be right. In the R.F.C. I think we all may be a bit too inclined to treat it as a game, a bloody dangerous game rather like your own sport of steeplechasing if you like but still a game, and it isn't, you know.'

'But I think it's that way of looking at it that keeps most of us going.'

'Perhaps, but you're a bit of a romantic, old boy. Those chaps in the balloons if they'd got down safely might have had vital information they could have handed on. Maybe it would have meant more of our fellows on the ground being killed. I wouldn't have done it, you wouldn't have done it, but that doesn't say we're right. It's war not a game. In war you kill your enemies or lose the war.'

'I don't like killing things. After the war if I get through I'm going to give up shooting. I may not even hunt, though the killing part of hunting is always exaggerated by those who've never done it. It's not so bad in a dog-fight where it's, well, sort of impersonal, but I still hate attacking two-seaters where you can see the poor bloody observer sweating with fright. Did you hear Conway in the mess the other day saying he could smell the observer's roasting flesh that afternoon when Shaw got one in flames? Can that be true?'

'Probably, if he said it. He doesn't hot-air much. He's a cold-blooded bastard. Can't say I take to him. But he's got guts. You have to hand him that. Bags of bloody guts. You know,' he looked keenly at Stephen, 'I get the feeling there's something between you two, that he's got it in for you. Could it be you've met before?'

Stephen hesitated. The whole affair between Conway and himself had been sitting on his shoulders like a black cloud ever since Conway had joined the squadron. Then he made up his mind. 'We've met all right,' he said. 'We were at school together. I was instrumental in getting him sacked.'

'So it was like that, was it? Can't say I'd have thought it of you, Stephen. I'd have given you credit for better taste.'

'No, it was *not* like that. Not the way you mean anyway.' Then Stephen told him the whole story.

'I see,' Clare said when he had finished. 'That explains a lot. Confirms what I always thought about the chap. Not at all my—or your cup of tea. You know—' he looked at Stephen and his lips twitched—'m'Colonel wouldn't have had him at any cost.'

Their eyes met and they both burst out laughing. It was in a way a sealing of their friendship.

'Hullo, what's this?' Stephen said.

A large touring car was drawing up by the squadron office. From it two figures descended.

'Brass hats,' Clare observed succinctly.

The figures went into the office and a few minutes later Uncle emerged and hurried over towards the mess. From there he went to the huts and gradually a stream of officers in various stages of dress and undress began to make its way through the rain towards the hangars.

Clare groaned. 'Another inspiring lecture from our esteemed General,' he said.

Brigadier-General Leatherhead, Commanding Twenty-Sixth Brigade R.F.C., was an ambitious soldier. Originally a gunner, very early on he had seen the opportunities for advancement offered by the infant R.F.C. and had joined it just before the onset of war. Going to France with the B.E.F. he was soon in command of a squadron. At that time squadron commanders were grounded and forbidden to fly. A stern disciplinarian and a competent administrator, he had quickly gone on to greater things and had rapidly begun to climb the ladder of promotion. Accompanied by his epicene A.D.C., the scion of a noble house whose succession he was protecting by making this appointment and by whom he expected to be rewarded after the war, the General had a habit of paying surprise visits to his squadrons with the purpose of 'keeping them up to the mark'. These visits were usually on

178

non-flying days and made by motor-car since neither the General nor his A.D.C. had any great love for taking to the air. Modelling himself on Trenchard, when he arrived he would address the pilots, urging them to even greater efforts that 'would sweep the Hun from the sky'. But whereas Trenchard, however wrong-headed and inarticulate he may have been, could in some way communicate his own vision and enthusiasm to the men he commanded and leave them feeling it was all worthwhile, as a result of which they would continue gladly to fly and die for him, Leatherhead possessed none of these qualities. Where Trenchard charmed he criticised and where Trenchard inspired he dispirited. Trenchard's visits to his squadrons did wonders for morale, Leatherhead's reduced it, leaving the pilots to whom he spoke sullen and angry and wondering whether to scoff or snarl.

He was decked out now in all the glory of the new R.A.F. uniform, the separate service having been formed on April 1. The uniform contained a considerable amount of gold braid and was looked upon by pilots in the squadrons as something of a bad joke.

'Fellah's turned out like a Mexican admiral,' Clare commented in his most penetrating drawl as the General and his A.D.C. entered the hangar.

'Looks like the Commissionaire at the Carlton,' someone said behind him.

The standard of turn-out of the members of 245 squadron R.F.C. made them resemble a band of pirates or condottieri rather than members of His Majesty's Armed Forces. Shaw, who arrived last, came in wearing shorts and pulling a khaki sweater over his head. Stephen and Clare both had on the G.S. tunics they had had made for them in London on Haynes' advice. These were now oil-stained and frayed and bound with leather on the cuffs. Stephen, in addition, was wearing a pair of shapeless and disreputable slacks. Clare, while retaining his beautifully cut breeches, wore golf-stockings with them and had a silk square wound round his neck in place of a collar and tie. Several of the others, who had been working on their guns, were in dungarees. Only one of the most recently arrived of the new men had the R.A.F. blue uniform. Few of them had had a hair cut in weeks. Conway, who had been about to leave for St. Omer, was the sole member of the squadron to be properly dressed. A strong and pungent aroma of castor oil hung over the whole group.

The General's nostrils twitched in distaste as he surveyed them. 'Now then, you men,' he began. 'I'm taking the opportunity of addressing you on the subject of the newly established Royal Air Force. As from April first we have been a third and separate service. We are our own masters, an independent branch of the Armed Forces. You may be assured that we shall be looked upon with some suspicion by the older services. I want to impress you that a higher standard of

179

dress and deportment than presently prevails will be demanded of you. I may say that I see few signs of either among you here. I shall expect a distinct improvement on my next visit.'

'Deportment,' Clare murmured to Stephen. 'Deportment, by Gad. Where the devil does he think he is?'

'Opening a parish bazaar,' said the unrepentant voice behind them.

The General walked towards the group and began exchanging a word with one or two. He spent a little time with Conway whom he appeared to have met before. When he came to Stephen he paused and began to look him up and down. 'Are you the officer who objects to shooting at parachutes?' he barked.

'Er, yes, sir, I think so, sir,' Stephen said.

'Don't you know that every German you kill shortens the war?'

'It seems rather like shooting sitting birds, sir.'

'Don't be impertinent. What's your fighting record? How many Huns have you shot down?'

The epicene A.D.C. was pulling at his master's sleeve at this point. The General disregarded him.

'Fifteen, sir—and one balloon.'

The General appeared to be rather taken aback by this reply. He glared at the A.D.C. as if blaming him for it. 'Fifteen, hrr humph,' he said. Then he peered at Stephen again. 'Are you the officer who won the race?' he said.

'Er, yes, I think I must be, sir.'

'I thought so,' the General said triumphantly, as if he had scored a point, thus overcoming his earlier error. He turned to the A.D.C. 'Dress and discipline poor. Make a note of that, Spenlove,' he said. He continued down the line, and turned to address them again. 'I want you all clearly to understand,' he said, 'that what I am about to say is an order and will be put in orders. When attacking balloons you will destroy the crew as well as the balloon. Attacks on the crew whether they are escaping by parachute or not will be pressed home. This is war, gentleman, and the only good German is a dead German. Do I make myself clear?' He thrust out his chin and stared belligerently at them.

There was a murmur from the group of pilots, whether of assent or disagreement it was hard to say. It occurred to Stephen to wonder just how many Germans the General had accounted for himself in his brief flying career. Leatherhead continued to gaze at them for a few moments, his angry glare being directed, it seemed to Stephen, directly at himself. Then he turned to Haynes who was standing beside him.

The squadron commander did not present any smarter or more soldier-like appearance than the rest of them. His battered cap with its skull and crossbones badge sat aslant on his head and he had on his oldest and most oil-stained tunic without either wings or medal ribbons. The General looked at him for a few moments in what was clearly intended to be an intimidating silence. Then he said in a loud and carrying voice: 'Far too much of a rag-time outfit this, Haynes. No real discipline. Smarten them up.'

Haynes flushed. 'This is a full-out squadron, sir,' he said. 'Not a hot-air one. I think you'll find our fighting record satisfactory. Would you care to see the scoreboard in the mess and our list of decorations, sir?' He stared pointedly at the General's left breast which was innocent of any ribbon save that of the Mons Star.

'I'm aware of the record,' the General said sharply. 'That is why for the moment I am overlooking certain matters. Make a note of that, Spenlove.' He stalked off and a few minutes later his car bore him away through the rain.

'Deportment,' Clare said, shaking his head. 'Deportment. Now I do really wish he'd tell us what he means by that.'

Two days later the Colonel commanding the Wing landed his personal S.E. at their aerodrome and walked into the squadron office. Lt-Colonel Clayton-Thomas was a tough Northcountryman with an armful of wound stripes on his sleeve and a line of medal ribbons on the breast of his tunic. Haynes and he knew each other well and there was both liking and mutual respect between them.

'What's up now, sir?' Haynes greeted him as he entered, for the Wing Commander's visits usually presaged the news of a nasty job, the announcement of which he did not wish to delegate to a subordinate or to convey by telephone.

Clayton-Thomas sat down in the chair Uncle pushed forward for him. 'The Brass Hats are worried about another push and they don't know where it's coming from,' he said. 'In case it may be here or hereabouts they want to pinch out the salient in front of Nieppe Forest. Fighter squadrons will give all support to the assaulting infantry by low-flying attacks on the enemy.'

'That's not nice but it's not new,' Haynes said. 'And it's not our front, sir, is it? You 'aven't come 'ere specially to tell us this. By the look in your eye there's something else.'

'There is. We've got to send down as many squadrons as we can spare to back them up. But that's not quite all. From intelligence and observation reports the Hun appears to have massed his supporting troops here.' The Colonel rose, walked to the wall and put his finger on the large-scale map that hung there.

Haynes and Uncle both joined him in front of the map. 'About ten miles over. I think I know what's coming, eh, Uncle?' Haynes said grimly.

'At the conference the Brigadier was asked to detail one squadron to attack them before the assault began. He chose you. You can take it as a compliment if you like.'

'I don't like. When is this to take place?'

'Tomorrow at dawn. It will be a squadron show.'

'What about an escort?' Uncle put in.

'The General says he can't spare planes for one. You'll have to find that yourself. One of your flights will act as escort. I have one other piece of news for you.'

'I hope it's better than the last.'

'Shaw has got his promotion to major, and command of a squadron. He goes to 402 in place of Drummond who's for Home Establishment at the end of the week.'

'So I'm losing my best flight Commander, too. 'Ell of a morning this is.'

The Colonel had a drink with Haynes in the mess and then walked with him to his machine. 'You've got old Leather's balls in a proper tangle,' he said confidentially to Haynes as he buttoned his flying suit. 'I've had him on the phone in a blazing temper giving me all hell about you. What happened when he was down here the other day on one of his social calls?'

'He was a bit rough on young Raymond about not shooting down parachutes.'

'He's putting all that in general orders. You know with Trenchard gone and all these changes in the new Service there are tremendous chances of promotion coming up. He doesn't want to be left out. So he's eating fire at the moment.'

'Eating fire, is 'e? Sounds more like 'ot air to me.'

'Take it steady. That's one of the reasons I wanted a word with you. He says you're a rag-time, insubordinate lot. No discipline, not a credit to the new Service.'

'Christ!'

'Chap called Conway commands one of your flights, doesn't he?'

'Yes. C. Flight.'

'Leathers knew him from the time he was commanding Ninety-First-Wing apparently. Only officer properly turned out when he was here, he says. Is he any good?'

'He's a damn good patrol leader but he's a rotten shot. Young Raymond is the best shot in the squadron.'

'Another Irishman. They like shooting things.'

''E doesn't. 'E's a queer sort of cuss. But I put 'im in for another decoration when 'e got 'is fifteenth 'Un. What 'appened to it?'

'The General said he was an insubordinate young pup. It was one of those new-fangled D.F.C.s that came up. One of the first. He gave it to his A.D.C.'

182

'Spenlove? That pouf. Wot'll the squadron say? I'd like to hear 'em.'

'Under no circumstances will you tell them. That's an order. But you can warn Raymond to mind his tongue in future when he's talking to senior officers. And, Haynes—'

'Yes?'

'If you want to know the worst of it the General is talking about sending you to Home Establishment with a bad chit. Get this job through O.K. whatever happens.'

'We'll do that,' Haynes said.

Haynes told the pilots about it that evening, stressing the necessity for them to mark their maps accurately and that the objective must be found and attacked at all costs. Only he did not put it quite like that. 'The bloody 'Uns 'ave got to be stopped,' he said. 'And we've got to find 'em and stop 'em and that's that.'

C Flight would go in first, B would follow and A provide the escort. 'This is a squadron job,' Haynes went on. 'And I shall lead.'

He looked tired, Stephen thought. There were lines on his face which had not been there before and dark patches under his eyes. The strain was telling on him as it told on all of them. He had the administration to contend with as well as the actual flying and he was driving himself too hard. There was no real necessity for him to go on this job at all. Many majors commanding squadrons would have left it to their flight commanders, and either Shaw or Conway was perfectly capable of leading the attack. But that was not Haynes' way. If dirty jobs were going he would not send men out to do them if he was not willing to do them himself. Stephen saw his eyes stray to the blackboard. The figures 45 now stood after his name. He must be one of the highest-scoring Camel pilots in France. Looking at his own score Stephen saw that he was still third on the list and now only one behind Shaw.

'Captain Shaw will be upstairs looking after us,' Haynes was continuing. 'And 'e won't be Captain Shaw much longer. Major Shaw 'e'll be any minute now. 'E's going to command 402 squadron at the end of the week or sooner. I've told Uncle to lay on lobster and champagne tomorrow night to see 'im properly off and wish 'im luck.'

There was a murmur of congratulation from the other pilots and Shaw smiled his shy, tight smile. A binge, Stephen thought, well, that was something to look forward to. It would be a pity, though, to lose the quiet, competent Shaw. He wondered who would get the flight. A stranger, probably.

There were dirty grey clouds down to about fifteen hundred feet next morning as the pilots ate their breakfasts and struggled into their flying suits. The cloudbase meant that they would cross the lines low down with all that entailed in the way of hate from the German ground troops.

It was not an enticing prospect, Stephen thought, as he walked to his machine. And he was right. Everything the Germans had they appeared to be throwing up at them through the morning mist. They weaved and twisted to confound the gunners' aim. The squadron spread all over the sky. And then, all at once, they were through it and forming up on Haynes again. No one seemed to be missing, which meant that they would be in full strength for the attack.

Following Haynes, they flew south and then turned east. Beneath them was all the desolation of an abandoned battlefield, a waste of shell holes and mud, broken houses and ruined roads. They were clear of enemy fire and the clouds were breaking a little. Shafts and patches of blue began to appear in the sky. From his map Stephen could see they were nearing their objective.

A minute or two later he saw them, almost directly in front of him. They were massed in the streets and on the outskirts of a small village—infantry and artillery and, on the road leading back from the village, cavalry. Yes, cavalry. The sun coming through the clouds was glinting on the tips of their lances. God, Stephen thought, the horses, the poor bloody horses.

Haynes waggled his wings and held up his hand. A red very light soared up from his cockpit and then they were all going down.

They seemed to have achieved at least some sort of surprise for the opposition at first was surprisingly light. Stephen found himself at rooftop height flying along the village street. He let his bombs go and pressed his triggers. Banking steeply he turned to rake the troops in the fields. Let someone else deal out death to the horses. Men in grey were running everywhere. A Camel came across in front of him almost hitting him. He zoomed, half-rolled and came down again. They had got machine-guns going now. A row of holes appeared in his lower wing. He kicked his rudder to throw off their aim and fired a burst in the direction of another one that was pumping up tracer. So far as he could make out there was pretty good devastation and disruption everywhere. Out of the corner of his eye he could see horses panicking and dashing about riderless.

His bombs and most of his ammunition were gone. It was time to be getting out. 'A reserve of ammunition,' he remembered reading in a recent directive headed *Fighting in the Air*, 'should be kept for the return journey when fighting far over the lines.' Someone had read it out in the mess to hoots of derisive laughter. Anyway, he was off home. It was the hell of a long way back.

He began to climb to get height. Looking around him he could see no other aeroplanes. The rest of the squadron had disappeared. Then he caught sight of them forming up above him and some way to the east. He opened the throttle to climb towards them and as he did so the engine coughed and spluttered. The rev counter needle went back and jumped around as the machine lost power and would not maintain her climb. Putting the nose down to level flight he began to nurse her homewards. It was clouding over again so there was a chance of cover but he was not happy about his situation. Seven miles over with a sick engine and not a friend about, he was just the sort of prey enemy fighters would be looking for.

Rat-tat-tat, that horrible ominous sound came from behind him and a stream of tracer flashed past. Looking back he saw an Albatros painted in stripes of black and white. He was caught; cold meat, miles behind the lines and no power. Where the hell was Shaw and the escort? Gone home to a second breakfast more than likely.

Even as these thoughts went through his mind a Camel came from nowhere through a gap in the clouds and fastened on to the tail of the Albatros. One sharp burst and the Hun seemed to stagger in the air. Then, out of control, it went plunging earthwards. Stephen saw it hit the ground and disintegrate. The other Camel came alongside and the pilot waved to him. It was Haynes. He should have known that quickness of approach and one deadly burst could have come from no one else. Haynes must have waited around to see if any of the squadron needed shepherding. It was typical of him to be the first in and the last out.

Haynes stayed with him as they approached the lines. Stephen was losing height, but only slowly. By coaxing the engine he was now pretty sure he could make it home. He waved to Haynes and pointed across the lines for him to go on and leave him, but the C.O. shook his head and stayed where he was.

A battle was raging below. Stephen could see figures running and tanks moving up. Perhaps because of the battle the fire directed at them was lighter than usual. Haynes was above and behind him weaving about. Stephen saw him wave again to him in encouragement. A moment later the propeller of Haynes' Camel stopped. Horror-stricken Stephen watched as the nose went up. Then it flicked over into a spin. Gathering velocity it hurtled past him. He had a single glimpse of Haynes slumped in the cockpit over the controls. The Camel struck the ground and burst into flames.

There was nothing he could do. Nothing. At first he would not accept what had happened, but it was all too true. His engine coughed again, recalling him to reality. The revs fell away, hesitated and picked up. His only task now was to try to get himself home but he never remembered doing it. His mind was numb with a sort of sick horror. Haynes had gone; Haynes the indestructible, shot down from the ground; Haynes, his friend and mentor; Haynes the Camel pilot *par excellence*, killed by a stray bullet from some bloody Hun machine gunner. At least no Hun pilot had got him, he was too good for them;

but there was small comfort in that.

As he landed and began to taxi in the engine gave a final cough and died.

There was a little group round the squadron office, most of them still in flying clothes, anxiously scanning the sky. Shaw and Clare stood apart. Stephen walked towards them pulling off his helmet as he did so.

'Thank God you're back,' Clare said. 'We wondered—'

'They've got the Major,' Stephen said.

'Haynes? I can't believe it.'

'It's true. Shot from the ground. He spun in and went up in flames. There's no hope. He's gone all right.'

They all crowded round him then, firing questions at him. Stephen felt a childish desire to burst into tears. 'He was dead before he hit the ground. I saw him as he spun past me. That's something, I suppose,' he kept repeating.

'Well done, chaps. Damn good show. I saw it all. I'll see the General hears about this. Damn sure I will.' A new voice broke into their discussions.

No one had seen the Colonel land and taxi towards them. True to his tenet of always being in the battle he had flown above them, watching the attack. 'Hullo, anything wrong?' he said then, seeing the sadness on their faces and noticing their silence as they turned towards him.

'The Major's gone,' one of the new men said.

'Gone—what do you mean?'

'Gone west, sir, I'm afraid,' Shaw said simply. 'Raymond here saw it all.'

Once again Stephen had to retell his story. 'He was looking after me as he did with all of us,' he said. 'That was his way. At least I can confirm his last Hun.' He could hardly speak for tears.

The Colonel looked past him at the little group of sad and despondent pilots. 'This won't do, gentlemen,' he said. 'No empty chairs. I suggest we adjourn to the mess for a drink.'

They trooped in after him and he told the mess waiter to put up drinks for them all. As the drink went down talk began to circulate again. Shaw took a duster and a piece of chalk from behind the bar. He handed them to Stephen. 'You saw it,' he said. 'You can confirm his last Hun. Go on. Chalk it up.'

Stephen walked to the blackboard. Against the name of Major H.B. Haynes, D.S.O., M.C. stood the figures 45. He rubbed out the 5 and wrote 6 in its place. There was a little cheer from the group of pilots as he did so.

When he came back, the Colonel drew him and Shaw to one side. 'There's a binge ordered in your honour tonight, Shaw,' he said. 'See that it goes on. I'll come down and take the chair.' He left them then and went out to his waiting S.E.

Shaw looked at Stephen and then at the scoreboard. He lifted his glass in silence and then said quietly as much to himself as to Stephen: 'Duncan is in his grave.'

'I never thought I'd hear Shaw quote Shakespeare,' Stephen said to Clare that night as they changed into their best tunics and slacks. 'Do you know the rest of it?'

'Can't say I do. I was never much of a one for the Bard.'

'I only know it because we did *Macbeth* at school and I was made to spout it. Here it is—dammit I can't remember it properly but it goes something like this: "Nor steel, nor poison, malice domestic, foreign levy, nothing, can touch him further." And that's true in a way about Haynes too. Bloody Leathers was after him. I heard Uncle telling Shaw about it. None of them can touch him now. Damn them all and damn and damn again all senior officers who have forgotten how to fly.'

'If they ever knew. Amen to that. We're bloody lucky to have Clayton-Thomas.'

'He's all right but how many Clayton-Thomases are there compared with the others?'

The champagne tasted sour in Stephen's mouth that night. He wished to hell they'd get on to whisky. He remembered that first binge after the race when he hardly knew how to drink and Haynes had roasted him for riding a rotten race. It seemed light years away now.

They were drinking the King's health. When they sat down all eyes turned to Clayton-Thomas at the head of the table.

The Wing Commander stood up. 'Gentlemen,' he said. 'I'll give you one toast and one toast only—Absent Friends.'

Every man who had flown with Haynes in the squadron that day or any other day rose to his feet and raised his glass.

18

After Haynes had gone, all the talk in the squadron was of who would get it. With a sinking feeling in the pit of his stomach Stephen thought that he knew. Once Shaw had left for his new post Conway was the senior flight commander. Moreover he had done well. He was the obvious choice and in a day or so his promotion to Major came through, together with the confirmation of his command of the squadron.

A new flight commander was posted to replace Shaw and Clare was given command of C Flight.

'You should have had these,' Clare said to Stephen as he watched the flight commander's streamers being attached to his struts.

'They're yours by right,' Stephen said in reply. 'You're a far better leader than I am.' Although by virtue of his score and his shooting Haynes would almost certainly have chosen Stephen and he knew that his passing over was deliberate he also knew that what he said was true. Clare was more of a team man, less of an individualist than Stephen and far more likely to think of the flight as a whole where Stephen would have used them as implements to help him add to his score. Apart from that Stephen did not want the paperwork and responsibility of a flight and he was genuinely glad for Clare's sake. The promotion to Captain that went with command of a flight meant much to Clare for they were evidence to the world that he had proved himself. 'Your Colonel will be pleased,' Stephen said, laughing, for it had become a joke between them now.

'Told me I'd never make a squadron leader if I lived till I was ninety,' Clare said. 'Put that or something like it in my confidential report. He'll say we're a rag-time lot in the R.F.C., I'll be bound, if he hears. Anyway, bugger the old boy, come and have a drink.'

In the mess they found Uncle standing at the bar staring into what looked like a very brown whisky. It was unusual for Uncle to drink much at any time and virtually unheard of for him to be at the bar in the morning.

'Hullo, Uncle, what's up?' Clare said.

'I've been sacked. I'm for home,' Uncle said.

'Good Lord, Uncle, why? You've been in since the beginning. We can't get on without you.'

'That's just it. He says I've been out too long. I'm too old. He wants a younger man. God, I'll be sorry to leave you chaps.' Uncle took a large swallow of his drink.

'Who's coming in your place?' Stephen asked.

'A chap called Baxter.'

'Baxter? Not Bill Baxter? Remember him, Clare? Chap who fainted?'

'Do I not. First time Haynes asked him to go up in a Camel, Uncle, he passed clean out. Hot-air merchant. Could it be?'

'It might well be,' Uncle answered. 'I gather he's done very little flying. He cracked a kneecap in a crash at Upavon and has a stiff leg. That's why he got the job.'

'Well I'm damned. There'll have to be a proper binge to see you off, Uncle.'

But there was no binge, for Conway frowned on binges and on his officers drinking. There were other changes, too, since Conway was determined to impress his personality on the squadron. One of the first of these was the removal of the individual scoreboard from the mess. It was probably significant, Stephen thought, that with Haynes and Shaw gone his name now stood at the head of it. Yet he could not help admitting that it was probably a wise move on Conway's part. Pilots who scored well did come to concentrate on their own score to the exclusion of everything else, and air-fighting was already becoming more a matter of tactics than of individual scores. He resented it because he felt that it was aimed at him and the sight of his name on the board was a constant reassurance to him. But he realised that with his name on top staring at him every time he entered the mess he might easily become obsessed with the ambition to keep it there to the exclusion of everything else. His total had gone up to seventeen now, not a great score when compared with the aces but good enough to be better than most, and he badly wanted to make it twenty before he died. For he was sure he was going to be killed. Somehow Conway would manage that. He was squadron commander now and he held every card in his hand. If he did not have him killed then he would break him or disgrace him because no one could stand the strain of war flying, especially low flying, indefinitely without leave or let up. Everyone had his breaking point and Stephen was beginning to think he was perilously near his.

Where Haynes had laughed and led, Conway ruled by strict discipline and fear. When he came into the mess to preside at dinner everyone stood up. He spoke to his flight commanders and few others. Conversation languished and officers, knowing that drinking and

189

high jinks were frowned upon, took to going early to their huts in the evenings. This was no harm in many ways for there were fewer hangovers in the mornings and, with the weather improving and the stretch in the days, flying hours were growing longer and longer. Those flying hours were filled, too, for Conway was determined to see that the squadron's time in the air was exceeded by no one. Any pilot who gave the dud engine signal and turned back from a patrol had to put in a full explanation in writing of the cause of the fault to the recording officer and have the fault verified. Yet at the same time he was merciful to the new men, refusing to throw them into the battle until they had been broken in gradually by their flight commanders and lectured on tactics and techniques of air fighting by himself.

So, although it was not the spirit of the old R.F.C. and it was not the way Haynes would have done it, the squadron prospered. The score reached 150 and there were messages of congratulation from Wing and from the General. There were few of the old original 245 left now. Most of the pilots though they feared Conway also admired him. Stephen hated him with every fibre of his being for, as he had guessed, the persecution went on. The squadron flew long hours and of the squadron Stephen flew the most. He felt so tired now he could hardly think. In order to sleep he had to drug himself with whisky and when sleep did come it took the form of nightmares in which Babs, the Bay, Conway and death in flames were horribly intermixed. Oddly enough his flying did not suffer. He felt alive only when he was in the air; and when he shot at Huns it was as if each time he was killing Conway. 'Burn, damn you, burn,' he found himself, to his horror, saying over and over again, when he got his eighteenth in flames over Roubaix. Though he did not know it, he, like the rest of them, was being hammered out on the anvil of war.

Clare confirmed that victory and they made their reports to Baxter who annoyed them ceaselessly each time they landed with petty questions and niggling cross-examinations. He had been as displeased to see Clare and Stephen as they were to see him and was just as fussy, grandiloquent and self-important as he had been at Ayr.

Uncle stayed on for a few days to help with the take-over and then packed his kit. By good fortune it was another day of rain and low cloud. Flying was washed out for B and C Flights, A being kept in waiting in case the weather cleared. Clare and Stephen borrowed the squadron tender and drove Uncle to St Omer. In the officers' club they stood him the best lunch they could procure, filling him with champagne and sole and filet mignon and washing the lot down with brandy. They then drove him to Dunkirk and the leave boat.

Uncle was a lawyer and even in liquor was careful of what he said.

190

But just before he reached the gangway he stopped and looked Stephen squarely in the eyes. 'Why does Conway hate you?' he said. 'What is there between you?'

'It's a long story,' Stephen said. 'Too long for now.'

The ship's siren went.

'I saw what was going on,' Uncle said. 'If ever anything happens and you want me I have it all written down. Don't forget.'

'I won't. Thanks again, Uncle. And thanks for everything.'

Uncle put out his hand. 'Cheerio, chaps. And happy landings.'

'Save a bottle for us at Murray's, Uncle.'

The siren went again. Uncle took his place in the queue of officers filing up the gangway. At its head he turned and waved.

'And to think we're exchanging him for Baxter,' Clare said.

They stopped at St Omer on the way back and had dinner and drank more champagne. After that they made their rackety way back to the aerodrome singing the squadron songs they used to bawl out all together in the days of binges and guest nights:

> 'In and out went the stainless steel,
> Round and round went the bloody great wheel,
> But this was a case of the biter bit,
> There was no means of stopping it—'

Laughing, they strolled arm in arm to the mess. At the door they were met by Baxter whose moustache was bristling with self-importance. 'What do you mean by going into St Omer?' he demanded of Stephen. 'You were on stand-by.'

'I was not. Morris was on stand-by.'

'That was this morning's list. The C.O. altered it just before you left. You should have checked. I'll have to see he hears of this—'

'Well, fuck you both then,' Stephen said, furious. 'I haven't had a day off in weeks. If he didn't know that you should have told him—not that I suppose it would have made any difference.'

'He wanted to take you out shooting parachutists,' Clare drawled.

'I shouldn't wonder, they're the only things he can hit,' Stephen said.

Baxter opened his mouth to say something, shut it again and then, making up his mind, decided to speak. 'Look, you chaps,' he said. 'Why are you so dead set against him? He may not be another Haynes but he's a bloody good C.O. Why can't you give him a chance?'

'Because he won't give me a chance,' Stephen said hotly. 'No. Not ever, never, see, Baxter, not in spades as poor old Hank would have said, and he killed him, too.'

'Good night, Baxter, that is your name, isn't it, I keep forgetting,'

Clare said airily. 'Tell him, dear boy, we'll meet in hell or whatever passes for it outside his squadron. Goodnight—Stephen, what is this dreary fellow's name?'

And, linking arms again, they swayed off together towards their hut singing untunefully another of the squadron songs from the time when they had been allowed to sing them: 'When I go out I always shout I'm buggered if I'll be buggered about. Yes, when I go out—'

'Apt, don't you think, apt—' Clare drawled as they reeled into the hut.

Next morning Stephen fully expected to be on the mat. C Flight did not have the early job and breakfast was almost over when he came in. That did not matter much for he rarely felt like eating these days. There seemed to be a lot of orderlies about polishing and brushing. A mess waiter brought him a mug of scalding tea. He sipped it slowly.

'I say, Raymond,' one of the new men sitting beside him said. 'That was your eighteenth Hun, the Albatros you got on Tuesday, wasn't it?'

'Was it? Yes, I suppose so.' He knew very well that it was his eighteenth kill but it didn't do to be publicly keen about it. Nevertheless the one thing he did seem to be clear about these days was his score. Involuntarily his eyes went to the board and then he remembered that it was not there any more.

'I don't seem to be able to hit anything. What am I doing wrong?'

'Hard to say. I don't think anyone can really teach you. Get close, that's the thing. And aim well in front if it's a deflection shot.' How many aeons of years ago was it since he had been asking Haynes these self-same questions?

'You make it all seem easy.'

'God,' Stephen thought. 'If you only knew—' His eyes went again to the non-existent scoreboard. He wondered if Haynes had ever felt like this. In a way this new man was looking at him as he had looked at Haynes. After all he was now the top scorer in the squadron. It was so funny he almost laughed. Fancy anyone thinking of him in the same league as Haynes. Only this chap had never seen Haynes. 'Don't fire till you see the whites of their eyes,' he said. 'That's the ticket. Hullo, what's up?'

Conway, followed by Baxter, had entered the mess. Everyone stood up.

'All right, gentlemen,' Conway said. 'Carry on.' Then he walked to the head of the table and cleared his throat. 'The squadron has been paid a signal compliment,' he said. 'We have been singled out for a visit by a party of Frocks'—he used the current senior officer argot for politicians—'who are visiting G.H.Q. They want to see units of all branches of the Service. We have been chosen as the Camel squadron. Carry on please, Mr Baxter.'

Baxter took the staff board he always carried from under his arm. 'Visitors arrive at 12.00 hours,' he announced portentously. All officers who possess R.A.F. uniform will wear it. Others—dress will be R.F.C. tunics and field boots or puttees. Slacks will not be worn. Officers will parade in front of the mess at 11.30 hours.'

'I shall expect a smart turn-out, gentlemen,' Conway said.

Stephen's dressing-down appeared to have been forgotten or at least postponed. He went slowly back to the hut where he washed and shaved. Then he put on his best tunic and Sam Browne.

Punctually to the minute the cavalcade of cars arrived. The Army Commander, a fighting little general something on the lines of Bobs Bahadur, who was universally liked and respected, was the first to alight. Next came the new chief of the R.A.F. in France and then Brigadier-General Leatherhead and his A.D.C. There were hosts of staff officers and myrmidons. Drab amongst all the glitter of uniforms and gleam of polished leather was a group of politicians in civilian clothes.

The Prime Minister himself was there. With a quickening of interest Stephen stared at his wide-brimmed hat, his flowing hair and the coat thrown like a cloak round his shoulders. He was said to be sympathetic towards fighting soldiers and to dislike generals, which earned him high marks in Stephen's estimation. As they approached he saw beside him another figure in Naval uniform. The dark blue and the four rings of a captain on his sleeve marked him out from the other members of the Prime Minister's entourage. The jutting beard emphasised the piratical air Stephen so well remembered. It was Andrew Massiter.

They greeted Conway first and then came down the waiting line of officers, stopping for a word here and there. When they reached Stephen they paused.

'This is the officer I spoke to you about, Prime Minister,' Massiter said. 'Lieutenant Raymond.'

Stephen was conscious of a pair of piercing eyes boring into his. 'How long have you been out?' Lloyd George asked him, the musical lilt of his voice coming through in even that short sentence.

'Four and half months, sir.'

'How many Germans have you shot down?'

'Eighteen, sir, and one balloon.'

'Eighteen! How old are you?'

'Seven—eighteen, sir.'

'Eighteen? I wonder just when your last birthday was?'

Stephen could hardly remember it himself. It had been at Ayr, he now recalled. Even his mother had written in her tall angular hand. He hoped he had answered her letter. There hadn't been much time for writing at Ayr or much inclination after it for that matter.

193

'You are Irish, Captain Massiter tells me,' the Prime Minister went on.

'Yes, sir, from County Kilderry.'

'And proud of it, I'm sure. Some of our best pilots are Irish— Mannock, McCudden, McIlroy.'

This chap's done his homework, Stephen thought. 'I'm hardly up to their mark, sir,' he said.

'Who can tell? Eighteen and a German shot down for every year of your age. Eighteen,' Stephen heard him repeat again to Massiter as the entourage moved on. 'Dear God of the valleys what are we doing to our young men?'

At the end of the line they talked again with Conway and then walked with him to where the Camels of the squadron were drawn up wing-tip to wing-tip outside the mess. After that they chatted together for a few minutes and then Conway called, 'Mr Raymond!'

Wondering what was up now Stephen walked forward.

'The Prime Minister would like to see a Camel flown,' Conway said. 'You're the top scorer in the squadron and he has asked for you. Get on with it.' Conway walked a few paces with him towards the line of machines. 'Put on a show for them,' he said. 'And make damn sure it's good—understand?'

Stephen nodded without speaking. He reached his bus and swung himself into the cockpit. The day was warm and the sun was shining. He did not bother with a helmet or flying suit. Pulling the single belt round his waist he clipped himself in.

The mechanics swung the prop. He taxied out and opened up. Then he was taking off in a climbing turn over the hangars and into the clear blue sky.

Stephen never fancied himself very much as an aerobatic pilot. He knew he could never turn a Camel inside out low down the way Haynes had done. Nevertheless he supposed he could do enough to impress these Frocks. He would have dearly loved to have dived on them and spreadeagled the lot, especially Leatherhead. Instead, he kept himself above five hundred feet and dived, looped, spun and rolled for them.

He had been doing this for about ten minutes when the engine cut out on the top of a loop.

Damn these bloody rotaries, he thought, they really were the very devil for giving trouble. But he was not really fussed or bothered. He had landed before with a dead stick and knew just what he had to do.

As he came out of the loop he saw he was over the far edge of the aerodrome. Putting the nose down he did an S turn to lose height. Another shallower one then and she floated in, touching down as light as a feather and rolling to a standstill a few yards away from the

194

waiting group. It was, he told himself, quite a pretty piece of flying.

There was castor oil, thrown back by the engine, all over his face, and on his best tunic, too, blast it. He took his cap from a waiting mechanic and, wiping his face with his handkerchief, walked towards the politicians.

'Very impressive,' Lloyd George said. 'What do you think of the Camel fighter, young man?'

'Splendid machines, sir.'

'Straight from the horse's mouth, eh, Massiter? I wish you well, my boy. Thank you, Major. It's been an interesting and instructive visit.'

The entourage began to move off. As Leatherhead passed by he drew Conway to one side. 'Very good turn-out, Conway,' Stephen heard him say. 'I'm glad to see you're licking them into shape.'

Then the cavalcade roared away in a cloud of dust to call on a tank regiment.

After lunch Stephen was summoned to the squadron office. Once more he fully expected to receive the postponed dressing-down for his absence the evening before. Instead Conway regarded him in silence for a few moments. His washed-out blue eyes were as usual totally expressionless. Beside him Baxter was industriously scribbling away.

'It seems you have friends among the Frocks,' Conway said slowly.

Stephen stood without answering, wondering what on earth was coming next.

'You're to go to Paris,' Conway said. 'It's a request from Captain Massiter M.P. who was with the Prime Minister. He knows you, it seems.'

'He lives near me.'

'I have no alternative but to allow you to go. A car will call for you in an hour. You are to report to Captain Massiter at the Ritz. But that's not all—'

Here it comes, Stephen thought, and he was right.

'You cut stand-by duty yesterday,' Conway went on stonily. 'What do you mean by it?'

'Morris was on stand-by.'

'He wasn't feeling well and I changed it. You're damn slack, Raymond, you always were. Why do you think I give you so much flying? It's to keep you up to the mark. If I didn't you'd take the chance of dodging duty as you did yesterday and as you've done all your life. I'm reprimanding you now and I'll see this goes down on your record. Understand?'

'Yes—sir,' Stephen said, seething inwardly.

'Baxter will make out your pass.' Conway heaved himself to his feet and walked out of the office.

Two hours later Stephen was on the road to Paris. He could not imagine what Massiter wanted him for but that did not matter. He was

195

away from Conway for a bit. Out of the blue a respite had been given him and he had a chance of seeing Babs again.

On the outskirts of the city he told the driver to pull up at a café. Going in, he telephoned the number Babs had given him. After much difficulty he got through. Fortunately it was another English voice that answered him. Babs was not there, she said. She was out with the General but was expected back soon. 'Is that Lieutenant Raymond?' the girl at the other end asked. When Stephen said it was her voice took on a conspiratorial air. 'I've heard about you,' she said knowingly. 'Where did you say to meet? The Hotel Britannique. I'll give her the message. How many *sales Boches* have you shot down now?'

'I've lost count,' Stephen said shortly and put down the telephone. He had been rude and he knew it but he hated being reminded once again and especially by a gushing woman when he was temporarily out of it that he had personally been responsible for the deaths of eighteen men, more if you counted the two-seaters.

Massiter had a suite at the Ritz. There was champagne in an ice bucket. 'And what do you hear from the Bay?' were his first words to Stephen as he filled their glasses.

'My father writes regularly,' Stephen said. 'He seems worried about the state of the country.'

'I don't think he need be. The Prime Minister tells me that except for a few isolated incidents everything is quiet. There have always been incidents in Ireland, you know, and always will be. The Rising was the act of a few fanatics. They had no popular support.'

'I'm afraid I'm pretty ignorant of politics, sir. I'm sure you are right.'

'Of course I'm right. Look at the number of Irishmen in the Forces. Even the girls are serving now.' Massiter was toying with the stem of his glass, not looking at Stephen.

'Yes,' Stephen agreed enthusiastically. 'My sister is a V.A.D. and Babs Murtagh is a driver.'

'That charming young lady you brought to Dunlay? She's doing her bit, too, is she?'

'Yes, sir. She's here. In Paris. She's driving General Hastings.'

'Indeed. And her father, I understand, is in the Flying Corps, too.'

'On Brisfits. That's our name for Bristol Fighters, sir. It was a good show, him getting on to them, he's so old. I suppose he's come through so far. I haven't heard lately.'

'He'll come through all right. His sort always do.'

Something in the way he said it made Stephen look at him quickly. He was in time to catch the sudden flash in those tawny eyes. Then it was gone and, catching Stephen's look, Massiter said lightly, 'An engaging rogue, Desmond, but a rogue nonetheless.' He smiled as he said it, but his eyes did not smile.

Stephen's mind went back to that Punchestown before the War. It was all so long ago now, so much had happened since, and he and Babs had been children then. But Desmond had done something mighty hot in that Conyngham Cup in which Massiter's horse had been beaten. Haynes had known about it, too. He had said everyone in racing knew. He wished he could remember just what it had all been about. It seemed ancient history to him but perhaps it wasn't to Massiter.

Massiter put down his glass. 'We'll go out to dinner. Maxim's,' he said. 'I told them to expect us.'

Seated at the table he gave his orders with brisk efficiency in fluent French. 'Champagne, I understand, is what you young men in the Flying Corps drink, and Krug, I think, will do very well,' he went on as he ran his eye down the thick and opulent-looking wine-list. The waiter came and filled their glasses. It was the best champagne Stephen had ever tasted.

From discussing the Bay and its people and finding out how little Stephen knew about the problems his father had faced and his own part in them, Massiter led the conversation round to the pilots' view of the way in which the air arm was being used on the Western Front.

The champagne, the heady feeling of relief from strain and escape from Conway, the anticipation of meeting Babs later on, all combined to make Stephen ready to talk freely. His pent-up resentment against the Generals who ran the air war from comfortable châteaux far from the stench of castor oil and the rattle of machine gun fire came surging to the surface.

'It's madness,' he said. 'This crazy policy of preserving the offensive at any cost and sweeping the Germans from the skies anywhere everywhere and at any price. I actually heard a General say that the other day. "Sweep them from the skies," were the words he used. As my first flight commander used to say we're at every conceivable geographical disadvantage, and he was right.'

'What did he mean?'

'We're flying into the sun almost all the time and the Huns have it at their backs. Then the wind—it's always behind us, pushing us into Hunland.'

'Can you enlarge on that a bit for me? I'm not sure I quite understand.'

'Look—the sun at their backs means that we can't see them against it and they can hide up there and come down on us when they want to. They can choose when to fight. Then the wind— we're made to do offensive patrols ten miles over. The Brisfits and S.E.s go in deeper, sometimes up to thirty miles or more. When we try to get back, often with crippled buses, the wind keeps pushing us farther and farther in. And we've no parachutes. They say the Huns have started using them but the powers on top won't give them to us.'

'We are told the air offensive must be maintained to press the Germans back and prevent them dominating the air.'

'Do they want to? Davis—that's my first flight commander—was a bit of a Bolshie but he had it all worked out. He'd been out before. He saw bloody April and the massacre last year of old F.E.s and B.E.s and he never forgot it. He said the Huns are far cleverer than we are. They know how to group their resources and use them where they are most wanted, instead of this business of what is it we do, I forget the word.'

'Attrition.'

'That's it. We fly three or four patrols a day deep into Hunland. If they had enough planes or their planes were good enough they'd murder us. Why do we have to do it? What's the point? Davis said it was to get the General another medal.'

The waiter placed a bottle of brandy before them. Stephen reached for it, tipped some into a balloon glass and drank deeply.

'That's Napoleon brandy or its near equivalent,' Massiter said mildly. 'You'll find it slips down rather better if you sip it.'

Stephen grinned ruefully. 'Sorry,' he said. 'There's not a lot of it about where I've just been.'

'The cult of the offensive,' Massiter went on slowly. 'It has bedevilled our military thinking since the Crimea. On the ground a whole generation has been sacrificed to it. Only now is it beginning to be realised that it prevails in the air, too. There is a similarity in thinking between the men at the top. They believe we can only win by a wastage of lives. They will never stop to count the dead or the cost. But the P.M. does.'

'Davis said they were like the Bourbons, they'd learnt nothing and forgotten nothing.'

'The ruling few have much in common with the Bourbons, certainly. I know that from my own experience.' The recollection of past injustices brought again a momentary flash into those tawny eyes. 'You mentioned superiority in machines just now,' he went on. 'Does that still exist? Are your machines still good enough? That landing of yours today, it wasn't entirely voluntary, I think.'

Stephen looked up, startled, to see the other man regarding him with a hint of amusement. He's shrewd enough, he thought. Too damn shrewd. He began to realise the full purpose of his invitation. He was being cross-examined to get at first-hand the fighting man's view of war in this new element, the air. Perhaps he had said too much; perhaps he should tread more carefully. Then he cast caution to the winds. To hell with it. He might be dead in a day or so. Almost certainly he would be in a week unless some friendly Hun got Conway first. He might do the other men some good by speaking out.

'The Clerget and Le Rhone rotaries are hellish unreliable and they're getting worn out,' he said. 'We're damn lucky to get through a patrol without one of us turning back with engine trouble. There's supposed to be a new Bentley engine coming along but we haven't seen it.'

'The Camel itself, it's a fine machine, isn't it?'

'It's a bloody good bus but like the engines it's getting worn out and out of date. The new Fokker is going to make us sit up. They say the Huns are just waiting for it. We haven't seen any yet but we've heard one or two have appeared down south on the Somme.'

'It's good, is it? Will it give them back air supremacy?'

'I don't know about that but it's said to climb faster than anything we've got and to turn inside a Camel. Why haven't we got Snipes? That's what all the chaps want to know. We were promised them ages ago. What's holding them up? The bloody strikers or the bloody politicians—sorry, Mr Massiter.'

Massiter smiled grimly. 'That's a question many people would like to know the answer to,' he said. 'I think perhaps it's neither but a combination of men and methods at the top. Well, this has been a most interesting conversation. Thank you for being so frank.'

Dinner was at an end. Stephen finished his brandy and they stood up to go.

'Where are you staying?' Massiter asked.

Stephen gave him the name of his hotel.

'You'll never get a taxi,' Massiter said. 'I'll send my car.'

As Stephen was borne through the darkened streets he was not thinking of what had passed between him and Massiter at the dinner table but of the immediate future and of Babs. If only she was there. She must be there.

Stephen ran up the well-remembered stairs. It was the same room as before. He threw open the door. A faint glow of light came from the bedside table. It fell on an aureole of russet hair spread on the pillows. Babs was waiting for him in the wide bed.

19

Two hours later Stephen woke up screaming. He was out of bed, standing at its foot, grasping the brass knob of the bedstead and pulling at it. Thick, black darkness surrounded him, and he did not know where he was. He held on to the bed for support.

There were no flames in the darkness. That meant that he was not on fire, that he was on the ground, safe, alive. He was sweating and shaking all over.

The light snapped on. 'Stephen, what is it? Stephen—' Babs, naked, her hair falling across her face, was sitting up in bed, staring wide-eyed at him.

'I dreamt I was going down in flames,' Stephen said. 'I was trying to pull her out of it.' He looked down at the ball of the bedstead in his hands.

'Come here, Stephen, come quickly.' She opened her arms and he went into them thankfully. Gradually and tenderly she comforted him and quietened him. But he could not sleep, nor did he want to. Sleep was beginning to frighten him.

'I'm finished,' he said to her. 'Done for. I'll never see the Bay again.'

'You mustn't talk like that, Stephen. You've come through all right so far. You're worn out, that's all. Aren't you due leave?'

'Leave? Oh, Babs, if only we could spend it together. Here, in Paris, with you. How wonderful that would be. I'm due for it soon if that swine doesn't find some way of stopping it.'

'That swine? What are you talking about? What is happening to you? Who is doing this to you, Stephen?'

Then, in a torrent of words, the story of Conway's persecution of him poured out. 'I can't go back,' he ended. 'I can't face it any more. Being with you has made me realise what being alive means. I know if I go back I'll be killed. It's only a question of time. It can't last. Clare and I are all that is left of the old crowd now. Let's go away together, Babs. Anywhere, it doesn't matter where, just the two of us together.'

'You don't know what you're saying, Stephen,' she said sadly. 'We can't go away, run away, more's the pity. You've got to go back.'

'I know,' he said miserably, burying his face in her hair. 'It wouldn't be so bad if it was only the Huns I had to face. But the thought of that swine sitting there finding extra jobs for me, waiting for me to crack. And he's winning. I *am* cracking. Look what I've just said.'

'Can no one stop him?'

'Only a Hun with a lucky shot. If they do get him I hope he fries in flames just as he's so fond of saying he wants the Huns to do. They got Haynes so maybe they'll get him. Why are the decent ones always the first to go?'

'Does anyone in the squadron know about it?'

'Clare does. Uncle Warmsley, the recording officer, did until he unstuck him and sent him home.'

'Can't you appeal to someone?'

'No. No hope. He's a damn good squadron commander. The General thinks he's God's understudy. They'd not believe me. All he's got to say is that I've cold feet and the General would back him up. Old Leathers has it in for me, too. God knows what they'd do. Put me in for a court-martial more than likely.'

He was out of bed again, now, pacing up and down the room, touching things, unable to remain still, shivering though the night was warm. 'It doesn't matter anyway,' he said savagely. 'I'll be the next to go. I know it. It's only a question of what day my number comes up.'

'Come back to bed, Stephen,' she said, softly pushing the sheets aside. Come back.' She reached for him and he came to her. A wave of excitement swept over him and he forgot his fears. Here was power and bliss and some sort of purification.

He made love to her again then, savagely assuaging his need. What he gave she took, responding to his passion with her own, trying to give back to him his belief in himself and in his chances, to restore to him the conviction that he would come through and that their love would last.

She had never forgotten what Oliver Martin, the Australian pilot, had told her. Those who believe in their star, who are certain they will survive, usually do, he had said. Those who think they are going to be killed almost always are. Somehow, she believed, she had to restore to Stephen the certainty of his own survival.

She had never loved Martin in the way she now knew she loved Stephen. Before Stephen, he had been her first and only physical lover. He had seduced her, if you could call it that for she had been ready and ardent to learn, and he had taught her. Martin had been a declared and faithless womaniser. She had known from the first that with him no permanent relationship was possible, nor indeed did she want one. But he had been skilled in physical love-making and had taught her to realise the raptures that lay in it. Personable, dashing, distinguished and considerate he had been fun to be with and had made her first experience a memorable one. And until that last night he had been marvellous in bed.

It was he who had told her that no pilot could go on for ever, that sooner or later nerves caught up with them all. He was on his way back to his squadron that night in Murray's when Stephen had seen them together. General Hastings had come over for some conference and brought Babs with him. Her evening was free and they had managed to meet.

As they drank champagne at Murray's and joined in the hectic gaiety of the scene she sensed that under the debonair, carefree exterior he was afraid. And, as if to prove it, later that night his sexual powers had betrayed and deserted him. He could do nothing. Angry and humiliated, he had dressed at dawn and left her, savagely blaming her for his failure. A fortnight later he was dead.

A fellow officer had forwarded a letter and a package he had left for her. He did not apologise for the words he had spoken in that grey dawn in the hotel room for apologies were not his way. But he did thank her for the wonderful times they had had together and sent her something he had picked up to remember him by. Opening the package she found inside a brooch in the shape of a pilot's wings with the letters AFC in its centre. The stones set in the wings glittered and shone in the light. The name in the lining of the box was Cartier.

Stephen moved and muttered in his sleep beside her. After they had made love he had fallen immediately into deep slumber. It seemed that sleep had come to him this time unhaunted by nightmares for he lay relaxed in her arms.

Light crept through the windows and began to flow into the room. She dared not move for fear of waking him. But she could see him quite clearly as the room grew brighter. The lines of strain had gone at least temporarily from his face. Sleep had brought him back to being a boy again.

Soon he stirred, stretched and sat up. He stared around him as if he did not quite believe in his surroundings. 'I've been asleep,' he declared triumphantly. 'And no nightmares. Babs, dearest Babs, you are a marvel.'

'We still have a little time to ourselves,' she said.

Later they took the Metro to the Champs-Elysées. In Fouquet's Stephen ordered champagne cocktails. There were a few precious hours left before he had to return to the Ritz and the car which would take him back to the squadron. It was Paris in early summer. Despite the war and the presence of uniforms everywhere, the old enchantment pervaded the air about them. The heat beat off the pavements, the sun sparkled through the leaves. They toasted each other and laughed together. Stephen, she saw, was himself again, or as near it as anyone could be who had been savaged by war.

'The two of us together in the Bay when this ghastly war is over,' Stephen said raising his glass. 'Babs, what bliss.'

'You'll be the leading G.R.,' she said, entering into his mood.

'Riding Bob Ferris' horses. I wonder how Bob is? Father never mentions him in his letters. I suppose they're racing still in Ireland. I never see the results, I never read a paper except the mags in the mess sometimes—' A shadow fell over his face again for a moment as he thought of the other life that could have been his and would await him if he survived. Then he said: 'Punchestown and the Big Double—do you remember?'

'Of course I do,' she said. 'We'll be back there again together, after the war.'

'Promise?'

'Yes, I promise, Stephen.'

Then it was time to go. On the pavement as they were leaving they came face to face with a major wearing the scarlet tabs of the staff. 'It's Harry! Harry French, it must be!' Babs exclaimed delightedly. 'Harry, how wonderful to see you again.'

'By all that's extraordinary after all these years to meet like this. It's good to see you, Harry,' Stephen said, putting out his hand.

The major stopped and looked them both up and down. 'You have the advantage of me,' he said icily. 'I'm afraid I haven't the pleasure of your acquaintance—either of you.' He looked stonily at Stephen. 'In the Flying Corps don't they instruct you to address Field Officers as "sir"?' he barked. Then he walked on.

'Well,' Babs said when she had regained her breath. 'Well! But that's Harry all right. I know it is.'

'Yes, it's Harry,' Stephen said. 'It looks as if he's still bitter about all that business at the Bay and his father. Major on the staff, too. He seems to have landed a cushy job. To hell with Harry French.'

'But,' Babs said. 'Why did he act like that?'

'Since his father robbed mine, if you ask me it is I who should be cutting him not the other way round. Like I said, to hell with him. I hate staff officers anyway. Come on, Babs.'

Back at the Ritz, Massiter insisted on giving them both lunch in his suite. There was more champagne followed by brandy and by the time Stephen arrived back at the squadron the warm glow brought on by these and the events of the night had not quite worn off. Babs had put new heart into him, he thought, and he felt better able to face Conway and the perils of the sky.

As he got out of the car Baxter popped up in the way he had, the clipboard as ever tucked underneath his arm. 'The C.O. wants you in his office straight away,' he said.

Entering the office Stephen came to attention and saluted. Conway went on writing for a minute or two and then looked up. He regarded Stephen stonily without any hint of expression appearing in his pale blue eyes. Stephen wondered just what was coming. Whatever it was was bound to be unpleasant.

'I'm putting you further down the leave roster, Raymond,' Conway said.

'But,' Stephen protested. 'I'm due after Captain de Vaux. That's in a fortnight—'

'You've had a rest—the best part of forty-eight hours in Paris with that Frock. You cut that stand-by. I'm putting Marks and Kennedy above you. They're both married men—'

So much for his hopes and vision of a leave in Paris with Babs, Stephen thought. 'I've been out far longer than either of them,' he said.

'I've mentioned your visit to the Frock to HQ. The General is not best pleased about it. He'll certainly confirm with Wing any action I take about your leave. C Flight has the evening job. You're on it.' He glanced at his watch. 'Take off in ten minutes. That's all.'

Inwardly fuming Stephen left the office. He might have guessed Conway would find some way of making him pay for that Paris trip. Now, when would he see Babs again?

Half an hour later he was over Houlthurst Forest, the smell of castor oil in his nostrils, the well-remembered bang of Archie under his tail, all the time twisting his head and neck to search for Huns, and trying to put hate-filled thoughts of Conway away from him so that he could concentrate on the job in hand.

So it went on during those long summer days. Stephen shot down his nineteenth and then his twentieth Hun. Conway drove them to fly in almost any weather and ever longer and longer hours so that often they took off at dawn, did three and sometimes four jobs a day and landed in near darkness. Of them all he drove Stephen the hardest but he did not spare himself. He put in as many hours as the rest of them and then returned to sit up late in the office catching up with his paper work. If the strain told on him he gave no outward sign of it. Occasionally when his sexual desires became overpowering he and his faithful chela, Baxter, would take the squadron car and spend an evening in St Omer visiting the officers' brothel. When this happened the raucous notes of the gramophone were heard again in the mess and the pilots romped like boys out of school. On his return Conway would expiate his guilt in ever more savagely hunting the Hun.

But if Conway showed no signs of strain others did. When he did succeed in sleeping Stephen found his nightmares came crowding back to him. Often in the night he could see Clare twitching as he too slept restlessly and tossed and turned and muttered. One of the flight commanders cracked and was sent home. A new man, after a bout of trench strafing, turned back from a patrol. On being brought before Conway he told him baldly he could not face any more of it. He was sent to base and recommended for a court-martial.

The machines, too, suffered from the almost ceaseless flying, and the ground crews could not keep up with the maintenance required despite, on occasions, working round the clock. The sleeplessness told on them, too, and their work fell off. As a consequence there was a spate of engine failures. These reached such a pitch that patrols were depleted. Conway was furious and, remembering the new man who had turned back without cause, he believed or affected to believe that not all of the dud engine signals that were given were genuine. He summoned his pilots to the mess and there addressed them. 'There are far too many reports of engine failure,' he growled. 'I've mentioned this before. As there are new men about I'm repeating my instructions and amplifying them. In future anyone leaving a patrol with a dud engine will report its cause in writing to the recording officer who will verify the report with the maintenance crew and submit his findings to me. If I am not satisfied beyond all doubt that the failure justified the pilot leaving the patrol then I shall put that officer in for a court-martial. Is that quite clear? Any questions?'

'I take it,' Clare drawled, 'that if we force-land in or near the lines Mr Baxter will go up and verify on these occasions, too?'

'He will—taking the pilot with him,' Conway said, glaring at Clare.

Two days later Stephen turned back from a patrol. Over Turcoing the engine spat, the prop spun once and then stopped dead. He was at seven thousand feet. Giving the dud engine signal he turned back. There was no hope of making his own aerodrome but he managed to get into a former RNAS station up north without much trouble. It turned out to be the home of the S.E. squadron which had been beside them in the early days.

Stephen was glad enough to be out of that patrol. He had a sore throat, his nose was running and his ears ached. Moreover his stomach was beginning to revolt at the constant inhalation of castor oil that permeated the Camel's cockpit and his neck now had a permanent ache from the twisting and turning necessary to avoid being bounced by the Hun in the sun.

When they examined the engine the S.E. mechanics told Stephen he had a broken ignition wire.

Conway could well try to query this as a doubtful engine failure, so Stephen determined to secure adequate confirming evidence and leave his squadron commander no loophole for laying blame on him. In the S.E. mess he borrowed a pen and a piece of paper on which he wrote details of the failure. Then he sought out the squadron recording officer. 'What's all this?' the recording officer said when Stephen put the paper before him and asked him to sign it. He was a man in his middle thirties wearing the single wing of an observer. His left hand had three fingers missing.

'Our C.O. has to have proof of engine failure if anyone turns back,' Stephen said. 'Otherwise we're in for a court-martial.'

'Court-martial, eh? That's a bit strong, isn't it? Who's your C.O.?'

'Major Conway.'

'Conway, that's 245, isn't it? I've heard of him. Bit of a slave-driver, isn't he?'

'That's putting it mildly.'

'Hang on a minute and I'll see what I can do.' He took the piece of paper from Stephen and left the office.

In a few minutes he was back, and was followed into the room by the squadron commander. Stephen jumped to his feet.

'Sit down, boy,' the squadron commander said. 'By Gad, it's the jockey!' It was Major Cutforth, still commanding the S.E.s since those long-ago days of the race against the Yeomen. 'What's up?' he went on. 'What's all this about?'

Stephen repeated his story.

'It's quite genuine, the ignition wire failure, I mean,' the recording officer said. 'I've confirmed it with the ack emmas.'

Major Cutforth looked at the paper. 'Major Conway is your C.O. now since poor old Haynes went west, isn't he?' he asked.

'Yes, sir.'

'Used to be on One and a Half Strutters. I remember him. A hard man.'

'It might be better if you were to sign that report, sir,' the recording officer put in.

'We'll both sign it or rather counter-sign it after this young feller, Raymond, isn't it, has signed first. And see that he gets a copy, Wilson.'

When all this had been done the report and its copy were handed to Stephen who pushed them into a pocket of his tunic.

'Come and have a drink,' the major said and led the way to the mess.

The windows of the mess hut were open and the sun was streaming through them. The gramophone was going and two pilots were playing ping pong. There was no ceremony. This was like the old days with Haynes. Seeing a stranger drinking with their major, one or two pilots drifted over and soon they were all into the inevitable argument about the merits of Camels and S.E.s.

After innumerable drinks Stephen took off again and returned to his base. He went first to the hut to deposit his sidcot. Clare was lying on his bed turning over the pages of an illustrated magazine.

'Anything happen after I turned back?' Stephen asked him.

'Nothing much. We saw a gaggle of Albatros. They cleared when we tried to get near them. Kennedy and Swainson chased a D.F.W. but he got away. What did you get up to?'

'Broke an ignition wire and landed at Roulandt.'

'Got your evidence for our revered and gallant Major?'

'Signed and counter-signed and a copy as well. It was that S.E. squadron who were beside us at Bessières. Cutforth is their C.O. Damn cheery crowd. I wish I was with them.'

'You'll wish it more when you hear what's in the wind for tomorrow. Aerodrome attack. Lessinghem, about twelve miles over. It seems the General has been told they've moved one of their circuses there and he's had the bright idea of knocking them out before they leave the ground. It's a squadron show.'

'And no escort, I suppose.'

'We're getting one this time all right. S.E.s at fifteen thousand and Dolphins above them. The General's sweating on his step. Thinks he'll make Major-General and a cushy home job if this is a success. There's another squadron coming in after us.'

Stephen threw his helmet and sidcot on to his bed. 'I'd better cut along and hand this report in,' he said.

'Are you all right, Stephen? You look a bit groggy to me, or is it those drinks of Cutforth's?'

'I've got a lousy cold, that's all.'

Going to the office he found Conway and Baxter there. Baxter took the report from him. 'What's this?' he demanded fussily.

'Verification of engine trouble as instructed. Broken ignition wire,' Stephen said. 'Both the C.O. of 332 squadron and the recording officer have signed it.'

Conway took the report from Baxter's hand and read it through slowly. When he had finished he flipped it across the table. 'Mark that and file it,' he said. Then he turned to Stephen. 'There's a squadron show tomorrow,' he said. 'We're to go in low, bombing Lessinghem. A circus has just landed there the General wants knocked out. See that your bus is O.K. I'm not going to have any engine failures tomorrow.'

During the afternoon Stephen's cold became worse. He sat in the sun outside the mess and tried to read but his head was so clogged up that his brain would not take in the words. After a bit he went across to the hangars and examined his bus. He had the mechanics start her and ran the engine up. It seemed O.K. Then he took her up and tried the guns on the ground target. There was nothing wrong there either. Flying cleared his head a bit so he climbed to five thousand and began to throw her around. When he landed Heal came up to him. 'Everything all right?' Heal asked. 'Guns O.K.?' He was always doing this now, Stephen thought sourly, for time had not cured his dislike of

Heal nor had he forgotten that lying report of Heal's about the gun stoppage. Now the armament officer was busy covering himself, he supposed. Soon the whole squadron would be so occupied covering themselves with reports, signing and counter-signing they'd be too busy to do any fighting.

'Yes, thank you,' he said. 'All seems fine.'

'You had a bit of trouble this morning, I hear. She should be all right now, though. Engine running smoothly?'

'Seems sweet enough.' He went back to the mess and drank two cups of tea. Between tea and dinner he began to feel light in the head and shaky on his feet. His cheeks and eyes were burning. At dinner he could eat nothing. After a couple of drinks he borrowed some quinine pills from Clare and went to bed.

During the night he sweated a lot and he thought he might have cured himself but when the batman shook him awake with his early cup of tea he found that his head was still heavy and his nose was so stuffed up that he could hardly breathe. There was heat behind his eyes, too. Feeling rotten he got up and slowly began to pull on his clothes.

Clare had been watching him as he dressed. 'You look awful, Stephen,' he said. 'Are you sure you're all right?'

'I feel a bit queer. It's only a cold. It'll pass.'

'Are you fit to fly?'

'Yes, of course I am.'

'I don't know so much about that. Look, I can sign you off and have the Wing M.O. have a look at you.'

'And what will Conway say to that? No, I'm all right, Clare.'

But his mind didn't seem to be working very well. He felt heavy in the head and confused in his mind and he could not face the usual breakfast egg.

The machines were lined up waiting for them. They would take off in flights, A leading. This meant C would go in last. Conway had announced his intention of bringing up the rear, no doubt, Stephen thought, to see that there were no stragglers.

He climbed in, settled his feet under the straps of the rudder bar, moved the joystick and pumped up the pressure. Automatically he went through the starting drill, took off and formed up on Clare's left.

Over the lines his engine began to miss. It would cough and kick, the revs would go back, and then it would pick up again. He saw Clare turn and look at him. What the hell could it be now, Stephen thought? A choked feed pipe? After a minute or two whatever it was seemed to have cured itself and he breathed a sigh of relief. Choked feed pipes had a habit of clearing themselves when you came in which would be just the thing to give Conway the chance of hammering him for leaving the patrol without justification. Then there was another cough from in front of him. Reaching out he switched over to the gravity tank. The engine began to run on again and for a moment he thought he had solved the trouble. An instant later it kicked and spat and coughed once more. He was beginning to drop back now. What made things worse was the fact that this was happening just when they were commencing to lose height for the attack.

It must be dud petrol, he thought, and Conway would never believe that or accept it as an excuse. Moreover it was all but impossible to prove unless you had it sieved and it did not always show up even then.

Another bout of coughing and spitting came from the engine. He saw Clare looking back at him again. In front of him the propeller arc grew suddenly visible as the revs dropped right away. Then, with one mighty hiccup, the engine finally died and the prop was still.

The next and most urgent thing was to try to get back. Putting the nose down he turned into the wind, towards the lines. He was at about three thousand feet and it did not take him long to realise that from this height and with the strong westerly wind against him he had no hope of making it. He was well into Hunland but just where was he? There was so much to do trying to maintain his angle of glide, keep her on an even keel and look out for lurking Huns that he could not spare time to unfold a map. He remembered an instructor once saying to him that you could not put on brakes in the air and stop to think things out, and this was one of the occasions when he was bloody well right.

Into this wind his ground speed must be close on zero. He was just not going to make the lines and that was that. There was nothing for it but to try to find a place to land. That meant he'd be a prisoner. Not if he could help it. If he could get down safely somewhere and find a hiding place he might be able to make his way back.

The wind was drifting him south and east as he lost height. He'd better make up his mind quickly where to put her down. To his left he caught sight of a green patch of forest. He might be able to lie up there if he could land near it. As he did an S turn towards it a semi-circular clearing at its edge came into view. That would do nicely if he could drop her into it.

'Concentrate, concentrate, now,' Stephen told himself. The wind sang through the wires. All else was still. He was utterly alone. No prowling Fokker had spotted him.

Another S turn, shallower this time. Left rudder and stick and a sideslip to lose what was left of his height. Straighten her and hold her, just touching the stick. The ground was rushing past. Stick back— now! The wheels brushed the grass and ran on. He was down.

He kicked the rudder to make the tail skid slow her but the clearing was even smaller than he had thought. The Camel ran on and, with a smashing of twigs and branches, buried her nose in the trees.

Stephen freed his belt and jumped down. He was unhurt and safe, for the moment at any rate. He took the watch and the Very pistol from the cockpit. In situations such as this the first duty of a pilot was to destroy his machine to prevent it falling into the hands of the enemy. The blaze would attract attention but they had almost certainly spotted him anyway. He fired the pistol into the fuselage behind the tank. In a few seconds the whole thing was a sheet of flame. Stripping off his sidcot he threw it into the blaze. From somewhere behind him came shouts. He turned and dived into the shelter of the trees.

The wood was denser and more extensive than he had thought from the air. Finding a path, he ran down it. The shouting behind him increased in volume. He wondered if anyone had seen him leave the scene of the forced landing. Perhaps they would think he had perished in the flames.

Leaving the path he pushed through the undergrowth, making his way further into the heart of the forest. The excitement and concentration of the landing had prevented him thinking about himself but now he began to realise that his cold or fever or whatever he was suffering from had weakened him physically and that he would not be able to go much further without a rest. His breath was rasping in his chest and his head felt like a ball of lead. Panting and gasping he leant against the bole of a tree.

After a minute or two he took stock of his surroundings. The tree against which he was leaning was a huge oak with spreading branches and thick foliage. The lower branches were only a foot or so above his head. Here was a ready-made hiding-place.

Reaching up he caught the nearest branch and swung himself on to it. He was now all but completely concealed from anyone below.

From some little distance away he could hear orders being shouted and there were crashing sounds in the undergrowth. The hunt was up, it seemed. They had not been simple enough to assume that he had died in the machine and when he thought about it he realised that even a cursory search of the embers would reveal that there was no body there.

They'd have to comb every tree in the wood before they found him, but it might be wise nevertheless to get higher if he could. The thick branches were almost like steps. He went up them and the leaves closed behind him. Finding a wide fork he wedged himself into it and settled down to wait.

Overhead he heard the sound of engines and the rattle of machine-gun fire. It was probably the squadron fighting their way home. He wondered how the raid had gone and whether anyone but himself had failed to return and what Conway would do about his absence.

The crashing and banging about in the undergrowth went on for some time. Then it gradually faded and died away. His position was cramped and uncomfortable but he dared not leave it. They would surely have left a guard on the wreckage and there would be patrols moving along the edge of the forest to catch him if he made a break for it.

He tried to doze the time away and failed. He could not rid himself of thoughts of Conway and what action he would take were he to succeed in getting back. Conway had been behind and above and must have seen it all; he would put his own interpretation on what had happened and no evidence to confound him could be got from the machine which was now a cinder. Perhaps he'd be better not to try to get back but to give himself up and become a P.O.W. To hell with that. He'd get back somehow and face Conway. Clare, too, would be sure to back him up.

About mid-day it began to rain. It was the soft, seeping Flanders rain which soaked into everything. In a few minutes it had penetrated the screen of leaves and began to drop on to Stephen. Soon his tunic was wet through and water was running down his back. After a little while he began to shiver despite the warmth of the day. He became alternately hot and cold and began to wonder if it was all another of his nightmares from which he would wake up in the hut with Clare gently snoring opposite him. Shivering and shaking he waited for darkness to come.

After what seemed an eternity day slid into evening and evening into night. He knew that he must leave his refuge and try to find food and shelter. With difficulty he climbed down from the tree. A watery moon came out and by its light he found a narrow track stretching away through the wood.

By now, what with cramp and cold and wet, his feet were not carrying him very well. He stumbled and wandered on, trying to work out from the North Star the direction he should take to bring him nearer to the lines and safety. But in fact in his muddled state he had very little idea where he was going.

Then he blundered out into an open space and at the same time the moon sailed out from behind the edge of a cloud, lighting everything up. He was standing at the edge of a field in which cattle were grazing. At the far side of the field were farm buildings.

Making his way round the field he came to a gate which gave on to a broad flagged path. The path was weed-grown and many of the flagstones were cracked and broken. It led to a flight of steps that brought him on to a terrace. Set back from the terrace was a long, low, stone-built house, its windows dark and shuttered.

By now he knew he could go no farther that night. His breathing hurt him, he was alternatively shivering and burning, and his legs would scarcely support him.

A gravelled path as uncared for as the flags below ran along the terrace. It curved round the far end of the house and Stephen followed it. Dimly he made out a railed bridge across an area and a tall door with glass panels shuttered on the inside. The whole place was dark and silent. The only sound was that of the cattle tearing at the grass in the field below.

There was a large, tarnished brass handle on the door. He turned it and pushed but it was firmly locked on the inside. Desperate now, he banged with his fist on the panels and then hammered his heels against the woodwork. Still no sound or response came from within. The rain had started to sheet down again and the moon was obscured.

At length he heard what he thought were footsteps approaching the door. They came to its other side and stopped. Then there was the sound of a lock turning and a bolt being withdrawn. The door opened slowly. As it did so he could make out the bulk of a huge figure standing a few feet inside it. Then he pitched forward into darkness.

20

Stephen never knew how long he remained between life and death. All his later memories brought him was a confused mixture of a sweating and burning body that somehow seemed to be his own, of tossing on a bed that felt as if it was on fire, of outbursts of delirium and cool hands that gave comfort. He remembered, too, later in his illness, being coaxed into taking broth and swallowing tablets though he never knew what they were.

Then one day he awoke fully conscious and with his mind clear. He was in a cell-like room, lying on a bed. The walls of the room were stone, there seemed to be neither window nor door. A lamp was burning on a table beside him.

As he lay there looking at the arched vaulting of the ceiling he became aware of a presence near him. Someone moved to stand by his bedside. He turned his head to look. Even to do that cost him an effort.

A tall, slim, fair woman was looking down at him. Cool, long fingers touched his forehead. She smiled at him and spoke. 'The crisis has passed,' she said in perfect English. 'Do not try to exert yourself. You have been very ill.'

He had no wish to do anything other than obey her. His limbs felt as if water flowed through their veins; to try to raise his hands was as if he were struggling with a great weight. All he wanted to do was to lie in peace in his present position. He closed his eyes and drifted off into a dreamless sleep.

When he woke once more the room was in darkness save for the glow of a red night-light beside his bed. As he struggled up from sleep he saw a section of the wall swing slowly inwards. Through the opening came the woman he had seen earlier. She had a lamp in her hand. She was followed by a huge man carrying a tray. On the tray was a steaming bowl of broth, a carved chicken, bread and a glass of wine. The woman indicated the table by the bed and the man placed the tray on it. Then she gave a gesture of dismissal and he turned and left. The section of the wall swung into place behind him.

She looked down at Stephen, a gracious smile lighting up her rather formal features. 'Can you eat?' she said.

Stephen struggled to sit up. Placing an arm behind his shoulders she helped him. Then she smoothed the pillows into a support at his back.

'Who are you? Where am I? How long have I been here?' Stephen said.

'It has been quite a time, my child,' she answered. 'And it will be longer before you are fit to move. You have been very ill. You have had pneumonia. It was our prayers and your health that pulled you through. You must be very strong.'

When he had eaten she took the tray and left. It was only after she had gone that he realised she had not answered his other questions.

The days passed slowly but with their passing his strength grew. As he recovered the visits of the woman became fewer and fewer. His meals were brought to him by the huge man whom he soon discovered to be a deaf mute. Every day the room became more and more like a prison cell. When he was able to get up and move about he examined it. Ventilation came from two hidden shafts high up in the walls. There was no window. The section of the wall which opened to form a doorway had to have some means of moving it from the inside for he had seen her use it, but try as he might he failed to find it.

On her rare visits she avoided answering any questions, smiling enigmatically and telling him he would learn everything when he was stronger. The deaf mute brought him books—Tauchnitz editions of English favourites. He read and ate and slept. But with the return of strength came a growing impatience to be out of the place, back at the squadron, to learn how the war was going and what was happening beyond the walls.

And then one day she came and sat by his bed. Her face was set and drawn. 'My husband wishes to speak to you,' she said. 'I shall answer your questions now and tell you something of what we are.'

Their name was de Kerouailles. Both of them had had English governesses. They had spent much of their time in England and spoke English fluently. Her husband had inherited this estate the year before the War. He was an aviator, too, she said. He had been a pupil of Chevillard who had taught him to fly. With Chevillard he had taken part in the early Hendon meetings. It was there that she had met him for she, too, had been interested in aviation and had been taken by a friend to watch the flying. In a short time they had become engaged and had married. And then, very soon afterwards, he had suffered a dreadful accident. The aeroplane he had been flying had crashed. Although his life had been saved he had been paralysed from the waist down. As soon as he had left hospital he had returned to his estates, taking her with him, and become a recluse. When the Germans had invaded and swept past, their life had become even more divorced

214

than before from all contact with the outside world. Alphonse, the deaf mute, was their only servant. He had grown up in the place and had been on the estate for years before they had come to it.

'And the Huns,' Stephen said. 'When they came, did they interfere with you? We were told stories of atrocities—'

'Mostly lies, I think. Here they behaved with the utmost correctness. Once they had ascertained the extent of my husband's injuries they left us alone. We had two officers, flying men as you are, billeted on us in the early days. Since then, no one. It is true they searched everywhere for you after your landing but of course they did not find you. In Napoleonic times this room was constructed as a refuge for priests. They failed to find them then; they did not find you now.'

'Then I can go?'

She looked at him steadily. 'You will never succeed in making an escape,' she said. 'There are Germans everywhere. We do not see papers. Hidden away here we know little more than you do. But Alphonse goes to the village sometimes. While he cannot hear or speak, he sees. He can make signs which my husband understands. There are stories of a coming British advance, he says. Come, my husband is waiting.'

The door in the wall brought them into a wine cellar where bins and racks were stacked with bottles. She led the way along vaulted underground corridors off which doors gave into empty and deserted kitchens, sculleries, cellars and servants' rooms. They went up stone stairs, through a door at the top where the deaf mute was waiting. She left them there, disappearing into another room while the deaf mute led him across an empty echoing hallway, threw open tall double doors and motioned him to enter.

It must have been daylight still outside but, as elsewhere in the house, the shutters were up. Light came from a crystal chandelier hanging from the ceiling. A polished mahogany table ran almost the length of the room. At the top of it, a man was sitting. Only his torso and head were visible. He was entirely bald and had a heavy greying moustache. Three places were laid at the table and immediately in front of him were two cut-glass decanters.

'You will take a glass of wine with me,' he said. Without waiting for an answer he reached out a hand and filled a glass. From the other decanter which was nearest to him he topped up his own glass. The liquid he poured into it looked dark and strong. It must be brandy, Stephen thought.

'You are fortunate to be alive or so I am told,' his host continued, pushing the glass towards Stephen.

'I want to thank you both for all you have done for me. I am deeply grateful.'

'Do not thank me. Thanks are for my wife. She has a fondness for

215

aviators. A fondness which has been ill repaid, at least until now—'
He was looking beyond Stephen into the shadows. She must have
entered without Stephen's hearing her and was standing behind him.
He heard the sound of her catching her breath as if she was frightened.
The man at the head of the table leant forward and pushed the decanter towards her. 'A glass of wine, my dear,' he said. 'To drink a toast to
your gallant aviator who came so opportunely knocking at your door.'

His eyes were looking at her over the rim of his glass, mocking her.
Without speaking she filled her glass and then went round the table to
her seat on his right. The doors opened and the deaf mute entered
with a tray. Artichokes were put before them and the meal began. It
was one Stephen was to remember all his life.

'I flew a Henry Farman,' de Kerouailles said abruptly. 'What was
the machine which brought you down from the skies to our door?'

Stephen was on the point of answering when he remembered the instructions to those who landed in enemy territory. Name, rank and
number, nothing more must be given. 'I'm afraid I'm not allowed to
tell you that, sir,' he said.

'Indeed and why not, pray? You are among friends. Good friends, I
think you must agree. Friends who have succoured you and saved
your life.'

'I'm very sorry sir, those are our orders—'

'Ah, he is cautious, the little aviator. Remember that, my dear. The
fly who has walked into your web is a cautious fly. How many Germans have you shot down?' The last sentence was barked at him so
suddenly that it took Stephen by surprise.

'Twenty,' he answered without thinking and the moment he had
spoken he could have bitten his tongue off.

'Indeed, twenty. So we have a skilled aviator on our hands. Perhaps
he is not so cautious after all, my dear. Twenty victories! An ace. My
dear, you have captured an ace.'

'Scarcely that,' Stephen murmured, embarrassed as much now for
her as for himself.

All the time the deaf mute, Alphonse, was padding round the table
refilling their glasses. His master's glass was constantly in need of it
and the level of the brown decanter sank lower and lower. His next
words gave Stephen some insight into what was happening in that
house.

'There was only one thing I ever found to compare with the sensation of flight,' de Kerouailles went on, holding his glass up to the
light. 'And that was the physical love of women. In the course of two
minutes and by one mistake I lost them both. My wife tends me and
succours me but she can give me neither of the things I most desire.
And I can give her nothing. I love her but I torment her for my life is
only a long torment which I wish to end and lack the courage to do so.'

216

He drank once more and sat staring down the long table. There was silence for a moment and then he broke it again. 'My wife was a passionate woman once,' he said. 'I could play upon her body as a musician plays upon a stringed instrument or an airman his craft in flight. It would respond to me as those things would respond to one who can master them and their art. It would sing or wheel or yield or come to vibrant life at my touch. But now I am only an empty vessel, my store of cognac my only consolation. I am dead from the waist down, dead, I tell you, dead.' His voice rose to a shrillness that was almost a scream and he slammed his glass on to the table.

The deaf mute refilled the glass. De Kerouailles drank and looked at Stephen over the rim. 'One of our gallant allies,' he went on mockingly, his voice normal again. 'How different from the other one. I wonder where he is now? Rotting or burnt, I trust. Shot down in flames by the guns of a Frenchman. That would be a truly appropriate end. Or perhaps he lives triumphant—like our little friend here with his twenty victories soon to be augmented by another on a different field.'

The meal was finished, the mute set coffee cups before them. He poured cognac into a glass in front of Stephen.

'*Eau de vie*,' de Kerouailles said as he watched Stephen's every movement. 'The water of life. It will give you strength for the combat to come.' He raised his index finger. Instantly Alphonse was behind him, his hands on the back of the wheelchair. Impassively he manoeuvred it from the table and pushed it down the room towards the tall doors. In a moment or two he was back. Taking the brandy decanter from the table he left, pulling the doors to behind him.

Stephen drank and then raised his eyes to look across the table at her. Her chair was empty. She had slipped away silently and unnoticed. He was alone.

A huge hand fell on his shoulder. It belonged to the deaf mute. He stood behind the chair, waiting. Then he escorted him back to the cellar.

Despite the fact that Stephen's thoughts were in a turmoil he drifted quickly into an uneasy sleep. A sound in the room brought him back to a drowsy wakefulness. The night-light, as always, was burning beside him. He sat up in bed and stared about him. The section of the wall was opening.

She slipped through the gap and pushed the door shut. Slowly she came towards him and stood in silence looking down at him. A candle, its tiny flame casting shadows in the still darkness of the cell, was in her hand. She put it down beside the night light.

She was wearing a thin dressing gown of faded blue silk, brocaded at the collar and cuffs. Her hand went to her throat and slowly, one by one, she opened the buttons of the gown. It fell away and slid to the

217

floor. Beneath it she was naked. His breath came in a gasp as he looked at her standing beside him. The lamp-light cast a sort of aureole around her, framing her against the surrounding darkness.

She raised her arms to arch them above her head as if making a votive offering. As she lowered them she reached out to extinguish the candle and the lamp. Then she ripped back the covers and threw herself upon him.

Her strength and her passion took Stephen by surprise. The aloofness and reserve she had displayed towards him before made the sexual ardour and hunger which now possessed her all the more astonishing. It was as if, driven by desperation for all those wasted years, she was determined to devour and consume him. Stephen had been celibate since that night in Paris. Moreover the suppressed sexuality that seemed to permeate the house had already stimulated something within him. He found himself as avid as she was. He took her fiercely and she groaned with pleasure, grappling him to her. Then, when it was over, satiated, they both fell into an exhausted sleep.

When he awoke both candle and night-light were lighting. The sheets were thrown back from the bed and she was lying naked beside him. It was as if she wanted to exhibit herself defenceless before him.

'You saw how he treats me,' she said without preamble. 'You heard what he said. He is mad. He made me do this. Tomorrow he will have me tell him every detail. It is part fulfilment for him for what he cannot do, part punishment.'

'Punishment?' Stephen said, puzzled. 'How—'

'It was one of the German aviators. Perhaps you could not grasp all he meant at dinner. Now I will explain. He was young, the German, so was I. He was handsome and he wanted me. My husband could do nothing. I was starved of everything, love, affection, the pleasures of the bed. Oh, yes, he was right when he said I was a passionate woman. You, too, know that now, little lover.' She raised herself on one elbow and stroked his cheek, softly. 'I slept with him—the Hun. I thought my husband would never find out. But he did. Alphonse knew. He told him, I think.'

'Could your husband not understand—?'

'Understand—with a Boche aviator? It was for him the ultimate insult. To his family, to his country, above all to his pride. I had to be crushed, humiliated. He gave me to Alphonse in our bed while he watched.'

'Alphonse, dear God, and what since?'

'It was only once and as a punishment. Perhaps as a punishment for us both. For, just as I had betrayed him, Alphonse had betrayed me. Betrayal is the greatest sin—'

'But now, this, he sent you?'

'He is unbalanced. Deprivation, pain, hurt pride and his own

218

terrors are driving him mad. When you dropped from the skies, since you were an aviator he seemed to think he could in some way live again in you. That is why he wished to talk to you about flying. And he knew I wanted you. I nursed you. I saw your body. I knew again what the loss of a man meant to me. I longed to do what I have done tonight. That is why I kept away from you. But he knew, that devil, he knew. He tortured me. He has a collection of erotic books with which he attempts to solace himself. Every night he took me to his room and made me pore over them. Then he sent me here. I hated him for what he was doing. But I had to come; I could not keep away. And now I regret nothing save that he sent me. There, my little airman, I have bared myself to you in more ways than one. Come to me again.' Her arms went up and around him and she pulled him down to her.

When he awoke again she was gone. He lay on the tousled bed thinking of her. He was exhausted. All the suppressed passion of years of torment and misery had been expended upon him in a single night. It had been altogether different from anything he and Babs had known together. There had been a kind of desperation about her. It had been a savage, wildly exciting and almost frightening encounter. On his back were deep scratches gouged by her nails and a scarlet weal on his shoulder which her teeth had left. The bed reeked of sex and of the scent she used.

That night she came to him again. This time her passion was more muted. It was as if the violence of their bouts of the night before had released and relaxed some of the tensions of her desperation. She was ardent and loving but the wildness and the fury had gone. Again when he awoke the bed seemed filled with her presence.

The days passed as slowly as they had done before but now almost nightly the door would open and she would come to his bed. Her splendid body and the ardour with which she gave it to him aroused him and satisfied him sexually. Beyond that she stirred no emotions in him. He was never remotely in love with her though he suspected she was deluding herself that she was in love with him. He implored her to help him get away. At first she was adamant in her refusal. 'I won't,' she said. 'I won't let you go.'

'Be sensible. The war must end sometime. I can't stay here forever.'

'Forever, forever,' she pouted. 'I have already experienced an eternity of shame and torment, mon petit. There is no forever, only now. That is a lesson I have learnt. Besides, the Boche will catch you.'

'That is a chance I'll have to take. You must help me.'

'No. Who would have thought such strength, such ferocity, such passion was in that body which was so frail when I first found it?' She looked at him under her long eyelashes and laughed and stroked him.

It was impossible to move her. She was alive again, she said. She had taught herself to live only in the present and now that the present had given her a chance of happiness she was not going to throw it away. Besides, she said, the monster upstairs would not let her set him free. He was taking a perverted pleasure in all that was happening.

So, for a while, it went on. And then, suddenly, her visits stopped. His only visitor was the deaf mute who brought him food and sometimes took him for walks on the terrace. During these Stephen wondered if he could make a break for it but always the mute was at his elbow, between him and freedom, silent, watchful and threatening.

After the mute had taken supper away one evening she returned. Sitting on the end of the bed she regarded him steadily, making no move to approach. 'I am frightened for you, mon petit,' she said. 'He is getting worse. All this has unbalanced him. It began as a game to torment me and to give him vicarious pleasure. But it has not worked out that way. What he makes me tell him about what we do together has started up again tenfold all the longings and cravings for his life before the accident. He knows, too, that you have awakened something in me. Instead of tormenting me he is tormenting himself. He has fancies. Sometimes he persuades himself that you are the Boche pilot. There is nothing he may not do.'

'So we must both escape.'

'No. Not both. I must stay here come what may. But you must go. I shall do what I can. But it will not be easy.'

'What is happening in the war?'

'The English are attacking everywhere. The Boche is falling back. The fighting in the air surpasses all that has gone before. It may be over soon.'

She crossed to his bed. Putting out a hand she ruffled his hair. 'I was mad myself for a little while, I think,' she said. 'He wants to keep you here a prisoner forever. But I shall set you free.'

More days passed and she did not come back. Stephen thought he would go mad. He re-read the Tauchnitz copies and then threw them away. He tortured himself thinking about what was happening on the squadron and whether Clare had come through. The walks on the terrace ceased. The mute now dumped his food in front of him and hurried away. Her last words about his being kept a prisoner forever ran round and round in his brain.

He began to lose track of time. Nothing could be learnt from the mute, and still she did not come. Was he going to spend the rest of his life here? Where was she? What was happening?

One morning, no meal came. Panic took hold of Stephen then. Perhaps the advancing armies had taken them away and left him here to die cooped up in this hole in the ground. He was sitting on the edge of his bed staring at the wall and fighting his fears when the door opened and she came in.

'He has *la grippe*, my husband,' she said. 'He is very ill. You are free. Hurry.'

'And Alphonse?'

'I found a sleeping draught my husband had. I put it in his coffee. But he is a strong man. I do not know how long it will last.'

Stephen was struggling into his tunic. 'The Boches,' he said. 'What about them? Where are they?'

She paused and laid her hands on his arms. 'The war is over,' she said.

'Over? We've won! They're beaten! When?'

'The Armistice was signed ten days ago. You're safe. You can return.'

She brought him out of the cell, up the stone stairs, and along dark passages where he had never been before. Here, sombre pictures of former and forgotten de Kerouailles stared down at them from the walls. Cobwebs wove patterns about pieces of buhl and ormolu whose inlay was flaking and gilt worn and tarnished. At length they came to the door giving on to the terrace through which Stephen had come the night of his forced landing months before. She pulled back the bolts and opened it.

The daylight hit Stephen almost like a blow in the face. He put up a hand to protect his eyes and, after a little while, stared about him, taking stock of his surroundings.

Below him was the narrow strip of field in which the cows had grazed, and beyond it the trees. Their leaves had fallen and, black and stark, on every side they crowded upon the house.

She led the way along the terrace and they came to the front of the house. A flight of wide stone steps, with weeds sprouting through the joins, went down to what had once been a spacious gravel sweep but which had now become almost entirely covered with thick, rank grass.

At the far side of this a pair of wrought-iron gates, sagging and broken, gave on to a driveway that entered the woods through an arch of trees.

'That will take you to the main highway to Lille,' she said, pointing. 'Go now.'

'What will happen to you?'

'Nothing. He is very ill. He may not recover. What we had could not last forever. I know that now. The War—The War is over. There is no place for madness or for dreams.' She turned and for the last time clung to him. Her hands were all over him, her mouth crushed against his, her tongue was probing him, seeking him as if it would devour him. Later he was to remember that it tasted of cognac. Tears were coursing down her face as she freed him. 'Think of me sometimes, little soldier,' she said.

221

Stephen ran down the steps. At the entrance to the woods he paused to look back. She was standing on the terrace, her hand on an ornamental urn, the grim bulk of the house behind her. She raised her hand in a last gesture of farewell.

When Stephen reached the road he found that there was a considerable amount of military traffic coming and going and he had little difficulty in flagging a lift from an A.S.C. lorry. This dropped him near the station in Lille. He made his way to the nearest café, ordered coffee and croissants and after them half a bottle of champagne. Drinking the champagne, he began to take stock of his situation.

He knew very well that he should go to the Town Major's office and report his return, but he had no intention of doing so. The daylight was still hurting his eyes, he felt shaky and queasy and he did not think he was capable of expressing himself clearly or giving a rational account of what had happened to him. He had no papers of any sort and the war had been over for ten days. All kinds of explanations which he was not prepared to give would be called for in the Town Major's office; he would have to render them in writing, in triplicate probably before senior officers who would bully and badger and snarl at him. He had to have some base, somewhere to sort himself out. As a first step he determined to get back to the squadron and find out what had happened while he had been away and how his absence had been dealt with. It meant facing Conway if Conway was still alive, but better Conway whom he knew than a host of red-faced, blustering majors and colonels from the staff.

Leaving the café he strolled around searching for a familiar face or anything which might help him locate the squadron. After a little while he saw a Flying Corps captain standing at a street corner looking about him as if waiting for someone.

'245 Squadron,' the captain said in answer to his query. 'They're at Limoye just down the road. I've transport coming along in a minute or two. We go past it, old chappie, if you want a lift. Here we are. Hop in.'

A Crossley tender had drawn up beside them. Stephen climbed up and sat down on the hard seat with a great feeling of relief. It was good to be back, to hear the old casual slang, to see the familiar khaki and to listen to the flat roar of the Crossley engine once again. The captain was chatting as they went. 'Back off leave, are you?' he asked and then went on without waiting for an answer. 'Been to London? Top-hole shows from all accounts. And the gals! What ho! They say if a virgin crosses Trafalgar Square all the lions roar and Nelson comes down from his pillar and lifts his hat! This is it—Limoye. Not surprised you couldn't find 'em. Everything's mixed up now *la guerre* is *fini*. Cheerio!'

Stephen stood for a moment at the entrance to the aerodrome, getting his bearings. The roadway curved away between a cluster of Nissen huts. But there was an empty and deserted air about the place as if the life had gone from it. The effell hung limply on its pole. No one was flying. There was no sound of engines being run up. Two Camels stood unattended in front of a farm building. On the farther side was a line of Bessonneau hangars but no sounds of activity came from them.

As he approached the machines, there came to him the familiar and well-remembered scent of burnt castor oil and flying dope. An all but overwhelming desire caught hold of him to get into one of the Camels, take off and fly again. He wanted to feel the air whipping past him, to dive and swoop and zoom, forgetting everything but the feeling of oneness with the machine, to escape to the cleanliness and mindlessness of the upper air.

As he stood there looking at the Camels, enjoying again their stubby air of purposefulness and power, he saw a figure walking towards him. It was one of the ack emmas who had been with the squadron from its first beginnings. Harris, Stephen remembered, was his name. He was a corporal now, it seemed, from the stripes on his sleeve. 'Can I do anything for you, sir?' Harris said, saluting. 'Were you looking for—' His jaw dropped as he recognised Stephen. 'Goodness, it's Mr Raymond. We thought you were dead, sir.'

'Not yet, anyway, Harris. It's Corporal Harris now, I see.'

'Yes, sir. Haven't been found out up till now. Glad to see you back, sir. But you'll find great changes here.'

'Captain de Vaux? Did he get through all right?'

'Major de Vaux, he was, sir. 'E got the squadron when Major Conway was promoted.'

'Good God, Clare a Major—but—was?'

'Shot down, sir. Three Fokkers got 'im. Day before the Armistice it 'appened. Turned back, 'e did, to 'elp one of the new men. 'E's missing, sir. No one saw 'im go in. But it's been a long time. Captain Mason 'as the squadron now, temporary like. But you wouldn't 'ave known 'im, sir.'

'And Mr Baxter?'

'Oh, 'e's still 'ere, sir.'

Harris directed him to the squadron office in the farmhouse. Sick at heart Stephen walked towards it. So Clare had gone as well. He was the only one of the old crowd left. When she had spoken of the fighting in the air intensifying over the last pushes, he had known the odds must have been building up against Clare but somehow he had always believed he would come through. Conway had been promoted and gone. That was one relief anyway. He pushed open the door of the office.

Baxter, just as before, was busily scribbling. Files and papers,

223

returns and reports, in-trays and out-trays, littered the trestle table in front of him. Hearing Stephen enter, he looked up and put down his pen. Stephen stared at him without speaking.

As recognition came to him Baxter went pale. It was almost, Stephen thought, as if he had seen a ghost from another war, another age, walk in, as indeed in some ways, life being so short and time so quick to pass in the R.F.C., he had.

'I'm real,' Stephen said. 'I'm reporting back for duty.'

Baxter reached out a hand which Stephen saw was shaking slightly and fiddled amongst a pile of papers and files. 'So, you've turned up again,' he said. He found the file he wanted and began to leaf through it. He was regaining his composure every minute. 'I don't know where you've come from,' he went on. 'But you seem to have taken your time about it.' He looked up from the file and Stephen thought he saw a gleam of satisfaction come into his eyes. 'You're under arrest, Raymond,' he said.

'Under arrest? What the hell for?'

Baxter's little moustache bristled. 'Cowardice and desertion in the face of the enemy,' he said.

PART THREE

TROUBLES

21

The actual charge laid against Stephen was of '*Misbehaving before the enemy in such a manner as to show cowardice in that he when on active service wilfully abandoned his flight and landed in enemy territory*'.

The court assembled in a building in Lille which had been used by the Germans as a military barracks. The President was a be-medalled Cavalry general. Stephen, sitting without his Sam Browne, his escorting officer on one side and the officer assigned to his defence on the other, ran his eye over the rest of them. There was a full colonel with staff tabs, a Sapper major, and someone in the garish new R.A.F. uniform so festooned with gold braid that Stephen could not determine his rank. He was wearing wings, so presumably he had flown. Stephen did not recognise him nor did his name mean anything to him. Probably a two-seater or bomber pilot, Stephen thought with the faint contempt shown by fighter pilots towards all other flying men. A young and fresh-faced captain completed the court, save for the Judge Advocate, a sallow-faced, serious-looking man wearing steel-rimmed glasses.

The prosecution witnesses were across the room from him. Conway, with the extra pip of a Lieutenant-Colonel on his shoulder and a D.S.O. now to add to the decorations on his chest, sat staring straight in front of him. Alongside him were Heal and Baxter, who had both metamorphosed into captains—and Davis. Davis, Stephen thought wryly, of all people the most ill-fitted to give evidence against a fellow-officer charged with cowardice. In fact Davis did not look too happy. He was shifting about in his seat and his fingers were constantly playing with his gloves or fiddling with his Sam Browne.

Bradley, the gentle-looking Gunner captain who had been assigned to Stephen's defence, looked them over too. He leant over to Stephen. 'A sorry crew from what you tell me,' he said. 'I wonder when the cock will crow thrice.'

Bradley, who was a barrister in private life, seemed to have grown in stature since he had entered the courtroom with his books and

227

papers. At first his retiring manner and quiet approach had persuaded Stephen that he would be of little assistance to him. He gave the impression of being a meek and mild, milk and water kind of chap, not at all the sort to take on one such as Conway. Now Stephen was not so sure. During the later conferences Bradley had appeared to know exactly what he was about. There was, too, an undeniable air of authority surrounding him as he sat, pen in hand, lightly tapping the table in front of him and surveying the scene with the bored expression of one who has been there many times before.

The Judge Advocate cleared his throat and began to read the order convening the court. When he had finished the President looked at Stephen and asked him the time-honoured words. 'Do you object to be tried by me or by any of the officers whose names have been read over?'

'No, sir,' Stephen said firmly.

The Judge Advocate then began to swear the members. Watching him, Stephen felt much the same as before his first flight in a Camel or his first encounter with the enemy. There was the same sudden dryness in the mouth, the same tightening of the guts, the same feeling of meeting the inevitable.

When he had first been placed under arrest the shock of it combined with the aftermath of his imprisonment had left Stephen depressed and apathetic and unwilling to do anything to help himself. What was uppermost in his mind was the shame he had brought on his parents and what they would feel, his mother especially, when they heard he was to be court-martialled for cowardice. They must have been notified by now that he was no longer missing but he could not bring himself to tell them what had happened.

At times he quite seriously contemplated suicide. That way out had been taken before, as he knew. A flight commander on a neighbouring squadron at Bessières had cracked up and asked to be sent home. On being told by a fire-eating squadron commander that it would probably mean facing a court-martial when he got there he had gone to his hut and shot himself. But suicide would mean an admission of guilt and, apathetic though he was, he was determined not to give up yet and allow Conway to claim a complete victory over him.

Nevertheless Bradley found him an uncommunicative and unhelpful client. All he would say during their early interviews was: 'The bloody engine conked out and that's the truth whatever the bastard says. Conway always had it in for me. He wanted to break me and now he thinks he's done it.'

Because beneath his gentle exterior Bradley was in fact an experienced and combative advocate, he sensed that there was more to be said in Stephen's defence than appeared on the surface and he became determined to dig it out.

228

The prosecution's case looked damning enough. Conway had had a distinguished and successful war career. There was nothing to suggest that he was telling anything other than the truth in his statement which was contained in the abstract of evidence. There he flatly declared that he was behind and above Stephen and in a position to observe him clearly. When Stephen left the flight and dived away his engine was apparently giving full revs and functioning perfectly. Moreover for reasons of his own he had kept Stephen under close observation from take-off and at no time had he seen any indication that his engine was faulty.

At first Bradley had been of the opinion that Stephen's nerve had given way under the constant stress of war flying, that he had in fact voluntarily left the flight and was now unwilling to admit it. He had made it his business to find out something about the new category of illness which the R.F.C. medicos were introducing—flying sickness debility, which in plain words meant war exhaustion and too much exposure to fear. The medical officer to whom he had spoken about it had gone on to say that no man could sustain indefinitely the strain of combat in the air especially if combined with constant ground strafing. Thus Bradley had been initially of the opinion that his only line to follow would be basically a plea in mitigation founded on this medical evidence and Stephen's unquestioned record of twenty victories and an M.C.

Then something happened to change his mind. During one of their conversations Stephen amplified his former statements a little. 'Conway hated me ever since we were at school together,' he said. 'He made me do more flying than anyone else in the squadron to try to get me killed or to break me. He didn't do either and now he's thought this one up.'

Bradley went away, picked up the abstract of evidence and read it through again. The accusation Conway made was of voluntarily leaving the flight but he had in his statement gone a little further than this. He had mentioned Stephen's return the day before with a broken ignition wire, stating that he had been far from satisfied about this but had given Stephen the benefit of the doubt. He had warned him, however, that further reports of engine failure on his part would be subject to an especially severe scrutiny and that this would apply more than ever to the following day's raid. He added that he had been for some time convinced that Stephen's nerve was going but that in view of his record he was prepared to give him every chance.

This did not at all reconcile with what Stephen had said. Putting the abstract under his arm Bradley went along to Stephen's room. 'Have you read this thoroughly?' he asked him, showing it to him.

'I haven't read it at all,' was the reply.

229

'Read it now word for word, especially Colonel Conway's statement. I'll be back in an hour. Tell me what you think of it.'

When he returned he found Stephen in a changed mood. Something had woken him out of his apathy. The abstract was open on the table in front of him at Conway's evidence. Some of the lines were underscored in pencil. 'The swine is telling lies,' Stephen said, pointing to the statement.

'Just how do you suggest that?' Bradley asked quietly.

'Leaving out my engine failure on that last show which I'll go into in a minute, it's the broken ignition wire the day before. I got signed confirmation of that from Cutforth, the S.E. squadron commander, and handed it in. It must be in the records somewhere unless he and Baxter tore it up or something. Is that possible?'

'Anything is possible in war but I'm afraid that wasn't necessary. There aren't any squadron records. I applied for them right at the beginning to check things up. The squadron office got a direct hit in an air raid just before the Armistice. All the records went west.'

'So they can say what they like?'

'As far as the records are concerned, yes, I'm afraid so. It comes down again to your word against theirs. Look, why don't you tell me the whole story?'

Stephen walked across to the window and, his hands thrust in his pockets, looked out across the flat industrial landscape. 'All right,' he said slowly. 'But it goes back a long way. Got a gasper?'

Bradley took a leather case from his pocket and handed it to him. Stephen lit up and dropped the match into the lid of a cigarette tin which did duty as an ash-tray. Bradley pulled a chair up to the table, opened a flat, barrister's notebook, and began to write as Stephen talked.

Two hours later, with the smoke thick between them, Bradley put down his pen. 'So that's it,' he said.

'Do you believe me?'

'That's a question you should never ask an advocate but in this case I'll answer it. There was something too glib about the evidence in the abstract, and the business of the missing receipt clinches it. He doesn't know it but he's pushing it a bit too hard. Yes, I believe you, but I'll be brutally frank with you. The question is, will the court? Once again we come down to the fact that it's only your word against his. Is there any possible corroboration of what you've just told me?'

'If only Clare were here. He was looking back when I dropped out. He must have heard the engine missing and seen the prop stop. I suppose there's no hope?'

'Precious little, I'm afraid, at this distance of time. Anything else?'

Stephen pondered for a minute or two. 'Yes, there is, now I come to think of it,' he said. 'Uncle Warmsley, the recording officer that

Conway sacked, he knew what was going on. When he was getting on to the boat he told me he had it all written down if ever I needed it. But I don't know how to get in touch with him. He was a solicitor in civvy street, I believe.'

'If he's alive we'll get him. If he's been demobbed the Law Society can trace him for us, if not the War Office will have to bring him out.'

'Won't this cost a fortune? I haven't any money.'

'There's a War Office Regulation by which they've got to contribute to witnesses' expenses. I'm not sure of the details, to be honest, and I imagine they'll be pretty stingy about it but, look, your people, won't they help?'

'I haven't told them anything. The disgrace, it'd kill them.'

'Do you mean to sit there and tell me they know nothing except that you're not dead?'

'That's right.'

'But, good God, man, if anything were to go wrong they'd never forgive themselves.'

'My father, perhaps, my mother would never forgive me.'

'If you won't write to them, will you let me? I'll tell them, which is true, that I believe you to be innocent. At the moment Warmsley is the only corroboration we have. It's vital we get him and to do that we may need financial help.' Bradley hesitated. 'You know, I do think you ought to write yourself,' he said.

'Very well, then. I'll write to my father. He'll understand, I think. It's only that it all seemed so hopeless—'

Bradley was flipping through his notes. 'That broken ignition wire,' he said. 'You got written verification from the S.E. major, and a copy, I think you said. What happened to the copy? You didn't hand it in, I suppose?'

'I left it with my kit. The Lord only knows what happened to it. It must have got lost or destroyed when I went missing, I imagine. Would it have helped?'

'It's not conclusive, nothing is conclusive in a case such as this but, yes, it would have helped. Conway didn't know of its existence, I suppose. He must have been sure when the records were lost that he couldn't be contradicted or he wouldn't have put that bit in. I could have used it in cross-examination. I've got to shake him somehow and it won't be easy.'

Three days later Bradley was handed a telegram which said: *Spare no expense. Travelling. Raymond.* Shortly afterwards he received confirmation that Uncle Warmsley had been located and would come out. Both these things gave him some hope. Money provided the sinews of war at law as well as in battle and if Warmsley bore out what Stephen had said then at least he had something to go on.

231

Courts-martial were said to be fair tribunals, and by and large they were, but where an officer was charged with cowardice they were inclined to lean towards the prosecution. An officer was expected to set an example and any leniency was held likely to be an encouragement to others to do the same. In the end, Bradley reckoned, much would depend on how he could deal with Conway in cross-examination. An all-out attack on an officer with such a distinguished record as Conway's would straight away alienate the court and ruin what chances he had. Conway would have to be led into error but what errors were there into which to entice him? His evidence of the actual incident with which Stephen was charged stood like a rock. Bradley loaded a large pipe, stared at his notes and wrestled with his problem. Of course if Major de Vaux had been there all might have been different but Clare had now been posted missing believed killed and Bradley was convinced that must be an accurate return.

22

Stephen was standing by the window some days later, having abandoned all efforts to read or play patience, which were the only methods available to him for passing the long hours, when his escorting officer was called to the doorway. There was a short conversation and then the other man turned to him. 'Your parent is here, Raymond,' he said to him.

'Father!' Stephen exclaimed.

But it was not his father; it was his mother who stood in the doorway.

'Your father has not been very well,' she said, entering the room and stripping off her gloves. 'And I'd like a chair, young man,' she added, giving the escorting officer one of her haughtier stares.

'Yes, madam,' he said and rushed to obey as people usually did when they met her bark and her air of command.

'I—I didn't do it, mother,' Stephen said as she sat down. He wished his father had come. He could have explained things to him. He did not know how or where to begin with his mother. There had never been any real communication between them. Even after what he had just said he could not foresee how she would take his denial. But her response was immediate and absolute. 'Of course not,' she snapped, sitting bolt upright on the hard chair. 'I never heard of anything so ridiculous. Who is responsible for bringing this absurd charge?' She glared for a moment at the escorting officer who opened his mouth to reply and then thought better of it. 'I shall have something to say to your uncle, the General, about all this, let me tell you.'

'You'd better see Captain Bradley, my defending officer, mother. He can explain it all far better than I can.'

'I have already seen him and I must say I am far from impressed. He appears to be a most ineffectual young man. You should have a K.C. from London. I intend to put that in hand immediately—'

'I don't know if that would be wise, mother. Captain Bradley is a qualified barrister, after all.' Stephen sought for a way of heading his mother off the subject until he could see Bradley himself. 'Mother,

233

how ill is father? And how are things at the Bay?'

'Your father has been having dizzy spells and a touch of gastric trouble. He is better but the doctor would not allow him to travel. He sent you a letter.' She opened her reticule and inspected the contents. 'Here it is.'

Stephen took it from her and put it on one side to be read at his leisure.

'And the others?' Stephen said. 'The Murtaghs? Do you hear of Babs?'

'Barbara Murtagh is married.' Honoria gave a disapproving sniff and her mouth shut like a trap.

'Married? Babs? She can't be—'

'Indeed she is and a more shocking performance I never saw. What Desmond was thinking of to allow it I cannot imagine. But then I believe he is in debt and in trouble again. That dreadful creature—'

'What dreadful creature? Mother, what are you talking about?'

'Andrew Massiter.' Honoria almost spat out the words. 'Married her in London three months ago. Now they're in South America on an extended honeymoon or some such nonsense looking after his interests there. Dunlay is shut up. It will be as well if he doesn't open it again. Marrying that child indeed. He's old enough to be her father—her grandfather if it comes to that.' Honoria sniffed again.

Stephen sat staring at the table unwilling to look up lest his mother should guess the extent of his hurt. Always through these long and desperate days he had clung to the thought of Babs. Memories of her, and of her warmth and tenderness, had been comfort and reassurance to him in all he was going through. And now she was married to Massiter, her youth and loveliness spent on an old man. Looking back, with the benefit of hindsight, all at once it became clear to him that Massiter had wanted her ever since the day they had sailed together to his castle; he remembered, too, how Massiter had cunningly questioned him as to her whereabouts in Paris and his pressing invitation for them to stay to lunch in the Ritz. What Andrew Massiter wanted he got, what he had he kept. Babs was gone and he was facing a court-martial. There was nothing left.

But his mother was speaking again. 'After you were posted as missing,' she was saying. 'I had a letter from a Captain de Vaux, a friend of yours. He sent it when he was on leave it London.'

'Clare,' Stephen said dully. 'He's dead. What did he say? Not that it matters now.'

'He was a nephew of the Earl of Mulcaster I understand.'

'Yes, mother. So he always told me.' Despite himself Stephen smiled. Trust his mother to get her social priorities right.

'Amongst other things he said he didn't think you were being fairly treated by your C.O. That's this wretched man, Conway, I suppose, and who indeed may he be?' His mother gave another of her contemptuous sniffs. 'He said that he had found this in your effects and he sent it on, telling me to keep it safely since it might be of use if you came back.' Honoria opened her bag again, took out a folded piece of paper and placed it on the table between them.

It was the copy of the certificate verifying the broken ignition wire signed by Cutforth and his recording officer.

When Honoria had gone, Stephen opened his father's letter. He was still filled with a burning bitterness and he sat staring at it for a few minutes before starting to read. He could not get thoughts of Babs out of his mind. Why? Why? Why had she done this to him? That devil Massiter. He began to wonder what he was like in bed. That led to other thoughts better kept away. He shuddered slightly and took up the letter.

His father, as always, gave him news of the Bay. The crops were in and it had been a good harvest. He had had a little stomach trouble. It was nothing but it had left him weak and that old ass Dr O'Byrne would not let him travel. Rogers had died during the summer and Mikey 'now very grown up and fairly responsible!' had fully taken over his duties. Then his father continued: '*I have, I'm afraid, what may be sad news for you, my boy. Barbara Murtagh has been married and to Andrew Massiter. Do not think too hardly of her—or of him, either, I suppose. She was home on leave after you were posted as missing and she came to see me. As time passed she had begun to give up hope that you were alive as indeed I fear we all had save your mother. She talked to me about you, saying that nothing mattered to her once you were gone. And it is said that Desmond only gave his consent to the marriage because Massiter threatened to reveal to the stewards the details of some racing scandal that occurred just before the war if he refused to do so. Massiter is a man of power just now and an intimate with the great. If the story is true and I have no reason to doubt it I fear the stewards would have had to listen to him and it would have gone hardly with Desmond. As you may know by now, he was shot down in June last and lost a leg. He is at home trying to get a stable together and I believe beginning to ride out again himself despite the loss of his limb. Whatever may be thought of his morals there can be no doubt that as a man he is indomitable . . .*'

Stephen had taken some crumbs of comfort from the letter. It was in his pocket as he watched Conway stride across the room to be sworn. He gave his evidence clearly and concisely. In fact, Stephen thought, he cut an impressive figure with his row of medal ribbons, the colonel's crown and pip on his shoulder and the general air of confidence and authority which surrounded him. Against all this Stephen wondered if he stood any chance at all. His own witnesses were pitifully few and what weight would his word carry against Conway's?

At least Uncle Warmsley had arrived. It was he who frustrated

235

Honoria's plan to bring out a K.C. He had known Bradley by reputation before the war and he satisfied her that it was far less likely to antagonise the court to have the defence conducted by a serving officer rather than a civilian barrister however eminent.

Bradley himself watched Conway closely as he took down his evidence. Conway was definite and damning, bringing out one by one the points against Stephen, culminating in the actual act of cowardice which he alleged. But, Bradley told himself, he's pushing it all a bit too hard, he's piling up too many old scores. Beneath it all for those with eyes to see and ears to hear was an undercurrent of hostility to Stephen. It was his task to bring that hostility into the open. He rose to cross-examine.

'Lieutenant Raymond has a distinguished record, I understand,' he said.

'I'm not sure just what you mean,' Conway answered aggressively.

'Twenty victories. Would you not agree that that is a distinguished record?'

'Others have far better scores.'

'That's not the point, Colonel Conway, nor is it an answer to the question I am asking you. Do you not agree that a score of twenty enemy aeroplanes destroyed constitutes a distinguished record?'

'Possibly. That is to say if they are accurate.'

Bradley paused. He risked a quick look at the court. The President had put down his pen and was staring at Conway. The Judge Advocate was making a note on the pad in front of him. This was a better beginning than Bradley had hoped for. He was on the verge of obtaining a disclosure of prejudice. 'Will you clarify that for me, Colonel, please,' he said.

'Raymond was very friendly with my predecessor, Major Haynes. I always felt that a number of those victories should have been credited to Major Haynes but that he allowed Raymond to take them. After I took over the squadron he did not score to any great extent.'

'But at the commencement of your time as squadron commander the squadron was employed in ground strafing mostly, I think?'

Conway hesitated then he said, 'Yes, that is so.'

'And in ground-strafing there are few opportunities for shooting down enemy machines?'

'Some skilled pilots manage to do both.'

'And what is your own score, Colonel Conway?'

'I understand I am credited with four enemy aeroplanes destroyed. I did not seek personal glory.'

'Quite so. But it is true, is it not, that at the time you took over the squadron and until he was posted as missing Lieutenant Raymond was and remained the highest scoring pilot in the squadron?'

'If the record says so—yes.'

'The record does say so. And this squadron was one of the leading Camel squadrons on the Western Front?'

'When I took it over I was far from satisfied with the discipline of the pilots. Lieutenant Raymond in my opinion was not a satisfactory officer from the disciplinary point of view. I had occasion to reprimand him more than once and shortly before he was posted as missing I did so very severely for his avoiding stand-by duty. Captain Baxter can verify this.'

Bradley had not wanted that answer nor did he like it for it might well indicate that Stephen had been dodging duty even before he went absent. He sought to recover his ground. 'Is it not the case that the stand-by was changed very late after Lieutenant Raymond had left for St Omer?'

'I don't recall that that was so.'

'Did you, yourself, change the stand-by?'

'I cannot remember, the matter was reported to me by Captain Baxter.'

'Whatever happened about that, will you now answer my question—in terms of enemy machines destroyed was not 245 Squadron one of the most successful on the Western Front?'

'In those terms, yes.'

'In war are there any other terms, Colonel?'

'Neither General Leatherhead nor myself was satisfied with the disciplinary state of the squadron.'

'Be that as it may the squadron was successful and Lieutenant Raymond was its highest scorer, and the holder of a Military Cross. Will you now agree that his was a distinguished record?'

'I should have thought that with his record he should have gained more than one decoration.'

He's not doing too badly, the brute, Bradley thought. He hasn't answered one question directly and he's fencing with me all the time. He's got in some neat stabs, too. But I can't really go for him yet, it'll only put them against me. Still I think the J.A. has got the message. 'Now, Colonel,' Bradley resumed. 'Would it be true to say that when you were in command of his flight and later of the squadron Lieutenant Raymond was given more flying hours than any other pilot?'

'Quite untrue.'

'You remember Captain Warmsley, no doubt?'

'Yes, he was my recording officer.'

'Exactly. And I have to tell you that he kept a record which he will produce showing that what I have said is correct. Furthermore, Captain Warmsley will say that he protested to you about it. Do you still deny it?'

'Emphatically. Warmsley would say anything.'

'Indeed. Why?'

'I sacked him.'

'Why?'

'He was too friendly with the pilots who needed pulling together and licking into shape. He took their side.'

'We'll pass from that for a moment. You told us in your evidence in chief about the affair of the broken ignition wire of Lieutenant Raymond's, and of his leaving a patrol the day before the raid. You said that you were profoundly suspicious of the truth of his explanation.'

'I was.'

'Yet in the abstract of evidence which I have here and to which I refer you, you say that in view of his record you gave him the benefit of the doubt. But from what you have just told us it seems you were suspicious of his record, too?'

'The abstract is wrong. I never said that. What I intended to say was that I gave him the benefit of the doubt until I saw how he behaved on the raid tomorrow. And I told him so.'

'But you didn't correct the abstract until now?'

'It didn't occur to me. I had other things to do.'

'Here we have an officer on the most serious charge that can be brought against him short of murder and you tell us that you did not correct your evidence during all this time because you had other things to do?'

'If I thought about it at all it seemed a minor matter. Besides I did not know what questions you were going to ask me.'

'Did Lieutenant Raymond hand you a certificate signed by the C.O. and recording officer of 332 Squadron verifying the engine failure and that it was due to a broken ignition wire?'

'No.'

'Do you swear that?'

'I do.'

'You never saw such a report?'

'I did not.'

Bradley picked up the paper in front of him. 'I'll read you this,' he said. 'It is as follows: *This is to certify that Lieutenant Raymond of 245 Squadron flying Sopwith Camel Scout No B9372 landed at Roulandt aerodrome at 0076 hours on 29.7.1918 with engine trouble due to a broken ignition wire. A repair was effected and Lieutenant Raymond was able to fly Sopwith Camel B9372 back to his squadron. Signed E.A. Cutforth, Major Commanding 332 Squadron R.F.C. D.R.S. Stanland, Recording Officer.* I'll hand this in but perhaps you would just look at it first.'

'Is that the original?' the Judge Advocate asked.

'No, a signed copy,' Bradley answered. 'Now, Colonel, did you see that or a copy of it?'

'No. It was never given to me. I should add,' Conway turned to the court, 'that the squadron records were destroyed in an air raid and Major Cutforth and his recording officer were killed in a motor accident returning from St Omer just before the Armistice. Anyone could have concocted that.'

'So you say it is a forgery.'

'I don't say that. I merely make that comment.'

'Assuming for a moment that it is not a forgery would it not strike you as extraordinary that Lieutenant Raymond having gone to the trouble of getting it would not hand it in to you?'

'I consider Lieutenant Raymond to have been a most devious officer. He had some connection with politicians, I believe. I cannot explain his actions.'

'Your squadron records were destroyed as we know but would it surprise you to know that the recording officer of 332 Squadron thought the whole affair so unusual that he wrote it into their records which I shall produce?'

'I can only repeat that I never saw it.'

'But you will, I assume, now agree that it cannot be a forgery?'

'When I see the records, yes.'

Bradley took a deep breath. This was the time, if ever, when he must introduce the incident at school to explain Conway's hostility to Stephen. There was the risk of antagonising the court on the grounds that he was dragging in old and dead wood and making an unjustifiable attack on the credibility of a distinguished officer. On the other hand he had to shake their belief in his evidence somehow and those last answers of Conway's had surely been an indication that his accusation was not as simple and straightforward as appeared on the surface. He looked at them again. The President was staring thoughtfully at Conway. The flying man was frowning at the table. The fresh-faced captain was looking puzzled and scratching his head. It was the President who held Bradley's attention. The look he was giving Conway was not a particularly friendly one. Bradley decided to take the risk. 'You and Lieutenant Raymond, Colonel, were acquainted before you met again on the squadron?' he said.

For the first time Conway appeared to be a little less than sure of himself. He hesitated before answering and actually shuffled his feet. 'We were at school together, if that's what you mean,' he said.

'In the same House?'

'Yes, I was House Captain.'

'I see. Was there any hostility between you then?'

'Hostility? I don't understand. I was much senior to him. How could there have been? I do remember him bowling very dangerously at me in a cricket match.'

For the first time in the cross-examination Conway had made a major mistake. He had volunteered information, said just that little

239

too much and given Bradley the opening he wanted.

'And did he faint at the end of the first over he bowled?' he said.

'Faint? Yes, I believe he did. A touch of the sun or something.'

'Touch of the sun? I suggest it was as a result of a savage beating administered by you to him the night before.'

'Certainly not.'

'Did you beat him?'

'He cut a cricket practice to ride a horse for some trainer in the fells. I administered punishment.'

'Was that a beating?'

'Yes.'

'How many strokes?'

'I can't possibly remember. Six, I expect.'

'I suggest that it was far more than six, that it was a ferocious and unnecessary punishment—a retributionary beating that confined him in the sanatorium for a week.'

'Nonsense.'

'Was he in the sanatorium?'

'He may have been. I don't recall.'

'He collapsed when he was bowling to you—dangerously as you have said. You remembered that quite clearly yet now you cannot recall whether he went to the sanatorium or not.'

Conway hesitated again. Then he said in a slightly less confident voice, 'I do remember now. He did go sick, I think.'

'So you did not take the trouble to find out?'

'I did not concern myself with the ailments of juniors.'

'I see. And a week later you yourself left the school?'

'Yes.'

'Before the end of the school term?'

'That is so.'

'Was this in any way connected with the beating, administered to Lieutenant Raymond and a subsequent investigation by the Headmaster?'

'No. I was offered a commission in the R.F.C. and I accepted it.'

'Colonel Conway, I must suggest to you that that is not an accurate version of what happened. I suggest to you that your father was asked by the Headmaster to remove you. Do you still say that your leaving abruptly in the middle of the term had nothing to do with the savage beating you had administered to Lieutenant Raymond?'

'If it had I was never informed of it.'

'Neither by your father nor the Headmaster?'

'No.'

'Colonel Conway, I propose to produce the Headmaster who will tell the court that in view of what you did to Lieutenant Raymond he advised your father to take you away quietly so as to avoid the scandal

240

of expelling you and furthermore that he also told you of that fact. Will he be telling an untruth if he says that?'

'He will be mistaken.'

The President took a half-hunter from his breast pocket and looked at it. 'I think, gentlemen,' he said, 'that we should now adjourn for lunch.'

'He's a tough nut to crack,' Bradley said to Stephen as they left the room.

'One thing about Conway, he'll fight to the last,' Stephen said. 'How are we going?'

'I think I've done enough to make them see there's something out of the ordinary behind it all but the trouble is he's managed to avoid making any really damaging admissions. Mind you, he's gone too far in denying that the Headmaster never told him he was sacked. No one is going to believe that.'

'He always goes too far. That's his trouble,' Stephen said.

'Let's hope he does it when he gets on to the meat of the thing after lunch. I'll have to try and shake him on that. In the end it comes back to the one issue—his word against yours.'

'I thought if there was any doubt the prisoner was supposed to get the benefit of it.'

'That's the theory anyway,' Bradley said thoughtfully.

In the anteroom of the mess the General was sipping his second pink gin. 'Who was that woman sitting at the back of the room?' he asked the Sapper colonel. 'Something damn familiar about her.'

'I wondered that, too, and took the trouble to find out,' the Sapper said primly. 'She's the mother of the accused, I understand, a Mrs Honoria Raymond.'

'Honoria, by Gad! Of course, I remember now. Ginger Delawaye's sister. I was at her wedding. Can't see any son of hers running away. He'd be too damn frightened of her. What do you think of it so far? All a bit rum, isn't it? Can't say I take much to that squadron commander fellah. And I'd have cut cricket, too, for a chance of riding in a race, don't you know. Beastly game cricket, always hated it.'

'I should think he did it,' the Sapper answered. 'Cracked up. Seen it happen in our own show. Sometimes with chaps you'd never believe it could happen to. They're an odd lot these Flying Corps merchants. In my opinion Colonel Conway was right when he said they were an undisciplined crew when he took them over.'

'They cut a bit of a dash,' the general said. 'But that's the way you want 'em for their sort of work. Wouldn't go up in one of those things if you offered me all Lombard Street.'

'Perhaps,' the Sapper said. 'But he's guilty all right if you ask me.'

If Conway's composure had been at all shaken during the morning he

241

had regained it after lunch and his evidence of the actual incident of alleged cowardice was solid and convincing. He had stationed himself above and behind the squadron with the avowed purpose of seeing that no one left it without adequate excuse and this applied especially to Lieutenant Raymond of whose anxiety to engage the enemy he had the deepest suspicions. According to him Stephen's engine had shown no signs of erratic behaviour, or of firing in snatches, nor had he seen the machine dropping back as a result of this and then catching up as the engine ran on again. He saw Stephen leave the flight. He had a perfect view and the engine had not then stopped. He had watched Stephen go down and effect a safe landing. No other machine had voluntarily left the flight. All except one which had been shot down during the attack had returned safely to the aerodrome. Nothing Bradley could do with him in cross-examination could shake him.

Baxter came next. He gave evidence of Stephen's general unreliability and corroborated Conway's account of his avoidance of stand-by duty which now appeared to be being built up into a major crime. But when Baxter came to the question of the certificate given by Cutforth and his recording officer he was on more dangerous ground and he knew it. His account of it was that the certificate had been handed in to him during Conway's absence, that he had filed it and in the general bustle of preparing for the raid he had overlooked mentioning it to Conway who had been correct in saying he had never seen it.

Bradley had more than an idea that this explanation had been concocted over lunch for the production of that certificate must have been a nasty surprise to them. 'Are you telling us that at no time did Colonel Conway see that certificate?' he asked.

'Unless he looked in the files and I'm sure he didn't, he could not have seen it,' Baxter said. But he did not look too happy.

'Colonel Conway has said that he told Raymond he was giving him the benefit of the doubt and warned him as to his conduct on the next day's raid. Were you present at that interview?'

Baxter hesitated, then he temporised. 'It's very difficult to remember after all these months,' he said.

'You seem to remember very well about filing that certificate. I'm sure you can remember this if you try. Just cast your mind back.'

Baxter hesitated again as if he was considering what answer would serve him best. Then he made up his mind. 'Yes,' he said. 'I was. I do remember now.'

'Was this before or after the certificate was handed to you?'

'Oh, after, I think.'

'And you knew the certificate was in the files. Why didn't you tell Colonel Conway about it?'

'I think I must have forgotten about it.'

'Did Lieutenant Raymond not refer to it?'

'No, I don't think so. I can't really remember.'

'Captain Baxter, here we have Lieutenant Raymond on the mat. He is told his excuse is under suspicion. That would be a serious matter for any pilot, don't you agree?'

'Yes, that is so.'

'Yet, according to you, having just handed in a certificate which gave him a complete answer to the charge he nevertheless said nothing about it?'

'I—I'm not sure now.' Baxter's eyes went roving round the room and finally rested on Conway. He gained little comfort, it seemed, from Conway's set and impassive features for his eyes darted off again, finally to rest looking down at his hands.

'And are you also telling the court,' Bradley went on, 'that you as recording officer said nothing about the certificate you had just received. Was it not your duty to produce it then and there?'

'I must have forgotten.'

'Forgotten? How long after you received the certificate was this interview?'

'About half an hour I should say.'

'And you had already forgotten receiving and filing this vital document which affected the honour of a fellow officer? You allowed him to accept a reprimand without saying anything and, further, he himself never offered that certificate as a justification or explanation? Are you telling the court that?'

'I—I—'

'Captain Baxter I must suggest to you that you are being something less than candid with the court and that the account of the interview which Lieutenant Raymond will give is the correct one. He will say that he handed the certificate to Colonel Conway in your presence, that Colonel Conway accepted it, read it and then gave it to you with instructions to file it, that there was no reprimand because in view of that certificate there could not be.'

Baxter put up his hand to his moustache. 'You must remember we were fighting a war,' he said. 'There was so much going on. Things happened so quickly—'

'Lieutenant Raymond was also fighting a war, Captain, and I would remind you, with twenty victories to his credit, he was fighting it not unsuccessfully. I now also suggest that in fact Colonel Conway saw that certificate and that when in his evidence before lunch he said he had not he was incorrect to use no stronger word?'

'I really don't think I remember it all very well.'

'Thank you, Captain Baxter.' Bradley sat down. 'That's one of them demolished anyway,' he said to Stephen.

Heal came next. His evidence was to the effect that Stephen was constantly complaining about his guns and his engines. He formed the opinion that Stephen was looking for things to go wrong. At the beginning of the squadron's term in France there had been several instances of his having left his flight before or just after crossing the lines. He thought that Major Haynes had his suspicions of him and on one occasion he had heard Major Haynes threaten to send Lieutenant Raymond home without his wings. He had heard that Lieutenant Raymond had returned with a broken ignition wire the day before the raid. As a result he had taken the trouble to ask him before take-off the next day if he was satisfied with his machine and Lieutenant Raymond had said that he was. The engine was running 'sweet enough', he had said. He remembered the exact words for they had stuck in his memory.

'You say that Major Haynes was suspicious of him?' Bradley asked.

'Yes.'

'Yet this morning Colonel Conway told us that Lieutenant Raymond and Major Haynes were close friends, so much so that Major Haynes allowed Lieutenant Raymond to take credit for some of his victories?'

'That was later.'

'Exactly. From the time Lieutenant Raymond started to score were there any complaints from anyone about Lieutenant Raymond leaving his flight justifiably or unjustifiably?'

'I think Colonel Conway did not trust him.'

'That's not an answer. Were there any complaints?'

'No. Not that I know of.'

'I'm glad you said that for I have his log-book here. Is it not also the case that he flew more hours and did more patrols than any other pilot?'

'I don't know.'

'Come now, Captain Heal, of course you know. You were the armaments officer. Answer my question. Did he?'

'He flew a lot, certainly.'

'Thank you,' Bradley said contemptuously. 'Now, one other question. You were with the squadron from the beginning when Major Haynes had it. Major Haynes was, I understand, an outstanding fighter pilot with a large score of victories?'

'Yes. At one time he was the top-scoring Camel pilot in France.'

'And he was at all times anxious and ambitious to increase his score?'

Heal failed to see where this was leading him. 'I think that would be correct,' he answered.

'You would know this, would you not, as armament officer, for I think it is true to say he took great trouble over his equipment especially his guns?'

244

'Yes, he used to say if he couldn't shoot he couldn't score.'

'And when he'd come down he'd say "another one for the blackboard" or "another two today, I'll pass Jimmy McCudden soon", or use some such words?'

'I have heard him say something to that effect certainly.'

'Major Haynes was a fine man and a splendid squadron commander but would it be true to say of him that he would be most unlikely to allow another pilot to claim any of his victories for himself?'

The trap had opened in front of Heal and he had no option but to walk into it. He hesitated for a long moment.

'You must answer the question,' the Judge Advocate said, looking up from his notes.

'I think that would seem to follow,' Heal said lamely.

The following morning Davis gave his evidence with every show of reluctance. There had, he agreed, been talk in the squadron early on about Lieutenant Raymond's keenness and in fact Major Haynes had consulted him about it. At that time he himself as his flight commander had had reservations concerning Lieutenant Raymond's qualities as a fighting pilot.

'Et tu, Brute—Christ! This from Davis!' Stephen thought.

'Thank you, captain,' the prosecuting officer was saying and commenced to sit down.

'I should like to add,' Davis went on in a quiet voice, turning to the President, 'that before I was wounded and left the squadron I had quite changed my mind. I had then formed the opinion that Lieutenant Raymond had become a more than competent fighter pilot and showed every indication of maturing into an outstanding one, should he survive. He was a brilliant shot and I know that by that time Major Haynes considered him quite the most promising officer he had.'

'No questions, thank you, captain,' Bradley said politely.

The rest of the morning was taken up with evidence from ack emmas and N.C.O.s mostly going towards proving that Stephen's machine was in perfect order and condition when he took off on the morning of the raid. That closed the case for the prosecution. It all depended on Stephen now.

And, in fact, Stephen did not do too well. All that was open to him was to tell his story and stick to it and, as best he could, this was what he did. But one by one the points against him were brought out and driven home. Did he not agree that Colonel Conway was in a position to observe him and his machine? Did he not agree that however much the defending officer had built up his record there were blemishes on it too? Was he really accusing Colonel Conway of fabricating the story because of some ridiculous incident at school years before? Was not the truth of the matter about that certificate that he had in fact given it to Captain Baxter and never mentioned it to Colonel Conway? And had not Colonel Conway at that interview warned him to make quite sure that his engine did not let him down the next day? Had not he himself told Captain Heal that it was running sweetly?

Warmsley followed to tell how he had kept a record of Stephen's flying hours and that he had been required to spend more time over the lines than any other pilot on the squadron. He had, he said, remonstrated with Colonel Conway about it.

'The personnel of the squadron was constantly changing at that time, I think?' the prosecuting officer said.

'There were changes when Colonel Conway took over, certainly.'

'And since Lieutenant Raymond was one of the, what I might call, old hands who remained, was it not reasonable for Major Conway as he then was to give him more duties?'

'Not to the extent that he did.'

'But to some extent anyway—breaking in new men and the like?'

'No. Breaking in new men as you term it would not take him on constant offensive patrols over the lines.'

'Was there any feeling against Colonel Conway when he took over the squadron?'

'His methods of command were different from those of Major Haynes.'

'And this led to resentment in certain quarters?'

'Possibly.'

'And did Lieutenant Raymond resent it?'

'I cannot say.'

'Colonel Conway has said that you were very friendly with the pilots?'

'I always considered myself to be.'

'And with Lieutenant Raymond particularly?'

'No more than the others.'

'Did Colonel Conway send you home because he considered he could not count on your loyalty?'

'If so he did not tell me. He said I was too old.'

'Nevertheless on your own evidence you admit that you protested on Lieutenant Raymond's behalf—took his side?'

'I thought that he was being given too much flying. I did protest. No man can stand the strain of too much war flying, especially low flying—ground strafing—indefinitely.'

'Well, that is rather what we are saying, isn't it?'

By that one injudicious answer Warmsley had destroyed much of the effect of the testimony he had given in Stephen's favour, and weakened, too, the admissions Bradley had wrung from the opposition.

The Headmaster came next. He had, he said, advised, to use no

246

stronger word, Conway's father that he should take the boy away as a result of the savage beating he had inflicted on Stephen. He had also told the boy himself what he was doing and why he was doing it. There was no question but that this was the true state of affairs concerning Colonel Conway's leaving the school and if he stated otherwise his memory must be at fault.

'Lieutenant Raymond was injured by this beating, you say?' the prosecutor said.

'Yes. He was in the sanatorium for a week.'

'It has been suggested that Colonel Conway bore animosity towards Lieutenant Raymond for what had happened but if there was animosity it would not have been all on one side, would it? I suggest that Lieutenant Raymond himself bore a grudge against Colonel Conway which he never forgot?'

'I cannot answer that; it is pure speculation,' the Headmaster said firmly.

At that point the court adjourned for lunch. Afterwards the Judge Advocate would sum up. Bradley went back with Stephen to his room. Though he did not show it he was a worried man. Almost all the points he had made appeared to have been turned very neatly against him by the prosecutor. It had been a gamble introducing that past history and it did not seem to have paid off.

At worst Bradley believed that he had done enough to have caused a reasonable doubt to exist in their minds, but even if he had would they give him the benefit of it? Conway's evidence had been unshaken while Stephen's was uncorroborated. He did not know what was in the minds of the court save that he was pretty sure the President disliked both Conway and the prosecuting officer and that the Sapper was dead against them, which might mean anything for Sappers were all mad anyway. Perhaps it would depend on how the Judge Advocate summed up, if they listened to him, and he had no idea how his mind was working.

As they entered the room they saw a figure sitting hunched at the table, a bottle of Stephen's whisky in front of him. Hearing them come in he raised his head to look at them.

For a long moment Stephen stared at him unbelievingly, Then: 'Clare!' he cried. 'Clare! God, it's good to see you! But where by all that's merciful have you sprung from?'

But it was not the old lazy, patrician Clare he had known. There was a black patch over his left eye and a horribly disfiguring burn on the cheek below it. One arm was in a sling. He looked shrunken and ill and the level of whisky in the bottle had sunk alarmingly.

'Heard you were in a spot of trouble, old boy,' he said thickly. 'So I thought I'd drop along. Noblesse oblige—what?'

'As your Colonel would say—'

Clare gave a weak smile. 'He's dead,' he said. 'Killed in one of the last battles in a tank of all things. Everyone's dead and I'm damn near it.' He lifted the glass to his lips and Stephen saw that his hand was shaking.

'What happened to you? Where have you been?' Stephen asked.

Slowly and with the help of whisky Clare's story came out. When he had been shot down he had been flying in a sweater and slacks underneath his sidcot and with no identification at all. German troops had pulled him out from the wreckage of his Camel but he had been badly concussed as well as being burnt, losing his eye and breaking an arm at the elbow. The Germans had done what they could for him but what with his concussion, being passed from field hospital to field hospital, in the confusion of retreat he had simply become lost amongst the muddle and misery of a collapsing and defeated army. In the end the hospital where he had been taken was captured but even then he had lain there virtually unnoticed and unclassified until someone had recognised him. It was weeks before they would let him go. In fact he had virtually discharged himself and made his way back to reclaim his squadron. It was then that he had heard of Stephen's courtmartial and had come along to help if he could.

'What's that bastard Conway up to now?' he said.

'He's accused me of deliberately leaving the flight. Do you remember the day of the raid on Lessinghem?'

'Nothing clearer, old boy. I saw your prop stop.' He poured himself more whisky. Some of it spilled over the rim of the glass.

Bradley drew Stephen aside. 'Can you sober him up?' he said.

'I hope so. Is it urgent? How soon will you want him?'

'Right away if he's going to say what I think he is. I'll put him up and knock the bottom out of their case—provided he's sober.'

'I'll try. How long have we got?'

'I'll see the prosecuting officer and tell him we have an unexpected new witness. They'll give us at least an hour before we sit. Probably more if I push it.' He looked doubtfully at Clare. 'But I'll want to get a statement from him and I must have him sober.'

'Send in some black coffee and I'll have a go.'

Bradley left the room and in a few minutes an orderly came in with a tray on which were a pot of steaming coffee and two cups.

Clare was now showing every evidence of being about to go to sleep. His head was nodding and his one visible eye was closed. Stephen shook him gently by the shoulder. Clare raised his head and looked vaguely at him. 'Where—? What—?' he began and then recognition came back to him. 'Oh, it's you, old boy, is it,' he said. 'Courtmartialling you, are they? Bloody shame.'

'Listen, Clare,' Stephen said. 'We want you to give evidence. Pretty soon, too.'

248

Clare sat up. 'Certainly, old boy. I'll tell them a thing or two. Never liked that bastard Conway. Man of no account. Dreadful fellow. Came from nowhere, I always thought. Glad to assist. Always one to help a pal—'

Stephen poured some coffee. 'Have a go at this, there's a good chap.'

'Lace it with whisky, will you, dear boy.'

'There isn't any. It's finished.' Stephen had taken the precaution of removing the bottle while Clare's eye was closed.

'If I must, I suppose I must.' Clare lifted the cup and tasted the coffee. He made a grimace as he swallowed. 'Hellish hot and smells of cheese,' he said. 'No, that's not quite right. Ever read Surtees? Of course you did, a horsey chap like you. My Colonel used to read a chapter every night before he slept and tell us all about it in the morning. Awful bore. Dreadful things, horses. Always hated 'em. That's why I left the regiment—or have I told you this before?'

'Some of it,' Stephen said. 'How is that going down?'

'It's not a question of it going down, dear boy, it's a question of it staying down.' He looked at Stephen through his one eye rather like a naughty boy. 'You wouldn't care to put some whisky in it? Are you sure there isn't any?'

'Quite sure,' Stephen said firmly. Time was running on.

'That being so I suppose I'd better stick to the noisome product. Never cared much for it. Pour me some more.'

His second cup went down and stayed down. He became noticeably more sober when he had finished it. He was starting his third with more protestations of distaste and saying that his duty led him down strange paths, when the door opened and Bradley came in. He glanced at Stephen who in turn looked at Clare and nodded. 'I think he'll do now,' he said. 'Over to you.'

Bradley sat down and opened his big notebook. 'Now, Major de Vaux,' he said. 'Do you remember the events leading up to the raid on Lessinghem aerodrome?'

'Only too well,' Clare answered. 'I'm not likely to forget them. It left me, I thought, the last of the three of us, the last of the old squadron, in fact.'

Two hours later they were back in the court room.

Bradley went straight to the heart of the matter. 'I propose to call a witness whom I have not had available until now. Lieutenant Raymond's flight commander who subsequently commanded the squadron. Major St Clare de Vaux, M.C.,' he said.

There was a stir amongst the witnesses. Both Heal and Baxter looked around them nervously. The N.C.O.s sat up. Only Conway remained quite still and unmoved, staring straight in front of him. Clare made his way slowly down between the rows of seats and was sworn. Then he turned to face the court. Even in his battered state with the patch over one eye, the disfiguring burn and the maimed arm, he contrived to give the impression that everyone about him including the President was as dust beneath his chariot wheels.

Bradley took him immediately to the heart of the matter.

'Major de Vaux, you remember the raid on Lessinghem aerodrome in July of this year?'

'I do. Very clearly.'

'On the way over the lines did you observe Lieutenant Raymond's machine?'

'I did.'

'Tell us what you saw.'

'Lieutenant Raymond's engine was coughing and missing. It began just as we crossed the lines. As a result he commenced to fall back. I took particular notice because Major Conway as he then was had issued instructions that anyone who left a flight without sufficient excuse or justification was to be court-martialled, and it seemed to me that Lieutenant Raymond might well have to turn back with a dud engine. If he did I wanted to be able to bear out that he had reason to do so.'

'Did he in fact then turn back?'

'No. He continued to try to keep up with the flight though in my opinion he would have been perfectly justified in leaving it. He was losing height and distance and I thought he might well find himself a sitting duck to any Fokkers that happened to be about.'

'What happened next?'

'As we were beginning to lose height to make our run into the attack Lieutenant Raymond's engine conked out—stopped completely, that is to say.'

'You're sure of that?'

'I saw his propeller stop.'

'Could he then have got back to our lines?'

'It would have been quite impossible from that height and with the strong westerly wind which was then blowing.'

The prosecuting officer rose to cross-examine. 'Was Colonel Conway behind and above your flight?' he said.

'Yes.'

'And as such in a better position than you were to observe Lieutenant Raymond's machine?'

'Possibly. I can only describe what I saw.'

'Saw? But you were in front. Do you have eyes in the back of your head?'

'In war flying that is very nearly what you do have if you are to survive and I had survived for some time. I was constantly turning my head to look out for Huns amongst other things. I observed Lieutenant

250

Raymond very well. In fact I waved to him when he left.'

'I see. So you are suggesting that your observation was more accurate than Colonel Conway's?'

'I'm not suggesting anything. I'm describing what I saw.'

'And this conflicts with Colonel Conway's evidence?'

'So I understand.'

The prosecuting officer was too wise to cross-examine Clare on the reason why Conway could or should have slanted his evidence against Stephen. He had heard Bradley's cross-examination and he could guess what Clare's answers to any questions on that subject would be. He tried to turn the trick the other way. 'You are a close friend of Lieutenant Raymond's?' he said.

'Very close. We were at Ayr together and shared a hut until the day in question.'

'And as you have told us you knew about Colonel Conway's threat of a court-martial for those who fell out?'

'Yes.'

'I suggest to you that your observation could only have been at intervals and not constant as was Colonel Conway's?'

'I observed Lieutenant Raymond at very frequent intervals. I was concerned about him.'

'Naturally. And I suggest that that concern has led you into mistaking Lieutenant Raymond's, I'll put it plainly, funking tactics, for engine failure.'

'Nonsense.'

'You were shot down yourself, Major de Vaux?'

'Yes.'

'And suffered multiple injuries. Was one of these concussion?'

'Yes.'

'And concussion frequently plays tricks with the memories of those who suffer it?'

'So I'm told, but I understand only for the events immediately before the accident. The raid was weeks before I was shot down.'

Then the prosecutor made his one great mistake. Seeking to clinch his cross-examination he said, 'Don't you find it strange, Major de Vaux, that Lieutenant Raymond's engine was the only one to suffer engine trouble out of the whole squadron that day?'

'I might if it was the case,' Clare answered.

'Just what do you mean by that?' The prosecutor had the horrible realisation that he had just asked one question too many.

'My own engine was spitting and coughing all the way back. I didn't think I'd make it and seriously considered landing elsewhere. However I did get back and I afterwards found it to be suffering from intermittent blocking of the feed pipe. I believe one other officer not in my flight, Lieutenant Daly, had much the same trouble but he was

251

shot down and killed the next day.'

There followed the final speeches, the Judge Advocate summed up and they filed out to await the verdict.

Inside the empty court room there was silence for a moment. The members then began to move in their seats and to shuffle their papers avoiding each other's eyes.

'Well,' the general barked. 'Junior first. You, boy.'

The fresh-faced Captain looked up. 'Not guilty,' he said quietly.

'Not guilty,' the airman added quickly.

'I don't see how we could convict now,' the Sapper said reluctantly. 'I concur. Not guilty.'

The full colonel agreed without further comment.

'We're unanimous then,' the general said. 'Never believed a word of what that chap Conway said, meself. Right from the very start. Tough lookin' customer. Couldn't see any son of Honoria's funkin' it. I must say though I believe that feller she married is a bit rum. Sits in his study all the time writin' history or some such thing. However.' He coughed. 'Mustn't ramble on. Not guilty of course. And, gentlemen, I think we should do something more since we're unanimous and in view of that Major Whatsisname, de Vaux' evidence. Agreed? Well, you, young feller, go and get them in.'

They all filed back into the court room as the orderly summoned by the young captain beckoned them in.

Stephen looked at the faces in front of him. His heart was pounding. They were all looking at him. Wasn't that supposed to be a good sign?

The President picked up a piece of paper from the table. 'We find Lieutenant Raymond not guilty of the charge laid against him and honourably acquit him of the same,' he read out.

In a daze Stephen found himself back in his room. 'Honourable acquittal! My hat that's something all right,' Bradley said to him. All Stephen could do was to blurt out his thanks in a few confused words. Someone was opening champagne.

His mother was there. For once he thought he detected a softening in her stern expression. Her eyes as she watched him, unaware that he was observing her, filmed over for a second and something approaching affection appeared on her features. 'Good God,' Stephen thought. 'She does care. It's not just family pride which brought her here.' Looking up she saw Stephen watching her. 'I'm proud of you,' she said quietly, as with a little gesture towards him she lifted her glass.

23

When Stephen returned to the Bay in the late summer of 1919 a brooding silence seemed to hang over the whole place. Even the people of the village and the farmers with whom he and his family had always been on the friendliest of terms appeared now to regard him almost as an alien. There was something withdrawn about them, as they were waiting for some fundamental change, some elemental catastrophe to take place.

Men gathered in little groups after Mass, there was whispered talk of a camp in the hills beyond Knockmaroon where 'the boys' gathered and drilled. A month earlier a successful raid had been made on the tender bringing mail and provisions out to the destroyers in the bay. It had happened in broad daylight. The crew and guard had been overpowered and tied up and their arms and equipment taken. The mail and stores had been left untouched. No one came forward to help the crew; no one afterwards named those responsible but everyone knew that Larry Rossiter was back in the hills teaching the boys the skills he had learnt in France, and knew too that it was Larry who had planned and carried out the raid.

If the Royal Irish Constabulary in Bellary were the only ones who did not know it, the reason was that they were being steadily and increasingly isolated from the life of the town and their sources of information. No longer did they mix freely as before with the community. It was the commencement of the period that was to lead to their all but complete boycott and their being for practical purposes prisoners in their own barracks. They carried out a few abortive raids and searches and then dropped the matter.

The guard on the tender was doubled and its members issued with ball ammunition but nothing further happened save that the tension in and around Bellary was raised to a higher pitch. Driving into town now, Stephen found that one looked constantly over one's shoulder, and in their own houses loyalists often found themselves all but unconsciously speaking in whispers.

Even Mikey had changed, as Stephen soon discovered. Fully grown

253

now and in charge of the staff, Mikey showed no desire to resume their old easy companionship. He refused all Stephen's suggestions that he would accompany him shooting as he used to do. Stephen had long forgotten his wartime resolution to forswear shooting. The war and his experiences had made killing and death commonplace to him. Looking back now he sometimes shrugged his shoulders at the boy who had suffered those scruples when Haynes led him down on to his first two-seater.

When Stephen attempted to draw Mikey on what was happening in Ireland and especially in the Bay he received evasive answers, or else Mikey would relapse into a wary silence.

Stephen's own return to the Bay had been delayed for the army, having given him an honourable acquittal, seemed singularly reluctant to allow him to return to civilian life. Resentful as he was at the way he had been treated, he put this down to prejudice amongst his immediate superiors. He knew too, that the stigma of a court-martial, despite his acquittal, would stick to him for the rest of his life and to that extent Conway had won even in defeat, and he brooded. Unfortunately he had plenty of time for brooding.

The squadron had been reduced to a cadre commanded by a captain whom Stephen did not know and had never heard of and who treated him rather as if he was some species of wild animal which had been passed as safe but was probably dangerous. Clare was in hospital in England having his arm, which had been hurriedly set by the Germans, broken again and re-set. He knew none of the few fellow officers left in the squadron, most of them had never crossed the lines or fired their guns in anger. Rather like a sixth form public schoolboy with new kids Stephen ignored them, drank whisky by himself and went on brooding. With this came the conviction that his demobilisation was being deliberately delayed probably by Leatherhead in the fear that were he to be let free he could do some damage to him with the Frocks. As a natural consequence there came to him a burning resentment against the system that allowed these things to happen.

First, he told himself, there had been Conway at Sellingham; then in the R.F.C. the only people who had treated him fairly or that he cared about had been an American, Hank, and two mavericks from opposite ends of the social spectrum, Haynes and Clare. Hank and Haynes were both dead, their lives lost, when you analysed it, the one due to Conway's murderous lust for killing and the other to Leatherhead's vanity and ambition in attempting to show what he could accomplish with an inadequate and unprotected force. And then there was his own court-martial engineered by Conway and assisted by his lackeys who were afraid to do anything else but back him up lest they might lose their own jobs. With a bitterness almost equal to that of Davis', he hated the whole lot of them, the gang that had controlled unchecked his life and other lives, the closed and magic circle of command and the acolytes who aspired to it at any cost.

When at last the orders came for them to fly their machines home to be 'reduced to produce' it was with a feeling of thankfulness that he climbed into his Camel and went through the starting drill for the last time.

'Switches off; petrol on; suck in!'

The mechanic turned the propeller.

'Contact, sir!' He snapped the switches on. 'Contact!' The engine fired and the propeller dissolved into the blur of its arc.

The sweet sickly smell of castor oil brought memories flooding back, of the deadly rat-tat-tat behind him in a fight, of Haynes, the incomparable, diving for a kill, of fun and laughter in the mess before Conway came, and of the companionship of Hank and Clare.

A figure came up beside the cockpit and saluted. It was Corporal Harris, the last of the old crowd. 'You're the only one of them left now, sir,' he said.

'It was all luck, Harris. Goodbye.'

'Goodbye! Goodbye!' Standing by the squadron office the new recording officer waved.

'Chocks away!' Opening the throttle he did not bother to taxi out but took off in a climbing turn, one wing all but touching the ground. Then he came streaming back across the aerodrome. At least he'd leave them in style. Stick back, the Camel again a live thing under his hands, he pointed her up into the blue.

Because he was the most experienced pilot he was expected to lead the others home. To hell with them. They could find their own way. Swinging round he flew across the landscape they had fought over those months before, recognising the old landmarks—Zillebeke Lake, Ypres, Dickebusch, Poperinghe. Away to the south from ten thousand feet he could see Kemmel Hill and the Forêt de Nieppe. Over the old aerodrome of Bessières he looped and spun for the last time and then set course for the coast.

When he landed at Lympne none of the others had turned up. 'They must have lost me,' he said to the duty officer, and flew on, contour-chasing, to Brooklands where he handed over his machine to be broken up. He slapped her on the side as he would have done a horse and walked away from her. Then he took the first train to London to seek out Clare.

Clare was convalescing with the help of a bottle of whisky when Stephen eventually ran him to earth on a short leave some weeks later. He was in one of his black moods. 'You bloody Irish are causing trouble again,' he said. 'Shooting policemen in the back. The latest one is an Inspector in a place called Thurles. What the hell do they want, anyway?'

'To get rid of you bloody English,' Stephen said without hesitation. 'And do you know, Clare, much of the time I can't find it in me to blame them.'

'You always were a bit of a rebel, weren't you?'

'Yes, when you go on like that. And when I go home they'll think I'm as English as you are.'

'By Gad, you are a rum crowd, damned if I understand you.'

'That's just the trouble, you don't now, you never did and you never will. But it seems to me I could say the same about you English. You wouldn't think people like Davis and that sadistic bastard Conway came from the same race. Have you heard anything about Conway, incidentally? Is he a Brigadier yet or whatever new rank our splendid young service has now invented?'

'I have heard about Conway, oddly enough. Ran across Davis of all people in Piccadilly the other day. He hasn't changed. Standing as a Labour M.P. at the next election. Anyway he told me. Conway's not a Brigadier or anything like it. He was refused a permanent commission because of what came out at that court-martial of yours. Someone met him in the R.F.C. Club or whatever they call it now. He was swearing vengeance against you. He's been de-mobbed—out—kaput. I should keep away from him if ever you meet him on a dark night.'

'To hell with him. The bastard did Hank in and did his best to do me in.'

The reference to Conway for some reason appeared to have raised Clare's spirits. Perhaps it reminded him of the old heady spirit of comradeship in a fighting squadron which peace had so rapidly blown away. 'He was a bastard, wasn't he?' he said. 'But a brave bastard for all that. Pretty well unsinkable if you ask me. I wonder what he'll do now? Something suitable with boiling oil in it, I should think. Come on, let's go to White's.'

White's Club had become Clare's home from home. There he drank quantities of whisky and talked about the war with other survivors of his own caste, maimed or whole. '"All over the club counting their scars sit the old fightingmen home from the wars",' one of these with a crutch and an empty trouser-leg misquoted Kipling to Stephen when Clare introduced them.

It was this veteran who turned out to be a Brigadier-General at the ripe age of twenty-five and the holder of the V.C. amongst other decorations who, on hearing Stephen's complaints about the slowness of his demobilisation, turned to Clare and said: 'Ridiculous. Wish I'd heard about it before. I'll have a word with my father. He'll arrange it for him in no time at all.'

'We—er—rather run things from here,' Clare said, airily sipping his third whisky. 'And do it rather better than those who think they do. All a question of helping one's pals.'

But it took another month all the same before Stephen was back at the Bay.

Not only did he find changes all around him but things were different at Bellary Court. His father seemed to have withdrawn even further into himself and his mother to be more commanding and strident than ever before, in which she was ably seconded by his sister. Ethel, too, had been released from whatever branch of the women's army to which she had belonged, Stephen had never bothered to ascertain the precise one. She was as rootless and dissatisfied as any demobilised officer and, as usual, she took her frustrations out on Stephen or tried to.

'What are you going to do now?' she asked him a day or two after her return when they met in the hall.

'Oh, I don't know,' Stephen said vaguely. 'Ride races, try to get going as a G.R., I suppose. I must go over and see Bob Ferris sometime soon.'

'Ride races,' Ethel gave a snort reminiscent of her mother. 'And where is the money coming from to keep you in luxury doing that, may I ask?'

Stephen had never really given a thought to money. The actual hard financial facts about the Sterling French affair had passed him by for he had been much too young to take them in. In the army he had always had enough for his few needs, his mess bill, drinks and the occasional spree. 'I expect I'll manage somehow,' he said lamely.

'Well, you'd better find out from father, then, just what is going on,' Ethel said in her sharp way. 'Mother knows nothing. That dreadful Hutton man seems to be in charge of everything. He has father completely under his thumb. Here he is now as it happens.'

Both of them turned to look towards the front door. Mikey was opening it and ushering Will Hutton in. Then he brought him upstairs, carrying the lawyer's gladstone bag for him, and they heard the door of Edward's study open and shut.

Greatly to his own surprise during the years of war, Will Hutton had found himself falling under the spell of the Bay. He had a power of attorney from Massiter to look after his affairs and this necessitated his travelling down to Bellary several times a year to supervise the administration of the Dunlay estate. Gradually, however, he found himself making excuses to return and paying more visits than were strictly necessary. Ever increasingly he came to look forward to the moment when the train would dive into the tunnel in the hills above Bellary. Then, a minute or two later, came the sudden burst into brightness and he would see the whole Bay spread before him, the scatter of white houses along its foothills, the shift of cloud and colour behind its peaks. Descending from the carriage, he would hear once again the lilt

257

of the voices; and the tang of turf smoke that hung over everything would come to his nostrils to tell him he was back.

Since Bellary Court was one of his principal's important investments, more and more, too, his ways took him there and to Edward's study, for a most unlikely friendship had grown up between the two men.

After a discussion about the rents and accounts they would move to a table where a chess board had been set up and there they would play indifferent chatty chess for Edward was a poor player who liked to talk between moves, and they would discuss the war, politics and the state of Ireland.

As Hutton soon came to realise—and it was a realisation which increased his liking for the man and his interest in his visits—Edward was one of the few representatives of his class and creed who perceived even if only dimly the changes which were taking place in the whole concept of Irish nationalism. Although he could not yet appreciate what would take its place Edward could and did see that any hope of a constitutional settlement to Ireland's problems had vanished with Redmond's failure and sudden death. In fact these, as Hutton knew, had left a vacuum in Irish politics, a vacuum which the men of violence were preparing to fill and, with Redmond's death too the tradition of paternalism in the councils of resistance and rebellion had vanished forever.

Always with his ear to the ground and his eye on the main chance, Hutton saw this early and clearly. Just as he had realised long before most of his contemporaries that the Land Acts had spelled the end of the influence of the landlords, so he now saw that a source of power and patronage differing in every way from that which had gone before was about to be created by the apostles of violence, and that they would call into being and then develop an entirely new Ireland. Already Hutton was putting out feelers and making contacts with such men who at that time were ignored or despised by most of his fellows.

Hutton was aware that the new men wanted no help from the likes of Redmond, or Ascendancy outsiders such as Wolfe Tone, Parnell and even Casement, for all their patriotism and dedication, had been. These had justified their leadership by superior class and education and all their efforts had ended in futility, humiliation and failure. The new men were either self-taught or had profited by the opportunities of education open to all. They repudiated guidance from outside themselves. Their catchword *Sinn Fein*—Ourselves Alone— was sufficient proof of that. They had learnt in the bloodshed of 1916 that a handful of dedicated men could disrupt a country and hold an Empire at bay. They believed with a fervence approaching fanaticism that freedom came only from the gun. Time and the times were

258

to confirm them in that belief, though no one, not Hutton, not even themselves, yet realised how strongly the time had run right for them.

They faced an England bankrupt of an Irish policy, drained of its best blood by four years of war, weakened by war debt and the problems of post-war resettlement, above all with the only man who might have carried through a rational plan for self-government concentrating his interests and energies at Versailles and elsewhere and regarding the sister island as a sideshow. Lloyd George's pragmatism played into their hands. Time again was to show how ruthlessly and successfully they were to use the cards he gave them.

'I'm worried about the boy,' Edward's voice broke into Hutton's thoughts. 'He seems, and perhaps I shouldn't say this to you, Hutton, to have developed Nationalist leanings. He was not well treated by some of the British during the war, you know.'

'I know,' Hutton said, who knew everything. 'The court-martial. But they acquitted him—'

'He says it was a false charge, that it should never have been brought. He sympathises at least to some extent with these men we have been talking about—'

'If he feels like that he'd be better away.'

'He won't leave the Bay,' Edward said sadly. 'I can't make him. I know how he feels.' It was not in his nature to impress his will upon others and especially not on this son of his who had gone away a boy and returned a man, a stranger and an embittered one at that.

'Tell him not to take sides.' Hutton's voice was suddenly harsh. 'The struggle now can have nothing to do with him or you, either, Raymond. For your own sake you must realise this.' His tone changed and he smiled. 'Sporting anachronisms, that is what you will be, those of you who remain, if you like, but that is all. Didn't you say he had hopes of success as a Gentleman Rider?'

'That is all that seems to interest him—that and the new politics.'

'Tell him to stick to racing.'

Edward looked up. 'Can he afford it? Can I afford it?' he said. 'You know what a duffer I am in business matters, Hutton. Will the boy be able to remain here after my time? People are already selling, you know. The Duchesnes down the Bay have gone. A farmer bought the property—'

Hutton hesitated. 'There is no financial reason given sensible management why he and his sons should not remain here for the foreseeable future,' he said. 'Politically it is quite another matter. If the new men gain power, win freedom, call it what you like, no one can predict the consequences for you and your class—'

Edward looked up and smiled rather sadly. 'That is a risk anyone who loves Ireland and the Bay as much as I do must be prepared to take,' he said.

'With all my heart,' Hutton said sincerely, and he was not a sincere man, 'I wish you well. And now, Raymond, I rather think I hold your queen in check.'

So it was that a few days later Stephen and his father had a discussion in Edward's study with the sun pouring through the tall windows and the mountains a running frieze in the background.

'I don't want to leave the Bay, ever,' Stephen said, looking out at the view he had dreamt about so many times during those tortured nights in France. 'And I want to ride races. Those are the only two things I have in mind, father.' But there was something else, too, though he did not mention it. He could not bring himself to believe that he had lost Babs forever. Sooner or later she must come back to the Bay. When she did he was certain somehow to see her again, and then he would learn from her own lips why she had done this to him.

'It's a bad time to begin to get into racing,' Edward said gently. 'I had Hutton here a day or so ago. He's a good fellow, despite what your mother says. He thinks that violence is only just beginning and that there is a new Ireland coming in which we have no part to play. Would you not be wiser to make a start in England? I'm sure your mother's relations could get you in somewhere as a learner in a stable—'

'I wonder could they, father. You know how they'd look at me over there. They'd say—oh, he's the chap who was court-martialled—without thinking of the verdict. I want no more to do with them. I'm an Irishman first and last. I know that now.'

'Maybe, but I wonder if your fellow countrymen know it, especially this new breed of violent men, the gunmen, Hutton calls them. You're young, you've been through a war, violence is no stranger to you. I know that from what you've gone through you may be tempted to ally yourself with them. I implore you not to. Don't take sides.'

'You needn't worry, father, I've had all I want of war. Let others do the fighting. I'll stick to racing.'

His father smiled slightly. 'They'll hardly stop that, I suppose, in Ireland, whatever happens,' he said. 'But how will you start? We've no horses here. I have always heard it is difficult to get going unless you have horses of your own.'

'Bob Ferris promised me rides before I left. Desmond, too, I'm sure, will help.'

'Desmond, yes, Desmond.' Edward looked thoughtfully at his son, started to say something and then stopped. There was silence for a few moments and then Edward coughed. 'Massiter is away a long time,' he said haltingly. 'But there is talk of his return. He is a man of power now, a difficult man, a dangerous man, and I fear he holds us all here in the hollow of his hand.'

There was a motor car in the coach house at Bellary now, an American Overland, with a tall jointed windscreen, a sort of flap in front of the radiator where the starting handle was and an absolute top speed of forty miles an hour. Two days later Stephen took it out and drove over to Bob Ferris.

'Glad to see ye, Captain,' was Bob's breezy greeting. 'Them Germans didn't kill ye, then?'

'Don't call me captain,' said Stephen quickly. 'I never got a flight. I never was one or near it, either.'

'Ye're all captains round here when ye come back from that Saxon Army. Are ye wanting to ride out for me, then? Ye'll be welcome though there's little enough here these days for ye to ride.'

Later they went round the horses. Bob had been right. There were not many of them and what there were were not an impressive lot. Stephen's spirits sank. He was not going to get very far riding any of these.

'That fellow might win a few races—small ones,' Bob said, his glance falling on a rakish chestnut with a big knee who looked like a cast-off from the flat. 'Small ones,' he repeated. 'We might get a maiden hurdle out of him in a month or two.' He sighed and scratched his head. 'The rest of 'em they wouldn't even run into a place if they started the night before.' Then he brightened a bit. 'But they do say Mr Massiter's coming back. He's promised me a few.'

'When is he coming?' Stephen asked, keeping his voice as indifferent as he could.

'I dunno. Charley Holmes, that's the new stud groom there, he told me that Mr Hutton said to have the horses and everything ready, that he might be back any time. Then again he said, with the way he is and the business that's in it you wouldn't know it might be a fortnight or it might be three months.'

On his way back Stephen passed the Murtaghs' gateway. Yielding to impulse he turned into it. The avenue was rutted and unkempt, large pot-holes were filled with water from the recent rains and the iron railings on either side were sagging and broken. Grass was growing on the gravel sweep in front of the hall door. Untrimmed creeper together with wistaria and passion-flower fronds grew across the first floor windows.

The maid who opened the door to Stephen showed him into the morning room where they had been that afternoon when he had said goodbye to Babs. Sarah was sitting in a chair by the fireplace, embroidering. She had aged, Stephen thought. There were lines about her face and neck that had not been there before and some of the lights had gone from her hair. Desmond, she told him, was in the yard and would be in presently.

'You've come back safely, Stephen,' she said putting the em-

261

broidery down and looking at him. 'You've changed, but then we all have. That dreadful war changed everything. We often thought about you. I had hoped—'

The door opeed and Desmond came in. He still used a stick but he managed well enough on his artificial leg which actually gave him an additional swagger in his walk. But he, too, had aged and there were lines of pain on his face. 'Well, young feller me lad,' he said. 'The last time we met we were putting one over on old Grig. He hasn't forgotten it, by the way. I should look out for him when you next go hunting. That is if there is any hunting with all this trouble brewing. There was that bad business in Fermoy and I see in today's paper another police-man was shot in Dublin.'

'They'll never stop hunting, will they?' Stephen said.

'They might do anything. The government are talking of intro-ducing military districts whatever they may be, in disturbed areas. Much good it may do them. There aren't enough troops in Ireland as it is and those I've seen seem a pretty poor lot. Anyway I expect you've come looking for something to ride, not to talk of Ireland's troubles. There's damn little here, I'm afraid, and won't be until I get some of the young 'uns going next year. But there's a four-year-old you can hunt if you like. I can't do anything yet with this damned leg—'

'I was saying to Stephen when you came in,' Sarah said, looking directly at him, 'that we had often hoped he and Babs—'

.'Massiter,' Desmond muttered, avoiding her glance. 'Massiter—'

'It should not have been done,' Sarah went on steadily and Stephen suddenly saw something approaching hatred for her husband, from whom she had suffered so much, come into her eyes. 'She was sold, sold into bondage.' She put down her embroidery and walked from the room.

Desmond sat on, staring at the fireplace. 'He did me, the devil, he did me,' he muttered half to himself as if Stephen was not there. Stephen felt he should escape but he could not. 'That damned hair-dresser—' Desmond went on. He was in fact living again for the hundredth time the scene between himself and Massiter which he would never forget.

Massiter had asked him to come to Dunlay shortly after his return to the Bay to discuss a matter of some importance. Puzzled and scepti-cal as to what could be of importance between himself and Massiter but interested to find out, Desmond had driven to the Castle. Massiter had been waiting for him in the library where he offered him whisky which Desmond had gratefully accepted for his leg was giving him hell. 'Well now,' he had said sitting down carefully and easing his leg. 'What is this great matter you want to see me about, Massiter?'

Massiter had looked directly at him and Desmond could still remember those tawny eyes and their steady, disconcerting stare. 'I want to marry your daughter,' he had said without preamble.

Desmond sat up with such a sudden jerk he almost spilled his whisky. 'You?' he said incredulously. 'You marry Babs? You're old enough to be her father.'

'Perhaps. Nevertheless I intend to marry her.'

Desmond laughed in his face. 'Are you formally asking my consent?' he said.

'Yes.'

'She's under twenty-one. You'll never get it.'

The tawny eyes did not move though Desmond saw something come alive in their depths. It looked uncommonly like a gleam of triumph and satisfaction as if Massiter had been waiting for this moment. 'Oh, but I think I shall,' he said, taking a folded paper from his pocket and handing it to Desmond.

'What's this?' Desmond asked contemptuously.

'I suggest you read it. It's an affidavit by a man called Thomas Kelly who practises as a hairdresser in Dublin under the name and style of André Lefèvre. You remember him? I rather thought you would. Please do read it, Murtagh. I've no doubt that you will find it interesting.'

Desmond opened the folded sheet of lawyer's paper and began to read. As his eyes went down the numbered paragraphs he went pale. They set out in complete, accurate and damning detail everything that Lefèvre, otherwise Kelly, had done in preparing and disguising Robin À Tiptoe for the 1914 Conyngham Cup.

'You have your choice,' Massiter said quietly when he had finished. 'Either you give your consent or that document goes to the senior stewards of the National Hunt Committee.'

Desmond made a desperate attempt to bluff it out and pass it off. 'It's five years ago, man,' he said. 'There's been a war since. No one would take any notice of this.'

'I'm advised that there is no Statute of Limitations in racing,' Massiter answered. 'Donal McManway is senior steward now. I happen to be acquaintained with him. He was seconded to the Ministry of Munitions for a short time. He is no friend of yours, Murtagh. It was a serious offence. You would be warned off—for life.'

Donal McManway—the fates, Desmond thought, were surely running against him. Just before the war McManway had got a fortune from some uncle in the city, bought Henry Barragy's place and taken a pack of hounds. He'd also owned a few good horses and made himself useful to the right people which was how he got elected to the committee even if he never rode the horses himself. It was quite true that there was no friendship between them for Desmond had laughed at the other man's pretensions and had dined out on his remark that the new master of hounds and member of the committee had never jumped a fence in front or ridden in a race in his life. It had been repeated back to McManway who in reply had been one of the first and harshest to criticise Desmond's initial reluctance to spring to the colours. Desmond could expect no mercy there. Massiter was right. He'd be off for life. 'You must give me time to think this over,' he said.

'I want an answer before you leave the house—the forms are there—'Massiter pointed to the desk.

Desmond read the affidavit again. It was totally damning. 'What guarantee have I got that you won't bring this up even if I sign?' he said.

'You have my word.'

Desmond's mouth twisted in a sneer. 'Do you really think I'd accept the word of a gombeen man?' he said.

'You may live to regret saying that,' was Massiter's reply. 'I may add that if you are an example of an Irish gentleman then I am glad I was not born one.'

Desmond walked heavily to the desk where the forms lay, picked up a pen and signed.

Massiter opened a drawer and took out an envelope. 'This contains the original affidavit,' he said, taking the document from the envelope and showing Desmond the signature. 'Since you have taken leave to doubt my word I shall show you how I keep it.' Putting the original and copy together he walked to the fireplace, struck a match and held it to the papers. The flames caught them, curled around them and consumed them. Massiter dropped the burnt remains to the hearthstone and crumpled them with his foot. Then, placing his hands behind his back, he turned to Desmond. 'Good day to you, Murtagh,' he said. 'Unlike you I always pay my debts. Edwards will show you out.'

And that was how Babs Murtagh was sold in marriage to Andrew Massiter.

Desmond came out of his reverie, shivered and then shrugged his shoulders as if to rid himself of something. 'All I can hope is that the Shinners do him in the day he comes back,' he said venomously. 'It would be a damn sight better for all of us than shooting those poor bloody policemen. Now where is that girl with the tea?'

264

24

In fact Stephen had far less inclination actively to ally himself with the policies and advocates of Sinn Fein than Edward, in his worry for his son, had thought. All he wanted to do was to stay at the Bay for ever and live in peace with his neighbours which he believed he could do when the present madness was over. He also wanted Babs Murtagh. He refused to think of her as Massiter, and he found himself longing for her ever more deeply as each day passed and she did not return, for the rumours about Massiter's impending arrival appeared to have been premature. In fact he was now said to be at Versailles occupying some position in Lloyd George's entourage, and a photograph which appeared in the papers clearly showed him, though unnamed, standing at the Prime Minister's elbow.

The madness, too, far from passing, appeared to be getting worse. As yet little of it had touched the Bay but the weekly, almost daily, shootings of policemen continued in other parts of the country. The authorities seemed powerless to protect them beyond, as Desmond had foretold, declaring certain disturbed parts of the country to be 'military areas'. This entailed putting such districts under a vague military control which stopped short of martial law and had the effect of satisfying no one save those whom it was intended to combat. The army were refused the full plenary powers they demanded yet the ordinary people, harassed by searches, stop points and raids were driven further into sympathy with the rebels. More sinister still, the failure to apprehend the gunmen or to bring them to justice led to a series of reprisals, official or unofficial no one seemed to know, in which houses of suspected sympathisers were burnt down and in some cases their occupiers beaten up or shot.

'It is only a question of time,' Edward said to Stephen, 'before it comes here. What is Larry Rossiter doing in the hills? He must be up to something.'

'Training, I expect,' Stephen said. 'Waiting until he's ready before he strikes. Never reinforce failure; always exploit success. A Napoleonic maxim never appreciated by our splendid leaders in the last unpleasantness.'

Soon they were to know what Larry was up to. A mixed police and military patrol scouring the hills looking for Larry found him and found more than they bargained for. They were ambushed. Three of their members were killed and the rest surrendered later being set free without their rifles, side arms or ammunition. Two nights later raiders with blackened faces came to one of the Rossiter houses, expelled the occupiers at the point of a gun and set fire to the house and the hay-rick behind it.

The following evening Stephen was in the study with his father. They were discussing what had happened. 'We seem to be able to do nothing right,' Edward said, unconsciously identifying himself with the Government as all loyalists did. 'Terror begets terror. Nothing is solved. Nothing is done save that human lives are lost. What is required is a political solution not a military one.' He looked at Stephen with his tired smile. 'I see they are even cutting down racing now—I never thought that would happen.'

'It's pretty hopeless in a way,' Stephen said. 'Bob can hardly get to the few meetings that are near enough because of the shortage of fuel on the railways. It looks as if we may even lose Punchestown again this year. Still, we did win a maiden hurdle with that flashy brute of a chestnut. I wonder, will they try to stop hunting here. They have stopped it in a few places. I want to hunt Desmond's four-year-old to-morrow. He's just beginning to go for me now.'

'Grig won't take kindly to stopping hunting—what's that?'

There was a sudden red glow in the sky showing through a gap in the curtain. Both of them went to the window and Stephen pulled the curtain aside.

Down the Bay against the dark background of cloud and trees they could see flames shooting up to the sky. As they watched, the conflagration increased in violence and spread until a whole area appeared to be on fire. A spray of sparks leapt up as a roof fell in.

'The Old Earl's place, they're burning it,' Stephen said.

Beside him Edward sighed. He walked wearily to his desk and sat down. 'Reprisal for the burning of Rossiter's,' he said. 'It almost had to happen. Well, he was an absentee. He hadn't been here for years. But he is only the first. What is to happen to the rest of us? Whoever wins this war, if it is a war, I know who is going to lose—the men in the middle, the moderates, like us.'

Looking at his father Stephen realised the full truth of an anxiety which had been gnawing at him for weeks. Edward was failing. There was a grey tinge beneath the skin on his cheeks; he had difficulty in standing for any length of time; he rarely left the study at all now except for meals and there he ate virtually nothing.

Neither his mother nor Ethel had appeared to notice it but then,

Stephen told himself grimly, they had never really concerned themselves about Edward, regarding him either as a cipher to be ignored or, if anything at all, then as a rather inconvenient appendage to their own affairs. That upset he had suffered before the court martial could well have been more than the doctor thought it was. Once or twice he had quietly suggested to Edward that he should see Dr O'Brien but his father had turned the request aside.

And there was Mikey to worry about, too. Mikey was up to something, of that Stephen was convinced. He wondered if Mikey had had a hand in the burning down of the Old Earl's place, for he had done one of his disappearing tricks that afternoon. Mikey would know every inch of the Old Earl's woods and the approaches to the house from Knockmaroon for he acted as beater when they took the woodcock shooting from the Earl every Christmas. If his mother or Ethel came to the conclusion that Mikey had dealings with 'the boys' there would be hell to pay. In fact he was not sure that Ethel did not already suspect something judging by some of the remarks she had addressed to him. It was a good thing in a way that both Ethel and his mother, like Clare, regarded servants as different and inferior beings from another world and took no real interest in what they actually were or did.

The following morning Stephen drove over to Desmond's to collect the four-year-old and ride him on to the meet. The roads were deserted. He passed no one save a solitary donkey cart bringing milk to the creamery. The man, whom Stephen did not know, touched his hat as he passed him but kept his gaze averted.

As he drove Stephen wondered how long they would retain the use of the car. In military districts one had to have a permit to drive at all even if one kept the car, for commandeering by one side or the other was frequent. They were lucky to have been out of the worst of it here so far, but if last night's burning meant anything it was the harbinger of trouble to come and if Larry Rossiter really got going anything might happen. Ethel was talking about getting the tennis courts at Bellary, disused during the war, cut and marked again. Did one play tennis during a revolution? What had the Russians done? Was this a revolution? The old military barracks at Kilderry had been reopened and a detachment of troops to occupy them was expected any day. Ethel would want to entertain the officers no doubt, that is to say if the regiment was smart enough. He smiled to himself as he drove on.

Leaving the car in a corner of Desmond's stable-yard he was crossing to the loose boxes when Thomas, the groom, met him. 'The mistress said would ye step into the house a minute before ye go,' he said. 'She's anxious to see ye. I dunno what it's about. She said she'd be in the morning room.'

Wondering what Sarah could want with him Stephen let himself in by one of the many back doors of the old house, walked along the stone passages to the main part of the house and entered the morning room.

Sarah looked up as he came in. A tray with a silver coffee pot and cups were on a table beside her. 'Thank you for coming in, Stephen,' she said. 'I hope I'm not making you late. Will you take a cup of coffee or would you care for something stronger?'

Stephen refused the offer of whisky. Sarah poured the coffee and handed him the cup. Then she looked at him steadily and their eyes met. 'Babs is back,' she said.

Stephen found that the hand that held the cup was shaking. 'Babs,' he said. 'When?'

'Yesterday. He doesn't care for too much communication between us but she managed to send word. She'll be out hunting today, Stephen.'

'I'll see her then,' was all he could manage to say.

'I'll drive to the meet in the dog-cart and try to bring her back to tea if she's alone. Stephen, I hate and fear that man.'

'Why did you let her do it?'

'He bought her. I don't know how it was done. We thought you were dead. There was no news of you. The night before the wedding she told me she didn't care what happened to her. Stephen, we must go or we'll be late for the meet.'

Stephen hacked the young horse on, full of eager anticipation. He was going to see her again. He didn't give a damn whether Massiter was there or not. To see her and talk to her and laugh with her was all that mattered for the moment.

At the meet Grig glowered at Stephen as he raised his hat to him. Grig had not forgotten that Yeomanry race. He swore at Stephen unmercifully whenever he got the opportunity and generally made things as uncomfortable for him as he could. It did not make for friendliness or enjoyment out hunting. Today Grig was in an even worse temper than usual. The previous afternoon he had received a note instructing him to stop hunting. It had been signed BY ORDER L. ROSSITER. Damned impertinence. As if he was going to stop hunting as a result of an order from that whippersnapper. BY ORDER indeed! Grig snorted and looked around for someone on whom to vent his wrath. Young Raymond, now, that flatcatcher, cheated them out of the Yeomanry Cup, he had. No wonder they'd court-martialled him.

Stephen knew nothing of what was going on in Grig's mind and would not have cared if he had. All he desired was to catch sight of Babs and he searched the little crowd assembled at the cross-roads. At first he could see no sign of her; then the Dunlay groom arrived on one of Massiter's big blood horses. Shortly afterwards the Rolls drew up with Babs alone in the back. He saw her glance round the meet, searching just as he had done, and then, over the heads of the crowd, their eyes met. He had expected her to smile in greeting but she did not. Her face remained impassive as she gave a little nod of recognition and turned to talk to her mother. Then, as Grig gave the word to move off, she crossed to her horse and the groom put her up.

Stephen pushed his way through the throng towards her. In a moment he had ranged alongside her. 'Babs,' he said. 'Babs, I've been missing you every day. How are things with you? I've got to see you—'

She still looked straight ahead. 'I'm all right, Stephen,' she said quietly. 'And you? Home from the wars at last?'

'Babs, where can we meet? Babs, look at me—'

'Everyone's staring at us, Stephen,' she said.

'Let them stare—'

'I think they've found, Stephen. Look out, can't you—'

As hounds gave tongue the big horse, excited by the music, gave a plunge and cannoned into Stephen. Then she caught him by the head and was galloping towards a small bank beyond which hounds were racing away on a breast-high scent. The big horse had been corned up awaiting Massiter's arrival and it had too little hunting and too little exercise. It was over-fresh, full of itself and a proper handful to ride in a fast hunt over this rough country. Watching him, Stephen saw that he hardly jumped one bank properly. Mostly he stood back and jumped big, kicking back disdainfully to carry him over any hidden gripe or ditch on the far side. With his strength he got away with it but Babs did not have an easy passage and even when scent deteriorated and hounds began to hunt more slowly he did not come back to her hand. At a check Stephen went up to her. 'That brute will kill you,' he said. 'Get off him. I'll ride him until he settles. You can have this fellow. I've got him going sensibly now.'

Something set the big horse off on another series of plunges. 'Don't be a fool, Stephen,' she said when she had him under control again. 'He'd murder me if he knew you were riding one of his horses.'

'Why did he send you out on that thing then?'

'That's his business—and mine, isn't it?'

Stephen could not make her out. He had longed for this meeting and now, when it had come about, she seemed withdrawn from him and almost hostile. Could it be she had fallen in love with Massiter and wanted no more of him? Stephen would not believe it—not until he heard it from her own lips and even then he would doubt it.

Hounds spoke again and began to run on. They were away from the rest of the field, on their own, downwind from hounds. The fence facing them was a tall narrow bank with stones in it. Crumbling and rotten, it looked a thoroughly unpleasant obstacle especially for a

269

horse that was too full of himself and had not settled.

The big horse threw a prodigious leap at it, did not bother to change his legs but gave the far side one of his cursory kicks. The bank was indeed rotten and the sod gave way where his hoof hit it. All might have been well had there not been a wide ditch on the landing side. The bank giving way tipped the horse up and destroyed the impetus of his leap. He hit the edge of the ditch, scrabbled for his feet and came down.

Stephen, having jumped the fence more sedately higher up, was beside Babs in an instant. 'Are you all right?' he asked.

'Of course I'm all right,' she said crossly, getting to her feet, the reins still in her hand.

'You may be, but the horse isn't,' Stephen said.

The horse had taken two strides and it was instantly apparent that he was lame.

'Damn,' Babs said. 'What now?'

Stephen looked about him. 'There's a pub near here if we can get to the road,' he said. 'We can put him in there and wait until you're picked up. The car is following round, I suppose?'

A bushed-up gap out of which Stephen pulled the branches and gorse cuttings to let them through brought them to a narrow lane which in turn led to the road. Half a mile farther on they came to the pub, a thatched house with a shop-front and the name FRANCIS FARRELL in faded gold letters on its headboard.

The woman of the house showed them into the parlour, a bare little place with a holy picture over the empty fireplace, a wooden table and three chairs. Ordering hot whisky for them both, Stephen left to look after the horses.

'I found somewhere to put them,' he said on his return. 'There's nothing much wrong with that fellow of yours, I think. He gave himself a bit of a bang when he fell, that's all.'

The woman came in with a tray on which were two thick glasses filled with dark brown, steaming liquid. They each took one. Babs sat sipping hers, looking steadily at him over the rim of her glass. The table was between them. She made no move to come nearer. 'What happened to you, Stephen, after you were shot down?' she said.

'I wasn't shot down. Nothing so exciting or glamorous. I had an engine conk out on me and landed behind the German lines. A Belgian family took me in. Then when I came back they court-martialled me. Is that why you're looking at me like that, Babs? Is that why you won't speak to me properly? If it's any interest to you I was acquitted.'

'I know all that. The Belgian family, who were they?'

'People called de Kerouailles.'

She was standing by the window now, her back to him. He put his glass on the mantelpiece and gazed into the empty fireplace. There

270

was a faded spray of newspaper in it. He read the headline—
BRITISH GAINS AT CAMBRAI, it said.

'You stayed on with them after the Armistice?' she said without turning round.

'What is all this? What are you driving at, Babs?'

She swung round to face him, her eyes blazing. 'She took you in,' she said. 'She kept you. She was your mistress. You were sleeping with her. She had practically to drive you out, hadn't she, to make you give yourself up and return to your squadron?'

'Who's been telling you this?'

'My husband—Andrew. He's been in France. He made it his business to find out.'

'Did he indeed. It would have been better, then, if he'd found out the truth and, having found it out, told it. When did he say all this to you?'

'Last night.' Babs' lips trembled. She remembered every word he had spoken. It was after dinner. He was sipping his port. The servants had left the room and she had stayed with him for he had told her he had something to say to her. They had discussed the question of hunting earlier in the day. He could not go, he said, for Hutton was coming down and there was important business to discuss. He had suggested that she, too, should stay at home, saying that it was a bad meet, the horses would be over-fresh, she would be unfit since she had not ridden for months and that in any event the weather was likely to be bad. He did not advance the real reason, which was that he did not want her to meet Stephen again, for Hutton had told him he was back. When he had married her they both had thought that Stephen was dead and out of their lives forever. He expected her to defer to his wish for she had been acquiescent in almost everything since they had married, too acquiescent, he sometimes thought, for he liked his women spirited, and it was the fire in her that had first drawn his attention to her. Now to his surprise he found that she insisted on going out. As they had talked about it it seemed to him that he saw a brightness come into her eyes that had been lacking so far in the months of their marriage, and he thought he could guess the reason for he remembered her and Stephen together in those days in Paris.

He had put down his glass and turned his eyes on her. 'You have not changed your mind about hunting tomorrow?' he asked her.

'No,' she said. 'It's ages since I had a day. I want to go.'

'If by any chance you are consumed with longing to see young Raymond again,' he said, choosing his words slowly and with care, 'I should curb your fancies. I made it my business to obtain access to the records of his court-martial. On reading them I noticed a gap in the time between the Armistice and his return to his squadron. No one else appeared to place any importance on it and it is lucky for him that

271

the prosecuting officer overlooked it. I had further enquiries made and found the lady who succoured him. She remembered him well, very well indeed. She was his mistress; he was besotted with her; she had to implore him to leave, virtually to drive him out, to compel him to return to his squadron.' His voice had grown harsh. 'He deserved to be court-martialled for that alone.'

'This French trollop—' Babs went on furiously. 'I thought you were in love with me.' She was angry; her eyes were filled with tears that were a mixture of rage and humiliation. He thought he admired her and longed for her more than ever before.

'I was and still am,' he said.

'Why did you do it?'

'They took me in. I had pneumonia. She nursed me; she saved my life if you want to know. I was grateful. He's lying when he says she had to drive me out. Her husband was a psychopath; he kept me locked in a cellar. When he got sick she set me free. Massiter would lie about anything to gain his own ends, I think.'

The fire died in Babs' eyes. She looked away. 'You may be right about that,' she said. 'He's ruthless to get what he wants and to keep what he has. I've learnt that.'

'You may as well know it all,' Stephen went on. 'All right, I did sleep with her. She was lonely and frightened, terrified of that mad husband. Can't you understand? And anyway, that Australian, Martin, what about him? Are you as pure as driven snow if it comes to that?'

She stared at him wide-eyed. 'Oliver Martin,' she said. 'How did you know about him?'

'I saw you together at Murray's before I went out. When we were, well, together, I knew—I guessed—'

'And you never said anything—oh, Stephen.' Suddenly she laughed and it was the old Babs again. 'We are a couple of damn fools, aren't we?' she said.

She came into his arms then as if she had never been out of them. His hand went up under her coat to her breast.

'These damn hunting clothes,' she said. 'I'm sorry to give you such a cack-handed approach.'

'Come away with me, Babs. We can leave—'

A discreet toot of a motor horn came from outside. She tore herself away and began to button her coat. 'That sneaky chauffeur' she said.

'To hell with him. Send him about his business—'

'I can't Stephen, I can't. Wait, Stephen. We'll be here weeks, months perhaps. Oh, Stephen, now that we've found each other again what are we going to do?'

There were voices outside. A knock sounded on the door. She picked up her whip and hat and was gone.

On his return to Bellary Court, Stephen saw Dr O'Brien's car drawn up on the gravel sweep outside the house. With a feeling of foreboding he put the Overland hurriedly away and let himself in. Mikey was in the hall, just inside the green baize door, waiting for him. 'Ach, the poor master,' he said. 'It's a sthroke he's been after having.'

Dr O'Brien was coming down the stairs. 'Is this true?' Stephen asked him.

'I'm afraid it is, Stephen. A slight stroke. His right side is paralysed. He may regain the use of it. Complete rest and quiet is what he needs now. I've sent for a nurse.'

'Can I see him?'

'Not now, Stephen. He's sleeping. Later. I'll be back first thing to-morrow. Let me know if there's any change.'

His mother and Ethel were in the round room. 'It's only slight,' Honoria said stoutly. 'I've no doubt he'll pull through.'

'What happened?'

'It seems he was sitting at his desk, writing. He must have guessed something was wrong. He rang for Mikey. When he came he said "I feel very strange" and slumped forward. We sent for Dr O'Brien who came immediately.'

'It would have been quicker if we'd had the Overland,' Ethel said tartly. 'But of course you had it out hunting.'

Stephen ignored this thrust. 'Shouldn't one of us be with him even if he is asleep?' he said.

'Dr O'Brien said he had a nurse coming. In fact I think that must be her now.'

When Honoria had left the room to deal with the nurse's arrival Ethel turned to Stephen. 'Vivienne Gnowles drove me into Kilderry this morning,' she said. 'She wasn't hunting. She's hurt her back or something. We had lunch with the Deverells. Do you know who was there?'

'No. Who?' Stephen was only half listening for his mind was on his father and his illness, and what it would mean.

'Harry French.'

'Harry French! I can hardly believe you. What the devil is he doing here?'

'He's been put in charge of the military at Kilderry.'

'Was he civil to you? He cut me dead when I met him in Paris.'

'He was friendly enough to me. If he's after anyone I think it's the Rossiters. He said one of them had cursed his father that day out hunting.'

'Old Bridie Rossiter. She's dead now. She cursed him all right. I remember it well.'

'He's dead nuts against them. He asked to be sent here because he

273

thought his local knowledge might help. He says they're going to step up activity—stamp the Shinners out.'

'He'll want to do a better job than they've done so far if that's what he's after,' Stephen said sarcastically.

'He thinks all of us loyalists can help a lot. We can give information about the movements of suspects, that sort of thing.'

'That's a damn good way of getting us shot or burnt down. We've got to live here. He hasn't.'

'What on earth are you saying, Stephen? Sometimes I declare I think you're half a Shinner yourself.'

'I'm Irish. I don't like what the bloody Black and Tans are doing in the other parts of the country. We haven't had them here yet, but if we do—'

'They're closing the R.I.C. barracks in Bellary, Harry said. He'll be in charge of the area. He says he'll be glad to come to dinner and tennis as soon as he's settled in. We can pass on the information then.'

'Look, Ethel, I've had enough of war, come to think of it I've had enough of the army. I think Harry French is only using you. Anyway I'm not going to act as a spy.'

Ethel went on as if she had not heard him. 'Stephen, what do you think of Mikey?' she asked. 'Could he be in with the Shinners? I've been watching him. He's always off somewhere and he never tells anyone where he's going.'

Stephen looked at her. 'You leave Mikey alone, Ethel,' he said. 'He and I have been friends since we were kids.'

'You'll be turning Shinner yourself next, I shouldn't wonder.'

'I hadn't thought about it but since you mention it I might do worse,' Stephen said, stung into taunting her.

Across the Bay a few days later another and different conversation was taking place. Massiter and Hutton were sitting over their port. Babs had left them and they were alone.

'I think I'll cut short this visit,' Massiter said, lighting a cigar. 'We've got through much of what we wanted to, far more than I expected, today. We can finish the rest in Dublin.'

Babs had given him her account of the day's happenings and, abridge them how she might, she had been forced to admit that Stephen and she had met and that he had helped her with the horse. Massiter had also seen his stud-groom, ostensibly to find out about the horse's leg. The stud-groom had already interviewed the chauffeur and the groom who had been in the car. They had told him they had found Babs in the pub with Captain Raymond as they insisted on calling him. How long they had been there they did not of course know. Massiter, however, had noticed a look on his wife's face when she returned. It was a look which could only be described as eagerness. He had not seen it since their marriage and he had drawn his own conclusions.

'It's a bad time to leave big houses empty,' Hutton said.

'You're thinking of the Sinn Fein campaign, I suppose?'

'Yes,' Hutton said laconically. 'I am.'

'I don't think we need worry too much about them. The Prime Minister assures me they are virtually finished. To use his own words to me, which I imagine he will employ in public later on, he says he has "murder by the throat". Also he's in the process of authorising the raising of a new force, an ex-officer *corps d'élite*. They will deal the murderers a final blow.'

'And how will they do that?' Hutton asked.

'By searching out, finding and destroying the gunmen and assassins.'

'I suppose it will sound very well in the House of Commons but it will be easier said than done. You've been away too long, Massiter. The time for that sort of thing has passed. Apart from the fact that they won't know an inch of the country they'll be asked to operate in they'll find every man's hand is against them. They can't succeed.'

'You really think I'm in danger of losing all this?' Massiter swept an arm around. The candlelight flickered and danced on the panelling and the pictures on the walls.

'Yes,' Hutton said soberly. 'I do. The Old Earl's place was burnt down, as you know, a night or two back.'

'Is there anything that can be done?'

'You might take out some insurance.'

'What do you mean?'

'Certain prominent Unionists in your position have been paying money into what let us call a fund. In return they are guaranteed protection for their houses.'

'Good Heavens! But this is hard to believe. Are you seriously telling me—'

Hutton took a folded piece of paper from his pocket. 'I have a list here. It is not complete but it will give you a general idea. I brought it with me because I thought it might interest you.'

'Can I see it?'

'Certainly.' Hutton handed him the sheet of paper.

Massiter ran his eyes over it. 'Good God,' he said. *Lord Donabate One thousand pounds and permission to occupy a derelict mansion house on the estate; Lord Brandon and Tralee, five hundred pounds. Donal McManway*—the senior steward—is this genuine?'

'Absolutely. The man who is likely to be the first Attorney General when Ireland wins her freedom obtained it for me. I thought you might be interested in seeing McManway's name on it.'

'I am indeed.' Massiter was already mentally filing the information

275

for future use. 'If I contribute, how will I know they'll keep their side of the bargain?' Unconsciously he was echoing Desmond's words to him before he signed away Babs in marriage.

'They'll keep it,' Hutton said drily. 'They have not had power long enough to become untrustworthy.'

25

Some weeks later Edward Raymond slipped out of life, in his sleep, as quietly and as unobtrusively as he had tried to pass through it.

The intervening period had seen an increase in Sinn Fein activity. Police barracks had been attacked and destroyed; ambushes had been set up and carried through; the harassment of all those connected with the Crown and the exercise of the Imperial writ intensified. The military had little or no success in apprehending those responsible who melted into the crowds or the countryside immediately after the perpetration of what were branded as outrages. It was frustrating for Harry French and his officers who, when off duty, behaved as if they were members of the peacetime garrison. They played tennis and golf and took tea or dined out at neighbouring country houses. Harry was often at Bellary and he and Ethel had become firm friends. It was through Harry that they learnt that a detachment of the new 'Auxiliary Cadets' was to be stationed in the area. Harry knew very little about their constitution or duties nor did he look on them with much favour. Their presence appeared to him to be a slur on the army's ability to contain the rebels and he had all the traditional dislike of the serving soldier for irregular forces. Given time, he said, and, glancing pointedly at Ethel, adequate information, he had no doubt that the army could do the job. They needed the unwavering support of all loyalists, he said, adding that if they could lay their hands on Larry Rossiter and some of his sources of information it ought effectively to curb rebel activities in and around Bellary.

But to lay their hands on Larry Rossiter or any of the leaders was just what the army could not do. These men knew the country, knew their 'safe houses' and knew too that they had by now the tacit if not the open support of nine-tenths of the population.

The weeks that had passed had been a period of intense frustration for Stephen. More and more was he becoming entirely out of sympathy with his mother's and Ethel's stridently Imperialist sentiments, often indiscreetly expressed, yet at the same time he could not bring himself to contemplate any open or active involvement with the

277

rebels.

No more than anyone else of moderate views could he approve of the gunning down of policemen in the streets of their own towns, yet at the same time the excesses of the Black and Tans and the pointless policy of reprisals carried out by the Crown forces together with the authenticated reports of 'shooting while trying to escape' and torture whilst in captivity appalled him.

To make matters worse for him, he found himself coming to believe that he had in his own household two active elements of the opposing forces operating in Ireland. He was satisfied that the friendship between Ethel and Harry French was not purely a social one and that Ethel was supplying Harry with what information she could glean or gather about rebel movements and intentions, and he now knew or thought he knew that Mikey was actively employed in some way, probably as a courier, by the Sinn Feiners. He had bought from Bob a young horse which he was schooling and bringing along, and one afternoon exercising along a mountain path he had caught a glimpse of Mikey on the road below him, crouched low over the handlebars of his bicycle, cap turned back to front, pedalling furiously in the direction of Knockmaroon on whose slopes Larry Rossiter was popularly supposed to have his hideout.

There was little doing in the racing world also. Punchestown had been abandoned for the second year in succession, the flat season was now well advanced which meant that fewer and fewer rides came his way, and Bob Ferris had roughed off most of his horses.

But worst of all was the problem of himself and Babs. Though she was so near he scarcely saw her. Once or twice they exchanged words at the few tennis parties which took place; she implored him not to write; there seemed no method of communication available to them. From his window he could see the tall tower of Dunlay Castle across the Bay but the stretch of water separating them might just as well have been the broad Atlantic. Almost daily he took out the twelve-footer and sailed down the Bay past the Castle, hoping that he would catch a glimpse of her. But the windows remained blank, the lawns empty. Once he thought he saw her getting out of the motor in front of the great door, but Massiter was with her and they disappeared quickly into the house.

Edward's funeral took place two days after his death. The cortège of carriages, motors, traps and donkey carts slowly wound its way up the road to the little church above Bellary where he could lie looking out at the landscape he had loved so well.

Stephen, Honoria and Ethel stood silently at the head of the grave watching the coffin being lowered into the earth. Stephen could not tell what the others were thinking; he himself was only beginning to realise what he had lost by his father's death and how much he was going to miss him. The upstairs study would be empty now; no longer would that gentle presence be there, always ready to discuss whatever mattered at the moment, quietly, sanely and without heat or rancour. He heard the clergyman drone on without paying him much heed. Instead he turned to look down to where the Bay lay in all its summer splendour below him. Perhaps his father was as well out of it; the troubles would intensify; he knew that in his bones. The peace around them was deceptive; the arrival of these new Auxiliaries, so far as he could hazard a guess, would only make things worse; their beloved Bay could be torn apart and all who lived there with it.

As the little group of mourners split up, a short stout man came bustling towards them. It was Arthur Merrett, the solicitor from Kilderry, Honoria's cousin. 'Well, Arthur,' Honoria said briskly. 'You'll come up to the house, of course. You have the Will, I presume?'

Arthur Merrett took out a large silk handkerchief and mopped his brow. 'Er, no, Honoria,' he said. 'I'm afraid I haven't. At least I have one made many years ago. There are provisions for lengthy minorities. I cannot think he did not make another—'

Honoria gave one of her high-pitched snorts. 'It would not at all surprise me if that was not just what he did or did not do,' she said. 'And what, pray, is this individual doing here?'

Will Hutton was approaching them. He took off his silk hat and murmured his consolations. Then he touched Stephen on the arm. 'I have the Will,' he said. 'You and I are the executors. When will it be convenient for me to see you?'

'You'd better come to the house,' Stephen said. He smiled slightly. 'If what you say is correct you could need a whisky and soda. You may not have a very friendly reception.'

When the Will was read it transpired that Edward had left everything to Stephen subject to rights of residence and jointures in favour of Honoria and Ethel. It was in a way, Stephen thought, Edward's vicarious revenge for all those years of ignominy and derision. Honoria was stripped of her power, for he was now the owner of the Bellary demesne such as it was and the Master of Bellary Court. That it would be a troubled inheritance he did not doubt but he had no intention of surrendering it by selling out or taking any of the easy ways of escape that might be offered to him. He intended to remain at the Bay and pass his days there as his father had done and his father before him.

'Well,' Honoria said when the reading of the Will had been finished. 'Well. It will take us some little time to digest this. When are you returning to Dublin, Mr Hutton?'

'I am spending the night with Mr Massiter at Dunlay. We have some business to discuss.'

'You will see me again before you go?' Stephen said.

'Of course. It is absolutely necessary.' Hutton rose to leave.

'You will get rid of that man,' Honoria said immediately he had gone.

'Why, mother?' Stephen asked.

'He is Massiter's lackey. It would be madness to allow him to remain in charge of our affairs. I can't imagine what your father thought he was doing. Arthur Merrett should have handled this.'

'Father liked him. He told me so.'

'Liked him! Fiddlesticks! He ingratiated himself with your father by allowing him to beat him at chess.'

'Just the same, mother, I think I shall retain him for the time being at any rate.'

It was the first open clash of wills between them. 'Very well, then,' Honoria snapped. 'But you will live to regret it and then you will remember what I have said.'

As he drove to Dunlay Hutton himself was wondering if there was going to be a conflict of interest involved if he continued to act for both Stephen and Massiter. But Hutton was above all an opportunist, and the time for a decision about that would come later, much later. Massiter's first words to him, however, as he joined him in the library, did little to reassure him.

'What happens at Bellary now?' he asked. 'Who gets the place?'

'I can tell you that without any breach of professional secrecy,' Hutton replied. 'In a month or so you could have it looked up for yourself in the probate office. The son, Stephen, it's all his subject to two jointures.'

'Jointures? Will he be able to pay them out of the place?'

'I should imagine so, if he's sensible.'

Massiter drummed his fingers on the big desk. 'For reasons of my own, Hutton,' he said, 'I should like that young man away from here. Will he sell?'

'From what little I know I think that's most unlikely.'

'Very well, we have a mortgage. Can we enforce it?'

'You can try to but it would be most unwise in the present circumstances. Any attempts to dispossess the Raymonds just now will only bring calumny and perhaps worse down on you.'

'On me? We have transferred the mortgage to the holding company. It could take the necessary steps.'

'I still think it would be unwise. No one knows what friends and connections that young man has. They tell me he has Nationalistic leanings.'

'I'm not surprised. He was court-martialled for cowardice and was very fortunate to be acquitted. There must be some way. I don't employ you for nothing, Hutton.'

280

Massiter just then had much on his mind. At the suggestion of the Prime Minister when his political career was beginning he had put money into certain companies to which, as he well knew, contracts for the supply of munitions and other implements of war had been carefully steered. The companies had prospered but that was during wartime; their affairs were not in such a healthy state now and it had been conveyed to him that a further injection of money was required. It had also been strongly hinted that an honour might be forthcoming if these and other contributions were made. Massiter badly wanted that honour; it would set the seal on his achievements and mark him out from his fellows. No one then dare point a finger at him as not being as good or better than the next man. That remark of Desmond's about the gombeen man' still rankled. But to obtain it his presence was badly needed in London.

If he were to go to London, as he felt he must, he could bring Babs with him, which would deny her any opportunity of communicating with Stephen. But there were objections to that course. In the first place if the honour was to be brought about or in plain language bought, then there would be comings and goings to the house he had taken in Lord North Street by people whom he did not particularly wish Babs to see. She might recognise some of them and use the knowledge of his purchase against him later on. Besides, he had a feeling that she would laugh at his ambition and despise him for it if she knew, and would certainly hold in contempt his means of obtaining it. Those companies, too, he wanted no word of what he was doing with them to leak out to anyone and who knew what a careless telephone call, for instance, could reveal to Babs were she to answer it? In addition, although he was satisfied that he had, through Hutton's intervention, protected his house from interference and destruction by the I.R.A., he had been told that this new counter-terrorist force had been given power to commandeer houses that were empty or occupied only by servants. If the Castle were to be left vacant that could well happen since they were due in the Bay any day now. The last thing he wanted was for his house to be occupied by a marauding crowd of tearaway ex-officers. To leave Babs behind would probably obviate that but then to leave her alone in the present circumstances was unthinkable, though, knowing her, she would probably insist that she was safe. Suddenly, looking at Hutton, he made up his mind. 'Hutton,' he said. 'Something very important makes it essential that I return to London for some days. I have no wish to submit my wife to the journey in these troubled times. Again I do not like leaving her here alone. You will have business no doubt with Raymond. May I suggest that you stay here for say a week while you transact that business?'

And am I to be gaoler too, Hutton said to himself sardonically, for it had not taken him long to scent out during the few days that he had spent with them that Massiter's young wife was dissatisfied. In his worldly way he had guessed at an affair or at least the makings of one. Massiter's first words to him, expressing his desire to be rid of Stephen, had confirmed these suspicions. With his delight in intrigue it occurred to him that the next few days might be uncommonly interesting and could moreover provide material from which he might derive both power and profit. He chuckled gently to himself. 'That would suit me very well,' he said. 'While I make a start in marshalling Raymond's assets and looking into the position there.'

'I have been thinking about that while we talked,' Massiter said. 'It seems to me that no possible objection could be taken to your conveying to young Raymond that the company which holds the mortgage would like to realise its asset and convert it into cash in these difficult times. Because I can assure you, Hutton, that that is what the company does require. It would at least set him thinking and it will be interesting to see what his reaction will be.'

'As you say,' Hutton replied. 'There could be no objection to that. I'll see to it.'

'I believe,' Massiter went on, 'that the women there would be easy enough to deal with. They have no real feeling for the place, or so I'm told. In the event of a sale I could buy in—or a nominee could purchase for me.'

Hutton regarded him with a look in which there was something as near to open admiration as he ever allowed to appear on his features. He had married the Murtagh girl. She was an only child and should therefore succeed to Desmond's house and lands. If Desmond had heavily mortgaged them as it was all but certain that he had, then Massiter could buy up the mortgages probably at a knock-down price at this time. And if Desmond tried to leave the property away from Babs as he might well do, then Massiter could have her oppose the Will. Were he to lose initially, by the use of his money he could carry through a series of appeals the cost of which would cripple the estate and almost inevitably force a settlement. And if a reasonable price for Bellary was dangled in front of Stephen then the women of the family, as Massiter had suggested, might well, in Hutton's opinion, bully him into accepting it. If this or even most of it came about, Massiter would end up owning virtually all the best land and residences of the Bay. And, through Hutton, he had protected his own seat. Hutton knew all about his ambition for honours and, he said to himself, a lord without a seat is like a jockey without a horse. He savoured his own witticism but he kept it unsaid, reserving it for retailing later on to his cronies in the St Stephen's Green club.

'That's all settled, then,' Massiter said. 'I'm obliged and grateful to you, Hutton. I shall be interested to hear from you just what you discover during the next few days.' The tawny eyes stared directly into

282

Hutton's who realised as plainly as if they had been put into words just what his extra-curricular duties were to be.

The news of Massiter's departure was known in Bellary immediately he boarded the train and was conveyed to Stephen by Mikey who remarked irreverently: 'Ould Massiter's gone off to London for a few days. Some says it's a week he'll be gone and some says more. And he's left her behind him with the solicitor.' He cocked an eye at Stephen and went off through the green baize door whistling, a tray of silver in his hands. Mikey, Stephen thought, had never really been cut out to be an upper servant or a servant of any sort come to that, and he was becoming less and less like one every day.

Stephen spent the morning with Hutton telling him what little he knew about Edward's private affairs and going through the contents of the safe and desk with him. Hutton told him that he intended to occupy the afternoon with the land steward discussing the stock, implements and crops and the values to be put upon them for probate.

As soon as lunch was over Stephen ran down to the boathouse and sculled out to the twelve-footer. And this time Babs was waiting for him, standing on the shores of Holy Island. As he approached he could see her figure silhouetted against the trees. There was a fair breeze and the little boat danced and cavorted against the waves. A squall tore at him and he paid out the sheet and laughed at it. It passed on, ruffling the water behind him. Soon he was near enough to see her wave to him.

There was a stone jetty running out from the shore of the island. She ran along this as he secured the painter to an iron ring let into the stone.

'Not here, Stephen,' she said, dancing on her feet as he reached for her. 'The boathouse. Follow me.'

A path led through the trees to where the boathouse stood above its slip. Because Massiter had dredged and enlarged the private harbour, the boathouse on the island was seldom if ever used for its original purpose. Since Massiter, however, disliked any of his property falling into decay he had renovated it, turning it into a place for picnics and a stopping point for expeditions when he showed visitors the sights and antiquities of the island. Even so it was a virtually forgotten part of the estate, especially in times like these when visitors were few and far between. Trees had grown up around it and its approaches. The path leading to it was moss-covered and narrowed by encroaching undergrowth. It was an all but perfect and secret rendezvous for lovers' meetings.

An outside staircase led to its upper storey. Taking a key from her pocket she slid it into the door at the head of this and threw it open.

Inside were upright basket chairs and long lounging chairs and cushions in abundance. Seascapes were on the walls and wicker picnic tables were dotted about. Best of all, two wide sofas faced each other across the room.

'Everything man could desire,' Stephen said, looking at her. 'And you.'

Then she was in his arms once more and their mouths were meeting.

Daily after that the little boat scudded down the bay. They were besotted with each other; they were young and they were reckless. It was easy enough for Stephen to avoid Hutton or to imagine he was doing so, for Hutton seemed always to be busy either at Bellary or Dunlay where he was locked away in its depths either in the library or the business room. Once Stephen mentioned him to Babs, wondering if he suspected anything.

'Old Hutton!' she said laughing scornfully. 'He's far too taken up with his law and his accounts and things. Anyway he's too old to know about us and this. Can you imagine him?' And they fell again to laughing together and spinning fancies about Hutton and the impotence of age.

But Will Hutton was neither as immersed in his duties nor as ignorant of life and lust and the sexual drives of the young as Babs and Stephen supposed. He suspected that something was going on under his nose but, being unacquainted with the layout of the Dunlay demesne, he could not divine where it was taking place. Reckless though she was, Babs took good care to cover her tracks when she approached Holy Island. She had been accustomed when at Dunlay to spend much of her time walking her dogs and now she would always come to the causeway from a different direction and at different times. The little jetty was well hidden from both land and sea, for trees surrounded it and a rocky headland blocked out any view from higher up the Bay. Nevertheless, other eyes than Hutton's did see the daily trips of the little boat down the Bay and their owners drew their own conclusions.

Hutton, however, had still no real knowledge or proof of what was happening to produce to his employer on his return. Even if he had he was puzzled as to how he should convey it. Massiter had only thrown out oblique hints and it would be, at best, a ticklish business telling a man of Massiter's calibre that he was being cuckolded. All that did not stop him looking for evidence. But, as the days went on and he failed to find any, he began to wonder if he had not been mistaken.

If they gave any more thought to the matter at all, Babs and Stephen felt themselves secure but, in fact, having found each other's bodies again and renewed their delight in them, they thought of little else. Nor did they pay any heed to what was happening around them.

The Auxiliaries had arrived and occupied a workhouse on the road between Bellary and Kilderry. These men in their strange medley of uniforms, dark Glengarry bonnets that carried the R.I.C. badge of a harp and crown in gold, service tunics, dark trousers or riding breeches, revolvers slung at their hips and rifles in their hands, immediately began to make their presence felt. They were mobile, far more so than the army who often had to rely for patrolling on bicycles or what transport they could scrounge or commandeer. Ex-R.F.C. Crossley tenders were put at the disposal of the Auxiliaries and the roar of their engines echoed often along the lonely roads. Their brief, it was said, was to make Ireland 'an appropriate hell for those whose trade is agitation and whose method murder'. In carrying it out they succeeded in making the country a hell for everyone including themselves. They issued instructions, amongst other things, that every house must have affixed inside its front door a list of the names and addresses of all its occupants, threatening that any error, omission or misstatement in the list could result in the immediate destruction of the house by burning. They rounded up 'suspects' and brutally interrogated them, and they incurred the immediate hatred of the whole locality by shooting and killing a boy who was working in the fields and who ran from them in terror.

If Babs and Stephen were blind to such things, Will Hutton was not. He kept in touch with his office in Dublin as best he could by the telephone which Massiter had recently installed. From these conversations, disjointed and frequently interrupted though they were by interference and breakdowns, and from the newspapers, he gathered that the Auxiliaries stationed in the city were stepping up activity there too. They were raiding houses of known and suspected sympathisers with the movement and were having some successes. It occurred very forcefully to Hutton that if that list of Unionist subscribers fell into their hands, then those whose names were on it might well be in danger from them and marked out for their reprisals, since even in the short time they had been operating they had gained the reputation of being no respecters of persons. He immediately burnt the copy which was in his possession in case it was found during a search at a stop point and then turned his tortuous mind to the problem of circumventing any danger to Massiter by reason of his name appearing on that list.

He considered making an approach to the Auxiliaries themselves to secure the safety of Dunlay. They would, he thought, be probably open to a bribe; most mercenaries were. The idea of buying protection from both sides appealed to him but he dismissed it immediately. The first commander of the Auxiliary company had shot himself accidentally in the foot when getting down from a lorry and had been replaced by another. He knew nothing of the character of the new man save he was said to have them under better control than many of the other companies, that he disapproved of drinking and had prevented his men looting spirit merchants and public houses. That apart, however, those who had come in contact with him held him to be a 'holy terror' and as ruthless and overbearing as the rest of them.

Still pondering his problem, Hutton found himself walking the corridors of the castle for he always thought best on his feet. It was a beautiful day outside. Through the windows of the upper gallery he could see the sun on the Bay and the colours of the mountains. At the end of the gallery he found himself facing the stairway that led to the roof of the tower. Climbing it he came out through the low doorway. He had never been here before and he gasped at the beauty of the panorama laid out beneath him.

The big telescope was in front of him. Idly he bent down and focused it, swinging it about to take in the vast view it revealed. It was almost by accident that the lens came to rest on the farther shore of Holy Island.

Stephen had just finished securing the twelve-footer. Straightening up, he jumped on to the jetty. Babs came out of the screen of trees to meet him and they embraced. Locked in each other's arms they went along the path to the boathouse and let themselves in. Through the telescope Hutton could see a blur of movement beyond the window but no more. Taking out a pipe from his pocket he packed it slowly and thoughtfully. One of his questions at least was answered. He sat on for a long time in the sun pondering on the folly of human beings and especially of youth. He smiled to himself as he thought how always that folly contributed to his way of life and gave him what he most enjoyed—the power to manipulate people.

The news must now, of course, be conveyed to Massiter on his return, and again, sitting there, he gave his mind to considering how best to do it, for it was clear that it would have to be done obliquely. He had little doubt, however, that when the time came he would find a way of wrapping up the truth yet conveying it in all its simplicity.

Much later, towards evening, he saw Babs crossing the lawn and entering the castle through the cloisters. He felt no pity for her, no compunction for what he was about to do. She had been foolish and reckless and those who were either or both had to abide by the consequences.

Although he was delayed longer than he had expected Massiter returned to Dunlay in a much better humour than when he set out. Things had worked to his advantage in London, far more than he had dared to hope. The injection of funds required by the companies had been less than he had been led to believe. In addition, from certain consultations he had had he was assured that the way was clear for an honour if not in the next list then the one after.

'Well, Hutton,' he said as, dinner over, they sat in the library, brandies by their side and cigars going. 'What have you to tell me?'

They were alone, for Babs had retired to bed early as she usually did, especially on the occasions when business associates were staying.

'I mentioned the matter of the mortgage to the Raymonds,' Hutton said. 'Casually of course and in the most general terms. You were quite right. The women, I think, would be glad to sell. The girl wants to go to England and lead the smart life. The mother only wants to be rid of it or so I gathered from what she said. They have no feeling for the place as the father had. But the boy is adamant. He refuses absolutely to sell or move in any way. And he is the owner.'

'Perhaps pressure can be put upon him as the administration of the estate progresses. There will be death duties and debts, too, I imagine.' Massiter abruptly changed the subject. 'How did you find my wife when I was away?'

'I scarcely saw her save at meals.'

'Indeed. And how did she occupy her time?'

'She went for long walks and busied herself in the grounds.' Hutton deliberately avoided Massiter's eye. He looked up toward a corner of the ceiling and blew smoke from his cigar. 'You have a boathouse on the island, Holy Island, I think it is called,' he said slowly. 'She appeared to spend much of her time there.'

There was silence between them for a moment and then Massiter's breath came out in a little hiss. 'Thank you, Hutton,' he said. 'I think I understand quite perfectly. You wouldn't care for another brandy? I believe I'll have one myself.'

The following morning after Hutton had been despatched from the station Massiter wasted no time. He, too, took a stroll in the grounds, a man in a panama hat and a reefer jacket, apparently walking aimlessly, enjoying the view and his possessions. Despite himself, however, his steps quickened when he reached the causeway. Climbing the stairs to the upper door of the boathouse he opened it and entered. What he saw told him all he wanted to know.

They had not even bothered to set the place to rights. The two big sofas were joined together and it needed very little imagination to realise that they had been used as a bed. As if to emphasize this, there were cushions at the head of them and the rest of the cushions were in disarray. There was an empty bottle of champagne—his champagne—on one of the wicker tables with two used glasses beside it. Looking at the place and the evidence that it offered of betrayal and illicit love, Massiter knew as surely as if he had seen them there that her partner had been Stephen.

What had taken place in the boathouse in his absence struck at the very roots of his self-esteem. He had been betrayed and between them they had destroyed everything for which he had worked and schemed. When they learnt of it as surely they would if they had not done so already, her family and their like would be able to laugh and sneer at him again—the gombeen man thinking he could raise himself to be their equal. Even the thought of the coming honour was as bitter ashes in his mouth. He was possessed by a cold consuming fury, all of it, or almost all of it, directed against Stephen. Had he not returned none of this would have happened; Babs would have settled down with him; with his ability and her connections they would have gone on together to undreamt-of reaches of power and position. Now he was a laughing-stock, the oldest one in the world, a middle-aged cuckold. His thoughts turned to ways of bringing about the destruction of Stephen and all he had, ways that would be far more certain and drastic than the mere calling in of a mortgage.

He did not have to wait long for an opportunity to be offered to him. Some days later a Crossley tender roared along the avenue by the private harbour, turned through the rock cutting and the rhododendrons and drew up with a screech of tyres before the great door. From its back spilled its complement of Auxiliaries. Spreading out, rifles at the ready, they took up positions on the lawn, eyeing warily the surrounding trees and shrubs as if they expected any moment a burst of fire to erupt from them.

Their leader got down from his seat beside the driver, crossed to the door and hammered on it with his cane. The door opened and the butler admitted him. 'Take me to your master,' he commanded. Then he followed the butler along the great hall, a burly, menacing figure that almost dwarfed the pillars, his Glengarry pulled rakishly down on one side of his head, the big Webley swinging at his hip.

'Good morning, Colonel,' Massiter eyed him coolly as he entered the library, taking in the crown and star on his sleeve, the flying brevet above the breast pocket and the line of medal ribbons below it. 'We've met before I think. I never forget a face.'

'In France,' Conway answered. 'You inspected my squadron with the Prime Minister. I recalled your name. That is one reason I came to you first.'

'You'll take something?'

'I never drink.'

'I should have expected,' Massiter said smoothly, 'that with your record you would scarcely be here. A permanent commission—'

'I was refused it.'

'Pity you did not come to me. I might have done something. However, shall we get down to business, Colonel? To what do I owe this visit?'

'I'm checking on loyalist or so-called loyalist houses. We have been informed that it is through their servants that the Shinners obtain

288

most of their information, especially in those houses where the military are entertained. Can you speak for yours?'

'My butler is English. So are the two footmen and the stud-groom. The maids are Irish, of course. It's possible that they might hear something but we guard our tongues in their presence.'

'I'm glad to hear it. Can you tell me anything of your neighbours?'

'General Gnowles is sound. I need hardly tell you that. He commanded a Yeomanry Brigade in France as no doubt you know.' Massiter appeared to hesitate though he knew very well what he was going to say. 'I wish I were so sure about those across the Bay—the Raymonds. The girl and the mother are all right. I hear, however, strange rumours about their butler. And young Raymond, too, is said to have Sinn Fein sympathies. He has just inherited the place.'

'Raymond was in my squadron. But you know that. You had him brought to Paris for some reason.'

'I remember. He ranted there about his senior officers and the conduct of the war in the air.'

'He was court-martialled for cowardice. He should have been shot. I felt we might meet again. Nothing you could say of him would surprise me. So he has a Shinner for a butler?'

'It's common talk.'

'They are evil men, sir. They must be exterminated, they and all who aid and abet them. I have heard my father say that papists are the infidels of Empire, that no man can be a true Englishman and yet put himself under the dictates of Rome. If he does he will put his church before his country. Root and branch, bone and sinew they must be ploughed up and torn apart.'

'Er—yes,' Massiter said. He had not expected this outburst and, not being given to rhodomontade himself, it rather took him aback.

During it Conway's face had taken on a look remarkably like that of his father when he was delivering one of the more ranting of his sermons. In fact some of the words he had used had been recollected from the last time he had sat in the all but deserted church listening to his father preach.

In the remote rectory in the fells after Conway's demobilisation and his failure to obtain a permanent commission, he and his father had discussed the matter of his joining the Auxiliaries.

At that time neither father nor son was entirely normal. Conway, like many another who had come out of those years of war and all but unbearable strain, was, although he would never have admitted it, suffering from what was known then as delayed shell shock. He had driven himself almost to destruction by his work with the squadron. He had taken no leave, he had kept late hours compiling and perfecting returns and reports; he had flown as many patrols as anyone save Stephen and more than the rest. When flying, he had pushed himself and his machine to the limits of their endurance. Just as at school his hopes had been centred on leading the school and the fifteen to tremendous triumphs so, after the war, all his ambitions had been placed upon gaining a permanent commission and making a success-ful career in the new service. Stephen, or so it seemed to him, had been responsible for frustrating him in both matters. Stephen was Irish. Just as he had truly hated the Germans, he really believed the Irish to be naturally evil and ungodly and he had come in a warped way to think that Stephen was an instrument of the powers of darkness. Were he to go to Ireland with the authority of an Auxiliary policeman and exercising the free hand they were promised, he could attempt to com-bat those powers as well as fighting against the hounds of Rome who threatened to destroy the English race and snap the bonds of Empire. And, he told himself, he knew where Stephen lived. It should not take much effort to seek him out.

The old man, for his part, was now all but mad in everything but outward appearance. He terrified his parishioners, emptied his church and lived alone without even a housekeeper, eating infrequent and frugal meals as a further penance and mortification of the flesh. Loneliness, sexual frustration, a sense of guilt, fear of impending death and the hell-fire to come had all taken their toll of him.

In some extraordinary manner he connected his son's disgrace and departure from school with the Irish, probably because he had learnt that Stephen was Irish, though he had long forgotten Stephen's name and all about him. In his muddled old mind he associated the Irish only with the dread religion he had been brought up to fear and hate and from that he associated them with all things evil. Then it was but a step to believing that by going to Ireland with the Auxiliaries his son would be wielding the sword of the Lord, as his predecessors the Elizabethans and Cromwellians had done. He encouraged Conway to enroll as if he were taking part in some holy crusade.

When Conway had arrived at the Curragh his rank and record made it certain that he would be given command of a company as the Auxiliary units were called. Once this had been confirmed it had been a simple matter for him to persuade his superiors to send him to Kil-derry and the Bellary area when the vacancy arose, for no one in that time of muddled thinking, divided command and diminished auth-ority knew quite what to do with the Auxiliary Division once it had been formed, where to position its companies or what directives for their operations to issue. Any application, therefore, from someone who actually knew his own mind was likely to be favourably received and Conway got his posting.

'Didn't you know? Make the place a hell for rebels,' a cynical Divi-sional Inspector of the R.I.C., who was supposed to be training them in police procedure, told Conway when he asked for instructions on

290

his and his company's rôle and duties. Those were the only operation orders he was ever to receive and by and large he was quite content to carry them out.

'The Prime Minister,' Massiter was going on, 'says he would like to place a ring around Ireland and sink it in the sea.'

'It's one solution.' Conway gave one of his rare smiles. 'Unfortunately it isn't practical. I wish it were and all in it—except loyalists of course,' he added quickly. Even as he said it he thought to himself that they could go too, the whole damn lot of them, you could never trust one of them, including this chap opposite sitting snug amongst his treasures. And Raymond was supposed to be a loyalist, wasn't he? He walked to the window and looked out. 'That's Raymond's house across the water, isn't it?' he said.

'It is his now. The father died a while back. They are very attached to it. It was the father's whole existence, you might say, and I understand the same applies to the son. The people who have lived here for generations have a tremendous family feeling for the place and their houses, you know.'

Conway's eyes swept the scene. The colours were brighter, the contours less rugged than those of the bleak fells amongst which he had grown up. The softness of it all, the langour and the beauty appeared to him in some way to make everything more alien and to epitomise the perfidy of the Irish. 'So Raymond is mixed up with them,' he said without turning round. 'I thought he might be.'

'It's possible. I merely repeat what I hear.'

'Then he too must be stamped out,' Conway said.

When the Auxiliaries had driven away, Massiter picked up *The Times* which had arrived with the post and slit the wrapper with a paper-knife. He was smiling to himself. He had reason, he thought, to be not displeased with the morning's work.

26

When the hammering on the front door began, Stephen knew it immediately for what it was. The dreaded 'knock in the night' from one side or the other was something for which every householder in those times consciously or unconsciously waited in fear. As it happened, when it came on this evening, he was not entirely unprepared for it.

Between tea and dinner Ethel had come to him in some agitation. 'Mikey's gone,' she said.

'Gone? What do you mean, gone?' Stephen asked her.

'Bolted, that's what I mean. Gone on the run. There's your precious friend for you.'

'How do you know?'

'I rang for him and he didn't come. Eventually Agnes answered the bell. She said that he'd gone off after lunch on his bicycle with all his belongings tied up in parcels around him. I went to his room. She's right. It's been cleared out. There's nothing left.'

'You went to his room, did you? Not for the first time when he was out, I imagine. And there was nothing there to help you?'

'It's none of your business what I do. The point is what are you going to do?'

Stephen went to the bell pull and tugged it. After an interval Agnes, the parlour maid, appeared. She looked as if she had been crying. 'Agnes,' Stephen said quietly to her. 'What's this about Mikey?'

'He's gone, sir. On the run. He must be.'

'Why do you say that, Agnes?'

'One of the mountainy men came for him, sir. One of them fellows from up behind Knockaree where the Rossiters are.'

'And he took all his belongings with him?'

'Yes, sir.'

'Now will you believe me?' Ethel said when she had gone.

'It certainly looks as if he's on the run.'

'Are you going to tell the Military?'

'No. It's a police matter if it's anything. There are no police. I'm certainly not getting in touch with those blackguards, the Auxiliaries.'

'Harry says this company are better than most.'

'They shot young Regan.'

'Harry says the new man in command of them knows how to handle men. He was a colonel in your show—the Flying Corps. His name is Conway.'

'Conway! Christ! Can it be?'

'Did you know him?'

'Of course I knew him. He was the swine who nearly did me in and then got me court-martialled. Does mother know?'

'I don't think so. Harry only told me today.'

'Today? So you've seen Harry today. You've been into Kilderry. It seems to me, Ethel, you're being a bit more agitated about Mikey going off than you need be. Just what have you been up to? You haven't been telling Harry anything about him by any chance, have you?'

'I don't like harbouring Shinners,' Ethel said and almost ran out of the room.

After dinner which was flung at them by the maids even more erratically than usual without even Mikey's haphazard direction, Stephen went to his father's study. He worked aimlessly for a bit, going through a list of questions Hutton had left him and then picked up the *Irish Times*. A mixed commission of labour stalwarts and left-wing radicals had arrived in Dublin to investigate the employment and behaviour of the Crown forces. One of the labour members was a Captain Davis, lately of the Royal Flying Corps. He had been the principal speaker at a public meeting in the Mansion House. He must be none other than his former flight commander, Stephen reckoned, and he was sure that he would have had something explosive to say. The opening words of Davis' speech indicated that his guess had been accurate. 'I am deeply ashamed of my country,' Davis had commenced, and he had gone on to make a vitriolic and unbridled attack on the British Administration in Ireland.

Once again, as he read, the old ambivalence gripped Stephen. Davis was almost certainly right but, just the same, Stephen thought, such sentiments came badly from one who had worn the King's uniform and was introduced as an ex-officer. Dublin was the capital of a country in open rebellion against the crown and a speech such as this could not but give active encouragement to the rebels. That brought him once again to think about Mikey and what, if anything, he should do. As a citizen and a loyalist, his duty was to report Mikey's absence on the run to the proper authorities whoever they might be. But he knew very well that he was not going to do it.

Apart from betraying a friend that would also mean that he would

293

be taking an active part in what was happening around him. As he had told his father that was something he was determined not to do and that determination was even firmer now that he had heard Conway was in command of the Kilderry Auxiliaries. Conway! Was he never to be rid of him? He felt sure that Conway's presence was no accident. These were lawless times and Conway had a gun in his hand put there by a crass and irresponsible authority. Clare's warning, given lightly enough that morning in White's, seemed far more weighty here in this remote and isolated part of Ireland where the rule of law no longer ran.

As he was turning the pages of the paper to the racing results, a noise outside, below the window, came to his ears. It was a slight crunching sound as if someone was trying to walk quietly in heavy boots. Putting the paper aside and turning down the lamp he crossed the room and drew the curtains.

Darkness was just setting in. On the terrace beneath him he could see quite clearly a soldier in full war kit. His rifle was slung across his shoulder, his back was towards the house and he was staring out over the Bay.

Turning away from the window, Stephen left the room and went to the head of the stairs. He was halfway down when the hammering on the door began.

'Open up!' a voice shouted from outside.

Stephen descended the stairs and crossed the hall to the door. 'Who's there?' he called.

'Open up in the name of the King!' came the answer.

Honoria and Ethel had followed him into the hall. Motioning them to stand aside, he turned the key in the big lock and pulled the door towards him. Led by Harry French, a mixed lot of soldiers and Auxiliaries crowded into the hall. At Harry's shoulder was a burly figure Stephen had no difficulty at all in recognising. Behind him he heard his mother give a little gasp. 'Colonel Conway!' she exclaimed.

'The same, madam,' Conway said with a savage grin. 'It seems we meet again—and I and your son also.'

'My family have suffered enough from you, Colonel Conway,' Honoria said, all the bark and sharpness back in her voice, for it took more than a knock in the night and a sudden invasion of soldiery to shake her nerve for any length of time. 'Perhaps you can explain this intrusion?'

For answer Conway reached up and ripped away the list of occupants from behind the door. Handing it to Harry, he said: 'The name of the man we are looking for should be there. If not we'll want to know the reason why.'

Harry glanced at it. 'Michael O'Sullivan, Then, turning to Honoria, he went on: 'Mrs Raymond, we have reason to believe that

294

Michael O'Sullivan, one of the servants here, your butler, I understand, is a wanted man, a known Sinn Feiner. This house is surrounded. I must ask you to hand him over into my custody.'

'My son is the master of this house. You should ask him.'

'He's not here,' Stephen said.

'Has he permission to be out? Is this his night off?' Harry asked sharply.

Before Stephen could reply Ethel said: 'No, Harry, it's not.'

'You don't believe this rubbish, do you?' Conway said to Harry. 'So called loyalists—they're as bad as the rest of them. I know Raymond's record. He was court-martialled amongst other things. I'll swear he's up to the neck with O'Sullivan. He's concealing him. Search the house.'

'Where's your warrant, Conway?' Stephen asked.

'This is my warrant.' Conway's hand tapped the holster of his revolver.

'I'm not surprised,' Stephen said contemptuously. 'It always was.'

'In a military area I have powers of search, arrest and detention,' Harry said. 'I must ask you to summon all the staff here. See to it quickly, please.'

Stephen went to the bell and pulled it. Agnes appeared almost immediately from behind the baize door where she must have been listening to all that went on. 'Will you get the servants in here as soon as possible, Agnes,' Stephen said to her.

When she had gone he studied the Auxiliaries. They were a tough-looking lot. Most of them had medal ribbons of one sort or another. The Glengarries, the mixture of khaki and black uniform and the heavy armament they carried gave them the threatening appearance they obviously courted and enjoyed. They stood around, staring about the hall, fingering their weapons and occasionally exchanging remarks in low tones. But they made no move to take independent action and kept looking at Conway as if for guidance. Obviously he had stamped his personality on them and had them in hand.

When the maids filed in, Mary, the youngest, took one look at them, threw her apron over her head and began to have hysterics. 'The Tans!' she wailed. 'Holy Mother of God, deliver us. They'll murdher us. Holy Virgin pray for us—we'll all be sthruck down and killed—'

'Be quiet child,' Honoria snapped. 'Pull yourself together. They'll do no such thing. I'll see to that.'

An Auxiliary, standing near her, gave a sudden guffaw. 'We'll only kill you after we've done with you,' he said.

Honoria turned on him. 'I'll thank you to keep a civil tongue in your head in this house,' she snapped. 'Colonel Conway, cannot you control your men?'

Conway ignored her. 'He's hiding somewhere,' he said to Harry. 'We'll have to search the place.'

Remembering stories of the destruction and looting by the Auxiliaries during their searches, Stephen said: 'I'm holding you responsible, Conway, if there's anything missing or any damage done when you search.'

'Responsible?' Conway looked at him and gave another of his savage laughs. 'I'm only responsible to King George V.'

'My men will carry out the search,' Harry cut in. 'Sergeant, take two men and search the house. Tell Corporal Lawrence to do the same with the outbuildings. Now, which is O'Sullivan's room?'

'I'll show them,' Ethel said.

'You'll do no such thing,' Honoria snapped. 'Agnes will.'

In an uneasy silence they waited for the return of the searchers. Then the baize door opened to admit the sergeant and his men. He saluted Harry. 'Nothing, sir,' he said. 'The room is bare, too. Stripped of everything.'

In a few moments the corporal came in with the same report.

'The bird has flown,' Stephen said, unwisely, looking at Conway.

Conway glowered at him. 'You got him away this time,' he said. 'However you did it. French, here, received information—'

'That'll do,' Harry said sharply, looking at Ethel as he did so. 'I'm leaving a guard on the house for twenty-four hours in case he returns. Goodnight to you, Mrs Raymond.' He saluted Honoria and turned towards the door.

Conway was the last to leave. 'You're mixed up in this somehow, Raymond,' he said. 'I guessed you would be. You're lucky the military were here. I'd have taken you apart.'

Before Stephen could answer his mother spoke, looking contemptuously at the burly figure opposite her. 'No doubt you would, Colonel Conway,' she said. 'It's what I should have expected of you. And let me tell you, as one who has been brought up and lived amongst soldiers all her life, you and your like are a disgrace even to that hybrid uniform you wear.'

Something flamed in Conway's eyes. His hand dropped to the butt of his revolver. Stephen looked desperately round for a weapon.

'Conway!' Harry was back at the Auxiliary's shoulder.

Conway's hand fell to his side. 'You exceed the privileges granted to your sex, madam,' he said, thickly. His eyes swept round the hall. 'I shall be back—alone.'

When they had left Honoria sat down heavily on the nearest chair. 'Well,' she said. 'Well. I never thought or wanted to see that man again. So it is true,' she went on. 'Mikey is one of them. I might have expected it, I suppose. He always wanted to be with guns. And you needn't think, Stephen, that I didn't know about those days that he

and cut back whenever he had time to think about taking charge and running the place. It all seemed so purposeless these days. Leaving the wood he came out on to a road which wound around a spur of the hills. Here he jumped in over a small bank and made his way through a series of cattle gaps to the schooling ground.

There had been rain overnight and the ground was softer than he expected. But the young horse jumped the schooling banks to his satisfaction. When he had finished he pulled down a stick in a gap and let himself out on to the road once more. No sooner had he replaced the pole and turned to mount the horse again than he realised he had lost a shoe. There was a forge, he remembered, about two miles down the road. It was a pleasant, sunny afternoon. The exercise and the fresh air had cleared his mind. His worries were temporarily put behind him. He walked slowly along towards the forge.

It was a small thatched cottage on the side of the road with a wide doorway giving on to its dark interior. The smith was in the act of pulling the wooden doors to when Stephen arrived. 'Bit early for you to be shutting up, isn't it, Danny?' he asked.

The smith, a stout, red-faced man with big shoulders, looked away from Stephen. 'Aye, 'tis that,' he said slowly. 'What's troublin' ye, Master Stephen?'

'I lost a shoe, schooling. Silly thing to do, I suppose, in this ground. Could you slap a slipper on for me, Danny?'

The smith hesitated. He pulled out a big, battered, metal-plated watch and consulted it. 'Aye, I will then,' he said, putting the watch away. 'Bring him in, Master Stephen. It won't take long. Ye're a bit away from home. I could hardly let ye go on without it.'

Stephen led the horse into the forge and the smith bent to his work. 'Are ye goin' back to the Bay, Master Stephen,' the smith asked him without looking up.

'Yes, as soon as you're finished, Danny.'

'You'd be going' through the Glen, then, I'd be thinkin'.' He was bending over the horse's raised leg and still he did not look up as he spoke.

'It's the quickest way.'

There was a pause. Silence fell between them save for the ring of hammer on iron. Still Danny, the smith, did not look up. 'Ye'd be wiser not to go home through the Glen, this evenin',' he said.

Stephen opened his mouth to speak and then shut it again. He was being told something by hints and obliqueness and he knew his countrymen well enough to realise that here was a warning he would be wise to heed. To go back through Brannigan's Glen was the shortest way home but he now knew that he was not going to take it. His mind ran over the alternatives. There was really only one. That was to thread his way through the series of lanes and bohereens that wound

299

their way across the shoulder of Knockaree. It was at least five miles longer but he knew every inch of the country from hunting over it so finding his way presented no problem. 'I'll go up by Carrigrue, then,' he said.

'Aye, 'twould be as well.' There was no other comment from the smith. He put his hammer down and straightened up. 'There it is now,' he said. 'That should hold him.'

Stephen took the horse to the road and swung himself up. Looking back he saw the smith closing the doors and then pulling his watch out again to consult it. Half a mile down the road he turned into a lane that led into the hills. There was a maze of lanes and little roads here but he held on without pause for doubt, picking his way through them as quickly as he could. The day was clouding over and with the clouds came an air of menace. No one was about in the fields, he noticed. The few cottages he passed had their doors closed and no sounds of life came from them, though the smoke curling up from their chimneys in one or two cases showed that someone was within. There was an almost tangible threat of trouble all about him. His way would take him along the shoulder directly above the Glen. He thought he could guess what was about to happen. He hoped he would get across the shoulder before the violence began.

As he turned into the lane that led to the crest the firing commenced. He had heard that particular noise too often before not to recognise it for what it was, and he had hoped never to hear it again.

The lane sloped steeply upwards. From his seat on the back of the horse as he came over the crest, he could see down into the Glen. The whole panorama of the action below was laid out before him almost as if he was flying over it.

The Glen was a shallow cutting through which a road ran. Trees and scrub covered one side, boulders and high stone-faced banks the other. It was an all but perfect site for an ambush.

Between where Stephen sat and the Glen itself was a rocky knoll and here the ambush party had mounted a Lewis gun. It was its rat-tat-tat, bringing back so many memories, that Stephen had heard on the lane below.

Two Crossley tenders were halted on the road, one of them slewed across it. Behind them their occupants were fighting back. But they were hard pressed and had already suffered casualties. Even as Stephen watched he saw a soldier stagger and fall. Between the two lorries a large man in a Glengarry was standing upright, apparently impervious to the bullets flying around him, shooting steadily with a rifle. Stephen did not have to see his features to know who he was.

And then he saw something else. Unknown to the attackers and unseen by them, an armoured car followed by another Crossley tender was coming up. Before they reached the actual scene of the fight they turned into a lane to the right. In a moment they were in a position to enfilade the whole ambush position. As he saw the turret of the armoured car swing round, just before the stammer of its Maxim began, Stephen almost found himself shouting a warning.

The troops from the tender were lining the bank beside the armoured car and, directed by an officer, were commencing to open fire. That man knows his business and the country, too, Stephen thought. He whipped them into that lane pretty quick. He could make a guess at who the officer was, too.

The tables were now turned with a vengeance. The ambushers were caught in their own trap. The Maxim was taking its toll and they were beginning to suffer casualties. The Lewis gunners on the knoll tried to bring the gun round to bear on the new threat. Then, seeing the armoured car, they appeared to realise the hopelessness of their situation. They slid off the knoll and, under its cover, began to break towards the hills.

The firing slackened. Stephen picked up his reins and started to make his way down the lane. He could hear the roar of the Crossley's engines coming up the other lane towards him. He had gone about fifty yards when a figure wearing a bandolier and carrying a rifle jumped down from the bank almost on top of him. The horse plunged and reared in fright. The man swung the rifle to cover Stephen. It was Mikey.

They recognised each other at almost the same moment. 'Holy God, it's Master Stephen. Where are they?' Mikey gasped.

'Down the lane on the right. Don't go down there or you're done for,' Stephen said. 'And don't cross that field or they'll get you for sure. Cut up the lane. I'll head them off.'

'Thanks be for ye, Master Stephen, I'll not forget this for ever, never fear.' Darting a glance over his shoulder Mikey ran up the lane into the hills.

The young horse had commenced to play up again. He was dancing about, throwing his head around and cracking his nostrils. Stephen talked to him and soothed him. That done he went slowly on, making his way through the twists and turns of the lane. It was too narrow, he noticed with relief, to take either the Crossley or the armoured car. As he reached the junction of the two lanes the tender roared up. Seeing him it pulled to a standstill. The officer beside the driver jumped down. He held up his hand. 'Stop there, please,' he said. 'Did you see any men making off?' Then: 'Oh, it's you, Stephen. What the hell are you doing here?'

'Exercising a horse. I seem to have got caught up in a battle.'

'See any Shinners running away?'

'No.'

'Will you get down. I'll have to question you. Take his horse

301

someone.'

Stephen was brought to the tender. The soldiers, he noticed, were in full kit even down to water bottles and entrenching tools. They were, he thought, about as ill-equipped for mobile or guerrilla warfare as they could be. Burdened as they were, how could they hunt Mikey and his like? Once they were off the road Mikey and the boys would have covered a hundred yards before any of these even got into their stride. He noticed, too, that they were not the tough, battle-hardened troops he had seen in France. All of them were very young and most of them looked frightened. They were staring around anxiously at this strange wild country as if waiting in dread for the next sniper's bullet.

Another tender drew to a standstill at the cross, pulling up with a scrabble of tyres. It was packed with Auxiliaries. One of them was binding a bloody handkerchief round a flesh wound in his arm; another was lying groaning in the back with two of his fellows bending over him. They were in an ugly mood.

Conway leapt down and strode across to them. He had a cocked service Webley in his hand. 'You got one of them, did you?' he said. 'By God, it's Raymond. So he is up to the neck in it. Just as I thought. Let's have him—' The Webley was raised to point at Stephen's chest. Stephen had faced death in the clouds many times but, looking into Conway's eyes and the film forming in them, he knew he had never been nearer to it than he was at this moment. Only one pressure was needed on the trigger of that big Webley for it to fire.

'He wasn't in it,' Harry said. 'He was coming back from exercising down the lane.'

'Do you expect me to believe that? I shouldn't wonder if it's he who is behind all these burnings and killings. Hand him over. We'll soon have the truth out of him.'

There was a little growl of agreement from the Auxiliaries behind him.

'May I remind you,' Harry said icily, 'that where there is a mixed force the military officer will be in command. He is in my custody. I'll take him in. I'll question him. Put that gun down. That's an order.' He turned to Stephen. 'Get into the tender,' he said.

Eyed by the Auxiliaries and feeling that every step might be his last, Stephen walked to the tender and climbed in. The soldiers were still nervously fingering their weapons. One of them was snapping the backsight of his rifle up and down. 'Stop that,' a corporal barked at him.

'We're wasting time. We'll get on,' Harry said.

'What'll I do with the horse?' the man who was holding him called.

'Shoot him,' Conway said savagely.

Without hesitation the Auxiliary beside him lifted his revolver, placed it between the horse's eyes and pulled the trigger.

302

The horse gave one high-pitched neigh that was all but a scream, reared up and then fell in a heap by the roadside.

Stephen sat for a moment stunned. Then he leapt to his feet. He was almost out of the tender and reaching for a rifle when many hands grabbed him. The Auxiliary's gun swung round towards him. There was a grin on his face and the eyes above it were cold and hard.

'Stand still.' Harry's voice rang out with all the parade-ground bark of command and authority in it. 'Keep him there,' he commanded the men holding Stephen. Then he turned on the Auxiliary. 'Put that gun away and get back to your transport,' he ordered. He had moved, Stephen noticed, to place himself between the Auxiliary and the lorry where Stephen was. He turned to Conway. 'What the devil did you do that for?' he snapped.

'He won't need it where he's going to when we catch up with him,' Conway said and laughed.

The lorries swept on round the roads, but their quarry had no need of roads. The countryside had long since swallowed up the ambush party. As almost always happened, the lorries made their way back to barracks empty-handed.

Stephen was brought into Harry's office. He was given a chair facing him and then they were left alone.

'All right,' Harry said. 'Did you see any Shinners and, more important, if you saw them did you recognise any of them?'

'No,' Stephen said.

Harry looked at him for a moment. 'I suppose I must believe you,' he said. 'You were lucky I got you first, not the Tans. You saw what they did to your horse?'

'I'm not likely to forget it.'

Harry stared steadily at him. 'You know,' he said. 'If you did see someone and if, mind you, I'm only saying if, he was your chap, O'Sullivan—that's Mikey, isn't it, the chap you and I used to shoot with sometimes—in your position I might, I only say might, mind you, have done the same myself.' He sighed. 'It's a bloody queer country,' he said. 'I hear the C–in–C calls it the finest open air lunatic asylum in the world. No wonder these bloody Auxiliaries can't understand it.'

'I thought you soldiers didn't like operating with them.'

'We don't. But up to now we've had to. Do you know what transport I've had? Twenty bicycles and one three-ton lorry. How can you carry on mobile patrols with those? Yesterday we got two Crossley tenders. They'll make us independent and they made all the difference today—together with the armoured car. It was on a tour and I bagged it.'

'Why did you come back, Harry? Do you hate us all?'

303

For the first time Harry smiled. 'I owe you an apology over that,' he said. 'I never knew what really happened about my father and I wanted to find out. My mother died a year after we left the Bay. Things were pretty hard then and naturally I was bitter. Ethel told me the true story. At least I found out, which was what I wanted to do.' He hesitated. 'But there's something more,' he said. 'Believe it or not I longed to see the Bay again. I remembered it and I wanted to know if it matched up to my memories. My mother too, used to say it was the most beautiful place on earth, that it haunted her always, even after she had left it.'

'Most people seem to feel like that. I know I do.'

'Somehow,' Harry went on, 'it seemed to haunt me too. At times in France I'd lie awake thinking about it. When the regiment was posted here I put in an application to rejoin from the staff. That was six months ago. I never thought I'd be doing the job I am but I'm a soldier and I've got to do it as best I can.'

'We were all kids together and now we're all caught up in it—you and I and Babs and Ethel and Mikey. I hardly know which side I'm on. I suppose the others do.'

There was a knock on the door. A subaltern came in, bent over Harry's desk and whispered in his ear. When he had gone Harry looked across at Stephen. 'It doesn't much matter now whether you saw anything or you didn't,' he said. 'We've got bigger game. They've taken Larry Rossiter.'

'Larry Rossiter, by God. How?'

'They forget I know the country almost as well as they do. I thought the fox might return to his earth. I sent the other lorry up to Corravore, the Rossiters' place. He was going back there to lie up, I suppose. They were lucky. They got there the same time as he did and they nabbed him. Most of my chaps can't shoot. They're nearly all recruits who haven't even fired a musketry course. It was the only old soldier of the lot who winged him.'

'Is he badly wounded?'

'No. Nothing. A flesh wound in the leg. The bullet went straight through.'

'What'll happen to him?'

'Taken under arms. He'll be court-martialled. He's almost certain to be convicted and that'll mean the death sentence.'

'Shooting?'

'I'm afraid so. They say they're soldiers and should be treated as prisoners of war. Perhaps they're right but that's not what our orders say. Look at it our way, Stephen. You get men shot down by assailants who melt into a crowd or a countryside, who don't wear uniform—'

'I still think your brass hats are bloody fools who can't see beyond their noses. Davis, my first flight commander, said they had a criminal disregard for all human life except their own. Though he's not much of a chap, either. He's a Labour M.P. now.'

'Sounds like one all right. Very well, Stephen, you can go. Keep out of trouble.'

'I hope I can,' Stephen said soberly.

And indeed it seemed that trouble was determined to pursue him. Hardly had he returned to the house when Agnes came to him in a state of some agitation. 'Excuse me, sir, ye're wanted in the gun-room, sir,' she said. 'There's someone there to see you.'

'Who is it, Agnes?'

Agnes looked everywhere but directly at him. 'He's below in the gun-room, sir,' she said and bolted down through the baize door.

Stephen went along the flagged passage. The gun-room was empty. He had not been there for months. There were no guns in the racks now for they had long since been surrendered to the R.I.C. for safe-keeping. Stephen wondered if he would ever get them back. The whole place was cold and bare and damp. He stood in its centre, frowning, remembering happier days. Then he heard a tapping at the window. Going to it and peering through, he could just make out a figure beyond the glass. After a moment's hesitation he opened the catch and pushed up the sash.

'It's me, Mikey,' a voice said. 'Is there anyone wid ye?'

'No, Mikey. I'm alone.'

Mikey clambered over the sill and dropped into the room. He grinned sheepishly at Stephen. 'Well, Master Stephen,' he said. 'It's thanks to you I'm here at all. If it hadn't been for you those Tans would have got me. I'd have been shot by now as like as not.'

'We've been friends for a long time, Mikey.'

'It's not everyone that'd have done it. I hear they shot your horse on ye.'

'They did, the swine.'

'Them devils. They should roast on the hot hob of hell every one of them.'

'Why are you here, Mikey? This house may be watched. You're taking the devil of a risk.'

'Risk, is it? Sure every one of your maids and all of them in the yard are looking out for to help us. Yer house is safe from us for what ye did today, Master Stephen, and you will never be touched but you'll have to get Miss Ethel out of here.'

'Why?' Stephen asked, though he was sure that he knew the answer.

'She informed on me that day I went on the run. I can tell you how I know. There's someone in the barracks that's helpin' us and tellin' us what goes on. That's how I got away in time. And they think it's her who told about the ambush. I might have left a bit of a sketch lyin' about. And Agnes says she's been goin' to my room when I was out. They'd never have got us that way if they hadn't been told about it.'

'You don't make war on women, do you, Mikey?'

'What if the women make war on us? Listen, Master Stephen, there's angry men out there. Men were killed today that wouldn't have been had things gone right. And Larry's been took. You've been in a war yourself—'

'Not this kind of war, Mikey.'

'Ye'll get notice tomorrow givin' you forty-eight hours to get her out. It was all I could do. She'd be better right out of the country. I'm tellin' ye this, now, so that you have a chance to get round her. I know Miss Ethel. I'd best be goin'. Goodbye, Master Stephen.'

'We'll meet again in better times, Mikey.'

'Aye, and go shootin' cock again.' He slid a leg over the sill and was gone.

When he had retraced his steps along the passage Stephen rang for Agnes and told her to ask his mother and Miss Ethel to see him in the upstairs study.

'What's wrong now?' Ethel demanded as she came in. 'Why am I summoned here like a servant?'

'I've seen Mikey,' Stephen said abruptly.

'I thought he was on the run.'

'He is. He took a chance coming back here to warn us.'

'Warn us of what, Stephen?' Honoria put in. 'I do wish you wouldn't speak in riddles.'

'I think Ethel knows very well, mother, and you had better know now, too. She's been giving information to the Military. The men on the run know it. Mikey came to warn me. Tomorrow we're being given notice that she has forty-eight hours to leave the country.'

'I won't go,' Ethel said defiantly. 'What will Harry think?'

'He'll see it as I do if he has any sense and I think he has. I've been with him today.'

'I can stay here. You can't order me out. I have a right of residence. Even beastly Hutton said that.'

Honoria looked at Stephen. 'You're sure what you are saying is true, Stephen?' she said.

'It's true all right, mother. Ask her.'

'Well, Ethel?' Honoria looked frostily at her daughter.

Ethel was silent for a moment or two. She was frightened and taken aback by the sudden impact of events. She went pale, looked away from them and her fingers plucked nervously at her skirt. Then she burst out: 'What if I did? Why shouldn't I? They'd murder us all if they could. Look what they did to those officers playing tennis in Galway—'

'Mikey had been with us since he was a boy,' Honoria said, inter-

306

rupting her. 'I should not have thought it of him . . . But you should not have done what you did in that way, Ethel, certainly not without telling me. What can they do, Stephen?'

'Anything, mother. Just anything.'

Honoria made up her mind. 'Very well, you must go, Ethel. You can stay with the Barretts in Kildare and then catch the mail boat the next day. Uncle George will take you for the moment in England. I'll send off telegrams now.'

'But, mother—'

'There are no buts, child. You will catch the Dublin train tomorrow morning.' She turned to Stephen. 'I can't let her travel alone, Stephen. I shall go with her.'

'Very well, mother.'

Honoria seemed to hesitate. Then she said, 'Stephen, should you come too? Will you be safe here?'

'Of course I will, mother.'

'Of course he will, mother,' Ethel echoed spitefully. 'Isn't he half a Shinner himself? Look how Mikey came running to him.'

Honoria disregarded this. 'I shall return, of course,' she said briskly. 'I do not intend to allow my pantry boy to drive me from my home. You will remember that, Stephen.'

'Yes, mother.' As always in these moments of stress and decision he could never do anything but admire her.

'What time does the train leave?' she was going on. 'Ten o'clock if it leaves at all, I believe. Well, Ethel, you'd better find Agnes and start packing.' She swept from the room.

When she had gone, brother and sister stared at each other for a moment. 'This is all your doing,' Ethel snapped at him. 'None of this would have happened if it hadn't been for your facing both ways.'

'If it hadn't been for my facing both ways as you call it we'd have been burnt out on your account and some of us might be dead by now,' Stephen answered.

Ethel tossed her head. 'I always hated this mouldy old place anyhow,' she said. 'It'll be a relief to be with people like the Barretts again, and Uncle George in England. They're part of the world. It's not like being half-buried alive down here.'

'You don't really give a damn what happens to this house and anything in it, do you?'

'No, Stephen, and I never did.'

'I hope your train leaves on time,' Stephen said politely.

28

About the time Stephen was returning from seeing his mother and Ethel safely on to the Dublin train, three men sat round a table in a 'safe house' in the hills holding a council of war. A teapot and three steaming mugs of tea were on the table in front of them. A picture of the Sacred Heart of Jesus looked down on them from the wall. Two of the men wore leather bandoliers and had service revolvers in holsters at their waists. The weapon of the third, a Parabellum pistol, lay before him on the table ready for instant use in case of surprise. A service rifle leant against the wall beside them, ready to hand.

'He'll be shot,' one of the men was saying.

Mikey paused in the act of cutting a loaf of bread. 'We'll have to get him out,' he said.

'How, Mikey, how? They'll bring him to the city for the court-martial. Could we ambush them?'

'Ambush, is it? They'll have armoured cars and the divil knows what. They're not going to let him go in a hurry.'

'We don't even know what way they'll be takin' him,' the third man said. 'There's nothing comin' out of Kilderry in the way of news now since they caught that soldier we'd paid to tell us what was goin' on in the barracks. That's why they got us in the Glen. They had him caught and silenced. Is the woman gone from Bellary, Mikey?'

'She was to go on the train today. I got word from the house. You're right, Jamesy, sure they could go ten ways when we'd be watchin' one.'

'What'll we do, then, Mikey?' the first man put in. 'If we haven't Larry we're done for. You've got some education, Mikey, from the big house but much good it'll do us on the run from them murderin' Tans.'

'Could we get into the barracks?'

'I hear they've put another detachment from the city into it. And an armoured car. The place will be stiff with them. We'd never do it.'

'Give us some more tea, Jamesy, till I think a bit,' Mikey said.

Jamesy poured the strong tea and they sipped in silence. Suddenly

Mikey sat up. 'Be the powers, I think I have it,' he said.

'What is it, Mikey? What have ye thought of?'

Mikey took a battered wallet from his pocket. Opening it, he pulled a piece of newspaper from it and unfolded it. Then, smoothing it out, he placed it on the table in front of them. All three bent down to look where his finger pointed.

It was the picture of Andrew Massiter standing at Lloyd George's elbow at the peace conference.

'That's ould Massiter, the divil mend him,' Jamesy said.

'Aye, and look who he's with,' the other man put in.

'Who's that?'

'It's the man himself. The Prime Minister of England. Lloyd George. Where'd ye get this, Mikey?'

'Below in the house. It was in one of them papers they get. They throw them away when they're done with them. I cut it out.'

'Ye did right. What have you in mind, Mikey?'

'Massiter and the Prime Minister must be very thick for him to get taken a picture of like that. Perhaps Mr Lloyd George mightn't take too kindly to shootin' poor Larry if we told him we'd shoot one of his best friends for him if he did.'

The others looked at him in admiration.

'True for you, Mikey, 'tis you that have the brains. When will we lift him?'

'Tonight,' Mikey said.

'Aye and on our way we can burn out old Gnowles. The Tans burnt O'Regan's last night. We said we'd burn house for house. And it's the O'Regans and the O'Reillys that his land was snatched from.'

'And he's huntin' them dogs too when he was told to stop. We warned him again the other day.'

'And we'll burn Dunlay round Massiter's ears while we're at it,' Jamesy said.

'No,' Mikey said. 'Orders from H.Q. We're to leave the house alone. But they didn't say anything about the man in it.'

'If Larry was here he couldn't have thought of better,' Jamesy said. He turned to the third man. 'Tadgh, lad, go and tell the boys what's on for tonight. We'll want another motor. Aye and a couple of spare tins of petrol, too.'

When Grig and Vivienne Gnowles came down for dinner that evening they found that the grog tray had not been laid out for their evening drinks.

'Ring the bell, my dear,' Grig growled. 'They must have forgotten. I don't know what servants are coming to. I suppose these days—'

Vivienne went to the bell and pulled it. There was no response. After a few moments she tried again with the same result.

'This is ridiculous,' Grig grunted. 'There must be someone about.'

'I—I'll go and see,' Vivienne said.

In a few minutes she was back. 'There isn't a servant in the house,' she said.

'What?'

'It's true. I've searched everywhere. The kitchen is empty. The range is out. No one. All gone. Bolted.'

Both of them looked at each other. They knew just what this meant. They were next on the list for destruction.

'There isn't even a gun in the place,' Grig muttered. 'I surrendered all mine to the R.I.C. when they called them in—like a damn fool,' he added.

'It would be no use anyway, Grig. Even if you could hold them off they'd get you in the end.'

'It's just one is so damned helpless—'

'We can only wait. Perhaps it's a false alarm. They may have got it wrong. Maybe it's someone else—'

But neither of them believed this.

'Those Auxiliaries at the workhouse,' Vivienne said as they ate a makeshift cold supper from a joint she had found in the meatsafe. 'Could we get a message to them somehow?'

'I want nothing to do with those thugs,' Grig growled. 'Damned ruffians. Rampaging around the countryside shooting into the air like a wild west show. Disgrace to their uniforms. Almost turn one into a Shinner oneself.'

'I just thought—'

'Know what they did?' Grig went on. 'They shot a fox at Drumgoon the other day and put his mask on the front of one of their damned lorries. One of them had the impertinence to point it out to me in Bellary. Damned young pup. Said they'd heard the Shinners were stopping me hunting so they thought they'd do a bit themselves.'

'They shot Stephen's horse, too, after that ambush—'

'Young Raymond—what was he doing up there? Up to no good, I'll be bound.'

'I must say from what Ethel tells me he is almost one of them himself. And yet he had such a good career in the war—shooting down all those German aeroplanes.'

'He was court-martialled. Never trust a chap who's been court-martialled. No smoke without a fire. Besides he and Desmond were mixed up in something very hot in a Yeomanry race—too long a story to tell you now, my dear.'

'Do you think we ought to try to move anything out—the pictures?'

'Get your jewellery together, my dear, and any personal valuables. I'll do the same and I'll see to the doors and the shutters. If they can't get in they may go away.'

310

Neither of them believed that, either.

It was about two hours later that the knocking in the night began. It quickly became loud and thunderous for the assailants had brought a sledge-hammer with them. Finding the door locked and bolted they swung it at the panels.

Grig stood in the hall watching and listening. The door, iron-bound by an earlier Gnowles to withstand just such an onslaught from the Whiteboys or the Fenians, seemed to be holding. 'Who's there?' Grig shouted.

'Open up, you old divil, or we'll roast you alive,' came from outside.

'Go to hell,' Grig called back. He was in the act of turning away when he saw the figure standing looking at him from the doorway that led to the basement stairs. It was a man wearing a trenchcoat. A cap was pulled low on his forehead and a scarf wound round his face hid all his features save his eyes. A long-barrelled Parabellum was in his hand. It pointed directly at Grig.

'How did you get here?' Grig demanded.

'One of your maids loosened a bar in a basement window for us. Open up now.'

'Damn you.' Grig took a step towards him.

'No, Grig, no,' Vivienne called out. 'I'll do it,' she said to the masked figure.

Going to the door she drew the bolts. Dimly, she could discern the figures outside. Four of them came in; two were carrying tins of petrol. The others had revolvers in their hands. 'Hurry now, we haven't all night,' the man with the Parabellum said.

The two men with the petrol cans went through the door on the right into the dining room. The table had not been cleared and the remains of the meal which Grig and Vivienne had taken were still there. Methodically they set about their task. First they ripped down the curtains; then they pulled up carpets and spilled out drawers looking for napkins and other material that would burn quickly. They put the Chippendale chairs on top of the long Regency table and threw the curtains and carpets over the lot. Opening the cans of petrol they poured their contents on to this pile of wood and fabric.

'Out now, the whole lot of ye,' the man with the Parabellum gestured towards the front door.

One man remained behind. Taking a box of matches from his pocket he struck several and threw them to where the petrol had already begun to drip from the table to the floor. Flames shot up-wards. He hurried from the house and joined the others on the gravel. 'She's away,' he said.

In a few minutes the fire had caught hold and the flames were roaring through the house. Nothing could save it now.

Jamesy, the man who had done the actual firing, began to move

311

away. 'Where are you goin'?' Mikey asked him, holding the Para-bellum to his side.

'I'm goin't to fire them kennels.'

Hearing this Grig moved in front of him. 'You'll have to shoot me first,' he said.

'Ye've been out with them dogs since we ordered ye to stop. You and your red-coats all over the country—'

'Arrah, leave him and his dogs alone,' Mikey said. 'We've done enough. There's more work for us tonight.'

The men walked to where the two cars stood a little way down the avenue. Getting in they started them, switched on their lights and drove away, leaving Grig and his wife standing looking at the blazing ruins of their house.

'We must try to save what we can,' Grig said making for the front door. Vivienne was about to follow when she saw that someone had come out of the shadows and was standing beside her. Turning, she recognised Bridget, her lady's maid.

'Well, Bridget,' she said sharply. 'Come to gloat, have you?'

'Oh, ma'am, no. I came back to see if I could help.'

Vivienne reached out to grip the girl's hand. Then she sat down on the grass and wept.

On the way to Dunlay, Mikey, who as author and originator of the plan, had been elected as leader, turned over his problems in his mind. He was not in the least worried about being intercepted by either the Military or the Auxiliaries, for they never moved by night. All the same it would be as well, he thought, to cut the telephone wire that led to the Castle if he could find it. He wondered if there would be diffi-culty getting in. He doubted it. Massiter had been guaranteed safety for his house; he would surely not anticipate any danger to himself. Amongst the loyalists, up to now, with a few exceptions, it was prop-erty not people that had suffered. There was, though, Miss Barbara, as he still thought of her. Master Stephen's friend. What did she want to go marrying that ould Massiter for? He liked Miss Barbara. Every-one did. He hoped that she would have gone to bed.

The moon had come out. Halfway along the avenue, before they reached the bridge he saw the telephone poles carrying the wires to the house. They were in a field beyond the railings. He stopped the car.

'What is it now?' Jamesy asked.

'Telephone,' Mikey said briefly. 'We'll have to cut it.'

'Has he one of them things? Bedad, Mikey, you think of every-thing.'

The pole was not substantial; there was a saw in the car. In a few minutes it came down bringing the wires with it and Dunlay Castle

312

was cut off from communication with the outside world.

Stationing his men as best he could about the Castle so as to inter-cept any of the occupants who might make a run for it, Mikey took Jamesy and Tadgh with him and the three of them approached the great door.

It was the English butler who opened it. Seeing the men in trench-coats, masks on their faces and revolvers in their hands, he backed away in dismay.

'We want the ould fellah—Massiter,' Jamesy said.

The butler, visibly trembling, led them down the great hall. 'Go with him, Tadgh. Keep him and the rest of them quiet,' Mikey com-manded as the butler opened the library door.

Massiter was smoking a cigar. He regarded the two men coolly. 'What do you want?' he said. 'I understood my house was to be left intact.'

'Your house, yes,' Mikey said. 'It's not your house we're after. It's you we want.'

'A Jesuitical piece of reasoning, I should have thought. Were you brought up by them, young man?'

'Jesuitical? What's that? What's he mean?' Jamesy said.

'I dunno. But ye're comin' with us, Massiter. We're goin' to hold you as hostage for Larry Rossiter's life.'

At that moment the door opened and Babs walked into the room. She was wearing a dressing gown over her night dress. 'I heard some-thing and looked out,' she said. 'There are men on the lawn—oh—' She stood back as she took in the scene. Then, in one moment she snatched up a poker from the hearth and swung it at Mikey. He caught her arm and they grappled. In the struggle the scarf fell from his face. 'Mikey!' she gasped as he held her. 'Mikey! What are you doing here?'

'You shouldn't have done that, Miss Barbara,' Mikey said.

'We'll have to take her now,' Jamesy said. His gun and his eyes had never moved from Massiter during the struggle.

'Aye. Go and dress, Miss—ma'am, I should say. Jamesy, go with her and stand outside her door. And don't waste time, ma'am.'

'So,' Massiter said when they had gone, looking Mikey up and down. 'You're young Raymond's butler—and his friend and ally, no doubt. Did he send you here?'

'Don't be talkin' nonsense,' Mikey answered. 'What would Master Stephen be doin' with the likes of us?'

'That's rather the question a good many people are asking just now,' Massiter said.

Ten minutes later he and Babs were in the back of a Ford car being borne into the heart of the hills.

29

The news of the burning out of the Gnowles' house and the abduction of Massiter and Babs horrified the loyalists of the Bay and it infuriated the Auxiliaries. Two outrages had been committed almost under their noses and they had done nothing even to interfere with them. If there was anything which bound these companies of *francs-tireurs* together and gave them some sort of *esprit de corps* it was a perverted pride in their ability to hold rebellion in check by brutality, counter-terror—and reprisal. These two incidents struck at everything they were supposed to be there for; they were a denial of their usefulness which was their only reason for existence. All next day they went rampaging round the country-side, beating people up, ransacking the houses of known or suspected sympathisers and achieving nothing, for they did not find Massiter and his wife nor did they receive any information as to their whereabouts. It was a hopeless task and those that thought about it knew it. They could only work by the map and many of their maps when they had them at all were out of date and inaccurate. They dared not leave the main roads. These held danger enough in this country where every turn might lead to a position admirably suited for ambush, but the side roads stretching away from them into the hills were uncharted deathtraps. The mountains, hills and valleys were every man's friend but theirs; their adversaries will o' wisps that melted into them.

That night there were mutterings in their makeshift mess. Looking at them Conway wondered how long he could hold them. He had no disciplinary powers at all, no sanctions he could apply. He was not even entitled to stop their pay for an offence. All he could do was to recommend dismissal or posting home and many of them wanted out, anyway. In the last resort he could only depend on the strength of his own personality and this evening he doubted if it would be enough for he had never seen them in a wilder mood. In any event he himself was savagely angry at what had happened. Basically he did not give a damn about the destruction of the Gnowles' house nor did he really care what happened to Massiter and his wife. They were Irish all of

314

them or half-Irish anyway and themselves suspect to some extent in his mind. What infuriated him was the flaunting of his authority by these impudent acts. And if his men went on the rampage on account of it in defiance of him what little control he had over them now would vanish. He looked down from the head of the table at his growling pack. Quite cynically he made up his mind. He would turn them loose.

He pushed back his chair and stood up. 'Good evening, gentlemen,' he said. 'I am going to my room. I shan't want you until morning.'

Hardly had the door closed behind him when they were on their feet. Buckling on their weapons they ran for the lorries.

The town of Bellary never forgot that night. Shooting into the air as they came, the Auxiliaries descended upon it. Pulling a Crossley tender across either end of Main Street, thus blocking it, they jumped down, making first for the pubs. Then, looting, breaking and shooting, they made their way along it. Soon the pavements were strewn with broken glass from the shop windows. Drunken Auxiliaries, many of them clasping bottles, reeled about the street shouting obscenities. Some of the inhabitants bolted through their back doors for the fields. Others hid from the violence as best they could.

At length satiated, in some cases frightened and in a few cases ashamed at what they had done, they made their way back to the workhouse. Had Mikey and the boys known it, the workhouse with all its military stores and equipment was theirs for the taking that night for it was guarded only by two sleepy and insubordinate Auxiliaries who had been left behind. Upstairs their commander was in bed reading the Book of Revelation. Hearing the tenders return he closed it and went to sleep.

Stephen learnt of what was to go down in history as the sack of Bellary as soon as he descended for breakfast. Yesterday, hearing the news of Massiter's and Babs' abduction, and guessing that Mikey must be mixed up in it somewhere he had spent the day wondering how he could get in touch with him. At the news of this fresh outrage, however, all thoughts of the other were momentarily banished from his mind and as soon as he could he drove down to the town to see what help he could offer. As he had half-guessed, the wild tales the servants had told him had exaggerated the truth. Only the main street had suffered. The other shopping street, Arthur Street, was untouched and in Main Street it was the public houses which had been the most damaged. One of them had been burnt out and its entire stock destroyed. Several shop fronts had been broken in and their displays looted and scattered.

The only thing to be thankful for, Stephen thought, was that his father was not here to see it.

315

The inhabitants were standing about in little groups talking or making efforts to clear up the broken glass and repair the damage. The looks which were directed at Stephen were mostly hostile. He stopped to talk to one man, a draper whom he knew well, who was standing arms on hips, staring at his smashed window and ruined stock.

'No, ye can do nothing,' was the answer to his enquiry. 'And you're not wanted here, Mr Raymond. Go back to your big house and your English ways.'

'I'm as Irish as you are, Pat.'

'Maybe, but ye lost nothing last night, Mr Raymond.'

There was little point in arguing. If that was how they felt he could do no good here. He turned and drove back to the house. A motor was standing on the gravel. Inside, Desmond and Sarah were waiting for him.

'Stephen—you've heard what has happened?' Sarah said. 'They've been taken. Andrew Massiter and—and Babs too. Can you help us?'

'Leave that gombeen man to rot wherever he is,' Desmond put in. 'It's Babs we want back. To hell with him. I hope they shoot him.'

'It's no good talking like that, Desmond. You allowed her to marry him. She'd still be with us if you hadn't—and now heaven knows what will happen to her. Poor Babs—' She took out her handkerchief and looked through the window across the Bay to where Massiter's tower rose above the woods that were already changing into their autumn tints. 'Mikey is on the run,' she went on. 'He must be mixed up in this. Can't you reach him somehow, Stephen?'

'I'll do anything I can,' Stephen said. 'You know that. But it will be little enough, I'm afraid. They might be anywhere.'

'They've hardly gone to one of their houses,' Desmond said. 'There'd be extra food involved. They'd have to shop for it. The neighbours, someone, would talk. It'd be the hell of a risk.'

'That's so,' Stephen agreed. The germ of an idea was forming in his mind.

'And with a woman involved they'd hardly be lying out,' Desmond went on.

'They must be somewhere,' Sarah said despairingly. 'You and Mikey used to shoot together. Can't you think of something, Stephen?'

'If I do I'll go to them. I promise you that,' Stephen said.

When they had gone he sat on, thinking, the germ of the idea growing and spreading in his mind until it became almost a certainty. Rochestown, the old, deserted haunted ruin in the hills, miles from anywhere; Rochestown where hounds had really started to run the day that Sterling French was killed. Funny how everything seemed to come back to that.

316

He remembered telling Mikey about it after he had returned from hunting and saying those deserted woods looked as if they would hold cock in hard weather. Greatly daring, he and Mikey had gone there to shoot and had penetrated into the ruins of the house. Although the rest of it was gaunt, ivy-covered and deserted and rooks flew in and out of the empty windows, the cavernous basement was intact. Climbing through a window in the area they had walked along its great, vaulted central passage and looked into the kitchens and servants' hall and rooms opening off it. These had survived untouched by the fire and were as sound as the day the house above them had been gutted in that wanton act of self-destruction. 'Bedad, ye could hide a regiment here,' Mikey had said.

It was the ideal hiding place. The country people would never come near it because it was said to be haunted. It was far too lost and remote for search parties of Military or Auxiliaries to penetrate to it.

After lunch, telling no one where he was going, Stephen took the Overland and drove into the hills.

The gate pillars of the old house were broken and fallen. Leaving the Overland in the grass-grown sweep between them he clambered over the ruined gates and began to make his way up the overgrown avenue. It was not easy going for trees had fallen across it and brambles and briars tore at him as he went. In places it was hard to find the path at all. Pushing branches and undergrowth aside, however, he pressed on. After he had been going for about five minutes a man suddenly stepped out from the bushes in front of him. He was carrying a service rifle which he levelled at Stephen. 'Put up yer hands,' he said. 'And keep them there.'

Obediently Stephen raised his hands. But his heart leapt. He seemed to have guessed right.

'What do ye think you're doin' here?' the man asked.

'I'm looking for Mikey O'Sullivan.'

'And why would ye be doin' that?'

'My name is Raymond. I'm a friend of his. I want to see him.'

'Raymond, is it? I've heard of ye. All right. Go on now in front. And keep your hands up.'

Soon they came to the ruined hulk of the house. It had deteriorated further since Stephen had been there years before. Storms and rain had brought down one gable and it lay in a heap of masonry and rubble in front of them. Sycamore and ash had sprung up inside its walls; briars and alder grew up to them and around them.

When they reached the rubble Stephen was ordered to stop. Another man wearing a revolver strapped to his thigh came round it. 'His name is Raymond. He wants Mikey,' his guard said.

'Raymond, is it? All right, I'll take him.'

Stephen was brought down a flight of stone steps, through a

doorway and into the vaulted central passage which was just as he remembered it. In a room off the passage Mikey and another man were sitting.

'Master Stephen!' Mikey exclaimed. 'What brought you here?'

'I came to see you, Mikey. I came alone. I thought you might be here. It seems I guessed right.'

'Did you tell anyone else where you were comin'?'

'No.'

'That's as well. What d'you want?'

'You have Mr and Mrs Massiter here. I came to ask you to set her free.'

'And keep the ould fellah? That'd suit your book, Raymond, wouldn't it?' the other man, who was Jamesy, said, looking insolently at him. 'We all know about them trips ye made to the island in yer boat and what ye were at.'

Mikey turned on him. 'Shut your trap,' he said. 'Mr Raymond did me a good turn, did us all a good turn, the day of the ambush and well you know it.'

'I know you don't want to hurt her. You owe me something, Mikey. You've just mentioned it.'

'I think I paid that back when I saved your house and got you to get Miss Ethel away. I don't think we can let the lady go.'

'She's no use to you here, Mikey.'

'Mebbe she is. They might listen to us more if they know we have a lady took. I'll have to talk to the others about it. There's a room down beyond, Master Stephen. They'll take you there.'

The room into which Stephen was brought was one of the old pantries. Its window was boarded up; there was a stone floor, a bed in one corner and a wooden chair. Light of a sort filtered through cracks in the boards over the window and there was a candle on the chair. Stephen sat on the bed, and waited.

It was an hour before Mikey returned. 'It's no good, Master Stephen,' he said. 'Even if I wanted to they wouldn't let me let her go.'

'Why not, Mikey?'

'She'd talk. They'd make her. We'd have to get out of here.'

'Is she here? Is she all right?'

'She's safe and sound and no harm will come to her. I promise you that, Master Stephen.'

'Can I see her?'

Mikey coughed. He seemed embarrassed. 'I fear ye can't,' he said. 'The boys say it wouldn't be proper like—'

'Christ—'

'Master Stephen,' Mikey hurried on, looking suddenly very young and unsure of himself and like a boy again. 'D'ye think will they shoot

318

Larry? You ought to know after mixin' with all those big people in the war—'

Stephen thought about that for a moment or two. In his anxiety for Babs he had not given any consideration to the reason for her kidnapping nor to the question of Massiter's ultimate fate.

'It all depends,' he said slowly. 'on how much the top people want Massiter. Or if he has papers or anything that might embarrass them if they were to come to light after his death, then they won't shoot Larry. They'll go on with a lot of high-falutin' stuff about not talking with treason and not yielding to blackmail but they'll give in just the same and find some way of saving their faces over it.'

'D'ye think ould Massiter is really that important?'

'He's one of the P.M.'s pals, that's all I know.'

'Then it's just waiting we'll have to be. By the same token, Master Stephen, I can't let ye go either. Ye'll have to stay here.'

'Why? I won't swing any weight for you with the powers that be. The other way round if anything.'

'Them Tans'd take you and beat where we were out of ye. But, Master Stephen, we won't shoot you.'

'Well thanks, Mikey. I rather hoped you wouldn't.'

They both laughed at that and Mikey left him.

The hours and the days dragged by. It was almost worse than being cooped up by the de Kerouailles. Here there was virtually no light in the little room and he had nothing to read except the current issue of the local paper, the *Kilderry Advertiser*, which Mikey brought him. Always his thoughts were tortured by what the next day would bring forth. He could not keep from himself the thought that if Massiter were to be sacrificed Babs would be free. But was it a freedom he and Babs could live with? Would not the knowledge of how it had come about poison the rest of their lives together? And if Massiter was to survive and be set free what would happen between the three of them, then?

And still the days went by and no news came.

At least he had time to think. He knew now beyond all doubt that whether it was with Babs or not he wanted to spend the rest of his life at the Bay. But there were other things besides Babs to be considered. Apart from the financial troubles which he did not entirely understand, the future for him and those like him looked terribly uncertain. He was now convinced that sooner or later the British were going to pull out. They had not played a single card correctly since the trouble started. The present policy of counter-terror had finally alienated almost the whole of the population including many of the less bigoted loyalists. It was an exercise in futility wasteful and expensive of men and material, doomed ultimately, and no one knew how soon that would be, to utter failure.

But when they did pull out, what then? Would the men who had bought power with their guns allow him and his like to stay on? Many had, indeed, already gone. Country houses were being sold for a song, mostly to farmers many of whose families had been dispossessed by one or the other of the plantations. Their contents were auctioned off cheaply while their owners sought peace to sleep quietly at night in places such as Cheltenham or Bath. What part, if any, would he be allowed to play in the new Ireland that would arise out of the present chaos? Might it not be that, whatever his wishes, he would have to go too, his lands being confiscated by the new state in whatever form it took? 'Take what you can and get out while the going is good,' had been the advice given to him by one member of his class at a dinner party some weeks ago. 'It's going to be worse than Russia, you'll see.'

But if he were to leave the Bay he would leave a large slice of himself behind him. No, he decided, he would not cut and run. He'd stay and face it out, if they would let him.

Then, one morning, Mikey came to the room. 'She's found out you're here,' he said. 'One of the lads let it out. She says she must see ye, that there's something she must tell ye. I dunno what it is. You can talk to her on the terrace. And, Master Stephen, don't be doin' anything silly like runnin' away. Two of the boys will be watching you.'

It was a clear, cool day with the first snap of the coming winter in it. By some alchemy of nature, some quality in the gravel on the terraces, they had remained almost intact and clear of weeds. Grandiloquent flights of steps led down to an overgrown and silted-up lake. Stephen was brought out to where, beside the steps, an ornamental fountain lay toppled and broken. He sat on its upturned edge looking out at the sweep of country stretching away below him. In the distance he could see the grim rocks of Castle Martin where Sterling French had met his death.

And then she was coming towards him. Captivity had told on her. She looked strained and drawn but the air of vitality she carried with her always was still there. 'Stephen,' she said. 'It really is you. I could hardly believe it when I heard you were here. How on earth—why are you here?'

'I guessed right, it seems. I came to try to get them to let you go. It didn't work, but I tried.'

'They said we only had a few minutes. Stephen—' the words came with a rush. 'I'm going to have a child—'

'Babs! But—'

'No, it's not his. I know. It's yours—ours—'

'Whatever happens now, Babs, you'll have to leave him.' Despite his decision to stay on and see it out temptation came to him and caught him. Here was a whole new set of circumstances. Even if he lost the Bay he would have her—and his child. They could make a

320

new life together somewhere. 'We can go away together.'

'You once wanted that. In Paris, do you remember?'

Paris, he thought. In peacetime without the dreadful feeling of the hours racing by before you went back to be killed. 'Paris,' he said. 'We could go there. Nothing now is ever going to be the same for us here.' Even as he said it he knew he was building castles in the air and her next words told him she knew it, too.

'It wouldn't work, Stephen. The Bay means everything to us both. You'd begin to hate me for taking you away from it. And he'll never willingly let me go. If we ran away he'd find some way of destroying us. He's ruthless and the power he has frightens me sometimes. He frightens me himself, too, Stephen. In a way I often think he hardly belongs to the human race at all. Some men are like that, I think. He's a sort of elemental. Stephen, why are we here? What is it all about? It's something terrible, I know, and I'm frightened.'

'Has nobody told you?'

'I know nothing.'

'And he hasn't said anything to you, either?'

'No.'

Well, full marks to him for that, Stephen thought. 'They're holding him hostage for Larry Rossiter's life,' he said quietly.

She put her hand up to her mouth. 'And us?' The full realisation came to her then. 'If they kill him—dear heavens—us—' She threw herself into his arms, weeping.

The guard stepped out from the shadow of the trees. Gently he touched Stephen on the shoulder. 'Time's up,' he said.

When she returned to the room she shared with Massiter she was still weeping. She looked worn and ravaged by strain, he thought, as he watched her, her youth and freshness tarnished by a torrent of emotion. Almost he allowed himself to be moved by pity for her. But pity was not something he would permit to influence him. Pity brought weakness and faltering with it and in any event, he told himself, she deserved no pity.

Despite the threat that hung over him he was enduring captivity far better than she was. In South America when he was fighting his way up he had been in many perilous situations and had emerged unscathed. He had a firm belief in his star and was convinced it would see him through. The threat to his self-esteem implicit in his wife's behaviour with Raymond frightened him far more than the physical danger in which he stood.

'You never told me why they had brought us here,' she said.

'It was not a matter for you to learn of—yet,' he answered her firmly.

He had still not confronted her with his knowledge of her unfaithfulness nor had he yet decided when he would do so or what course of action he would take in regard to it. Divorce was out of the question. He was not going to allow his name to be dragged through the courts and expose himself to public humiliation. Somehow he would ruin Stephen; on that he was determined. He had never loved Babs; love was another emotion he distrusted. She was lively, gay and attractive; she enjoyed a position in the Bay which helped to consolidate his own. In bed she had yielded herself to him with something he was acute enough to realise was near to desperation. He would keep her, he thought, and compel her to adorn his property and position, but that would be all. For his physical needs he would find solace elsewhere as he had done before. A flicker of fear rose within him at the thought that she might herself decide to leave him, to throw her cap over the windmill and bolt with young Raymond. Raymond—it all came back to him. A surge of almost uncontrollable fury rose in him as he repeated the name to himself.

'How did you find out?' he asked her.

'Stephen told me,' she said and the moment she uttered the words she regretted them. She saw the flame in his strange eyes at the mention of Stephen's name and his lips tighten into a bitter line.

'So,' he said. 'He is here, is he? He is behind all this. I should have guessed it.'

'He's not! He's not!' she shouted at him. 'He's as much a prisoner as we are. He came to try to help us.'

'Do you expect me to believe that?' he said contemptuously. 'He's been in it since the beginning. He and that Mikey fellow of his. Conway was right. They should have kept him when they had their hands on him after that ambush and beaten the truth out of him.'

'How can you say things like that?'

'I think I have every right to say them.'

Their eyes met and, staring into his, she knew that he had somehow learnt everything about herself and Stephen. She began to weep again.

'Tears will not help you,' he said to her. 'You have a murderer for a lover.'

'It's not true. I know it's not true. He came here to help us.'

'No doubt that's what he told you. It's lies, all lies. He was court-martialled for cowardice.'

'Yes—and honourably acquitted,' she flung back at him.

'The President of the court was a family friend. They look after their own. They despise me because I'm an outsider—the lot of them do, including that precious father of yours.' Driven by emotions which were strangers to him and which he found for once he could not control, for a moment he had let the mask slip. Resentment, envy, jealousy were all having their way with him. He had stretched the truth in his reference to the President of the court-martial, embroidering a chance remark he had overheard in a club and stored away for future reference. He had always twisted truth for his own ends. It was an easy way to fool simpletons. But he had not reckoned on, nor had he in the short space of their married life yet divined, Babs' fierce capacity for loyalty. 'You swine,' she said quietly. 'Now I know my father was right about you. You are only a gombeen man. Now I hope they kill you.'

'He will never get you,' he said savagely, biting out the words. 'What I have, I hold. Remember that.'

They sat on in silence, hating each other. A meal was brought to them. She pushed it away untouched. He forced himself to consume his portion; he would not display any sign of weakness before these people, and a lack of appetite must surely be that.

The tension between them built up until the room seemed suffused with it. Babs sat on her hard chair staring into space, fighting with herself to keep from screaming, to restrain the urge to fling herself at him, her fingernails flailing at his cheeks.

An hour passed in this way. The afternoon was beginning to draw in when they heard footsteps coming to the door. It was flung open and Mikey stood on the threshold. They both turned to him. Babs found herself shivering in dread of what might come. Massiter rose to his feet and stared levelly at Mikey. 'Well?' he said.

'You can go now,' Mikey said quietly.

'What's happened?' Babs breathed.

'He's not being shot. That's enough for you to know, isn't it?'

They were brought out of the basement, along a path that wound its way through the tangled woods and shrubberies. In a few minutes they reached the road where a Ford car waited for them.

Then they were taken on a tortuous trip along side-roads and by-roads until eventually they reached the back entrance to Dunlay. Here they were dropped to complete their return on foot.

At the Castle, Babs went without speaking to her room. Massiter made his way to the library. Sprawled in his armchairs were three Auxiliaries who had been left as a guard by Conway after the kidnapping. Their accoutrements and weapons were in a heap on his desk top; an empty decanter stood on a side-table with beside it two bottles of whisky they had bullied the butler into producing for them. All three had glasses in their hands and one of them was smoking a cigar taken from the open box on his desk. The windows were closed and the reek of stale cigar smoke and consumed spirits was everywhere.

Massiter stood for a moment surveying them with distaste. 'May I ask what the devil you think you are doing here?' he barked.

One of them scrambled to his feet. 'Glad to see you back safe and sound, sir,' he said. 'We've been keeping an eye on the place for you.'

'And making free of my cellar and cigars at the same time, I see. Is the telephone repaired?'

The Auxiliary who was on his feet muttered something about a land line being through to the workhouse.

'Then get your commanding officer on it and tell him I want to see him as a matter of urgency,' he said. 'And then—get out.'

Meeting the blaze of his eyes, the Auxiliaries, who were not accustomed to take orders from anyone save Conway, and not always from him, picked up their weapons and bandoliers from the desk and shuffled from the room.

Massiter strode to the bell pull and tugged it. After a minute or two the butler crept in through the door as if unsure of what he was going to meet or what he would see. At the sight of Massiter alone by the fireplace he straightened up. 'You're back, sir, and unharmed, thank God for that. Oh, sir, we've had a terrible time with those men. And the mistress—is she safe, too?'

'She's in her room,' Massiter said curtly. 'Get this place cleared up at once, Bates. It looks and smells like a bar parlour.'

'Yes, sir. And those men?'

'They're either going or gone. I've sent for their commanding officer. Tell someone to run me a bath while this mess is being cleaned up.'

Lying in the warm water a little later Massiter allowed his thoughts to run over what he had seen and heard during the last few days. Violence, he thought, violence was all about him. It had crept into the Bay almost unawares to shatter the peace and quietude which its inhabitants so much loved. It was implicit in every attitude of those three young bruisers he had just banished from his library. Conway was possessed by it. There must be springs of it, too, in young Raymond with that tally of enemy machines shot down to his credit. One of the lessons Massiter had learnt from the war was that violence lurked behind the most unlikely exteriors. The apparently meek and mild, the soft-voiced, the seeming innocents were frequently the true exemplars of it, once the chips were down, as the Americans said. Raymond, he was beginning to recognise, was one of these and all the more dangerous on that account. But violence in others could be harnessed and used. And that was what he was determined to do now. That was why he had sent for Conway.

Downstairs again, he poured himself a whisky and soda. Sipping it, he turned over the pages of the *Illustrated London News* noting the space given to atrocities in Ireland. After a little while he put the magazine aside, and unfolded an ordnance sheet of the country to the north of Bellary. He was studying this when Conway was shown in.

'I don't admire the conduct of the riff-raff you sent along as a guard, colonel,' he said, cutting short Conway's congratulations on his safe return.

'I'll speak to them,' Conway said. 'But I would remind you these are picked men. Each of them has been decorated for gallantry in action.'

'So no doubt were the followers of Genghis Khan and Attila the Hun. However it was not that I wished to speak to you urgently about.'

'So I imagined. Information is what we badly need. Can you help us?'

Massiter crossed to the open ordnance sheet and Conway followed him.

'It was here I am all but certain they held us prisoners.' Picking up a pencil, Massiter laid its point at a place on the map: *Rochestown Ho* (*in ruins*) were the words where the tip of the pencil rested.

Conway leant forward and studied the map. 'It's very remote,' he said after a moment or two. 'And no approach roads worth the name. To take it would mean a military operation with more men and transport than I can muster. And they will have cleared out by now more than likely.'

'I agree but it is still something to bear in mind that they have a hide-out there.'

'More important, did you recognise any of them?'

'I did. The leader was Michael O'Sullivan, Raymond's butler.'

'I'm not surprised. He slipped through our fingers when we raided the house. We should have had him then with any luck. Anyone else?'

'Would you be interested to learn that Raymond himself was there?'

'Very much. He was not a prisoner, I take it?'

'So far as I am aware he was there of his own free will and on the best of terms with the rest of the gang.'

'So,' Conway said. 'It's clear enough now. O'Sullivan got away from Raymond's house when we almost had him. Raymond was at that ambush in the glen. I should have taken him then only that mealy-mouthed feller French stood on his rights.'

'French's family once lived at the Bay. Did you know that?'

'I did not but nothing would surprise me in this country. As for Raymond turning up where you were held prisoner it confirms that he is one of them. How did he know where to go if he's not? He knew because he's in it up to the neck. It may even be he is the brains behind all their operations.'

'Perhaps. But remember I'm only reporting to you what I learnt up there.' Massiter was choosing his words with care. 'The evidence is not absolute by any means. You must draw your own conclusions.'

'I've done that already,' Conway said grimly. Almost unconsciously his hand dropped to the Webley on his hip, his fingers closing round the butt, as if to reassure himself that the source of his power was intact. 'The gun is all the evidence you need round here,' he said.

'Of course he may be on the run with the rest of them. On the other hand he may not know I learnt of his presence there. If so he may well return.'

'And keep up the pretence of being a loyalist. At all events wherever he is we'll flush him out. You may be assured of that. I'm obliged to you, sir.'

When he had gone Massiter sat on staring into the fire. No one could point a finger at him for what he had done. He had merely stretched the truth a little and to his own ends, as was his custom. Perhaps he had not even done that for Stephen's every act since his return smacked of suspicion. Perhaps he was indeed in league with the rebels. At all events, Massiter reassured himself, the cards had fallen his way better even than he could have hoped; having been dealt them, he had made the best possible use of them. Crossing to the desk he selected a cigar and, striking a match, went through the ceremony of lighting it. As he sat on, savouring the flavour, darkness began to creep into the room. A footman entering to draw the curtains found him sitting in his chair, the tip of his cigar glowing, a small cloud of smoke surrounding him and a look of satisfaction as of something well accomplished on his hawklike features.

After the Massiters had gone Mikey waited a little and then went along to the room where Stephen was. 'They've given in,' he said. He was jubilant and brandishing a paper in his hand.

Stephen sat up. 'What? Do you mean—'

'They're not for shooting him, anyway. They're saying' now that he wasn't taken with arms on him at all. And there's no way of tellin' he was in the ambush because no one saw him there. He's not to be court-martialled. He's to be interned.'

'Very neat,' Stephen said. 'Saves everyone's face. I wonder what Harry French and the military will have to say. So Massiter can go—'

'They've gone,' Mikey said. 'An hour ago. And you can go now too.'

They pulled the Overland out from under the trees where it had been hidden. As Stephen was getting into it, Mikey touched him on the arm. 'Watch yourself now, Master Stephen,' he said. 'There's some of them in the Bay sayin' ye're a Shinner yourself and that you've gone on the run. Go home to the house as quick as ye can. And stay on the back roads.'

The Overland was slow to start but they pushed it for him.

Dusk was falling now and night coming on. He picked his way along side-roads and short cuts, making for his house and the Bay. As he came over the saddle that guarded the entrance to the Bay, the beauty of it, as always, caught him by the throat. The air was still,

326

there was no movement anywhere. Despite the failing light he could see down the full length of the great sheet of water to where the three rocks of the Cat, the Kitten and the Dog lay across its entrance. On either side the mountains were blending into the gloaming and beginning to take on their purple shades of night. Below him a stream in which he had fished for trout ran brown and foaming over a little fall, making its way to the sea. Stephen sat on for a few minutes, drinking it in. As he watched darkness sweeping over the countryside of hill and heather, rock and mountain he knew beyond all shadow of doubt that he would never leave the Bay. Babs had been right. If they were to make a run for it they would end up both of them longing to get back, each of them blaming the other for their absence and hating themselves for it.

He put the Overland into gear and drove down the winding road that spanned the saddle and would lead him to Bellary Court.

Darkness had fully fallen when he came to the back entrance to the Bellary lands. The avenue wound its way through the home woods and past the walled-in gardens. As he left the woods he saw the glow in the sky. It took him a moment to realise what it meant. Then, with a sick feeling at his heart, he knew. Bellary Court was on fire.

His foot went down on the accelerator. The car bounded forward, rounded the turn above the stable-yard and slithered to a stop. Leaving it, Stephen ran towards the blaze.

The ground-floor rooms were all alight. Flames were shooting upwards and thick oily smoke from the petrol that had been used was billowing out of them. He stood and stared at it helplessly, the leaping flames signifying the end of all his hopes and dreams.

A noise behind him made him turn around. A Crossley tender was drawn up at the edge of the gravel sweep. In the light cast by the burning house he could see standing beside it a burly menacing figure in a Glengarry. Instantly he knew it was Conway. Then the figure strode towards him and he saw the service Webley in his hand.

'You did this, you damn swine,' Stephen said.

Conway gave a short savage laugh. 'You've come back,' he said. 'Back from your Shinner friends. You've no base for your spying for them now. I've seen to that.'

'What the hell do you mean?'

'You've been with them in their hideout. All along you've been playing false, Raymond. I guessed it from the minute I came here. You've never run right since the first time I knew you.'

'You're mad. You and your kind, you're all mad. The only things you think of are violence and killing, like the time you murdered those poor sods on the ground in the last show. Destruction, firing this house—'

'You Shinners fire houses. I lost a man yesterday—shot in the back.

An eye for an eye, a house for a house—and a life for a life.'

'Can't you see, you fool,' Stephen said desperately. 'All I've been trying to do is to stop this ghastly business, to prevent it getting worse—'

Could this really be happening, Stephen thought. He had tried to be uncommittted, not to take sides, to be the man in the middle. It seemed he had failed utterly both for himself and others as his father had said men in the middle always did. It might have been better had he thrown in unashamedly with Mikey's lot.

'"Make Ireland a hell for rebels," that's what they told us,' Conway was going on. 'And you're one of them. You always were. You haven't changed,' The muzzle of the big Webley came up.

Stephen's mouth went dry as it had always done in the skies over France the instant before action was joined. But now he was not sitting behind a pair of Vickers; he had not even his skills as a pilot with which to defend himself.

Behind him a ceiling fell in with a crash. Sparks showered around them and the blaze intensified. The house which he and his father and their fathers before them had loved so well was in its death throes. Tomorrow only stark walls and charred chimneys would remain. Never again would he sit in the great window and look down the Bay watching its colours of sea and hill, heather and mountain, cloud and sky, shifting and changing under his eyes.

Conway laughed again, and Stephen heard the click as the hammer of the Webley went back. He had Stephen at his mercy and he knew it. He was savouring the moment for which he had waited so long. In the jumping light of the flames Stephen could sense the madness behind his eyes.

If only there was some way of distracting his attention, Stephen thought. If he could turn away those eyes for an instant and make one lunge forward...But there wasn't. Conway's glance held his with that fixed, fanatic glare. The muzzle of the Webley never wavered. Death was very near. 'Get down on your knees, you scum,' Conway said.

At that moment a voice rang out from the shadows behind them. 'Stay where ye are, Master Stephen,' it said. 'Don't move now....

'Put 'em up, Conway!' And a figure stepped forward to the edge of the firelight.

Instantly the Webley swung away from Stephen. Two shots crashed out almost simultaneously. For a second as Conway stood erect and apparently untouched Stephen thought that his saviour had missed and that he was still at the Auxiliary's mercy. Then Conway took a step backward, a look of horrified incomprehension spreading across his heavy features. His body swayed and he staggered. His hand had dropped to his side and he struggled to lift and level the big revolver once more. As he did so another shot tore his chest apart. Slowly, like a tower falling, he collapsed to the ground and lay still.

The other man stepped full into the light of the flames. It was Mikey.

328

The long-barrelled Parabellum in his hand was pointed to where Conway lay a few yards away. With gun still poised, Mikey approached the body slowly. Then, bending down, he picked up the Webley and pushed the fallen man with his foot. He did not stir. Conway had fought his last fight. He was dead.

'You've evened the score now anyway, Mikey,' Stephen said shakily. 'I thought he'd got me at last.'

'Aye. Well lucky for ye we heard about him and his tricks almost as soon as ye'd gone. They drink, these devils, ye know, and when they drink they talk. He told some of them what he was at and Neligan, who has the pub near the old workhouse, heard them braggin' about what he'd do to your house and you, too, if you were there. He got the message to us.'

'We'd better look out. There may be some of his chaps about.'

'No. He said he'd do it all himself. Wipe the slate clean this time, he said.'

A Crossley tender was drawn up at the far side of the gravel sweep. It was empty save for some petrol tins in the back and an open box of .45 ammunition on the seat beside the driver's. 'We might as well take the lorry,' Mikey said with a grin. 'He'll not be needing it where he's gone and it'll come in handy like.' Then he turned to Stephen. 'Ye'll have to come with me, Master Stephen,' he said. 'No one's going to believe ye didn't kill him. If ye stay here they'll all be after you—soldiers, police and the Tans too. They'll never let you live after this. Whether you like it or not ye're one of us now.'

Stephen turned to look at his ravaged and burning house with the body of Conway lying beside the holocaust he had started. Mikey was right; that was all too clear. It was bad enough to have been holed up with 'the boys' at Rochestown. That alone would cast suspicion on him, which Massiter was certain to do nothing to disperse. His implication in Conway's death would clinch the authorities' conviction that he was concerned with and active in support of the rebels.

He sighed again. He had tried to avoid taking sides, to keep to the middle way, not to make any decision. One was being forced on him now and he knew what he had to do. He looked again and for the last time at his burning home. 'It seems you're right, Mikey,' he said sadly. 'There's no other way.' Putting his foot on the step, he climbed into the tender.

Mikey started the engine. The wheels spun on the gravel as he swung the tender round to point the way they had come. The engine roar rose to a crescendo and then died slowly away amongst the echoing hills.

JOHN WELCOME

John Welcome, a retired solicitor, now divides his time between the family home in Kerry and his own Georgian house in County Wexford, Ireland, where he keeps horses and cattle. His interests have always lain in the sporting world of horses, fox hunting and steeplechasing that form the background of his novels, and he is a member of the prestigious Irish National Hunt Steeplechase Committee, the governing body of steeplechasing in Ireland.